QUEST FOR THE GOLDEN ARROW

Also by Carrie Jones

Time Stoppers

★

Need

Captivate

Entice

Endure

With Steven E. Wedel

After Obsession

TIME STOPPERS

QUEST FOR THE GOLDEN ARROW

CARRIE JONES

BLOOMSBURY
NEW YORK LONDON OXFORD NEW DELHI SYDNEY

First published in the United States of America in May 2017
by Bloomsbury Children's Books
www.bloomsbury.com

Bloomsbury is a registered trademark of Bloomsbury Publishing Plc

For information about permission to reproduce selections from this book, write to Permissions, Bloomsbury Children's Books, 1385 Broadway, New York, New York 10018
Bloomsbury books may be purchased for business or promotional use. For information on bulk purchases please contact Macmillan Corporate and Premium Sales Department at specialmarkets@macmillan.com

Library of Congress Cataloging-in-Publication Data
Names: Jones, Carrie, author.
Title: Quest for the golden arrow / by Carrie Jones.
Description: New York : Bloomsbury, 2017. | Series: Time Stoppers ; 2
Summary: In the enchanted town of Aurora, Annie, one of the last of a magical line of humans who can control time, and her mystical creature friends must save Annie's beloved new guardian, Miss Cornelia, from the wicked Raiff.
Identifiers: LCCN 2016037695 (print) • LCCN 2016050250 (e-book)
ISBN 978-1-61963-863-1 (hardcover) • ISBN 978-1-61963-864-8 (e-book)
Subjects: | CYAC: Fantasy. | Magic—Fiction. | BISAC: JUVENILE FICTION / Fantasy & Magic. | JUVENILE FICTION / Action & Adventure / General. | JUVENILE FICTION / Humorous Stories.
Classification: LCC PZ7.J6817 Qu 2017 (print) | LCC PZ7.J6817 (e-book) | DDC [Fic]—dc23
LC record available at https://lccn.loc.gov/2016037695

Book design by John Candell
Typeset by Westchester Publishing Services
Printed and bound in the U.S.A. by Berryville Graphics Inc., Berryville, Virginia
2 4 6 8 10 9 7 5 3 1

All papers used by Bloomsbury Publishing, Inc., are natural, recyclable products made from wood grown in well-managed forests. The manufacturing processes conform to the environmental regulations of the country of origin.

To my daughter, Emily Ciciotte, the brilliant magic warrior who made this story and all my stories possible. Without her, there would be no me. And vice versa, because . . . you know . . . I'm her mom.

1

Pomegranates Cha-Cha

When Annie Nobody, the youngest Time Stopper currently in existence, awoke that frigidly cold winter morning, she was already happy. It didn't matter that her always-messy hair stood up in tufts that resembled hay bales. It didn't matter that a good amount of sleep residue resided by her overly large eyes. She just wiped it away without a second thought. And it certainly didn't matter that her room seemed abnormally cold as a ghost floated in front of her face, dramatically blowing air out her transparent nose. Annie just squared her shoulders and smiled at the ghost's worried face.

What mattered was that she, Annie Nobody, the same girl who earlier this week had been an orphan, abandoned (unwanted and very unloved) at a foster home where the family only cared about money, was now in a magical town that she and her new friends had just saved from a crow monster and trolls the night before.

What mattered was that she *had* friends now.

And a job. That is, if one could call being a Time Stopper a job. Miss Cornelia had promised to teach her all about being a Time Stopper. Miss Cornelia was the matriarch of Aurora, fond of rainbow skirts, and full of wrinkles. She was a Time Stopper, too.

In all her years, Annie had never felt more at home than she was at Miss Cornelia's Aquarius House. And last night, Annie actually had the best night's sleep she'd probably ever had in her life. She even had her own bed, which was pretty awesome. She rubbed at her eyes again as the ghost huffed at her.

"Wake up!"

Annie sat up straight. "Sorry! Why? Did I sleep too late?"

"No questions!" The ghost twirled around in a frantic circle, wringing her transparent hands together. "NO questions. Not allowed. No, they aren't."

Annie bit her lip. She'd forgotten that questions always sent the ghost, the Woman in White, into a small tornado of tizziness.

"Sorry," she whispered.

"Apologies are lovely, but they get you nowhere," the ghost whispered into Annie's ear.

Her breath tickled.

The ghost retreated up toward the roof. "Things are happening!"

"What sort—" Annie broke off her question, but it was too late.

"QUESTIONS!" The ghost began to whirl into the ceiling, frantic. Her head and left shoulder disappeared completely while the rest of her dangled there, spinning. Her long white dress and petticoats fluttered as she rotated, out of control, for several moments.

"Thanks for stopping by," Annie called after her, because she honestly wasn't quite sure what else to say. Sorry, obviously, wasn't good enough.

Suddenly, a man's voice boomed into the room. "Stopper! Do you have any idea how much our heads hurt when you stop time? It's like railroad cars are driving through them."

"Ah, the pain . . . the pain . . . ," sang a wispy woman.

A barrage of voices echoed "the pain . . . the pain . . ." just as dozens of ghosts crammed into Annie's bedroom.

Like the Woman in White, these ghosts were translucent and very dead. They stood half on the bookcases, dangled from the ceiling lights, and floated arm to arm along her bed. Some overlapped onto each other, body parts taking up bits of the same space. A young girl, with a teddy bear pinned to her dress, slid along the edge of the bookshelf. Some stern men in Revolutionary War outfits, missing limbs and with big black holes in their chests, craned toward her as she stared. A man who wore a doctor's stethoscope paced back and forth through several ghosts dressed as nuns. Some friars knelt on the floor, hands clasped in prayer, rocking back and forth. The doctor kept checking his watch and looking at a thermometer.

Annie had never seen them before. She wondered where they had all come from. Annie was still a little confused about what was happening. She'd never seen so many ghosts and so early in the morning. She was almost half-convinced she was still dreaming.

"Hello, and how do you do?" Annie greeted the pack.

"We are here," one of the stern ghosts said, "to implore you not to stop time unless absolutely necessary. It gives us all a headache."

The little girl ghost toddled over to Annie's chair beside the bed, reaching out her arms to be picked up. Annie hesitated and grabbed her, pulling her up with her onto the bed. It was like taking hold of air, but she cradled the transparent form in her arms. The little ghost cuddled in and whispered, "I'm Chloe. Head hurts sometimes."

It broke Annie's heart.

"I'm sorry," she said in a soothing tone.

The child turned solid for a moment, and Annie kissed her cheek. The girl smiled.

"We need you to not stop time again," the doctor ghost demanded.

The ghosts murmured among themselves.

"I can't promise that," Annie said, thinking about the

Raiff and his dangers. Sure, they'd gotten the Gnome of Protection back, but the Raiff was still out there in the Badlands, hoping to find a way to come back and hurt them, a demon ready to unleash his trolls and the rest of his minions. "I might—I might have to . . ."

"We could help her if she needs us," a nun said.

"We are not supposed to interfere in the world of the living," the man said stiffly, as the group of friar ghosts began murmuring louder prayers.

"Fiddlesticks," said the Woman in White, reappearing again, perfectly dry, but with a piece of seaweed draped over her shoulder. She plucked it out and put it on the merboy Farkey's hair. "We do all the time."

"A vote, then?" The doctor ghost raised his hand. "All in favor raise hands. Those without limbs may say 'Aye.' "

Most hands shot in the air and a few "Ayes" rang out.

The ghost turned back to Annie with an air of ceremony. He smiled at Chloe and her teddy. "We promise to help you if the need arises."

The old ghost reached into the pocket of his waistcoat and pulled out a solid gleaming brass bell.

"The bell!"

"He gave her the bell!"

"Oh, goodness me."

"My head . . ."

"A promise is a promise."

Annie took the heavy bell in her free hand.

"It summons us," the ghost doctor said. His voice was solemn and deep. "Ring the bell and we will help you. Use it instead of stopping time if you can."

"Thank you," Annie said in what she hoped was a solemn and respectful voice. "I will only use both if necessary."

As soon as Annie said the words, the ghosts disappeared. If it wasn't for the bell in her hand, Annie would have thought she'd imagined it all.

The Woman in White popped her head back into the room. Wet tears drenched her cheeks and leaked onto Annie's quilt, creating a damp puddle spot as quickly as if there had been a torrential rainstorm. "Learn from your mistakes, Annie, dear little Nobody. Learn from your mistakes and the mistakes of others. For he comes . . . he comes soon . . . and my poor Cornelia . . ."

"Miss Cornelia . . ." Annie tried to make the name less of a question and more of a prodding.

"She goes!" The ghost sobbed once more, unleashing a waterfall onto the end of the bed.

Annie leaped out from under the covers, standing on the bed, reaching up toward the ghost as the rest of her began to spiral into the cloud-painted ceiling. Panic overwhelming her, Annie attempted to grab the ghost's disappearing left ankle.

"What? What do you mean? Who goes? Where? Where does she go? Do you mean Miss Cornelia?"

But the ghost was gone, leaving behind a wet bed and a confused Annie.

"Please come back!" she called after her.

Tala, the huge white dog who had helped to save Annie from her foster home, woofed his agreement, but the ghost didn't return.

She jumped off the bed, kneeling next to Tala. Her arms wrapped around the dog's chest and she buried her face in his fur. Home. She was home. Whatever the Woman in White was carrying on about probably wasn't that important. It couldn't be.

With her friends Jamie and Eva and Bloom, she had saved the town last night. Annie had done what she once might have thought was impossible: they had stolen a force field–producing gnome from trolls and battled—and defeated—a terrifying crow monster. They and all of Aurora were safe. Nothing could go wrong now. They'd even had a party and celebrated both the victory and Jamie's thirteenth birthday.

"Obviously," Annie said to Tala, stroking his muzzle, "I am being a worrywart."

He nuzzled her chin.

"Right?" she asked, her voice rising with worry.

Tala gave a tiny woof.

"Good," she said, staring into his big brown eyes, and for a split second, they reminded her of something familiar, somehow. "You are the best dog ever. Now let's get some breakfast."

Down the hall from Annie, James Hephaistion Alexander woke up and dressed quickly; a strange feeling of dread seemed to only be growing, tightening his small chest.

He tried to push the anxiety out. Maybe he was just anxious because he was used to being anxious? He had lived with trolls all his life, and not just trolls, but trolls pretending to be his relatives, trolls that were just waiting for him to turn thirteen so that they could eat him. That was enough to make anyone anxious.

But it felt like more than just a habit.

It felt real.

It felt as if things were about to go terribly bad somehow, if they hadn't already, which made no sense because everything was all right now.

Hurriedly, he started to put on his shoes. Aquarius House seemed like the sort of home where people wore shoes inside. Old and Victorian, rambling along multiple corridors, the house exuded magic and welcome and mystery all at once.

Someone banged on the door with a fist.

"Are you awake?" Eva challenged in a grumpy, demanding voice.

He sat on the edge of his bed with one shoe dangling from his toes, too shocked to answer.

"Jamie! Have you gone troll or something, or are you awake?" she hollered.

He checked his skin. It was still a dark shade of brown. His wrists were still bony. Jamie had always been skinny. His father and grandmother only let him have a couple of minuscule cans of Vienna sausages a day. It was hard to build up muscles let alone fat on that kind of diet. A pat to his head confirmed he still had hair.

"I am not a troll," he announced, feeling quite relieved. "I am still human!"

"Are you naked?" she demanded through the closed door.

Jamie hopped up. "What? What? No!"

"Then why don't you open up the freaking door? Freaking word, Jamie. You are as rude as a freaking arkan sonney, I swear. Are you just going to skulk in your room all day like some Manx fairy hedgehog or something?"

Eva kicked the giant wooden door open and trotted into the room, grabbing Jamie by his ear, tugging him toward the door and the hallway. "I mean, I know we're friends, but you have got to stop hiding from the world. You've got to go out there and announce yourself, you know?"

Jamie's shoe fell off.

Eva did not notice. "I mean, freaking word, Jamie. You are a hero now, you know? Just like me. Although, obviously not as mighty as me or as brave or whatever. But you are a hero. You've got to act like one. Every morning you have to roar hello to the sun like this . . ."

She proceeded to do a pretty decent lion imitation, releasing Jamie's ear so she could pound her chest for effect. Jamie scuttled back and grabbed his shoe.

Eva stopped roaring, braced her stocky frame in the doorway, and peered at Jamie, a triumphant smile filling her face before she said, "That was a pretty good roar, huh?"

"Amazing. An amazing roar." Jamie knew Eva was big on flattery. He and Annie had talked about that a lot.

"I could teach you how to do it?" Eva suggested. "We could have roaring lessons."

Jamie hopped around and then leaned against the wall, trying to get his shoe on. "Well . . . I don't think I'm really a roaring type."

Eva scrutinized him. Her arms crossed her chest. "No, you're more of the studying, quiet type. The smart type like SalGoud, only with actual emotions."

"Maybe," Jamie admitted, thinking of his young friend the stone giant and his penchant for books, history, and quotations.

"That's too bad." Eva coughed behind her hand. "Bor-ing."

Jamie decided to ignore that statement rather than argue about it, which, he realized, probably just proved Eva's point.

Once his shoe was on, she grabbed his hand and tugged him down the hallway. "Come on. We have a day to adventure with. No school. A weekend. Life is freaking good!"

She was so enthusiastic about it, pretty much bounding down the velvety wall-papered corridor, that it was hard for Jamie to remember the tight feeling in his chest—the feeling he'd always get right before his grandmother screamed at him and threw cans at his head, the feeling he'd always get right before his father and grandmother would play catch, making him the ball, the feeling he'd had right before he watched his grandmother turn into a real, certified monster.

That feeling was doom.

That feeling was dread.

That feeling was oh-my-gosh-something-is-horribly-wrong.

And even as he followed Eva down the hallway of Aquarius House, that feeling was spreading. The house appeared slightly less fancy and elaborate than the day before. It was as if the magic keeping it all together had started to wilt.

"Good morning, Aquarius House," he said to the wall-papered hall.

G d mor ing, Jami appeared in shaky script writing along the walls.

He did not like the look of the greeting, which was missing letters and trailed away into swirls before fading away completely. Usually, the walls were a stickler for perfect grammar and liked using upbeat punctuation.

Jamie pushed his concern out of his mind for the moment and quickly caught up with Eva, who wasn't much of a runner. The thing about Jamie was that he was actually quite fast. He was all knobby knees and close-cropped hair, short straight nose, and thin arms, but he was in actuality stronger than he looked and much faster than people expected. Living with his fake grandmother and pretend father had taught him how to dodge meaty fists, outrun kicks, and sidestep thrown cans. He could bob and weave and evade pretty much all kinds of blows. It came from all the chores the Alexanders had made him do.

He hadn't had to do one chore at Aquarius House. He blinked hard at the realization. How was that even possible? To not have to clean toilets with toothbrushes or cook meals or pick up random chicken feathers off the floor? It seemed impossible, but it felt *sooo* good to not have to do work, or be yelled at, or hit in the back of the head, or anything horrible.

Nobody kicked or threw things at him here in Aurora.

"Eva . . ." He stopped following her down the hallway.

"What?" She put her hands on her hips and tapped her foot.

"Why are we hurrying?"

"Because this is my first full day as an official, glorious hero and I don't want to miss it!" She glowered at him as if she couldn't believe he hadn't figured it out.

Annie and Tala sat at the kitchen counter, which was all shiny and deep-colored, waiting for the bread to pop up from the unicorn-shaped toaster. Nobody else was there and an odd quiet settled over the room.

When Annie opened the refrigerator, none of the food items sang out like they had the night before. The cartons of eggs and blocks of cheese and butter just rested there stock-still like regular cartons of eggs and blocks of cheese and butter. Even the milk stayed in its jug and refrained from yodeling. Everything seemed profoundly un-magical. Annie found it unsettling. She'd been looking forward to a bacon serenade or a pomegranate cha-cha, to the obvious evidence of happy magic.

"Maybe the food is just asleep," she whispered to Tala as she quietly removed the orange juice and shut the refrigerator.

Tala whined.

"Don't you think?" Annie whispered.

His tail drooped.

She poured herself some orange juice and got him some water, which he elegantly lapped out of a sparkling bowl decorated with frolicking dwarfs.

Eva burst through the kitchen door just as the toast popped up. She snatched it out of the toaster and shoved a piece into her mouth.

"Eva," Annie started, wanting to tell her about the missing magic. "Things seem a—"

"Delicious!" Eva announced, crumbs scattering everywhere as she interrupted Annie. She then took another bite as Jamie followed in behind her.

Annie's heart lifted to see him.

He smiled at her while Tala barked out his objections at having his toast stolen.

"You're a dog. You don't even need it toasted," Eva declared, throwing a floppy piece of bread at him.

It hit him in the muzzle and plopped down onto the counter. He barked one more time and, using his nose, nudged it toward Annie, an offering.

"You eat it," she told him. "I'll make some more. Do you want some, Jamie?"

"Yes, please, but you don't have to make it for me," he said, settling into his seat. "Where is Gramma Doris?"

"No idea," Annie answered, thinking about Aquarius House's enchanted cook and their biggest maternal figure after Miss Cornelia. "I just got here. Besides that, I'm not sure why, but things seem a little off today."

"Off? Nonsense! Today is a super amazing fantastic day for celebrating US. Last night's party was just the beginning. And Gramma Doris is sleeping like a vampire in Alaska, probably," Eva said through a mouth full of toast. "Brounies can't handle too much of a party. Not important. ANYWAY, what is important is how we should all celebrate our first day as bona fide heroes."

She chugged some orange juice out of the container, not bothering to get a glass.

Annie raised her eyebrows at Jamie.

"I've seen worse," he admitted.

She had, too. The Wiegles, her last foster family, were not known for their table manners, or any manners, actually. She shuddered, remembering.

"Would you like a glass or something, Eva?" she asked, taking one out of a cabinet.

"That's just more work. You have to wash a glass." She dropped the juice back on the counter. "I'm done anyway. No worries!"

She belched.

"I'm supposed to say 'excuse me' after that." She belched again, wiping her mouth with the back of her forearm as she put the glass back in the cupboard.

They all waited for Eva to say "excuse me."

And waited.

"What?" Eva demanded, glaring at them.

"You're supposed to say 'excuse me,' remember?" Annie gently prompted.

Eva threw her hands up in the air just as more toast popped out. "Excuse me!"

She snatched the toast out of the air and tossed one slice to Annie and another to Jamie. Annie handed hers to Tala. He refused it.

"You look hungry," she said.

He shook his head.

"Halfsies," she insisted, ripping the toast into two. "I'm not eating my half unless you do."

The dog gave up and scarfed down his half.

Eva turned to Jamie, exasperated. "She's too nice. I mean, it's good to be nice and everything, but you've got to take care of yourself, too, Annie. You're the Stopper and all. Stoppers have to stay healthy and keep their magic up."

Jamie put more toast in the toaster and began wandering around the kitchen, pouring more juice, finding some cereal and apples. "What happens if they don't?"

"Let me help you, Jamie." Annie took the apples from him and washed them in the sink even though they seemed as if they were already pretty clean. "Yeah, what happens if Miss Cornelia or I . . ." She couldn't figure out the best way to say it.

Jamie finished for her. "Get sick or something?"

"Yeah," Annie agreed, flashing him a thankful smile. "What then?"

"Well, Miss Cornelia's magic is part of what holds Aquarius House and Aurora all together. The Gnome of Protection, obviously, shields our town from the eyes of evil and keeps people who have never been in here out."

"Wait," Jamie interrupted. "But the Raiff . . . He used to live here. Does that mean he can come in?"

Eva staggered backward, hands dramatically clutching

each other over her heart. "Seriously? You guys remember nothing. The Raiff is in the Badlands. Miss Cornelia put him there after the Purge. It weakened her to do so. It took a lot of magic. In fact, it weakened all of us."

Annie and Jamie exchanged a glance.

"And that means?" Annie prodded.

"AND THAT MEANS!?! DUH!" Eva stomped around in a circle. "It means that that evil Raiff monster can't come back, nor can all his people. He is stuck there."

"But I read—" Annie started.

"What do you mean, 'you read'?" Eva interrupted, hands back on her hips.

Annie shrugged. "There are all these books in my room, and they all want me to read them. They sort of beg every night when I go to sleep. It would be rude not to read them."

"Look, Stopper, if you worry about hurting books' feelings you are just Way . . . Too . . . Nice," Eva insisted. She tweaked the unicorn horn that was the lever on the toaster with each word to make her point.

"Plus," Annie continued, "they are teaching me things."

"That is not very heroic of you," Eva countered. "Heroes act. They do not read."

"Of course they do." Annie appealed to Jamie for help.

"Books teach you things that you don't know yourself. They let you feel things. Every time you read a book with a hero in it, you become that hero." Jamie poured the cereal into bowls and then added some milk.

Annie remembered to say "thank you" for the cereal. Eva was too flabbergasted to be polite. Plus, it took a lot for Eva to ever remember to be polite.

"I can't believe either of you." Eva shook her head and started eating, not pausing to chew before finishing her sentence. "I'm going to have to do a lot of work to make forever heroes of glorious glory out of you."

Annie gave up trying to argue with the dwarf and stirred her cereal and told them what she'd read last night. It was a book about portals and the history of Aurora. The book said that portals can transport beings from one place to another. Miss Cornelia had cast the Raiff over to the Badlands through a portal, trapping him there forever.

"There was a lot of science in the book. I didn't really understand some of it," Annie admitted reluctantly.

"I'll try to explain the science parts to you," Jamie offered and then added, "If you want."

"Stop being so shy!" Eva pounded her fist on the counter. "The two of you. Freaking A. It's all reading books and being polite and being all self . . . self . . . self-depreciating?"

"Deprecating," Jamie corrected. "Actually. Self-deprecating."

"Whatever!" Eva roared. "Own your awesome! Be like me. Strut it out! Come on. Let's practice our struts."

Annie shirked. "Oh, no . . . that's really okay."

Eva yanked Jamie off the chair. "Work it, James

Hephaistion Alexander. Work that strut. Own your awesome. Come on."

Jamie gave Annie a tortured save-me look as Eva forced him to push out his chest and stand up straight and swagger toward the refrigerator. Annie collapsed into giggles. Tala whimpered in doggy sympathy.

Annie desperately searched for a way to save him from Eva's strutting lesson.

"Wait!" she announced. "Eva! You said that Miss Cornelia's magic keeps Aurora and Aquarius House running. But the stuff in the fridge isn't singing anymore. What does that mean?"

Eva stopped midsashay. Her mouth dropped open. Jamie reached over and gently closed it for her.

"What do you mean, Annie?" Jamie asked. He silently mouthed the words, "thank you."

Annie cleared her throat and stood up, walking over to the fridge to demonstrate. "I was trying to mention it before, but what I mean is that yesterday when we were in here all the food sang and stuff when we opened the fridge. Today? It's all quiet."

Eva and Jamie hustled over. Annie opened the fridge. They all peered inside. One tiny radish whispered sadly, "Rad-ish-es are de-lic-i-ous."

Eva jumped back, windmilling her arms to try to keep her balance. She failed, falling with a thud next to Tala, who used his thick, doggy muzzle to push her back up to a standing position.

"Oh, no!" she whispered.

"Oh no what?" Annie asked, steadying her on her feet.

"Something's off with Miss Cornelia's magic."

"What do you mean?" Annie stared into the dwarf's eyes. Annie was fearless and intense.

So intense that Eva looked away as she said, "The inanimate stuff in the house starts losing its magic if Miss Cornelia starts losing hers. Like, I mean she's been losing it forever, but it's super gradual. Like the food doesn't sing quite as loudly as it used to and stuff, but it still sings. Or the walls stop bossing you around constantly and only do it sometimes. Or the mosaic on the ceiling in the library doesn't move."

"But . . . ," Annie urged.

"This is different, isn't it?" Jamie said, putting away the cereal bowls as he spoke.

Annie agreed. "The whole place feels different. She must be sick or something or just suddenly really weak or . . . or . . ."

"Or missing," said a voice from the door. Bloom, the very last elf, stood there, his perfect blond hair glowing radiantly despite his worried expression. "I think Miss Cornelia is missing."

Feelings Schmeelings

Eva rushed at the elf until she stood a mere inch away from him. Her nose came up to his belly, but the height difference didn't bother her at all. "YOU will not be saying such things! That's ridiculous."

He scoffed, leaned on the fridge, and said calmly, "You're ridiculous, Eva."

"*I'm* ridiculous?" She poked his stomach with her index finger, but it was solid and didn't indent much. "I'm not the one saying that Miss Cornelia has gone missing! Miss Cornelia can't go missing!"

"Why not?" Bloom rushed to the window, peering out it this way and that as if searching for enemy invaders.

Eva huffed out a breath but didn't answer.

Annie's voice softened the atmosphere of the room. "Yeah, why, Eva? Is it impossible somehow?"

"It's impossible because we got rid of the crow monster! The gnome is back and so our town is protected from bad things that want to do us harm!" She stomped her foot so vigorously that the salt and pepper shakers shook and let out a tiny, weak squeal. "Do none of you remember what we did last night? We saved the town from that bird monster thing! We returned the gnome! We're heroes."

Jamie and Annie exchanged a glance as Bloom declared there were no visible threats at the perimeter of the property from what he could tell from the faulty vantage point of the kitchen window.

"Are you seriously still not getting it?" Eva threw her hands up in the air and stomped away toward the counter. She hopped up onto the stool and then the counter's surface. "There are no threats in town. Nobody would take Miss Cornelia. And she wouldn't just 'go missing' by herself. It's ridiculous to even think that." She pointed at Bloom. "You, elf, are ridiculous."

Bloom's face reddened. "Enough with that word, Eva!"

"Then tell us why you're saying ridiculous things!" she demanded.

"I just had a feeling," he admitted.

Eva scoffed and muttered, "Feelings schmeelings . . . Pshaw. Elves are as bad as humans, I swear. Always going on about feelings."

Annie, Jamie, and Bloom just stood there for a moment, awkward and insulted.

"Feelings are good things," Annie whispered to Jamie, "aren't they?"

"Of course they are," Bloom answered, gliding purposefully toward the counter. "Feelings are what let us know there is trouble coming. Feelings are what make us remember how to be kind and how it feels when someone"—he stared pointedly at Eva—"is not kind to you."

Eva harrumphed.

"I get feelings about things a lot," Jamie admitted, remembering how he felt coming down for breakfast and the dream he'd had last night about a woman with swirly skirts, whisked away on a horse. Maybe that had been about Miss Cornelia.

Annie jerked back to attention. "And what do you feel now? About this?"

Jamie thought for a moment. "I agree with you, Annie. Something is off. Something is very off. The house doesn't feel the same, but I can't tell if it's because Miss Cornelia is sick or tired or missing or—"

"SHE IS NOT MISSING!" Eva roared, jumping off the counter and landing with a thud at Annie's feet. "The gnome is back in town so we are protected. How can you all not get that?"

There was a tiny silence. Annie cowered a bit by the refrigerator, and Bloom refused to make eye contact with anyone. Only Jamie was brave enough to break it.

"Because there were two monsters we saw that day. Well, two evil things at least . . . ," he began.

"That's right!" Annie hit her head with her hand, totally upset for not thinking it herself. "There was the crow monster but also that dark horse. Remember?" she appealed to Bloom and looked to Jamie for backup. She didn't appeal to Eva because she knew how stubborn she was. "It was huge and felt really mean and evil.

"And it obviously *was* since it was running with the crow monster," said Annie. "Maybe the horse is still here in Aurora. We should find Miss Cornelia and ask her."

Eva rolled her eyes. "You just said she was missing! Now you want to find her! How about instead we just eat third breakfasts and bask in being heroes for a bit?"

"Because something is wrong, Eva!" Bloom said. He pulled out his dagger, stared at it, and then resheathed it on his belt. "I know I'm supposed to be positive all the time because I'm an elf, and you are supposed to be negative all the time because you are a dwarf, but I cannot ignore this."

"Whatever. The only evidence you have that something is wrong is your feelings." Eva glared at him. "Feelings are not evidence! Feelings are silly."

Jamie thought this was interesting since Eva was exhibiting a lot of feelings herself right then—frustration, rage, annoyance.

"Are you *afraid* to fight another monster?" Bloom asked, eyes squinting as he stared at her.

It was a brilliant move because Eva was all about being brave even though she had a tendency to pass out sometimes when she was really scared.

Bloom asked again, "Is that it, Eva? You just want to sit here and do nothing because you are afraid of a big horse?"

Eva took the bait. "NEVER! Eva Beryl-Axe would never fear to fight a monster!"

"Well, there you go, then . . ." Bloom smiled, and spread his arms triumphantly. "Let's all look for Miss Cornelia and find out about that horse."

"Sounds like a plan," Annie agreed. She power fist-bumped Bloom's outstretched hand a bit awkwardly and then bumped Jamie's fist and reached out to Eva.

"'Sounds like a plan,'" Eva mimicked, but she fist-bumped Annie back. "Everyone always agrees with the elf. Always."

Despite her grumpy misgivings, Eva followed them out of the kitchen and into the hall, ready to hunt for Miss Cornelia.

Nearly four hours later they had searched the entire house, or at least all the rooms that they could find, and hadn't located Miss Cornelia anywhere. They asked the mermaids in the foyer fountain, the fairies, everyone they came across. Nobody had seen her. They hunted for her in the library, the front rooms, the kitchen, and assorted bedrooms.

Annie didn't feel right snooping around other people's rooms. Before Aurora, this would definitely have been a reason for her to get kicked out of a foster home. She had grown up trying really hard to obey people's house rules, and even though Miss Cornelia was always saying that Annie and Jamie had a forever home here in Aurora, she still worried about misbehaving and disappointing everybody. There was a niggling doubt that filled up her heart: What would happen if she did something really wrong?

Or worse, what would happen if Miss Cornelia really was missing? Who would be her foster mother, or foster grandmother, or . . . oh, whatever Miss Cornelia was? Would Annie have to leave? Would she have to go back to living at a place like the Wiegles' again? A place where she was a nobody, meant to act like she didn't exist? A nothing?

"I will *not* be a nothing," she whispered as the others moved on to search another room.

Panic filled her heart. They had to find Miss Cornelia, and they had to find her soon!

As Eva and Bloom headed down the dark corridor toward the front stairs, Annie gently pulled Jamie aside.

"What is it?" he asked, head tilting slightly to the left.

"I'm really worried," Annie admitted.

"Me, too." He petted her arm awkwardly. "But I'm sure it'll all be okay."

"But what if it isn't?" Annie asked, peering down the hallway where Bloom and Eva were arguing about something.

Again. Eva was stomping and had even emphasized her points with her ax. "What if Miss Cornelia is sick or something? She's kind of old. What if she dies? I mean, I know we've only known her for a little while, but I kind of feel like . . . like . . . I love her."

The words were hard to say.

"You're biting your lip. It's bleeding," Jamie said gently.

"Oh!" She stopped and wiped at her lip with the back of her hand.

"It will be okay, Annie." He sighed out the words. "I mean, we have to believe it's going to be okay."

"Yeah," Annie agreed with him. "But, I don't know *how* to believe that it's going to be okay, you know? I mean there were all these ghosts in my room this morning and they seemed . . . like they knew something was happening. So, how do I believe it's all okay?"

"You'll believe it once we find Miss Cornelia." He elbowed Annie in the side as they started walking again. It was a hearty rah-rah elbow that was much braver than either of them actually felt. "Right?"

"Right." Annie took his arm as they descended the stairs to join Eva and Bloom. "And no matter what, we have each other."

"Right."

She just hoped each other would be enough.

The rest of the morning passed and still they were no closer to finding Miss Cornelia. When the front door opened and Gramma Doris bustled into the house, carrying an armload of groceries, the children mobbed her, demanding if she knew Miss Cornelia's whereabouts.

The stout, gray-haired woman handed her groceries to Jamie and Eva and bustled to the kitchen, taking off her coat and hat, all business. She was in charge of feeding everyone who lived at Aquarius House as well as whoever tended to show up for the evening meal, which was always served backward starting with dessert and ending with appetizers. Still, she paused and offered them her soft, kindly face as she said, "Why, no, I haven't. But Corny is a busy woman, you know. Perhaps she went into town? It's nothing to panic about. Why are you panicking?"

So, they told her about the food in the fridge, the walls' missing letters and not telling them updates about the day, and how Jamie and Bloom both just had bad feelings about things. Eva scoffed at that part.

Gramma Doris opened the fridge, nonplussed. "Well, let's see."

"HELLO, DORIS! WELL, HELLO, DORIS! DON'T YOU WANT TO MAKE A PIE TODAY? . . . DORIS!" sang out the eggs and milk.

"Yes, of course," she told the fridge. "Momentarily." Shutting the refrigerator door, she turned back to the children, smiling. "See? Nothing to worry about."

"But couldn't that be your magic?" Annie asked quietly. "You're a brounie, so you have household magic, right?"

Gramma Doris hopped onto one foot and pulled a grape out of midair. "I do, dear. I do. But I really think it's all okay. It is lovely of you, yes . . . yes . . . lovely of you to worry, since it shows you care . . . If you are so worried about Cornelia, why don't you go look around town? Judging by your stressed faces, you need to get out in the fresh air. And take some cookies with you!"

She snapped her fingers and a large canister popped its lid off. Chocolate chocolate yum cookies soared up and onto the counter by the sink, marching in a line into a waiting paper bag. Once it was full, Gramma Doris handed it to Jamie. "There. Provisions."

They thanked her and went to the front room to gather boots and coats. The world was wintry cold and still covered with snow from last night's storm.

As they took their coats off pegs, Bloom opened the shoe closet and hopped backward.

"We'll see if this magic still works," he said as he hustled out of the way.

"What magic?" Jamie asked.

Bloom didn't need to answer. It was obvious as the boots marched out of the closet by the front door in perfect lines. There was every kind of snow boot Jamie or Annie could imagine.

"Look!" Eva did a little jig, spinning and stomping

around in a happy circle. "That's Miss Cornelia magic right there. RIGHT THERE!" she insisted. "And it's perfectly normal go—"

Her voice petered out as the boots all fell over on their sides and flopped about like fish yanked out of the ocean water. Then the boots stopped, completely still.

"Oh," Eva whispered, grabbing her ax. "That's not good."

"This is what I've been saying!" Bloom sighed, exasperated, hauling boots out of the pile for each of them, muttering things such as "This looks like your size," and "Why doesn't Eva ever just believe me," and "Harrumph."

They headed first to town, trudging through the long snowy driveway that descended from Aquarius House, which was perched at the top of the hill, and then down to the town proper, full of its rock walls and wooden buildings. Jamie surveyed the landscape as they walked, but spotted nothing out of the ordinary, even for a magical town. Snow-covered blueberry barrens rolled gently to one side with a random tree or boulder sticking up out of the land. The ocean, gray and rough, full of wind-induced whitecaps, was a bit more distant. Thick Maine forests full of overgrown Christmas trees rolled up into the somewhat mellow mountains of Acadia National Park and the rest of the island.

"Let's try Canin's first," Bloom said, referring to the gruff, not-so-friendly werewolf who ran the general store in town. "I'm not sure we're ready to take this to the mayor yet, and Canin always knows what's going on in this place."

"Miss Cornelia will be fine," Annie whispered insistently without making eye contact with him or the others.

Bloom put his arm around Annie's shoulder, hustling her into Canin's shop. "Of course she will. Of course."

Eva and Jamie followed them inside.

Despite the fact that Canin looked anything but jolly, the doorbell to Canin's store rang out "For He's a Jolly Good Fellow" as they entered the dust-filled establishment. His wild white hair sprang out from beneath his Red Sox baseball cap in unruly tufts. His practically nonexistent lips didn't even begin to twitch into a half smile as the door slammed shut behind the kids. However, he did manage to lift one bushy eyebrow up toward the bill of the cap and grunt out a hello.

Jamie thought this was probably progress, since just yesterday Canin was inspecting him for signs of troll and Annie for signs of cowardice. A grunted greeting was at least slightly better than that.

"Hello, Canin!" Bloom sang out in a chipper, elfy way.

"Hello," Canin said again, sniffing at them, his wolfish ears back.

Eva saddled up toward the counter like a cowboy heading up to the bar, all swagger and confidence. "Look. We're here on business. These companions of mine"—she gestured back toward Jamie, Annie, and Bloom—"think that something might be up with Miss Cornelia. They have quote, unquote *feelings*. They think the magic is off. We've hunted all throughout Aquarius House. Can't find her. Asked Gramma Doris. She's not worried, but she hasn't seen her. So now we're here . . . asking you."

Canin chewed on a pencil, inserted the whole thing into his mouth, and then spat it out. All that was left of it were toothpicks. "Asking me what exactly?"

"If you have seen her. If you feel like the magic is off," Annie blurted.

"Gramma Doris said we were worrying about nothing," Eva said. "I think she's right . . . Maybe . . ."

"Worry is never about nothing," Canin grumped. "Sometimes it's pointless because you can't fix things. Sometimes it's pointless because what you're worrying about isn't real. But just because something isn't real doesn't mean it's nothing. Get me?"

He glared directly at Annie. She was too intimidated to tell him the truth, which was that she didn't understand what he was saying at all, actually.

"You make no sense," Eva blustered.

"Eva!" Annie scolded. "You're being rude."

"Honest, I'm being honest," Eva corrected, fiddling with a box labeled "Cantankerous Canine Dog Treats of Happiness."

Jamie cleared his throat. "What do you think, um, sir?"

The shop seemed to get closer to them as Canin filled up his lungs with a long, harsh, raggedy breath. Even the ceiling seemed to be sucked down a couple of inches lower. As usual, Canin's store was full of strange products nobody had ever heard of before, all containing magic potions for one purpose or another. A gallon of Ancestral Memories fell off a nearby shelf and rolled into Bloom's foot as they waited for Canin's answer.

"Should we be worried about Miss Cornelia?" Annie's voice squeaked. Canin made her nervous.

Everyone stared at her. She took a frightened step backward, knocking over a bar of Pretty All the Time Soap and a plastic jar of As Big as You Wish. Eighteen mice scurried from under the floorboards, lifted up the soap onto their tiny shoulders, and marched with it back into a hole in the wall, chattering excitedly. Another followed, rolling the jar into the hole.

"Drunken unicorn blood," Canin sputtered. "As soon as those mice get that jar unscrewed, we're going to have giant mice around town for the next twenty-four hours. Everyone better hide their cheese."

"Sorry," Annie whispered.

"You better be!" Canin growled. He slammed both his hands down on the counter. The force burst the cash register's drawer open. It rang as it hit the wall and money fluttered out into the air, turning into birds. Canin growled again, rattling off a string of random mutterings about bat poop and vampire vomit.

The children raced around the shop, helping him catch the money. They let the one that fell in a vat of Instantly

Hairy Hairiness stay there. Nobody wanted to risk their fingers becoming instantly hairy hairiness.

As soon as that was taken care of, Canin sighed. "Obviously, the store's magic still works."

"Which means . . . ," Annie prodded.

"Which means that if Miss Cornelia is gone, or if something has happened to her, she is not dead." He paused and looked thoughtful.

"But?" Annie asked.

"But, my dollar bills have never tried to escape before. The mice have never just stolen something so blatantly, and that means . . . that the magic is most definitely off."

Silence descended on the shop. Even the mice stopped skittering in the walls. The bags of semitransparent daggers no longer rustled. The cans of conjure dust no longer hummed.

"Which means?" Annie whispered, grabbing Eva's free hand (the one without the ax) and squeezing it.

"It means that something is wrong with Miss Cornelia." He refused to make eye contact with them, staring at the ceiling. "It could just be age. Her . . . her sorrow has made her weaker and so has her age, but now that Annie is here she should be getting stronger, happier."

Annie's heart dropped. She had failed somehow, hadn't she? Was she not what Miss Cornelia expected? Was the lessening magic somehow her fault? Everything was always her fault. That's what her last foster people had thought.

Braving herself up, Annie strode across the store and placed her hands on the high counter, going up on tiptoe, and said in a clear, sure voice, "The first step is to find Miss Cornelia. To look everywhere. To see if she is hurt or weak somewhere."

Everyone stopped what they were doing and turned toward Annie.

"I mean, isn't it?"

Bloom tightened his cloak around his neck. "It is."

"We should go throughout the town and ask if anyone has seen her. Isn't that what we were already doing?" Eva asked.

It was.

"But now we have Canin to help, right?" Annie turned back toward him. He was shoving on his winter coat.

"I will take the far houses. I am faster than most of you. As you ask, get others to help you. Try not to panic anyone . . ." He hustled them out of the little store, locking the door behind them.

"I thought nobody locks their doors in Aurora," Jamie whispered to Annie.

"Apparently he does," she answered as Canin raced off, "and the mayor."

"That was different," Jamie said. "There was a monster that night."

"True," Annie agreed, but somehow it didn't feel different. It felt bad, just like now.

3

Bossy Girls for the Win

The children split up into groups of two, with Tala heading off with Annie and Eva. They rushed from house to shop to tower to burrow, asking if anyone had seen Miss Cornelia that morning. Nobody had.

"This is a waste of time." Eva plopped on the rock wall, not even bothering to brush the snow off the top.

"What else can we do? I wish we could send out an all-points bulletin like the police or the FBI . . . ," Annie said.

Eva panted a little bit, short of breath. After a moment she bounced off.

"I've got it!" she yelled. "Follow me!"

She scurried off back toward her house, yanking open the small door, and rushing in a hobbling sort of way toward a wooden cupboard. Jerking open the bottom doors, she started hauling out steel pots, biscuit makers, axes, a scythe-type weapon, and a doll.

"That is not mine!" she shouted, face flushing as she pulled out the doll. "Look away."

Annie pretended to glance away, but managed to see out of the corner of her eye as Eva kissed the doll's fabric cheek and fixed her black hair before squirreling her away into a pot.

"You can look now," Eva declared as she pulled out a bunch of rocket-shaped tubes with large candlewicks sticking to the end. "Take some of these."

She smashed an armload into Annie's chest. Annie grabbed them with a tiny harrumphing noise.

"Do you think I'm bossy?" Eva asked, seemingly switching the topic out of nowhere as she grabbed some tubes and kicked the cupboard door shut with her boot.

Readjusting her load, Annie took a moment to figure out how to respond. "I think people always call girls bossy, and if boys do the same exact thing, people say they are leaders."

Eva squinted at her.

"I'm saying you're a leader, Eva," Annie explained as she tried not to drop anything.

Eva head-butted Annie's arm so hard Annie staggered back into the edge of the couch. "I knew I liked you."

Annie wanted to rub her arm, but her hands were full. "Thanks?"

"Anytime. Want me to head-butt the other one so the

pain ain't lopsided?" Eva hopped around a bit, excitement filling her face. "These are fireworks."

"No, I meant thank you for liking me." Annie cleared her throat. "Um, are you sure we should be doing this? Where I used to live, lighting fireworks was illegal, and it's sort of dangerous."

Eva froze. "Are you kidding me?"

"Um . . . no."

"You're in Aurora now, Annie. Different rules. Danger is everywhere. Kids are allowed outside to play. We are supposed to explore. Wow. Sometimes you are so . . . human."

Annie never realized "human" could be an insult. She thought about that a bit as she followed Eva back to the street and then halfway up the hill to Aquarius House. The dwarf finally stopped in a blueberry barren, dropping the fireworks in a big heap on the snow.

"Now, help me set this up," Eva ordered, and Annie assisted her as she placed the long cylinders in the snow at appropriate angles. Some had zigzag edges. Some were covered in teal polka dots. Some seemed to quiver and bark like dogs.

Eva inspected their handiwork. "That looks right . . . I think . . . Yeah . . . Well, let's hope."

"Hope? Doesn't it have to be—"

Eva cut her off, running between the firework rockets with a giant match. She lit them all and dived backward, knocking Annie to the ground. Tala growled and leaped away with them.

"Hold your ears!" Eva yelled.

Tala buried his head in the snow. Annie managed to untangle herself from Eva just before eight resounding explosions shook the entire field.

Boom! The red rocket full of stars vaulted into the sky spelling out Attention! Horns seemed to bellow from the word.

Boom! Another rocket flew up, creating a picture of Miss Cornelia's face.

Boom! More words as another rocket exploded.

Have you seen me?

Boom! Do not panic. this rocket said.

Boom!

But things might be bad.

Boom! Another picture of Miss Cornelia's face as the words fizzled out.

Have you seen me?

Boom! The polka-dot rocket spiraled into the sky and dissolved.

"Crud," Eva cursed.

Boom! The last rocket launched into the sky and dissolved into bright spiraling lights.

Do not panic, okay?

But Miss Cornelia, please come home.

Eva sat up, smiling, removing her hands from her ears.

Tala pulled his head out of the snow. "That worked brilliantly, if I do say so myself."

"So now what do we do?" Annie asked as the last of the fireworks dissipated.

"I, Eva Beryl-Axe, the leader, not the bossy girl, think that we should go back to Aquarius House and wait."

Jamie and Bloom had taken the other side of town, quietly going from house to burrow to lawn chair in an attempt to get information about Miss Cornelia in a nonterrifying way. They were just outside the library's stone gates when Eva's fireworks lit the sky.

Bloom gasped. "Well, that was subtle."

Jamie agreed. He straightened his coat. His stomach rumbled; he was already hungry again. "I guess we might as well just go back."

They had barely returned to Aquarius House and taken off their winter clothes, and Bloom had just started arguing with Eva about the fireworks, when the front door burst open and a mass of townspeople crowded inside. Jamie was not big on crowds, not used to them at all, being from Mount Desert with a year-round population of fifteen hundred spread-apart people.

As three hags gathered around the boot closet and some fairies fluttered up to the ceiling, Jamie staggered backward and said, frightened, "Annie . . . ?"

"It'll be okay, Jamie." She glanced at Bloom for reassurance, most likely, but from what Jamie could tell the elf looked as overwhelmed as Jamie felt.

"No worries," Bloom whispered.

"What the heck?" Eva bellowed, jumping up on the banister of the staircase as several furry Big Feet ambled inside followed by a plethora of dwarfs and shifters and vampires, covered completely in black cloth to keep them from the sun's burning rays. "Seriously? What are you all doing?"

Mr. Nate, Jamie's former librarian, and Helena, the baker, rushed inside. She fussed with his hat, whisking the flour off it, and then she began scraping chocolate off his face.

"We saw the message," Mr. Nate said.

"We saw the message!" the fairies and pixies twittered, repeating his sentence in high-pitched bell tones. "We are scared! We are alarmed! We are terrified."

"There ain't no reason to be terrified," Eva announced, waving her ax around.

"Miss Cornelia! Where is Miss Cornelia?" some mossy rocks were yelling.

Eva tried again. "Hello! Do NOT be TERRIFIED or I will smite you or something!"

Nobody paid attention to her. Some of the fairies started hyperventilating. Others muttered and swore, yelling out their worries as the hysteria grew greater and greater. One hag plucked out her eye, releasing it into the air where it jerked around, flying left and then right, straight up and then spiraling down.

"Really! We are not going to freak out here!" Eva yelled, stomping her foot so hard that she lost her balance. Bloom caught her.

"Let me down!" she grumped.

"Of course." He dropped her on the floor next to a crying hedgehog wearing a yellow-and-orange superhero cape.

More shifters, as well as Canin and some stone giants, rushed inside the room. The mermaids and mermen swam to the surface of the fountain. Farkey, one of Jamie's favorites, winked at Jamie. Jamie was too scared to wink back, but he gave a little wave. It didn't feel like a time for winking anyway, but who knew what mermen winking even meant. Maybe it meant don't worry. Maybe it meant the lobsters are jerks today. Who knew?

Jamie offered Eva his hand to help her stand. She glared at him and climbed back up the banister. It creaked a bit under her weight. She started taking all sorts of things out of her pocket and dropping them onto the stairs or onto the heads of the creatures surrounding her—a sausage link, a plant, a piece of gold nugget, a bag of dirt, and finally a whistle. She clasped the whistle and brought it to her lips, blowing hard three times.

Everyone was quiet.

"Finally," Eva muttered, removing the whistle. "I expected more from all of you. Carrying on like this ain't helping, and I expect Miss Cornelia would say that, too. Wouldn't she? Oh, don't you glower at me, Odham Norton-Dog." She pointed at a scowling boy. "You know I'm right. Now, everybody listen to me, Eva Beryl-Axe, recent hero of glorious awesomeness. I am asking you all, right this second, if any of you have seen Miss Cornelia this morning? Do NOT speak!" She yelled as people started raising their voices, babbling over the top of one another.

She blew her whistle again.

People stopped talking, but it was a bit more slowly this time, Jamie noticed. It was as if they really didn't want to be quiet or listen to the young dwarf balanced precariously on the banister.

"How about this," Eva suggested. "Raise your hand or your paw or your fin or whatever if you did indeed see Miss Cornelia this morning."

Nobody raised anything.

Annie pushed her way up the staircase to have a better look.

"Anyone? Surely, someone must have seen something?" she called out into the crowd.

Nobody raised anything, but then there was a slight splash in the fountain. The merboy Farkey tentatively lifted his tail fin.

"Yes . . . Mer . . . Merperson? I don't know your name, I'm sorry," Annie said.

"Farkey." He cleared his throat and repeated. "I'm Farkey."

"Farkey. It's good to meet you."

Annie was always polite, Jamie realized, even in a crisis.

"Did you see Miss Cornelia this morning?" Annie asked.

"Um . . . no . . ." He cleared his throat again as the crowd started murmuring and mumbling over him.

"Please be quiet, everyone!" Annie asked with her tiny voice.

Eva blew the whistle again, eliciting some angry moans from all the shifting dogs who found high-pitched whistle noises offensive.

Once everyone was silent again, Annie continued, "But you saw something, didn't you?"

"It was more like I heard something," Farkey agreed. He looked nervously around. "Everyone's staring at me. Does my hair look okay?" His wet hand fluttered up to his unruly hair.

"It's great. Very full of volume. No tangles," Annie assured him. "And everyone is looking at you because . . . because . . ."

She appealed to Jamie for help.

"Because we want to hear what you have to say," Jamie finished for her and tried to give Farkey a reassuring look.

Farkey cleared his throat again. "It happened late last night. It sounded like a door opening and clothes being rustled. I was . . . was on the surface, drying out a little, trying to keep the mold at bay. My flipper has been having an issue."

"So, a door? And rustling clothes? Is that all?" Annie asked. She leaned closer, listening.

"More like the swirling of skirts. And a horse. It smelled like a horse was outside, and there was the sound of something heavy being moved around."

Jamie's mouth dropped open. A horse? The dark evil horse *was* still in Aurora.

For a moment nobody said anything, and then the room burst into chaos and ranting and worry. Even Eva's whistle couldn't quiet anyone.

"Miss Cornelia's been kidnapped!" someone shouted.

"Don't jump to conclusions!" a Big Foot argued.

"We're doomed!" the fairies and hags all started yelling.

"What do we do?"

"Where did they take her?"

"And who?"

"And why?"

"And how?"

Annie moved toward Jamie and Bloom. "It was that horse. The one with the crow, I bet." She turned to Farkey. "What else did you hear?"

"Heavy footsteps going out the front door."

"But you don't know for sure it was Miss Cornelia, do you?"

"It was dark, and I couldn't see. But it smelled like her," Farkey said sadly, shaking the water out of his hair. "Plus, I smelled someone else, someone spicy. That's all I know. I'm sorry."

"You have nothing to be sorry about. You're being super helpful," Annie said.

"No. I'm sorry that I didn't realize earlier. That I-I didn't put it all together. I was too busy being sad about the mold and my hair and . . ."

"It doesn't matter," Jamie said, patting Farkey's shoulder, and then awkwardly wiping the wetness off his hand. "You've told us now. Right?"

Jamie took a deep breath and surveyed the large front room, which was absolutely crammed full of magical creatures, most of whom were arguing or having hysterics. It was sort of pitiful. He'd expected more out of magical creatures somehow.

"The Stopper Girl, Annie. She should tell us what to do," a hag insisted. "If she's a real Time Stopper and all."

"She's a real Stopper," said Eva. "I've seen it! You calling me a liar?"

Eva bounded off the banister and began thumping her chest up against the hag's stomach in what was meant to be an intimidating move. The hag seemed unfazed, as if threatening dwarfs were normal occurrences in her day. Maybe they were. Jamie didn't know.

What Jamie did know was that he wanted to turn and

run away, just run right out of the front room, up the stairs and into his bedroom, slamming the door behind him, go back to sleep, and start the day over.

"Settle down, everyone!" The mayor strode into the room purposefully, unzipping his bright red parka as he smiled.

Relief flooded Jamie. The mayor was in charge here. Not him, not Annie. Surely the mayor would fix everything or tell them what to do to fix everything.

"What is all this about?" the mayor asked.

"Oh, great. He's going to talk forever," Eva muttered.

Annie edged closer to Jamie, protectively.

"Don't worry," he whispered. "It's the mayor. He'll fix it. It's his job. The town where I lived has a mayor, too. That's what they do."

Bloom cleared his throat and called out over the murmuring crowd, "It's Miss Cornelia, Mayor. We think she has been kidnapped. Nobody can find her, and the magic in Aquarius House isn't quite right."

"Or in the town!" shouted out a broad dwarf with black hair. He scratched at his nose. "The Belles are fluttering around yelling 'Emergency' in that silly accent and then just disappearing. Poof! That ain't right."

"And the Gnome of Protection is blowing bubbles," Miss Helena said, brushing flour out of her hair. "The bubbles smell of rotten eggs."

People gasped and started talking all at once.

Farkey whispered in Jamie's ear. "I smell the spice smell again. Right now."

"What?" Jamie yelled the word, too late realizing that drawing attention to himself was not a good idea.

"It's his fault," one of the hags shouted, pointing a long, crooked finger at Jamie. "That troll boy has a hand in this! I know it!"

Jamie thought fast, trying to determine if he could run out of the crowded room without anyone stopping him; it didn't seem likely.

"Jamie hasn't done a thing!" Annie shouted, gripping his hand hard and keeping him by her side. "He's been looking for Miss Cornelia all morning."

"Looking for her, eh?" a mossy rock said. "How'd he know she was missing, then?"

The rock raised an eyebrow. Jamie didn't know rocks could have eyebrows.

"Unless he's the one who took her!" the rock continued.

People started clamoring about, shouting and edging toward Jamie. Annie pushed him behind her, and Bloom helped block him from the angry townspeople. Jamie stood on the rim of the mermaid fountain, teeth chattering. He clenched Annie's hand, tottering on the edge.

"Don't be ridiculous!" Eva shouted, but nobody listened to her. Instead they just inched closer, yelling.

"Put him in the dungeon, we should."

"No, that's too good for him, coming in here, messing with our Stopper."

"Once you live with trolls, you can't be good. Being near that evil? It wears off on you."

"He's not even magic. He don't belong here."

Annie's heart seemed to growl. She yelled as loudly as she could, "Stop it!"

"You should all be ashamed of yourselves," Bloom muttered. "I am so ashamed of you."

The crowd didn't seem to care about shame or anything else. Then, SalGoud, Ned the Doctor, and Gramma Doris pushed through the doors, hair askew, coats half-unbuttoned, and faces all drawn down into upset lines, making them horribly concerned looking. Jamie doubted they could help. There were so many people upset, so many people yelling, so many people wanting to blame him.

"Jamie has nothing to do with this," Annie yelled, hopping up to the statue in the fountain so that everyone could see her and she could see them. "Just because he is not magic does not make him evil!" Her voice grew stronger. "Do you know who is acting evil? All of you! You're making snap decisions, laying blame, and pointing fingers at Jamie—and what has he ever done to you? I'll tell you what he's done. He's saved you. Risked his life for you! And this is the way you repay him? You're all being nasty anti-troll bigots, and he is not even a troll! He's just a boy, a brave, human boy. I am ashamed of you! And Miss Cornelia would be ashamed of you, too. She loves Jamie. He helped save all of us. He's a hero!"

Annie drew in a deep breath, hair wild about her face and eyes fierce. She had never seemed so magical, never seemed so powerful, and Jamie had never heard her yell so loudly, not ever. She climbed down from the fountain and stood defiantly next to Eva.

"A hero of glorious gloriousness," Annie finished.

The creatures were quiet.

"She's right, you know," Ned the Doctor said in a serious, calm voice. "As Johann Wolfgang von Goethe said, 'There is nothing more frightful than ignorance in action.' "

SalGoud, the young stone giant, adjusted his glasses farther up on the bridge of his nose and said, "Or as Sir William Drummond said, 'He, who will not reason, is a bigot; he, who cannot, is a fool; and he, who dares not, is a slave.' Will you all be slaves to your fear? Do you not dare to reason?"

Ned the Doctor patted SalGoud on the back. "Or this one from Emma Goldman, 'Someone has said that it requires less mental effort to condemn than to think.' "

"Good one!" SalGoud said, beginning another quote as soon as Ned the Doctor thanked him.

"They can go on like this all day," Eva grumped, crossing her arms in front of her chest, but putting her ax away.

Just as she grumped, the room shook. Everyone went

silent. Annie's eyes grew wide and she turned to Bloom. "There's something . . . Something is coming . . . I can feel it."

Bloom pulled out his dagger. Eva grabbed her ax once more, and all around the room, dwarfs unsheathed their weapons. The mermaids and mermen, even Farkey, dived into the fountain, terrified, as the room rumbled and the water stirred. Dwarfs stood strong while Big Feet hugged stone giants, who hugged shifters. Some pixies cowered by the chandelier, hiding behind the flowery bulbs.

"What is it?" Annie whispered, leaping off the statue to the floor next to Jamie.

Jamie pointed to where she just was. "The fountain."

The water blackened and bubbled. A watery figure started to form from the droplets. The room gasped as the air vibrated. Some creatures ran back outside into the snow.

"Ah, it'll not be him again," Gramma Doris muttered, making the sign of a heart above her chest. "Lovely, dramatic timing, he has."

As she spoke, the water formed a man. And the man had a face. A face they all recognized.

"The Raiff," Bloom whispered, his skin whitening.

"I see you remember me, even those whom I haven't met. How lovely." The image smiled.

Someone shrieked. Eva fainted, but luckily Bloom and Jamie had been expecting it, and they caught her before she hit the floor. Some other dwarfs were not as lucky.

The mayor strode forward, forcibly knocking some

smaller vampires out of his way. He stood face-to-face with the Raiff's water embodiment.

"He's not really here, right?" Jamie whispered. "This is just magic, but not his real self, right?"

Helena grabbed his shoulder. Her hand trembled. "Right."

"What do you want, demon?" the mayor demanded, puffing himself up to his full height and sticking his broad chest out so much that it seemed like the seams of his parka might burst.

"I have someone you want." The Raiff reached out into the air, his arm and hand disappearing, and pulled a bound woman beside him. Even though she was watery and blurry, it was obvious that it was Miss Cornelia. Annie's world spun and for a second she thought she might faint next to Eva, but then anger made her bones solid. What had he done to Miss Cornelia and how had he gotten her?

"You scoundrel!" the mayor yelled. He put his hands on his heart. Annie had never heard anyone use the word "scoundrel" before, but it fit. "How dare you?"

"I dare because I can!" The Raiff's quiet words were much more frightening than the mayor's yells.

"What do you want?" the mayor pleaded. "Tell us. We'll give you anything. Let us have Miss Cornelia back."

"Her!" The demon pointed at Annie. "I want the Nobody."

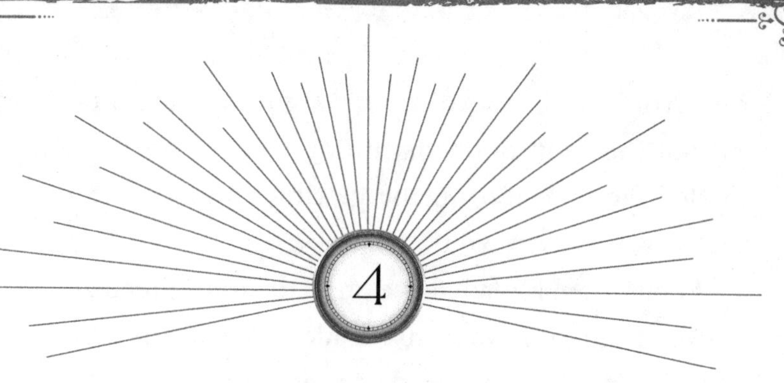

Wanted: Dead or Alive

The Raiff's demands echoed in the crowded room for only a split second before Megan, a hag Annie and Jamie's age, pushed Annie from behind, forcing Annie forward. "Take her!"

Canin snarled and snatched Annie's arm, yanking her backward and away from the fountain. Tala hopped in front of Annie, too, ears back, and growling. They were protecting her as if the Raiff's watery image could somehow snatch her away.

"Megan!" SalGoud yelled out. "Don't do that!"

"We should trade her. She's no good as a Stopper anyway. We need Miss Cornelia!" Megan reasoned, eyes flickering.

"Don't you dare!" Gramma Doris yanked Megan away

from Annie and shooed her through the remaining crowd and out the front door, slamming it shut right in Megan's startled face. "You'll not be getting any of our Stoppers, you . . . you demon, you!"

"Looks like I already have one," the Raiff preened.

Even though he was only made of water, the evil rolling off him was strong and made Annie sick.

"No," she managed to say, "Megan is right. You should trade me for Miss Cornelia. You should—"

Canin covered his mouth with his hand and whispered, "Hush," into her ear. "Say no more."

"Exactly!" the demon agreed. "Send Annie over and I will return the old—"

"Don't send Annie. Do not!" Miss Cornelia gasped behind him. "Look for the Big Foot to find the . . . the dragon . . . the elves . . ." Her voice fizzled out, and the image exploded into a million drops of water, all raining down on the creatures cluttered in the hall.

The Raiff and Miss Cornelia were gone, leaving only the faint smell of rotten eggs and fear.

"Dragon!" The crowd rumbled and panicked even more. Fairies rushed to the front door and scanned the skies.

"There are no dragons . . ."

"Why would she say 'dragon'?"

"Are they in the Badlands? Does the Raiff have a dragon?"

Canin released Annie, who fell to the floor in a sobbing

heap. Her arms circled Tala's doggy side. "Let me go . . . You should just trade me . . . You should just make me go . . ."

"We will do no such thing, young lady," said Gramma Doris. "We will get Miss Cornelia back, and YOU will not be the price that we pay. He probably wouldn't trade in the first place, just wants you both, he does. Demons don't keep their word anyway. Just like pirates, they are . . . You ask the Woman in White. No, don't ask her anything. She'll just disappear," Gramma Doris ordered as her ears went pink. "Ned, take Annie to rest. Right now. I will send up some nice tea later."

As she hurried to the kitchen, Gramma Doris muttered under her breath, "Why would Corny mention Big Foot and elves? She . . . Oh, she must be under such stress. Poor thing . . . Poor wonderful woman . . ."

The mayor eyed the remaining folk in the front room as Ned carried Annie's sad, small frame up the stairs. The dwarfs had all fainted straight away, as they tend to do under moments of extreme duress. The shifters couldn't stop shifting, and they blinked in between forms, causing a strobe light–effect on the rest of the crowd.

"Someone start resuscitating the dwarfs," the mayor ordered. "There will be a Council meeting in a half hour. Mr. Nate, you fill in Miss Cornelia's seat, since you somehow qualify as a magical human—barely. Town Hall. Be there."

Mr. Nate froze for a second. The mayor strode away.

"Mr. Nate?" Jamie nudged his friend who had been his

only confidant when he first discovered the whole troll family business. "You okay?"

The man shook his head. "I'm terrified. Come with me? Please . . ."

"But . . ." Jamie noticed Annie and Doctor Ned retreating up the stairs, and he really didn't want to leave Annie's side. He needed to talk to Annie about what Farkey had said. Someone with the spicy smell had been there when Miss Cornelia was kidnapped. And that same someone was in the room right this very moment. But who?

Jamie was torn between his two friends. But Mr. Nate's already gaunt face seemed to have skinnied itself down to the size of a pencil. He had done so much for Jamie. He had looked out for Jamie before Aurora, and if it weren't for Mr. Nate, he probably would have been troll food already. There was really no decision to be made.

"Okay, Mr. Nate," Jamie said with completely fake bravado. "Let's go face the Council."

As Jamie and Mr. Nate entered the Town Council Chamber in Aurora's Town Hall, the atmosphere became balmy. The swirling ceiling fans seemed to pump out tropical, humid air. Some snakes slithered along the radiators, basking in it. Some fairies were defogging the windows with their breath and tiny glittery rags, getting glitter everywhere, which caused the vampires in attendance to sneeze from the dust. Parkas, winter hats, sweaters, and mittens were cast aside, resting next to their owners or in jumbles on the floor. Dozens and dozens of scarab beetles scaled one of the walls, turning it into a black, glistening, moving plane.

"Well, that's strange," Mr. Nate said, voice shaking. "Never seen that before."

They were the last to arrive. Several town residents sat below the stage, perched or lounging on the long, heavy wooden benches. The Town Council had already taken its seats. The Council was the political body that made decisions for Aurora. Board members included representatives from all the major creature species. There was a fae (Arrius Herman), a magical human (Miss Cornelia), a giant (the Mayor), a hag (Walburga Wakanda), a shape shifter (Leodora Leksi), and a dwarf (Nicodemus Metal Smith), as well as a non-blood-sucking vampire (Aelfric Darling).

Next to Arrius Herman, the fae, Miss Cornelia's seat was vacant.

"Come on up, Mr. Nate!" the mayor bellowed. He had positioned himself at the head of the long wooden table.

Mr. Nate hesitated.

"It's okay," Jamie whispered.

"What if—?" Mr. Nate's voice broke off.

Jamie cocked his head to the side. "What if what?"

"What if I make the wrong decision?" Mr. Nate finished.

He was wringing his hands together, twisting them one way and then the other.

"You won't. No decision is wrong if it comes from a place of good, right?" Jamie helped Mr. Nate shrug off his coat. "Go on. You can do it."

With a quick nod, Mr. Nate climbed up the three side stairs to the stage and landed between Arrius Herman and Walburga Wakanda, the hag. A long yellow snake bared its fangs at him but didn't strike.

Jamie didn't think Mr. Nate even noticed. Jamie settled himself on a bench next to Miss Helena, who smelled comfortingly of sugar and vanilla. She handed him an éclair.

"Thank you," he murmured.

She petted his knee. "Anytime, sweetie."

A dwarf in front of them snorted and whispered in a super loud way to his companion, "I wouldn't be feeding him. He'll be troll soon enough."

Helena kicked the dwarf in the center of his back, sending him landing on his rump. He roared, turning around. "Why—why you—"

She pointed a spatula at him as he sputtered at her. "I would not say anything against our young hero, if I were you. Not if you ever want any of my chewy cinnamon bialys again."

Up on the stage, the mayor called the meeting to order, which caused Leodora Leksi to tap her well-manicured nails on the table and mutter, "Finally."

"We are here today under dire circumstances, to determine the fate of our town and its Stopper, Miss Cornelia, who has been abducted and somehow taken to the Badlands."

"How was she even abducted? I thought the town was protected again since the gnome has been returned?" demanded Nicodemus Metal Smith.

"Something or some *things* must have snuck in undetected during the time the gnome was gone," drawled Aelfric Darling, who looked not too happy to be there. He pulled off his cloak, exposing vampire-pale limbs. "It is dreadfully warm in here. Can someone fix that?"

"I am afraid not. We aren't relying on magic for heat but an actual furnace, and nobody knows how to use a thermostat. No worries. Take off another layer." The mayor's large hand waved the worry away, dismissing it. He began pontificating again, explaining that they needed to decide on a course of action, finishing with, "The Raiff suggests a trade: young Annie, our untested and untrained Time Stopper, for the more experienced benefactress of the town, Miss Cornelia."

"Well, it's not hard to see where his loyalties lie," Helena murmured, pulling a red velvet cupcake out of her large zebra-print purse.

"But . . ." Jamie jumped to his feet. He didn't even know where to begin.

"Do you have something to say to the Council, young man?" the mayor asked.

"Y-y-y-es," Jamie stuttered. "Two things came to Aurora. There was the crow, which Annie defeated, and there was also a dark horse. We saw it, and it felt like evil. It's still out there, somewhere. So you see, we can't give up Annie. We just can't."

Jamie sat down again and cleared his throat.

"I agree with the mayor," said Aelfric, adjusting his shirt so it hung perfectly from his shoulders. "There is no way young Annie can protect this town. With Miss Cornelia, we have thrived since the Purge and—"

"You would send a young girl to the Badlands? In trade with a demon?" Leodora interrupted. Her golden mane of hair seemed to thicken with her anger. "How could you?"

"It is our only option," Aelfric countered. "And she is untrained. Her power is untested."

"She saved us just last night!" Leodora stood up, hair rippling around her face. "Who are we to determine the fate of another being? To force this poor, defenseless girl into the lair of the Raiff?"

The mayor appealed for calm.

"Yes, she did save us," Mr. Metal Smith added, "with the help of a dwarf. Let's not forget the dwarfs!"

The Council erupted into a quarrel between Leodora and everyone else. Only Mr. Nate and the hag, Walburga Wakanda, remained quiet. Finally the mayor asked, "What say you, Walburga?"

The chamber went silent.

"Well, one of my kind has foreseen that the girl will fall with evil. Perhaps this is what she meant. The prophecy."

"No!" yelled Jamie, jumping out of his seat again. "No! You can't just trade her. How do you know the Raiff will even keep his promise? He could just hold on to both of them. And hags are only right seventy-six point five percent of the time. Everybody knows that."

The mayor hemmed and hawed as if he was pondering it. "There is no other way, but yes, we have no assurance of the Raiff's promise."

"But you're still going to do it?" Jamie asked, stunned.

"Young man, you are not a representative of this Council and you are speaking out of turn." The mayor gestured to those at the table. "Only the Council is allowed to speak, to determine the outcome of our town, our Stoppers' fate, our—"

"It's like Ms. Leodora said. Shouldn't Annie be allowed to determine her own fate?" Jamie interrupted. "You have no right to just send her there to die or be tortured. Haven't you even thought about why the Raiff would rather have some untested Stopper instead of Miss Cornelia? There has to be a—"

"Remove the young . . . man—or is it soon-to-be-troll?—from our meeting, please." The mayor snapped his finger and a giant named Red Nose and another, furry man grabbed Jamie by the arms, hauling him out of the building. They hadn't even let him put his coat back on as they dumped him in the snow.

Helena bustled out after him, helping him get his winter things back on.

"Don't you worry, now," she said. "Mr. Nate will vote with Ms. Leksi. Don't you worry." She yanked his hat down over his ears. "But maybe you best go find Annie and tell her to hide." She looked anxiously over her shoulder back toward the erupting yells inside the Town Hall. "You know . . . just in case . . . That sweet little girl wouldn't last a day in the Badlands . . ."

Someone in the hall yelled, "Over my dead body!"

Helena gave Jamie's nose a tweak and turned him toward the road. "Yep. Why don't you tell her to go hide? Maybe you should hide with her. Yes, I think that is a very wise idea. Hide, young James. Hide!"

Luckily for Annie, Bloom had followed her to her room where she was supposed to be resting. Annie did not want to stay in bed. Annie did not want to have any "nice tea" later. She wanted to go to the Badlands and trade herself for Miss Cornelia somehow.

But then she thought about the Badlands . . .

And how the actual name of the place had the word

"bad" in it. Although she supposed Badlands was better than EVILlands or TORTURE-YOU-FOREVERlands.

But then she thought about how Miss Cornelia was there . . . Miss Cornelia of the swirling skirts and kind eyes . . . Miss Cornelia of the *I will give you a home, Annie* . . . Miss Cornelia of the *You belong here with me, Annie* . . . Miss Cornelia whose hugs seemed magic because they were so full of love.

"Bloom, why does the Raiff need a Stopper at all?" Annie asked and offered him some of the tea that was on the side table.

"Only a Stopper can open portals and travel back and forth. Once humans or creatures go through a portal, it's a one-way kind of thing. There is no coming back." He paused.

"Unless you're a Stopper. Or with a Stopper."

"Right. Or with a dragon, you can open it up and anyone can come through, but it stays open. You can't close it again, I don't think. Both can bring people and creatures back with them. That's probably what the Raiff wants. He needs a Stopper to open the Badlands portal and bring him back to Aurora."

"So if he already has Miss Cornelia, why does he need me? Can't she just open it?"

"Maybe she won't."

"And if she refuses?"

"He will torture her. Like he would torture you." Bloom

took the tea and sipped it. "I think she would die before she would do it, Annie."

Annie gritted her teeth. It didn't make sense. She didn't even know how to open a portal. And sure, she wasn't as strong as Miss Cornelia obviously was, but how was the Raiff so sure that he could torture her into doing what he wanted?

"There's got to be another way," she insisted.

"I don't know of one." Bloom flopped on the floor, flat, arms spread wide.

Annie sighed. "And what about dragons?"

"They're all gone, Annie. There are no more dragons. Humans hunted them into extinction centuries ago," Bloom said, still on the floor.

Annie let out a big sigh. She remembered reading about that now. "Books. Maybe our answers are in a book!"

Bloom closed his eyes. "Books don't know everything, Annie."

"Magical books do," she insisted. She wondered who wrote magical books.

"And magical writers," Bloom said, as if it was the most sensible thing in the world. "Elves used to write them, but we're all gone now, like the dragons. Stoppers did, too. An occasional brounie. They write cookbooks mostly, but . . ."

"So the magic gets into books because the writers have magic in them?" Annie asked, getting out of bed and perusing the books in the room.

"No. Yes . . ." The boy sat up. "If you think about it, all

books are magic and so are writers because they make you believe in stories, see images, and all that. Right?"

"Right," Annie said, but she wasn't fully listening. She was sure there had to be a book here that could help them, and if not here, then maybe in the library. But none of the titles seemed to be related to what she needed. *The Goofy Girls' Guide to Gastronomical Prophecy. 1,000 Ways for Even Nitwits to Reverse a Hex. The Magical Unicorns of Moravia.*

"Books!" she announced, clapping her hands for attention. "If any of you have anything to do with going through portals to the Badlands or about dragons, could you please make yourself known?"

She waited a moment.

She waited another moment.

"Please?"

A book toppled onto the floor. She snatched it up as Tala sniffed it cautiously, and she read the spine. "*A Guide to Dragons.*"

The prickle of worry that had built up in her chest was getting larger and larger by the second. She had thought that the books would help . . . For a second, she had thought that dragons might be the answer. She thought Miss Cornelia had given them a clue.

Annie pivoted around, excited. "Someone must know where the portal is. We just have to find it, go to the Badlands, rescue Miss Cornelia, and then all of us together will conquer the Raiff. After that, Miss Cornelia and I can make a portal big enough to get us all back."

Bloom's mouth dropped open.

"What?" Annie asked.

"You've seen the residents of this town, right?" he scoffed. "They are hardly an army, especially without the elves."

"They are brilliant and magical and awesome," Annie countered.

"They are also not-so-brilliant and semi-magical and annoying." Bloom shook his head. "You do remember the hags, right? And the dwarfs? Have you ever seen a fairy try to fight a troll?"

"If there was a fight, they'd pull together. They would have to. Isn't that what happened during the Purge?" Annie insisted, bringing up the biggest battle in Aurora's history.

"Annie," Bloom whispered. "We lost in the Purge. We almost lost everyone. We lost all the elves except me. If it wasn't for Miss Cornelia finding the strength to banish the Raiff, we would have—"

Annie wasn't listening. She caught sight of another book wobbling on the edge of a shelf. She grabbed it. "What's this? *Portals to Other Worlds*? Bloom!"

He hustled over. His expression changed from worry to wonderment. "Oh, this is fantastic!"

Annie flipped through the book and found the index. Aurora was in there. She turned to page 98 and began to read.

"What?" Bloom asked anxiously. "Did you find something?"

"There's a portal," Annie said, eyes wide. "There's a portal right here in the barrens."

The book said that there were fewer portals in the world than there had been. It said that regular people, the nonmagical kind of people, break the portals when they cut down trees and mine in the mountains that hold them. Some creatures don't need portals to leap from land to land. They just leap. But they can't take others. According to the book, that's why there are so many reports of aliens and demon dogs and giant bats. Those are the leapers, but they can't bring companions with them. Only themselves. Stoppers are different. When they open a portal for real, instead of its being like a one-way door or even a door with locks, anything can go through.

Annie shrugged on some boots that she didn't even remember taking off and snatched the ghosts' bell off the top of her nightstand. Then she pulled open the nightstand's drawer. A shiny, sharp knife with intricate etchings rolled to the front. Miss Cornelia had said it was called a phurba and would keep her safe.

She tucked the phurba into the waistband of her jeans and grabbed Bloom's hand. "Come on! We've got to go!"

The duo ran down the stairs, and Annie pulled open the front door—only to see Jamie standing on Aquarius House's doorstep. And there was an angry mob of townspeople not far behind him.

5

Monsters

Jamie's head spun. He had tried to warn Annie, like Helena had suggested. But he wasn't fast enough. Only moments after he left, the Town Council had made its decision: to find Annie and take her through the portal to the Badlands. To the Raiff.

"Get her! Get the boy, too!" someone roared.

Cheers of agreement sent shivers into Jamie's heart.

"Annie Nobody!" the mayor yelled in his normal jolly tone, as if he were just stopping by Aquarius House for a social call. "Just the Stopper we were looking for. It is your duty to trade places with Miss Cornelia. If Miss Cornelia bends . . ."

"Even she cannot withstand the Raiff long," came an answer.

Was that Canin? Jamie gulped. He had sort of imagined that Miss Cornelia could withstand anything. She seemed like a little tree, solid. Then Jamie remembered the night he witnessed his grandmother turn troll, battering down the beautiful trees as she and her troll posse barreled into the forest by their house. Those trees seemed unbreakable, too.

"I am not in favor of this plan, Mayor. I am horrified that you think it is okay. Cornelia would—" Canin argued surprisingly passionately for someone who hadn't given Annie, Jamie, Eva, or even Bloom much mind.

"Cornelia is not here, Canin!" The mayor's voice dropped down low, but it became so much more threatening.

"I'm well aware of that," Canin ruffed back, obviously unfazed by the mayor's tone.

"The plan is for Annie to open the portal and exchange places with Miss Cornelia. It's the only way. We can't go to the Badlands, because we can't come back. The only ones who can cross both ways are the merpeople."

"The merpeople!" Canin explained. "How does nobody know this?"

Jamie and Bloom gazed back at Farkey who was floating in the fountain. Farkey gave a slight nod.

"There are certain things that only the Council knows. The Council thought it wiser—" the mayor began.

"The Council is full of—" Canin roared.

"CANIN! Language and tone. I am the mayor. Respect."

"Yes, you keep reminding me. And I show respect when

respect is due." Canin stepped closer to the mayor. "If what you say is true, then why can't the merpeople go in and bring Miss Cornelia back on their own, without Annie?"

At that, Farkey dived headfirst and stayed underwater.

"They can't cross with others, not using their own magic. It doesn't work. We've tried. And they can't launch a ground raid to retrieve Cornelia because they can only be out of the water for a moment or two at a time."

Canin growled. "So we do what? Give the Raiff the poor kid? She won't be able to resist him. And in the meantime he'll have more time to torment Miss Cornelia?"

"Torment isn't the word for it," the mayor answered.

They stood in silence for a moment.

The mayor broke it. "We have no other choice."

Canin roared. "If you give them Annie and she opens the portal, then the Raiff can escape. He will come back with his minions. We will be overrun. It will be like the Purge, only this time our Stopper will be weak. There will be no hope for us."

"There is always hope," countered the mayor. "We have no other choice. The Council has made its decision, and we will deal with the consequences. We will do whatever it takes, deal with whatever it takes to get our Stopper back."

A horrible, sinking feeling overcame Jamie.

Perhaps it was because her world was suddenly tilted and askew again that Annie didn't really know what exactly to think. She was only recently thrust into this magical world after a lifetime of living in one foster home after another. She'd always been so unwanted. And then finally—finally!—she came to Aurora, and she had actually believed all that good could be true, and now—AND NOW—poof! Miss Cornelia was gone. And everyone was willing to trade her for the real Stopper.

"It's okay. I'm not important," she muttered, catching a snowflake on her hand. "I never am."

Aurora felt more like home than any town she'd ever lived in, but she felt she'd let her new friends down. She should have known Miss Cornelia was in danger. She should have thought about that horse they'd seen with the crow monster. Tears threatened and the mean voice in her head said, *Stupid girl. Coward girl.*

Annie closed her eyes and imagined the struggle. Large dirty ropes bound Miss Cornelia. Slumped down about her ankles, her rainbow socks signaled pain. Loose strands of hair strayed from her bun. Fierceness glistened in her eyes. That horrible horse laughed and gnashed its teeth.

"Don't give up, Miss Cornelia," she whispered. "We'll find you."

Annie's stomach dropped. It hurt that they'd be so willing to give her up. They *wanted* to give her up. And nobody believed that she could defeat the Raiff and come home with Miss Cornelia. Even Bloom hadn't been so sure about it.

"Annie, if there was any other way, we would go, too. We would protect you and ensure we get Cornelia back. But we can't." The mayor puffed up his chest. "Maybe you can trick the demon."

Bloom's mouth dropped open. "The Raiff is not someone you can trick."

"Miss Cornelia did once," Aelfric countered. "She got him and most of the trolls in North America through the portal."

"That was Miss Cornelia! She was . . . she is . . ." Bloom's face reddened.

"Brilliant," the mayor finished for him, "and so are we. We might not have a complete plan yet, but we'll get one and all will be right again with our little town." He gave a jolly, forced laugh that echoed throughout the barrens and then fell flat. "Just you see. Now come along." He whisked the children ahead of him with a broad sweeping arm.

"Is the portal far?" Annie whispered, her voice quivering. It was so cold that she had lost feeling in her piggy toes.

"It's an oak tree in the barrens. It stands tall and has lived for centuries. It's a good portal," the mayor answered in the same sort of voice he used in meetings. Annie knew he was trying to comfort her. He was a large man, and even if he was bombastic, he radiated warmth. The heat coming out of his body warmed her slightly, despite the awful cold. "It's okay to be afraid, Annie, but remember, we *will* be there with you in spirit."

They galloped on with Aelfric and Canin in the lead. Annie had no idea how they could see at all. Every once in a while Canin would stop and tilt his ears as if he was listening for a trail. Tala walked beside Annie, occasionally pressing his side against her right leg and making a small growling noise. Jamie walked on her other side. His lip trembled and Annie wasn't sure whether it was from rage or fear or cold. It didn't seem polite to ask in front of the others.

"Does he know what he's doing?" Annie asked the mayor, nodding toward Aelfric.

"He's a good tracker. The secret is in the ears."

Annie nodded, but she felt as if they were walking into a horrible nightmare. The dark night seemed to push against her, grabbing her, shaking her. She wondered if they'd fall off one of Aurora's cliffs or land in a trap.

"Cold, Annie?" the mayor asked, his big pillow of a hand on her shoulder. He wiped the half inch of snow that had accumulated there.

"She needs to keep up," Aelfric said. "It'll be colder in the Badlands. Unless it's hotter. I hear that it can be as hot as the fire pits of Mount Forgeolympus, the dwarfs' ancient lair. But either way, if she hopes to survive at all, she needs to keep up, be tough. Cold can't bother her."

"She is keeping up. We aren't all elves and vampires, you know," Canin gruffed back, his voice getting louder. "You are too hard, Aelfric."

"I survive," he answered.

"But at what cost?" Canin asked.

Aelfric stopped and turned around. He glared over Bloom's and Annie's heads at Canin. In the darkness, she could see his eyes glint like an angry predator's.

"Are *you* lecturing *me*?"

"You two act like children." The mayor sighed. His hand still rested on Annie's shoulder.

"I am saying nothing, Aelfric." Canin sniffed at the air.

Aelfric twisted around. "I can hear what you're saying without words."

Bloom interrupted the argument. His hand grabbed his bow, and he notched an arrow in it quickly. "Shhh. Something comes."

The mayor glanced over at the trees and then down the road. He pulled a massive sword from his parka. It glinted, reflecting the snow. They all froze. Annie held her breath and clutched Jamie's hand in hers. Aelfric's nostrils flared quickly, and his fangs popped out with a slight clicking noise. At her side, Tala sniffed the air. The mayor's stomach rumbled. She prayed that they would stay quiet. Canin doubled back, and the mayor's hand tightened on her shoulder, giving her tiny hope.

"What is it?" he whispered.

Bloom crouched to the ground and listened. "Trolls. Close."

"How many?"

"Five."

"How did they get past the gnome? I said we shouldn't follow the road," Aelfric grumbled. "But did anyone listen? No. They never listen to the vampires, do they? Giants and elves. Giants and elves."

The mayor shot him a look.

Bloom suddenly grabbed Annie's leg and sprang back up from where he listened to the ground.

"They're very close, Annie."

"How close?" she asked.

"Run!"

He snatched her hand, pulling her and Jamie along, and raced off the road into the barrens back toward Cornelia's.

6

Trolling for Tutus

Annie hoped that Bloom could see enough in the darkness to know where they were running, because she certainly couldn't. Dashing through the scrubby hills dotted with boulders, the low-brush blueberry bushes scraped at her ankles and tangled up her feet. Behind them, Jamie, Canin, and Tala rushed, keeping a second line.

Even as they ran, Jamie was trying to sort everything out. "Wait. Someone kidnapped Miss Cornelia, Canin. It wasn't the Raiff, but one of his henchmen. It seems like lots of evil things might have snuck over here when the gnome was gone."

Canin thought for a moment. "That's not the only way evil can get in the town."

"What? I thought the town was protected when the gnome was here."

"It is . . ."

"But?"

"But someone can invite them in."

It took a moment, but then Jamie thought of the person with the spicy scent who had been there when Miss Cornelia was taken, and he understood. "But why would someone bring trolls into Aurora?"

"Because they are working for the Raiff, that's why."

They ran until Bloom stopped, suddenly dead still. He put his finger to his lips.

They ducked down low. Canin, Tala, and Jamie crouched beside them.

A horrible stench filled the air, just an absolutely foul stench, like the locker room at the YMCA mixed with old shrimp shells. Annie tried not to gag. Bloom covered her mouth and nose with his hand. She jumped, surprised at the mint leaves he held inside his palm. The leaves' fresh scent helped to keep her from coughing. All her senses were heightened now; a crunching, shuffling noise along with the sound of rocks breaking and being crushed between massive teeth broke the air in front of her.

Bloom pointed. Darker shadows formed against the night sky. Trolls.

Annie shrunk into herself as two trolls shuffled through the barrens. Trolls grew enormous, like two professional basketball players stacked up on each other. These monsters were as wide as garage doors. Everything about them was foul—their teeth, their smell, their manners. Even though she could only smell them slightly through Bloom's minty hand, the odor was still strong enough to remind her of gas station toilets.

One of the trolls bent and scooped up a massive boulder. Smashing it into his mouth, the troll began to chew. Pebbles sprayed in all directions and some of them hit Annie and Bloom, like tiny bullets piercing their skin.

"Ouch," Annie said.

The troll stopped munching.

Jamie gasped.

Canin clamped a furry hand over Jamie's mouth, but Jamie was too scared to make a noise, too horrified that people would think he was like his grandmother and father.

Never, he swore. *I will never be like them.*

And then he made a promise. He would go with Annie. He would find Miss Cornelia and rescue her. That would show them—it would show everyone.

In the snow in front of Jamie was a small vial shaped like a long test tube. Its liquid contents sparkled and shimmered like a disco ball. *This must be magic*, Jamie thought. *But what kind?* Not knowing what else to do, Jamie plucked it up from the snow and tucked it into his pocket, like every lucky penny he came across.

"Hear noise? Disgustopuke? You hear noise?" one troll

asked. His voice was hysterically high-pitched, squeaky like a church soprano who couldn't quite hit the notes.

The other grunted in reply.

Canin's eyes grew big. His lips stretched up, exposing a full, sharp set of wolf teeth. He released Jamie's mouth and pushed him forward, urging him to crawl.

Canin pushed Jamie forward again. It took all of Jamie's willpower to get himself to move.

"I hear noise," the troll said again.

He began to toddle toward them. Annie peeked at Bloom. His face shone white in the darkness. Jamie's mouth flapped wide open. Bloom yanked Annie's hand and started crawling away, creeping over the snowy bushes. Jamie and Canin followed. Above them, a group of bats swooped. She hoped that if they were vampires, they were the good kind.

"Hear crawling," the troll said.

They stopped. They were absolutely, totally caught, Annie knew, but she wasn't about to be part of a troll fondue. It might have been fruitless, but she was not going to just die without trying. Standing up, she pulled out the phurba Miss Cornelia gave her, ready to fight. She could feel power surging through her.

I am not a wimpy person. I am a Time Stopper, she thought. *I will fight.*

The trolls stepped closer, their stench overpowering.

Whew, do they need deodorant, she thought as Bloom stood beside her. He notched an arrow in his bow and pulled it back. Canin and Tala growled behind them. Jamie slowly stood.

The trolls were almost on top of them, coming closer, smelling worse. Three yards away. Two. A loud masculine voice broke the silence, "Yoo-hoo, trollies. Over here! I have some nice tutus for you."

"The mayor," Annie whispered.

A troll grunted and squeaked out, "Hungry. Rearfungus is hungry."

"Oh, but these are nice tutus," came the mayor's voice. He was probably a good three hundred feet away, but his voice carried well and it attracted the trolls. They glanced in Annie and the others' direction again and then turned.

"Tutus?" Annie whispered.

"Trolls like to dress up," Bloom explained. "Occasionally."

Annie tried to digest that particular piece of information as she stood ready with her phurba, heavy in her hands. The closest troll leered just yards in front of her and Bloom. She strained her neck looking up toward his head. All he needed to do was lean forward and he could grab them in his meaty fist. Her weapon hand trembled.

Bloom swayed from the stench of the trolls. So did she.

"Come on," yelled the mayor. "Lovely tutus, which I am sure you will like. They are pink and purple and very, very shiny, frilly tutus."

Annie tried to imagine the gigantic warty trolls in frilly

little tutus. She didn't have much of a chance to conjure up the visual image because suddenly a large dark bat and Tala appeared. The white dog reared up on two legs and placed his front paws on Annie's shoulders. The bat landed on Annie's hair and hissed into Annie's ear with a voice that sounded a lot like Aelfric's, "Run. We will hold them off."

"But the mayor . . . ," Annie said.

"He will be fine," the bat said, fluttering up into the night sky. "Go. Canin, Tala, come with me."

Tala slammed his body back to the ground, turned, and left, only looking back once. Canin howled and morphed, his body quickly shuddering into wolf form. It happened so quickly that Jamie and Annie weren't quite sure it even happened. He howled once more and loped off.

The children did not hesitate. They stowed their weapons and ran.

Annie, Jamie, and Bloom raced as quickly as they could through the snow to the Beryl-Axes' house. They needed Eva, who would never forgive them for letting her miss all the action. That is, if she didn't faint and miss it anyway.

At every sound, every twig crack, Annie imagined a troll or a demon or a vampire ready to pounce. She clutched Bloom's hand as they ran across the barrens. Jamie raced alongside.

Something crashed behind them. Something screamed,

high and piercing. *That has to be a troll's scream*, Annie thought. She refused to believe it was anyone else's. Still, she crossed her fingers and hoped Tala, Canin, the mayor, and that somewhat creepy vampire guy, Aelfric, were all right.

"Maybe we should go back," Annie said, gasping for air as she ran; every breath felt like someone had stuck an ice cube into her lungs.

"We'll be a distraction," said Jamie.

"What do you mean?"

"Annie, do you remember? Trolls like to eat elves and Stoppers. It's rare they get us, though," said Bloom.

"Why?"

"They trip on their boas, and it's hard to run fast in a tutu."

Annie laughed at his joke, so he wouldn't feel bad, but she was so worried that the laugh came out sounding more like a cough . . . a sad, scared cough, actually.

Storm clouds thickened the air and really darkened everything, but Annie spotted something glowing on the road below them. She stopped. Maybe it was cars. Maybe someone could help them out. Maybe the sheriff had come or the Maine State Police.

Then she remembered. This was Aurora. Sometimes she couldn't believe how easily she forgot about the rules of Aurora. Regular people couldn't just find it and be there to rescue them. They had to be their own rescue.

"Bloom?" Jamie had seen it, too, and his voice made the elf's name into a question.

Along the road, a series of hay carriages swayed and bumped. Enormous trolls heaved and pulled each of the carriages in the caravan. As the convoy passed beneath them, screams and cries shrilled out from the beds of the carriages. Leaning forward, they spied faces of pixies and fairies. Iron bands bound their tiny legs, burning their skin.

"Horrible!" Bloom said and he began to run down the hill.

Jamie caught him by the arm, counting the trolls. "There are too many."

"We can't let them take them!" Bloom said, stopping. His hand jerked to his forehead and he pulled off his hat and used it to brush the wet snow off his face. His hand trembled.

It was then Annie realized that this was part of what had happened to Bloom's parents. She closed her eyes and saw what felt like a dream. A lovely woman with long, braided blond hair held hands with a tall man whose eyes twinkled like Bloom's. Their wrists were bound, but their fingers clung to each other. Sadness settled in their hearts. It made an ache right in the middle of Annie's chest and tasted like old snow. That same sorrow was burrowed into Bloom's heart. She could feel it.

She shook the image out of her head. She would not let the Purge happen again. Not on her watch. Miss Cornelia might not be here, but she was, and she had to do what she could to keep this town—and its people—safe. She remembered her promise to the ghosts, and knew they would understand.

"We won't let them take them," Annie told him. She grabbed his hand and Jamie's. "Hold on to me."

"What are you going to do?"

"Just don't let go."

Annie closed her eyes and cleared her head. The circles of her palms tingled. The power was there, so much it almost hurt. It pulsed through her body like blood, racing. *I am a Time Stopper*, she thought. She could do this. It had to work. It just had to.

Every single nerve she had sang out in a different way, and she could feel it; the changing vibrations within her matched the changing vibrations in the world. She hummed. She trembled. She sang with it. It was power and magic and it was Annie. Jamie shifted his fingers to Annie's wrist as she bent down and wrote the word on the snow, and in the loudest voice she could muster she yelled, "STOP!"

And in that instant the world did.

Her word echoed across the barrens. A snowflake paused in mid-descent right in front of her nose. The convoy stilled. The wind disappeared.

Next to her, Bloom and Jamie still touched her hand and wrist.

"You're certainly not a one-timer," said Jamie.

She smiled as Jamie let go of her wrist and started down

the hill to the road. "Come on. We should be quick. I don't know how long it will hold."

They followed her, running so fast downhill that it was like flying, gravity pulling them along. Annie loped so quickly she could barely stop and slammed into the caravan. Her parka scraped along the splintered timbers on the side, and she slid underneath the wagon wheels on the slippery road.

"Annie." Jamie's face was terrified. "You okay?"

She nodded, blushing and brushing the snow off her legs. Bloom helped her up.

Annie started to say something, but stopped because of the poor fairies. Their wings drooped, and their faces were ashen and gloomy. She knew that they weren't dead, but they looked it. They seemed as if all their dreams had been crushed, like they finally summoned up enough courage to run for class president and then only received two votes.

She stroked the head of one with her gloved pinkie finger. "Oh, the poor things."

"Trolls take the life out of them," Bloom said, face grim and ashen still. "I hate trolls."

"'Hate' is too nice a word."

"Despise, then."

"That's better."

"Loathe?"

"That's good."

"What would they do with the fairies?" Jamie asked, looking over at the massive bulk of a troll near them. He shuddered. A smile was frozen on the troll's face, revealing nasty teeth.

"Put some in cages and torture them. Make them sing for them. Rip their wings off. The others, the lucky ones, they eat."

Jamie gulped and didn't know whether to cry or slash one of the trolls' throats. He'd never heard Bloom be so harsh and cold. "You sound more like Eva than you."

"I'm sorry, Jamie. This is a hard world." Bloom turned away.

Annie thought of Walden Wiegle, her last foster brother who had been so consistently cruel. She said, "All worlds are hard."

"No, I'm sorry . . . I . . . I'm sorry that I was so angry. My anger made me weak," Bloom explained, looking down at his feet.

"It's okay. Everyone gets angry. Everyone gets weak." Annie helped Jamie free a pixie from a troll's grasp, uncoiling the beefy fingers.

"You aren't now." Bloom swallowed hard.

"Neither are you." She grimaced and climbed up into the carriage bed. Foul with green troll ooze and slime, the hay made her descent slippery. Several cockroaches had been stopped in the midst of tormenting the fairies with their long antennas, tickling them. Annie cringed. She couldn't imagine what the fairies and pixies were dealing with. The echoes of their screams still rang in her ears.

"First we have to get the irons off," she said, reaching out toward the leg of a lovely little fairy, whose dress seemed to be made of daisy petals. The thin metal easily snapped off. She moved on to another. "Fairies aren't very strong, are they?"

"Not really. They can't stand iron, though, or aluminum foil," Bloom answered, snapping off the band that kept a pixie prisoner. "It's like the strongest metal to them."

Jamie snapped off another band. "We need someplace to put them. We could bring them back to Eva's."

Along with a sequined red evening gown, the troll closest to Annie had a huge sparkling red purse with a snap lock. She crept nearer and grabbed it out of the troll's slimy hand. Green ooze caked her fingernails. Warts and hair sprouted out of her knuckles.

"Ughhk," Annie moaned, backing away.

She dumped the contents of the purse onto the ground. Strawberry-breeze lip gloss, two cockroaches, glittery purple eye shadow, three long hunting knives with wooden handles, and an Avon Skin So Soft moisturizing spray fell out. She shook her head. Trolls. Go figure.

"We can put them in here," she said, showing Bloom and Jamie.

Together they crammed in the pixies and fairies as fast as they could. It wasn't very dignified, but they couldn't think of a better way.

As they worked, the Woman in White floated by.

"Oh, you've done it again, haven't you? Twice in less than two days, that's powerful. Most can only stop time once a week, if that. But, oh, Annie, my head . . . my head . . . You need to refrain from this type of behavior if you can. Oh, my head! The ache of it. *Aaiee.*"

"I'm sorry," Annie said, folding another fairy into her coat pocket.

They had run out of room in the purse. As it was now they couldn't shut it. Little legs and arms stuck out at all sorts of angles. Bloom put a few of the fairies in his hat. Jamie stuck some in his pockets.

"Just let us get to the house where it's safe. I won't be long," Annie pleaded. The ghost's bell was still in her pocket. She almost felt like she didn't deserve it.

The Woman in White moaned and echoed Annie's words, floating upward so that she sat on a troll's head. Her dress floated down past his nose.

"I won't be long. I won't be long. That's what the Captain said. Oh, my Captain. Captain! Captain!" Her wails echoed in the quiet. "Blackbeard . . . Oh . . . that wretched, wretched . . ."

Annie, Jamie, and Bloom worked as swiftly as they could, double-checking to make sure they hadn't missed any of the little winged people. Then they struggled to tie up the trolls with some chains they had persuaded the Woman in White to bring them. She'd found them on the sea bottom.

They thanked her and left her moaning about pirates and deaths at sea. Then they walked toward Eva's little burrow house, purse full of pixies and fairies swinging over their shoulders, as time hitched back into place. One by one, the grateful pixies and fairies flew off into the night, twinkling like stars in the black winter sky.

They got to Eva's house at the same time as Canin—who shoved them through the door and slammed it shut behind them. Eva's dad was out on patrol, and her mom was still on vacation, sunbathing in Hawaii.

"There's no lock!" Canin growled. "Why don't these dwarfs have a lock?"

"Because they feel safe?" Jamie offered.

Canin whirled on him and growled, fangs showing.

"Not saying it's a smart idea!" Jamie said, backing up with his hands in the air. "Just saying it might be why."

"No one is ever safe," Canin sputtered. "Help me block the door with this table."

"How is Tala? The mayor? Aelfric?" Annie asked, terrified of the answer.

"Fine. They were all still alive last I saw them," Canin said as together they hauled a thick wooden table toward the door and flipped it over. Battle axes, hammers, and tankards of some sort of ale spilled all over the floor, making a huge mess. Annie immediately started cleaning it up.

"Don't bother with that now!" Canin ordered. "Get more things. We need to barricade the door."

"Against the trolls or the townspeople?" Bloom asked.

"Both." Canin hauled over a couple of chairs. "Potentially both."

Jamie grabbed a bench, but it was too heavy to lift. He began to drag it across the floor and bumped it into a lumpy pile of blankets. The blankets shot out a swear word. A doll tumbled out, and Eva hopped to her feet, rubbing her eyes. She pushed the covers over the doll, hiding it in a not-very-discreet way.

"What the heck is happening?" she demanded. "Why does it smell like wet dog in— Oh, hi, Canin."

"Help us, dwarf," Canin ordered.

"He's not the nicest, is he?" Eva said, yawning and completely calm despite Jamie and Canin's intrusion into her house and their agitated state.

As he dragged the bench over, Jamie quickly explained what had happened since he last saw Eva back at Aquarius House when the Raiff appeared in the fountain.

"Oh," she muttered gloomily, "when I passed out. My dad must've brought me back here."

"It doesn't matter if you fainted, girl," Canin declared. Exasperation seemed to make him even furrier. "Just help us secure the property."

Eva groaned. "That's a sissy's way out, that is. Hiding. Securing the property. What say you: We go out and fight those trolls? What say you: We go out and tell everyone that the mayor is being an idiot about trading Annie? Dwarfs ain't into this hiding thing. Dwarfs rush into battle."

"Dwarfs are foolhardy," Canin countered, looking through the chest of weapons.

"Dwarfs are brave!" Eva roared.

"Dwarfs are loud," Jamie whispered as he hammered some boards over the small windows. Not that a troll could squeeze his or her monstrous bulk through a window, but still . . .

Something thudded against the door.

Everyone froze.

Something knocked on the door, a tight *rap-rap-rap.*

Eva's mouth opened to say something, but Bloom clapped his hand over it. She bit him. He muffled a yell.

"No one silences a dwarf," she whispered, handing Jamie a massive, ancient ax. "This was my great-uncle Baron Beryl-Axe's, the greatest of all Beryl-Axes. He killed a pirate with it. Make him proud."

Bloom hopped around in a circle, shaking his hand.

"I didn't even bite hard," Eva scoffed.

The knock came again—*rap-rap-rap.*

"Should we answer it?" Annie whispered, pulling out the phurba.

"Yes," Eva whispered back as Canin simultaneously said, "No."

Jamie noted that Eva actually whispered, which was not a good sign. She was scared.

Rap.

They tightened their grasps on the handles of their weapons.

"Come out, come out, wherever you are!" called a high-pitched voice from beyond the door.

"Trolls," Canin mouthed the word.

They raised their weapons.

"I'm going to count to three," called the voice, sickening sweet.

Annie wondered if she should stop time again, but she worried about the ghosts. It seemed unfair to do it too often. Jamie's heart thumped hard against his chest. Canin seemed to be turning more wolflike. Fur sprouted out of his cheeks, and his shoulders seemed broader, more muscular.

"One . . . ," called the voice.

"What do we do?" asked Bloom.

"Stand our ground," Eva answered.

"Everybody hide," Canin ordered as his fingernails lengthened into claws.

"Two . . . ," the voice sang.

"It's too late to hide," Eva said. "And dwarfs don't hide."

"I want you to hide!" Canin snarled.

But it *was* too late. Jamie, Annie, and Bloom knew Eva was right.

"Three!"

And the door burst open.

7

Mini Magic

Eva had a tendency to pass out when presented with trolls, but she must have been getting braver because she didn't even sway when the trolls bashed down the door to her home. In the seconds that followed the splintering of the wood, Eva pretty much stayed stock still, surveying everything. Only her nostrils flared. Jamie had never seen her still before—except when she fainted.

"Hide!" Annie yelled, scuttling beneath a bed, but it was far too late.

"You dare enter a dwarf home?" Eva raged. "You dare ruin the door that my ancestor built out of the sacred trees of Ag—"

"Dwarfs. So talky-talky," muttered a troll, ducking to fit into the room. "My ancestor did this. My ax did that. Blah. Blah. Blah."

"And they taste awful," said another, smooshing her huge body through the gaping hole that was once a door.

"We taste fantastic," Eva boasted and then thought better of it. "Not that I would know . . ."

Jamie pulled at Eva's overalls. "Eva, is there any way to get out of here?"

"We stand and fight, Jamie." Eva glared at him.

Canin growled. He'd transformed completely again, no longer a man at all, but a huge gray wolf with glowing yellow eyes and canine teeth that seemed as long as Jamie's forearm. He took a step away as Canin's back legs tensed and ears flattened against his skull. Bloom whipped out his bow and an arrow.

"Great. Canin's going to have all the fun," Eva muttered just as the wolf flew through the air, flinging himself against the lead troll's chest. He hit him dead center, and the troll wavered a bit, flailing his arms, knocking over assorted pictures off the wall.

"No! You will NOT disrespect the great Beryl-Axe that way!" Eva roared, lunging forward and attacking the troll's shins. She wasn't tall enough to reach anything else.

The three of them toppled to the floor in a snarling, frantic mess even as Bloom shot an arrow at the other troll. It bounced off his chest. Annie crawled out from under the bed and started attacking the nearest troll's feet.

I have to do something, Jamie thought, *but what*?

His weapon felt wrong in his hands. No. He didn't have

to use the ax even if Eva *had* given it to him. He dropped it on the floor.

"Eva! Canin! Bloom!" he bellowed. "Stand back! Annie!"

None of them moved away from the trolls.

"Taste my ax, you mean face of boogerness!" Eva yelled despite the fact that the troll had grabbed her in his fist and she couldn't actually swing her ax, or move her arms, or do anything but dangle there as the troll used that same fist to try to punch at Canin's rapidly attacking body. Another fist grabbed up Bloom. Annie stabbed at the troll's toes. He complained of the tickling, but otherwise didn't seem to pay attention.

Canin darted out of the way of the fist, knocking over a table.

"Not the Table of Awesomeness! Agh . . . you broke the leg!" Eva hollered.

"I'll be breaking your legs in a minute," the first troll said. "Puke-o-rama," he addressed the girl troll, "are you going to help me or just stand there watching?"

"It so funny, though. Little dwarf in your hand. Blondie elf in the other. Crazy wolf going all over the place, and little girl tickling your toes," Puke-o-rama said, smiling a ghoulish smile full of grayish-green teeth.

"I AM NOT FUNNY!" Eva roared. "Jamie! A little help here."

"I'm trying," Jamie said, remembering the magic vial in his pocket. He wasn't sure what it was exactly, but judging how the contents were sparkling and purple, he figured it was some kind of enchantment.

"I crushy crush you, dwarf. You talk too much." The troll kicked Canin out of the way and began to squeeze Eva's stout form in his even stouter fingers.

"JAMIE!"

Canin whimpered in the corner and leaped back toward the troll, biting at his legs.

"I'm trying!" Jamie pried at the cork in the top of the vial.

"Why are you playing with that? Oh my unicorn pickle turds. You dropped your ax! GET YOUR WEAPON!" Eva demanded, but her voice fell into a pained squeak. She gasped. "Dwarfs do not squeak," she squeaked.

"I make dwarfs squeak and cry, and then I eat them," the troll said. "Even though you taste gross."

"We. Do. Not. Taste. Gross," Eva insisted, trying to kick him. He held her above his head and opened his mouth.

"NO!" Bloom yelled, twisting in the other hand, trying to escape.

Annie gave up stabbing and tried to push the troll over. He didn't budge.

"You need to share," Puke-o-rama said. "I get half."

"You can have the wolf or the boy."

"Boy. Wolves are too furry. It gets stuck in my teeth," she said. "Want tickling girl, too."

Eva was now directly above the troll's open mouth. Her eyes bulged.

The cork popped out of the vial. A large purple mist began to stream out of the tube as Jamie hurtled the tube at the trolls.

The mist twirled and twisted into the face of a hag and screeched out the word "SMALLER" just as it hit the trolls and engulfed them.

Poof!

They were gone.

And so were Eva and Canin.

And so were Annie and Bloom.

The mist evaporated. Jamie stood alone among splintered furniture, scattered weapons, and barren floorboards. Jamie staggered against the far wall, tripping on abandoned weapons. His breath came out ragged.

"Eva?" he whispered.

Nothing.

"Canin?" he whispered. "Annie? Bloom?"

Had he killed them? The world spun. His hand went to his eyes. He couldn't have killed them, could he? No . . . no . . . Panicked, he uncovered his eyes and dropped the vial on the ground. It shattered. "Oh no . . . Oh no . . . Oh no . . ."

Something touched his foot and climbed right up onto his shoe. It was a wolf, a tiny wolf that looked exactly like . . . no, it couldn't be . . .

"Canin?" Jamie asked, gently picking up the wolf and holding it in the palm of his hand.

The wolf growled.

"Oh, you are definitely Canin." Jamie cringed. "That means . . ." He put Canin on the mantel of the fireplace where it seemed Canin would be safe. Being careful not to step on anyone, Jamie began searching the room for the others. Over by the door, he found the two trolls, angrily bashing their heads against each other.

"Too small. Your fault," said the male one.

"No. Yours." Puke-o-rama bashed him with a splinter.

"Enough!" Jamie snatched them both up and plopped them into a KISS ME, I AM DWARFISH earthen mug, which caused them both to start swearing at him and his ancestors as they tried to break the mug with their heads.

"That has got to hurt," Jamie said to Canin. Canin woofed, which Jamie figured meant he agreed. He sighed and moved the mug over to a shelf. "Now, where are Annie and Bloom and Eva?"

Jamie had moved one step away from the shelf when a cracking noise froze him in place. A sharp pain pierced his ankle. Grunting, he staggered backward. Something below him gave a battle whoop, and the pain happened all over again.

Jamie hopped up onto his other foot, knocking against the shelf and smashing it off the wall. Trinkets, medals of glory, chunks of gold, and the mug the trolls were trapped in tumbled to the ground. Finally, the pain abated enough for him to look for the cause. A toothpick. Someone had stabbed him in the ankle with a toothpick. No, not someone. Eva.

She stood there, glaring at him.

"You stabbed me!" he accused.

"You made me small!"

"I was saving you from the trolls."

"YOU MADE ME TINY!" She shook her miniature-size ax at him. "And look at my ax!"

"I was saving you!" he insisted, flabbergasted. He stomped away to the front door, righting things as he went, searching for the trolls that had toppled out of the mug. "You really aren't nice, Eva."

Anger coursed through his veins. Where were the annoying trolls? Why couldn't he just find them? Why couldn't Eva be grateful? Frustration rippled through him. He roared like some sort of monster.

And stopped.

He took a deep breath.

"Jamie!"

A voice!

He peered down. Eva stood by the broken mug and pointed across the room. "The trolls are hiding behind the Fluffy Pillow of Happy Slumber and the Doll of Beddy-bye Land. Say nothing of it! Ever."

The trolls scattered as soon as she spoke, but Jamie scooped them up and placed them inside another mug.

"Try not to break that one," Eva said. "There's a lid over there." She gestured toward the back of the room. "Also, you're missing the elf and the Stopper still."

The trolls objected to their captivity, of course, but Jamie ignored their flailing limbs and name calling. Instead, he verified that Canin was still on the shelf. Jamie transferred him to his pocket and searched for Annie and Bloom. He found them in a pile of dust by the broken leg of the Table of Awesomeness. He picked them up, apologizing even as they sneezed.

"It's—*achoo*—okay." Bloom sneezed. "You had to do what you could."

"It was—*achoo*—a good—*achoo*—idea, sort of," said Annie. "It's just kind of weird being so little and so sneezy."

Jamie tucked them into his front coat pocket and grabbed Eva.

"Dwarfs do not get carried," she announced. "This is humiliating."

"There is nothing wrong with being small, Eva. You say that all the time."

"But this isn't small. This is pixie size." She harrumphed. "How long is this going to last exactly?"

"I don't know . . . Let me look at the label."

"What?" she roared. "You didn't look at the label first? Seriously? Are you freaking kidding me?"

She began grumbling. Jamie stopped listening, focusing

instead on finding the broken vial and reading the label, which he did aloud. "It says results may vary."

Canin howled. Bloom just started to laugh.

"May vary! What does that even mean?" Eva demanded, thudding her fist against Jamie's chest.

"I think it means it depends—" Jamie began.

"Depends on what?"

"Good question." Jamie shrugged. "I don't know. We've got to . . . We have to find someplace to put the trolls in case they get big again."

He exhaled deeply, feeling suddenly very large and very responsible. Annie, Bloom, Canin *and* Eva were under his care now, and he was the least magical of everyone. He couldn't even throw a potion right. How was he going to protect them? It seemed impossible. He picked up the ax Eva had tried to get him to use before. He swallowed hard and set off into the night.

Jamie scurried out the door of Eva's house and then stopped dead still on the front walk. What if the trolls grew back to their normal size and attacked? He was completely unprepared.

"What are you stopping for?" Bloom climbed up to his shoulder and leaped up to his earlobe. He dangled there, swinging back and forth. Eva joined the elf. It was a little disconcerting, but at least she wasn't stabbing him with toothpicks anymore.

Jamie cleared his throat and explained his predicament.

"Just kill them," Eva insisted. "Squish them or step on them or something."

"I can't do that." Jamie shook his head, nearly flinging off Eva. She let go of his ear, landing next to Canin who was currently pacing back and forth on Jamie's shoulder and sniffing the air. Annie poked her head out of the pocket and then seemed to think better of it and ducked back in.

"Why the heck not?" Eva bellowed. "They'd kill you and then they'd suck the marrow right out of your bones, and would they think about it? Would they regret it for just one second? Let me tell you, they would not."

She began to make bone marrow–slurping noises to demonstrate the disgustingness of the trolls. It worked; Jamie cringed, but it still wasn't enough. He had no idea how he could hurt them when they were so small, so weak compared to him. It would be like squashing an annoying puppy, an ugly, annoying, smelly puppy. Okay . . . an ugly, annoying, murderous, bone marrow–slurping puppy.

"I can't. They are powerless. If I killed them now, I'd be worse than them," Jamie tried to explain.

"Are you going to eat them?" Eva demanded. She pointed her ax blade at him.

"No."

She swung her ax around in a circle. "Then you are hardly worse."

"Eva!" Bloom scolded.

She grumbled and plopped down into a seated position

on Jamie's shoulder, crossing her arms over her chest after she laid her ax in her lap. "I don't agree with you."

"I figured that out," Jamie muttered.

"And I am really cranky that I am basically the size of a crayon," Eva said, and Jamie imagined he actually saw steam come out of her ears. "How can I wield a mighty ax when I am the size of a crayon!?! A CRAYON!?!?!"

"I can't blame you for being cranky, and I'm sorry." Jamie checked inside the mug to make sure the trolls were still there. They tried to spit at him, but they didn't have enough force and the spittle just flew straight up and landed back in their faces, which unleashed another volley of curses and threats. Jamie put the lid back on the mug, which smelled vaguely like hot chocolate mixed with troll sweat, so basically it smelled like hot chocolate mixed with old tuna fish. It was not a good smell.

"First things first," he said. "We need to get these trolls somewhere that they can't escape even if they grow again. Is there a jail anywhere around town?"

"No," Eva said. Then she clapped her hands together and almost did a merry jig. "But there is a forgotten room."

"A forgotten room?" Jamie asked.

"It's like a dungeon, but kind of worse," Bloom said. "Come on. Let's go."

Jamie and his passengers trudged through the town, sticking to the shadowy street, always listening for signs of monsters.

"Where is everyone?" Jamie whispered as they tiptoed by Tasha's Tavern. The structure's windows were shuttered closed.

"Good question." Eva climbed up to the top of Jamie's head and sank into his hair. "I can't see anything. Also, your hair smells like coconut."

"Sorry."

"No, it's nice," Bloom offered. "Coconut is a good smell."

There was a strange pulling sensation along his scalp, and after a moment Eva shouted. "Okay, I built a platform."

"Out of my hair?" Jamie interrupted. His free hand went to his head, feeling around.

"Yes, out of your hair. Watch out! You're going to knock me down. Canin, Annie, come up here with us," Eva demanded.

The wolf scurried up to the top of Jamie's head via his earlobe and hair. Once there, he howled long and achingly sad. The sound ripped into Jamie's heart. Annie gasped.

"What is it?" Jamie whispered as he lifted Annie out of his pocket and up to the platform. She caught Bloom's hand and pulled herself on.

"I still hate heights," she whispered.

"You're being brave," Bloom answered as Annie tried to console the howling Canin.

"What's going on exactly?" Annie asked, petting the wolf's head.

"Everyone's hiding," Eva said. "Or something. But that makes no sense because dwarfs don't hide. And everyone still wants to send Annie to the Badlands. Once the troll panic is over, they'll be coming back for her."

"You've said a lot of things about dwarfs, and I'm pretty sure you said that they don't get carried," Jamie teased, trying to make them all forget about the trade. It didn't seem to fully work.

She made a harrumphing noise. "I'm not *getting* carried. I'm taking a ride. Big difference." She cleared her throat. "Okay, almost there . . . The oubliette is right past the library and to the back of it, hidden in that copse of pine trees."

An owl hooted in the distance.

"Where is it?" Jamie whispered. Everything felt too dangerous to talk in a regular-volumed voice.

"A door is in the trees," Bloom said.

And there was, right in the middle of the trees, a large, red wooden door painted with all sorts of sad words like "***sorrow***," "***regret***," "***what happens when you are evil***," and "***past mistakes should not be future ones***." The door itself was sort of suspended in midair. Nothing was on the other side.

Reaching out, Jamie tentatively touched it with his finger. It didn't sway. It stood there, or suspended there, solid.

"You've got to knock three times," Eva said. "Then it opens."

"Three times?"

"What did I just say?"

Jamie didn't answer. Instead, he knocked against the word "***loss***" three times and took a step backward, nervously. This incited Eva to make a dismissive snort. Jamie decided he didn't care. The entire place spooked him.

"Good job, Jamie," Bloom said. "Good knocking."

"Stop trying so hard to be encouraging," Eva shouted. "And Annie, stop petting Canin. He's fine. And you are not going to fall. And even if you did, Jamie's not that tall."

"He seems tall now," Annie whispered.

Slowly the door opened with a great creaking noise.

"Yes?" A scorpion man stood before them. His head, arms, and chest resembled that of a normal human, but from the waist down he had the segmented, armored body parts of a scorpion, including a giant stinger.

It took all of Jamie's will not to take another step backward and run.

"H-hi . . . ," he stuttered out. "I'm James Hephaistion Alexander and I-I . . . um, I have some trolls in a mug for you."

He held out the mug. The scorpion man took it from him, removed the mug's lid, and peered in with distaste as the trolls began to shout for him to let them out. He ignored their pleas. "How unsightly. Did you shrink them thus?"

"I did."

The scorpion man lifted his eyebrows and re-covered the mug with an emphatic smack. "With personal magic or with premade potion?"

"Premade potion," Jamie answered. Eva was being uncharacteristically quiet. Everyone else was, too.

"And the dwarf and shifter, the elf and the Stopper?"

"They were in the way."

The scorpion man scrutinized Jamie's face. After a moment he answered, "It has been known to happen. The spell will wear off eventually. I suppose you would like to leave the trolls with me in the oubliette for safekeeping."

"Um . . . yes . . . if possible." Jamie cleared his throat. "Is the oubliette the forgotten room? That's where Eva and Bloom said would be a good place."

The scorpion man motioned for Jamie to follow him through the door. Peering inside before he stepped through the threshold, Jamie had to blink hard to understand what he was seeing. A passageway made of some sort of sandstone, the kind he imagined pyramids were built out of, headed into the tree. Along the sandstone were drawings of ankhs and stars, men in ancient robes. Most of the drawing was made of thick black paint, but there was some red and gold mixed in. Two eyes stared at him from the far end of the hallway.

"Enter if you like," the scorpion man said.

"Eva?" Jamie whispered. He hated to admit it, but he was kind of freaked out.

She had passed out.

"Seriously?" Jamie plucked her off his head and stared disbelieving at her snoring form.

"I tend to make the dwarfs nervous," the scorpion man said. "They are a mining species. They don't really like scorpions."

"That's too bad," Jamie offered.

"It is what it is." The scorpion man gestured one more time for Jamie to enter, so he did, taking a large breath. The air was so much warmer and dryer. It was how he imagined desert air would feel. There wasn't a trace of the Maine cold.

"Wow." Jamie let out his breath. "This is really nice. Bloom? Annie, you okay?"

"Thank you." The scorpion man led him down the hallway as Annie and Bloom whispered that they were fine. "I'm afraid I don't have many visitors. People like to forget what this place is. I think they fear if they think too much of it, that they, too, will be punished here. So, they choose to forget. I find creatures, be they human or magical, prefer to forget the darker parts of their own history so that they don't have to feel guilt over it."

"Is it very dark here?" Jamie asked.

"Very." Scorpion Man cleared his throat. "Sometimes,

however, we must do things to ensure the betterment of all. As is the case with you at this juncture, am I right?"

"I don't know what to do with the trolls," Jamie admitted. "I'm afraid they'll go back to normal size and hurt us."

"Me, too!" Annie said from the platform in Jamie's hair.

"And you don't want to kill them?"

"No," Jamie admitted. "It doesn't feel—right."

"Even for you, elf boy?"

"Even for me," Bloom said. He held Annie's hand, and tightened his grip.

"I hope someday when your fate is in the hands of another, they offer you the same mercy, young James Hephaistion Alexander, and you, Bloom the elf, and you, Annie the Stopper. Now tell me what is happening out there."

"Do you not get to leave?" Annie asked. She felt a bit braver now that they weren't moving. Jamie's head still seemed impossibly high, but Bloom's hand gave her strength.

"No. I am not made for winter weather in Maine."

So, Jamie told him what had happened, about Miss Cornelia's abduction, the trolls in the town. Annie explained her own part of the story, as did Bloom.

"And you? What of you?" the scorpion man asked Jamie.

"I was raised by trolls," Jamie admitted. "They wanted to eat me."

"But you are not troll yourself?"

"I'm only thirteen. I have a whole year before I know if I'll change." Jamie stared at Eva's sleeping form and switched the subject. "Can you tell me where you're going to put them?"

It might be his fate someday, too, he realized, if he turned troll. What could they do other than kill him?

"The forgotten room is not truly a room. It is more of a shaft, which descends into a tiny chamber, wide enough for only one full-size troll, so if they transform back to their normal size, it shall be quite tight and terribly uncomfortable. I lower the prisoner down myself and shut a trapdoor behind me. If they are to be retrieved, I retrieve them via rope. It is much too high for even a troll to climb out. Plus, their kind cannot climb. Once they are full size, they shall be trapped there in their separate forgotten rooms until they are released."

"Will you release them?" Annie blurted.

"Of course not." The scorpion man eyed Annie and then focused on Jamie. "Do you wish this to be their fate, James Hephaistion Alexander?"

Regret filled Jamie's stomach. "Is there anywhere nicer?"

"Only death."

"Oh." Jamie couldn't just kill them, not when they were tiny and defenseless. He closed his eyes and thought hard for a second. "Okay. Please take them and thank you."

"I think it may be best if you five did not stay to watch," Scorpion Man said, "but I would like to convince you to have some tea. As I once said and believed, 'No beast is more savage than man when possessed with power answerable to his rage,' but that was before I knew of trolls and of demons. It was a gentler time despite man's own ancient ferocities."

The scorpion man's long nose seemed to go beyond his thin mouth. He had a full beard that wasn't to the point of birds nesting in it secretly, but was pretty lush and a good week past the stubble stage. There was an air of otherworldliness about him, Annie decided, that wasn't just because of his scrambling, multiple scorpion legs.

"The legs are disconcerting to you, aren't they?" the scorpion man asked.

"Oh, no!" Jamie lied. "I was just thinking it must be hard to keep track of everything you are doing when you have so many . . . so many . . ."

"Appendages. It is a bit, but it's quite useful. I can write multiple thoughts at once." The scorpion man sat down and illustrated, taking an old-fashioned fountain pen in each of his hands and legs and scrolling out a bunch of lines on papers.

"Wow . . ." Jamie came forward. "What does it say?"

"It says, *Welcome, Catcher of Trolls*, on this one." The scorpion man pointed to a piece of paper on the floor, by his lowermost left foot. On this it reads, *I am quite pleased to make your acquaintance*. On this one it says, *Would you like some tea?* And so on."

Using all of his legs, he picked up each paper and crumpled it, while still holding the assorted pens in the little claws at the end of each appendage. Jamie shook his head.

Even though he'd been in Aurora for a couple of days now, sometimes it was hard for his mind to come to terms with the things he was seeing.

The scorpion man's tail rattled a bit.

"Tell me about the trolls out there, young James. Unlike your namesakes you have never been trained to be a boy warrior. You could not even kill these two trolls that had just put you and your friends in mortal peril. You chose to confine them instead."

"Maybe that's because I'm a troll." It was hard for Jamie to admit. "Maybe I didn't want to kill them because I am like them."

"If you were similar in temperament to the trolls, you would have killed them without thought or remorse, young Jamie. Being the same species does not prevent you from killing others of your species. Think of the humans and their constant wars and killings. They kill each other, do they not?"

Jamie had to admit that they did.

"Do you think it is harder to kill an unstoppable army of monsters? Or one-on-one?" Jamie asked, turning to meet the scorpion man's gaze.

"It is a man's character and how easily it is influenced that makes one good or evil. For one such as you, it appears that it is harder to deal with evil one-on-one because your heart softens at the possibility that the evil may be good."

"You mean because I couldn't kill the trolls and had to bring them to you?" Jamie's hand dropped to his side.

"That does not need be a weakness, Jamie. Your kindness can be a strength."

"Not in war."

"Even in war." The scorpion man placed Eva and Canin in a tiny box with glass sides. The bottom was cushioned. Bloom hopped in and held out his arms to catch Annie, but the scorpion man took her gently down instead. Then he handed the box to Jamie. "'Perseverance is more prevailing than violence; and many things which cannot be overcome when they are together, yield themselves up when taken little by little.' I find myself telling people this quite a lot."

"Is that what the Raiff is doing by stealing Miss Cornelia? Chipping away at us? At our strength?" Jamie placed the box on his shoulder, and the scorpion man quickly latched it to him, securing it with thin pieces of twine.

"Perhaps."

"I never asked you your name," Jamie said after he thanked him.

"I never gave it to you, young James Hephaistion Alexander." The scorpion man cleared his throat. "Names hold much more power than we realize. For instance, once our new Stopper decides she is not a Nobody, her strength will triple or more."

Annie gasped.

The scorpion man smiled at her and continued, "And for you—your name is a key to your power. Hephaistion was a great logician only known to have one temper tantrum, which is really saying quite a lot, and devoted to Alexander, his king and his best friend. Their friendship was epic, young Jamie. Do you think you are capable of being such a friend?"

"I hope so."

The scorpion man gently placed a hand on Jamie's head. "As do I."

"As for the other last piece of your name, Alexander, that name has been widely used in the time since Alexander's death. Alexander the Great was a fearless king, willing to lead his troops into skirmishes with elephants, willing to calm the wildest of horses, willing to do anything for his best friend, Hephaistion, willing to conquer the world for glory, and to create an empire."

"I don't think I'm like him at all," Jamie said. "He sounds more like the Raiff to me."

"I can see that . . . I can see that . . . But for Alexander to create an empire that was strong, it was essential to protect his people, to keep them safe."

Jamie felt lost. The scorpion man must have sensed it, for as he brought him to the door he said, "Your companions will probably reconstitute to their original sizes, twenty-four hours past the moment they became small. So you still have a bit of time to keep that dwarf manageable." He winked.

"'Courage consists not in hazarding without fear; but

being resolutely minded in a just cause.'" The scorpion man stretched. His human arms lifted high toward the ceiling. "Don't worry too much about the Raiff's motives; his intent is your destruction, the enlargement of his empire, the reclaiming of this town. You cannot change that intention. He is a demon."

Jamie's heart sank. He wished Eva and Canin were awake to hear all of this.

"But you may know my name." The scorpion man pulled himself to his full height, towering over Jamie. "I am Lucius Mestrius Plutarchus, or at least that is what the Romans called me. And I am pleased to meet you and sorry to see you go. Allow me to give you this timepiece as a token of luck for your quest, young James Hephaistion Alexander. May you have the strength and resolution of your namesakes, but more importantly, may you have the loyalty and kindness."

The scorpion man placed a golden clock face into Jamie's palm. And with that, he pushed Jamie out the door and shut it firmly behind him.

Jamie turned around. The door was still there, but now it had a sign.

No guests allowed currently. We are quite busy. However in case of troll emergency or other major issues, please knock three times on the nearest tree.

"This town is so weird," Jamie whispered, and decided that this was probably the biggest understatement in the world.

Jamie—with Canin, Annie, Eva, and Bloom in miniature form—agreed that the only way to save Miss Cornelia was to go through the portal. They headed back to Aquarius House, knowing that's where the whole town was probably waiting for them. And they were.

The first person they saw when they pushed open the door was Aelfric, all gaunt and scared looking. His hair stuck up straight in angles, and he had an injured Tala in his arms. The dog's leg was stuck in a cast, and he was unconscious. Annie screamed, jumped out of the box, despite its height, shimmied down Jamie's leg, and rushed to Tala as Aelfric laid him out on a couch and related what had happened.

The mayor had arrived at the portal first, but trolls were ripping it apart, tearing the tree limbs down. Tala had attacked them, valiantly, but the destruction had already occurred. One troll managed to throw the brave dog into a rock, snapping Tala's front leg.

"It's been reset already," Aelfric said, trying to calm down a frantic Annie. "He has been given a Sleep the Pain Away and will be fine. No more fighting for him, though. You are—you are even smaller than normal, I dare say."

"What will we do?" Annie buried herself in Tala's soft white fur. "What do we do without a portal?"

Aelfric sighed, exhausted, and flopped down next to the box that Jamie set down. "Nothing. There is no other way. The people are already panicked because of the troll attack."

"Can we make a portal? How about the mermen? What sort of portal do they go through?" Bloom asked as he climbed out of the box.

"What happened to you?" Aelfric asked. "Are you all shrunk? Even Canin?"

"Don't ask," Eva grumped as she climbed out, too.

Aelfric paused and decided not to ask again due to Eva's attitude. Instead, he answered Bloom's question. "They don't go through a portal. *They* themselves are a portal, similar to the Loch Ness monster's abilities."

Someone shouted from the foyer. "The fairies are all accounted for!"

Aelfric stood up again, wiping his hands. "Well, it's all up to you now, Miss Time Stopper. You need to find a way to the Badlands. You need to bring Corny back to Aurora. Do you understand?"

Taken aback, Annie stammered, "No . . . No . . . Not at all. What do I do?"

"Well, let's put it this way. Your Stopper guardian is gone. It's just you and this boy who might be troll. If you two want to keep yourselves safe, then I suggest that you find another way to get to the Badlands and do it soon. Because I may not be able to persuade the citizens of Aurora to be patient much longer."

Bloom jumped to her defense and shouted at Aelfric. "Not everyone feels the way you do! Gramma Doris . . . Mr. Nate . . . Ned . . . Helena . . ."

Aelfric laughed and said knowingly, "Brounies, a stone giant pacifist, and an inept human can hardly stand against the will of the many. I am warning you . . . find a way to trade places, Annie, or all of you will be doomed. The town is out to get your young Jamie friend. They are terrified because of this attack. They don't think you're Stopper enough to stop this."

"But . . . but how?" Annie stammered.

"You're the Stopper! You need to figure it out!" He pointed his finger at her and stormed out of the room. "I'm just a vampire. That's what Canin always tells me anyway."

Annie and Bloom gaped at each other, stunned.

Jamie hauled Tala up the stairs to Annie's bed as Annie, Bloom, and the others followed. Thankfully, they resized there, Bloom added some leaves to the dog's cast to help him heal, and Annie searched books for answers until she finally just gave up, desperate. Jamie and Eva started to look sleepy. The last twenty-four hours hadn't been easy. Annie wished she could ask Miss Cornelia what to do, anyhow, somehow. She plunged her hand into Tala's fur and focused.

Annie could sense that Miss Cornelia knew she was looking for her. In the image in the fountain, the old woman had straightened her back up. And even though Miss Cornelia's eyes were hidden behind the dirty rag they used as a blindfold, they'd focused right on Annie.

Annie concentrated and decided to try something new. She had nothing to lose.

The portal is gone, she said in her mind. *Tell me what to do.*

And then, to her shock, the answer came flying back into her head with the exact same voice and perfect grammar and diction that made Miss Cornelia's speech patterns so remarkable.

Find a dragon.

A what?

Find a dragon. He will carry you.

Are you okay?

Be brave, Annie. All will be fine. Find the dragon. Gran Pie will lead you to the dragon . . .

Pinned to Tala's side and completely confused, Annie shook her head free of the vision even as Bloom's face hovered above her.

"What happened? What just happened? Your eyes were blank, Annie, completely blank, and the room seemed full of magic." Bloom took her by the shoulders and said, "Jamie, something is wrong with Annie! Eva!"

Jamie and Eva were asleep and didn't wake up.

Annie blinked hard, staring up at his concerned face. "I . . . I just saw Miss Cornelia . . . We have to . . . We have to find a dragon and someone named Gran Pie."

Bloom didn't question, just thought for a second. "Gran

Pie is the eldest Big Foot. There are no more dragons. But if there actually *is* a dragon still alive somehow, she will know."

Annie tucked Tala gently into bed, leaving a note for Jamie, who had fallen fast asleep the moment his head hit the pillow, and Canin and Eva, who had also passed out, snoring, on the couch. It explained what had happened, politely asking them to take care of Tala while she and Bloom were gone.

Bloom and Annie scurried out of the house to the edge of the woods where Gran Pie liked to hang out and cross the road multiple times. Big Feet were somehow very into that. That's exactly what they found all of her eight feet of furriness doing.

Gran Pie hid behind a tree for a second, before coming out, squinting at them. She put her nose right up to Annie's ear and sniffed it a bit. Annie held her breath. Big Feet smell like human feet that have been in sneakers too long. It was not a pleasant smell.

"Have you seen any trolls?" she blurted in a deep, rumbling voice.

"I think we're fine for now. Um . . . Miss Cornelia told me to ask you about a dragon. She is in trouble. All of Aurora is in danger from the Raiff. There is no other way. Please, Gran Pie. We need to find a dragon," Annie said. "We were hoping you could help, please. It's important. Miss Cornelia's life . . . and all of our lives . . . depend on it."

"Find a what?" Gran Pie said, wheeling around to face Bloom who gave a half shrug.

"A dragon," Annie repeated. "I need to find a dragon. Please."

"Dragons are extinct," Gran Pie said, grabbing Annie by the shoulders and peering into her eyes. "There are no more."

"Annie had a vision," Bloom replied. "Miss Cornelia specifically told her to ask you about a dragon."

"If I can find a dragon, maybe it can take me to the Badlands. I think that's what Miss Cornelia wants me to do. We have to rescue her," Annie said, knowing how ludicrous the words sounded.

"You want to ride a dragon to the Badlands?" Gran Pie shouted. "Oh, my word. You are going to get yourself killed. You can't tame them, you know. They have to like you, and if they don't like you they will just step on you or breathe on you, and then it's all over. Kaput. It's the end of you. Ack. I hope I never have to see that day. No. Dragons are no good. No good at all."

Gran Pie's furry hands pointed at the air, and she gesticulated all over the place. Her voice shook the trees, and several pine needles fell to the forest floor. Little puffs of steam came out of her mighty nostrils. She paced away, furious.

"She's not too hot on dragons, is she?" Annie asked.

Before Bloom could answer, Annie tried to mollify the Big Foot. "Gran Pie. Are dragons still alive? Just tell me where I can find one. You don't have to go on it. I do. It's my only way to the Badlands."

"Rrraaahhh!" Gran Pie roared in frustration and stomped off again, yelling back over her shoulder. "Are you listening to anything I'm telling you? No dragons. No. No. No, dragons are not to be trusted. They are reptiles. They have no fur. No fur! They lay eggs. Eggs! And they leave their young. Just leave them. They are not to be trusted. Not at all. They breathe fire. Just a sneeze from them is enough to singe off all my fur. A dragon!"

Bloom's eyes lit up.

"They're supposed to be extinct, which means they are good hiders . . . So . . ." Bloom was thinking quickly. "A dragon would be by the sea, I think. I've never seen one, though. Dragons are shy."

"Dragons are not shy. They are hermits, completely antisocial," Gran Pie huffed.

"Kind of like your kind, right?" Bloom teased.

"We come when we are called," she retorted.

"So will the dragon," Annie said, her voice so calm and sure that both Bloom and Gran Pie stopped arguing and looked at her as if she wasn't the girl that they thought she was. Annie didn't mind. She wasn't sure exactly *who* she was or who she was meant to be, but she knew she was getting closer. "Where's the dragon, Gran Pie? There is one alive and in Aurora, isn't there?"

The monster's shoulders slumped in defeat. "Miss Cornelia sent you to me?"

Annie and Bloom exclaimed that she had. Bloom went

down on one knee. "Yes, and we will keep it secret if we can, Gran Pie. We will try."

The Big Foot sighed. "Bloom was right. The dragon is by the sea, if he is there at all. They wander, you know."

"He will be there. There is no other choice. Tell us how to find him," Annie said, putting her hand on the Big Foot's elbow. She couldn't reach her shoulder. Then she remembered her manners and added, "Please?"

Gran Pie shook her head.

"Pretty please?" Annie was begging now.

"No."

"Pretty please with a pine tree on top?" Bloom stood up.

"I will take you. I will not show you. What sort of guardian am I if I let the two of you wander off by yourselves to get shish-kebabbed by a fickle dragon?"

The cold weather and storm had frozen the cove water to ice near the river and then out into the bay about two hundred yards. But the tide had already begun its work to change it back to pure water again. Great heaves had lifted pieces of ice into tiny pyramid shapes, layering one chunk of ice onto another. Rocks pocked up out of the whiteness like little islands. Past it, the open water stayed still and dark gray. The mountains of Mount Desert Island and Bar Harbor lay beyond. Past that waited the Gulf of Maine and the open sea.

Bloom lit the way with hovering balls of light as they

followed the river until Gran Pie decided it was no longer safe. Then they stepped on the snowy shore beneath the great cliffs that stretched out on either side of the river. Annie scanned the rough, cracked granite faces searching for a dragon's home.

The sea smelled salty and was full of mudflats where clams and mussels hid away from draggers' nets and pickers' buckets. They stopped at the pebble beach below the cliff's face.

"Where now?" Annie asked Gran Pie.

The Big Foot wrung her hands, jerking her head about. "Have I told you I hate dragons?"

"Only a million times," Bloom answered.

"Let me tell you again."

"No!" the children shouted at the same time.

"It's just . . . How can they live out here? There are no trees? No forests? Just these horrible gray cliffs and the sea." Gran Pie shuddered.

Annie did not feel like disagreeing with a Big Foot, but she thought the sea was beautiful in its own solemn way. She loved the forest, but there was something so majestic about the ocean.

Above them three gulls circled and called hello. Gran Pie answered them back, sounding remarkably like a gull. "*Sqwark. Kreee. Swqua.*"

A gull came down and perched on Annie's head, and then began to squawk back at Gran Pie. Gran Pie answered.

"Scree. Mi-noo. Scree."

Annie prayed the gull would not poop on her head. *Don't poop. Don't poop. Don't poop*, she chanted.

To Gran Pie she said, "What is the gull saying?"

Gran Pie motioned for the gull to wait and then looked down into Annie's eyes, smiling. However, the smile of a Big Foot is anything but comforting. It was like the smile of the lunch lady when she doled out some putrid green slop on Annie's tray at school and told her that it was pea soup.

"The gull and I are having a conversation about the dragon," Gran Pie said. "I was asking her if she perhaps knew whether or not the dragon was home."

A series of high-pitched bird noises interrupted the beast. The bird switched her footing on Annie's head and craned down to look into her eyes.

"The bird wants me to assure you that she will not actually poop on your head. She is far too civilized. She will poop on you, however, if you start acting mean," Gran Pie said.

Annie blushed. Bloom started laughing. She would have elbowed him if she thought she could without disturbing the bird.

"How does she know I was thinking about that?"

"Birds can hear thoughts," Bloom said.

Annie's blush turned a shade deeper. "Oh."

"What the lovely bird was explaining"—Gran Pie reached out her arm and the gull landed on her finger and she stroked it—"is that the dragon is indeed home and in a decent mood, which is a very good thing, let me tell you, because you don't want to bother a dragon when it's annoyed or cranky. Although, I would say that even when they are in a decent mood, they are terribly cranky."

Suddenly scared of meeting this dragon, Annie's eyes pleaded with the Big Foot. No matter how grumpy Gran Pie was, having her near made Annie feel safe. It was like having a super-size teddy bear that could talk. Okay, maybe not as cuddly.

"Oh, and I forgot to ask you? Are you good at riddles?" Gran Pie stared at her as the gull flew off Gran Pie's finger to land in Annie's hair.

"At what?"

"At riddles."

"I don't know." Annie tried to think of riddles. She couldn't think of any.

"Dragons love riddles. You can bribe them with riddles. Try to think of some."

"Oh, okay," Annie looked at Bloom. "Do you know any riddles?"

"A few."

"Tell me one," Gran Pie demanded.

Annie bit her lip. "Um, er . . . what's black and white and red all over?"

"That's no good. That's too easy!" Gran Pie blustered and reached out to grab the gull on Annie's head.

"What's the answer, then?"

"A newspaper."

"No, it's a zebra with a sunburn."

Gran Pie rolled her eyes, and the gull made a long series of annoyed chattering noises. "That is not a good enough riddle for a dragon."

Annie had had enough of this dragon bashing. "Please, just tell me where to go."

Gran Pie pointed. "Walk along the tide line. Go to the double boulders. One is shaped like a giant beaver, to remember the beaver's sacrifice for man. When you get there, turn. Anyway, just follow the gull down the beach. She will lead you."

"That's it?" Annie pushed her hair back behind her ears.

"That's all you need." Gran Pie looked away from them and out to the sea. Dark clouds tumbled across each other off the horizon. Bloom gave her a thumbs-up.

Annie knew he was being brave for her and she smiled, heart soaring. "Okay, then. Let's go. Thank you, Gran Pie, for your help."

"Remember: dragons—no matter what I think of them—are rare. This one is the rarest of all, because it is not supposed to be. Secrets are kept hidden and safe for a reason. Stories and histories are woven together in such a way so that time can march on. Corny, of all people, knows this, and she is the only one for whom I would ever reveal the dragon. It is for her and for her alone that I am telling you this. Remember well."

Annie turned and started off, but two large hairy arms wrapped around her in a Big Foot hug, which, by the way, is much, much bigger than a bear hug and much, much tighter. Annie couldn't breathe. Big Foot fur surrounded her nose and teeth. She closed her eyes and fought back a sneeze.

Gran Pie swayed with her, rocking back and forth. Then one arm shot out and caught Bloom up in the embrace as well, smooshed right up against Gran Pie's belly.

"Oh, my poor wee brave ones," she crooned. "The sacrifices you make and don't even know it. My brave, brave little elf, the last one left, off to face the hideous dragon to save poor Miss Cornelia from the wicked talons of the Raiff. Oh, I wish I could go with you, you sweet, sweet things. Two new friends with bonds greater than—"

"You are smothering them!" a shrill voice interrupted, the Woman in White.

Gran Pie reluctantly let them go.

"And you know dragons are not all that bad," the ghost said, hands on her hips.

Gran Pie snorted. "Not if you're a ghost and already dead."

Gran Pie wiped at the tears that collected in her eyes.

"You children should go," the Woman in White said, floating over toward Gran Pie and holding her. "She gets emotional. I'll take care of her."

Gran Pie had started to sob, horribly racking sobs that shook the trees. Annie touched her arm. "We'll be fine."

"Oh, so brave."

"Go!" the Woman in White said, ethereal hand pointing down the shore. "Time runs short. Go!"

The gull took flight and the children ran after her. Stopping, Annie turned around one last time. Gran Pie waved good-bye. It reminded her of an overprotective mother seeing her kindergartners off for the first day of school.

"Be careful!" she yelled. "Think of a riddle!"

But a riddle was the last thing on Annie's mind.

The trip was not too long. They passed more seaweed and discarded mussel shells, a giant mound of dark sand, and some broken-apart crabs. Their shells bleached from the air and sea's workings. The old wooden hull of a long-ago ship lay on the beach, also broken apart, but in the middle, its supporting beams sticking up from the sand like giant ribs.

"They say that was Blackbeard's," Bloom said in a low tone.

"The pirate?"

Bloom nodded.

"In Maine?" Annie thought pirates were just down in the southern Atlantic waters, like in Charleston, South Carolina, Florida, and the Bahamas, not in cold, boring Maine.

"He came to Aurora." Bloom shuddered.

The gull turned left and brought them right to the face of

a huge, almost sheer granite cliff that went up at least four hundred feet. It had no trails up, only cracks and crevices and outcroppings. The gull began spiraling higher, the way gulls do when they fly, twirling in looping circles.

Annie and Bloom craned their necks to watch her ascent. She went halfway up to a place where there seemed to be a dark hole in the cliff's face. She hovered there for a moment and then soared back down. The sun caught her wings, making them shine.

The bird landed on a boulder in front of them. The boulder was shaped like a gigantic beaver with a big flat tail attached. That's what Gran Pie had said to look for. Annie stared up at the sheer cliff.

Her heart sank. "All the way up there?"

The gull squawked.

"I could never climb up there," Annie said, apologizing. "I'm afraid of heights."

"Afraid of heights? I thought you did gymnastics?" Bloom said.

"The uneven bars aren't *that* high," Annie said, craning her neck to look all the way up.

When she climbed things, her head always became all dizzy and swirly. Even when she was on top of a mountain and looked down, it felt like her breath all whooshed out of her and that she'd faint. Bloom's tree home was about as high as she could go without stressing. Even being in Jamie's hair had twisted her stomach in two.

Annie turned away from the cliff. Storm clouds thundered over the sea. They came quicker and quicker, gaining power as they moved across the sky. The dark rolling mass of them gobbled up the blue as it moved closer and closer.

Annie despaired. She was no good at adventure or at being a hero. She kicked at an old clamshell. She felt so bad for Miss Cornelia since she was the one who was supposed to rescue her.

She scooped down and picked up a clamshell and hurled it at the rock face. "Yoo-hoo, Mr. Dragon! Or, Mrs. Dragon. Yoo-hoo! Hello!"

She grabbed a mussel and threw it, jumping so hard her feet left the beach for a moment and she was airborne. The mussel barely went up halfway. Hardly missing a beat, Bloom took a handful of clams and tossed them right into the dragon's cave, lost in the dark.

"Show-off." Annie laughed, smiling at him. Sea glass, purple and blue, had been under the mussel shell. She scooped it up and put it in her pocket.

"Dragon!" he yelled. "Would you mind coming out, please?"

Nothing moved.

"Hello, dragon! Dragon!"

"Dragon!" Annie yelled.

"Excuse me, Mr. Dragon."

Nothing happened.

"Dragons need doorbells," Annie said.

"Or hearing aids." Bloom whipped another shell into the hole far above their heads.

"Or manners. Do you think he's just ignoring us?"

The wind began to pick up. Their arms and voices grew tired. Annie closed her eyes, and a desperate Miss Cornelia appeared. Her face was bruised and looked as if it had been bludgeoned. Annie gasped. They were trying to break her spirit.

What had Miss Cornelia told her at the house? It seemed so long ago.

Annie, you can be brave.

Cannot. Cannot, the other voice in her head droned on.

Annie shut it out. *Enough!*

"Okay." Annie sighed. "I'm climbing."

"But you're afraid."

"There's no choice." Annie shrugged.

Bloom put his hand on her shoulder. "I go first, then."

By the time they began their climb, the sun had already moved midway across the sky, keeping just ahead of the storm clouds that were trying desperately to catch up. The granite cliff soared up straight and defiant against the ocean.

Bloom's feet sprinted up the cliff, already a good twenty feet above her. The bottoms of his shoes had no treads like boots or running shoes. They were smooth and seemed to meld with his feet. He scurried up the massive stone face easily, gracefully using the tiniest of holds as if they were gigantic ladder steps.

Annie wiped her hands on her pants and then rubbed them together. They were red from the cold. She let out a low whistle as she scanned the rock's face.

"Darn elves," Annie muttered.

I can do this. She brushed some hair from her face with her left hand. There was nothing else to do with it at the moment, since she couldn't find a handhold. Then she spotted a crack. *Okay, there.*

She grabbed the crack and began her ascent. Tucking her body tight against the cliff, she struggled to find places to put her feet and hands. But slowly she located them and began climbing up. The wind began to blow against her, but she clung to the cliff's gray and rocky side. Then she just kept climbing. One inch, then two.

"You okay, Annie?" Bloom called down.

He had stopped to wait for her and was crouched on one foot in what seemed to Annie to be more of an impossible position than those of human contortionists.

"I'm fine," she said, pulling up another inch or two with her arms. "Having the best time ever. Can't believe people actually pay to do this."

Annie came up a few steps more. The muscles all along the tops of her arms burned from the effort of heaving her body up over the rock ledge. Her fingernails, although never long, were broken and cracked in tiny parts, and barnacles and rocks scratched at her fingers and hands making little cuts. She wondered how far she'd come. She peeked down to see, without thinking about it. That was a mistake.

"Oh," she murmured.

The world swirled. They'd climbed about 150 feet. The beach looked so far below her. The clamshells were just black pebbles. The five-foot swells were tiny splashes. Her head churned, and her stomach came up to say hello to her tongue and teeth. She pressed her face into the rock ledge again.

Don't look down. Don't look down.

"Annie, are you all right?"

"I looked down," she whined.

"Okay. Okay. I'm coming down to you. Don't look again, okay?"

"Uh-huh." Her fingers trembled.

"You don't need to come back down. I'm fine."

"I'm coming."

Annie gulped and her fingers shook more. They could barely hold on, and the rock beneath them crumbled. A piece fell into her mouth. It tasted like metal dirt. She spat it out and heard it fall to the beach below. She knew she had to move, to find a place for her foot. She had to stop being a wimp and climb up. It wasn't safe where she was with her handhold crumbling away and the hard world so far below her. If she fell, she would be cracked in half like those crabs they'd seen as they walked, dropped from gulls' beaks and split in two. She would be split in two. Her stomach fell back down to its proper place. *I will not think that.*

"Okay, I'm coming up, Bloom," she said. "No more wimpy Annie."

"I'm almost there. You wait."

But Annie didn't listen. She had something to prove to Bloom and to the voice inside her head. She thought of Tala and how much she missed him, missed putting her hand in his soft fur, kissing his big black nose.

Her right foot squirmed along trying to find a hold. She crept it up at a forty-five–degree angle. There was something there, a little nook. *Yes, that would be good. There. Right there.* She shifted her weight to it just as the gull came swooping by.

The gull landed on her shoulder screeching encouragement much too loudly into her ear.

"I know you are trying to be nice," Annie said. "But that really isn't helping."

She reached her left hand over on top of her right, and shimmied her left foot up another four inches into a tiny groove that ran up and down the rock wall.

"In fact," she said with a grunt, "it's very, very distracting."

"*Craawkk,*" she said, lifting off her shoulder and soaring up toward Bloom.

Some little rocks crumbled away from beneath her left foot, but it held.

"What I need right now, Mrs. Gull, is some luck."

Luck, said a voice inside her head at precisely the same time the gull squawked and blasted out some poop that landed right on her head.

That little disgusting surprise was too much for Annie, who had been barely hanging on as it was. Her hand shot up to her hair to feel what happened, letting go of its precious hold.

That was all it took. She fell, scraping her cheek as she ricocheted off the cliff. Screaming, and arms flailing through the air, Annie fell back into a terrifying, weightless free fall. Bloom was above her on the rock wall. He was frantically reaching for his bow while holding onto the cliff face with one hand. He was a master archer. Bloom could shoot an ant off a tree branch three hundred feet away if he had to, but she knew whatever he tried to do wouldn't make it in time. She would die. Miss Cornelia would be all alone against the Raiff.

Annie closed her eyes, but her mouth opened in a silent scream and in it were the names of everyone she'd already loved: Tala, Miss Cornelia, Bloom, Jamie, Eva. The wind whooshed by her and the ground rose up. The seagull landed on her shoulder squawking hopelessly in her ears.

Luck, luck, luck.

Annie just kept falling.

8

Grady O'Grady

Falling is nothing like jumping. It is a freewheeling lack of control. It is a skydive without a parachute, and it is terribly quick. It was too quick for Annie to think of anything intelligent to do to save herself. If she stopped time it would do no good. She only stopped it for other people—not herself—so theoretically she would have just kept falling while the rest of the world stopped. And when she reached bottom and smashed—kaput—into the hard beach rocks below her, sprawled across the one that resembled a beaver, she would be dead.

So, luckily for Annie, she really thought of nothing as she fell except the faces of the people she loved. She thought, too, of how she'd failed Miss Cornelia and Jamie and everyone. She quickly wondered if it would hurt when she hit the boulder. She imagined it would, quite a bit, actually. That only made her squeeze her eyes shut tighter.

Because her eyes were clenched closed, she was completely unaware of what was happening in the world around her. How Bloom had laced an arrow with hands far quicker than any man's. How he just had it notched when from above him came a monstrous flapping noise. How he refused to pause and look, and instead he shot the arrow down, hoping to latch onto Annie's jacket. How he had let go of the bow and put it around his arm, along with the end of the rope, so that he could clutch a rock, praying that his hand would hold and he would not be pulled over when the arrow hit Annie's coat.

Because Annie's eyes were closed, she didn't witness how Bloom's arrow, while exactly on track, completely missed her jacket and didn't even lodge into her pant leg. In fact, it didn't hit Annie at all.

Instead, Bloom's arrow sank into the scaly end of a dragon's tail.

The dragon soared down, underneath Annie, pulling the arrow's rope . . . which was still wrapped around Bloom's wrist . . . with it.

The elf's mouth opened in a wide O, and he shouted "Annie!" as he plunged off the rock face and swung through the air above the rocky surf, attached to the dragon by the rope's long tether.

Annie opened her eyes at the sound of her name. Bloom

was falling toward her. And then she landed with a hard thump that forced her eyes back closed and made it feel as if her entire brain had smashed into the top of her skull. Her cheek scraped against something hard.

I have died, she thought. *I am dead.*

Then she realized what that meant. *Oh no, I'm going to be a horrible ghost like the Woman in the White. I am going to be stuck forever searching for the dragon. I will never have peanut butter and fluff sandwiches again. And I'll go twirling off, shrieking when anyone asks me questions . . . And—*

She was listing all these things in her head when she suddenly heard another voice. It wasn't like the mean voice that sometimes told her she was stupid. It was a low, mellow voice that reminded her of kind men who drank too much Scotch at night when watching old cowboy movies and baseball games.

Hold on, we'll get your friend, it said.

Out loud, and much to her surprise because she didn't usually talk to the voices inside her head, she said, "Okay."

She twisted onto her belly and grabbed something solid that she assumed wrongly was a beach rock. Her head throbbing, she expected to see sand and coral bits, maybe a piece of a broken shell or bones bleached white by the sun. She hoped she didn't see bits of her broken, dead self.

My bones will be like that, she thought with a shudder, *unless Bloom buries me.*

That thought was entirely silly, because Annie was not, in

fact, dead and facedown on the beach with her ribs cracked open. She did have a bit of a concussion and was dizzy, but she was very much alive and very much on the back of a medium-size, red dragon, whose deep color reminded her of a Patagonia fleece.

"Ahhhh . . . ," she said, clutching at the spine she'd previously believed was a rock. The dragon! She had found the dragon! Or rather, the dragon had found her and saved her life.

Annie had landed near the dragon's neck. She scurried up to him and sat astride just in the nick of time, because three seconds later Bloom landed on the dragon's back, plop, right where she'd been a moment before. He, of course, landed on his feet, being the confident elf that he was. He had more grace than a cat.

Nice landing, the mellow, gravelly voice in her head said.

Thank you.

Annie's eyes widened as Bloom sat down. "I heard you say that, but your lips didn't move."

Bloom smiled but didn't say anything else. Annie took one hand off the dragon's scale to hold her head. Her cheek wound was bleeding. She hoped she wasn't brain damaged.

"I don't understand," Annie said to Bloom, who was busy unwrapping the rope from his wrist.

The dragon swooped down to almost beach level and crested out over the sea toward the storm. He then flapped his large wings and swung back toward the cliff.

Going up.

Annie gulped as the world flew past them and they soared up way past the cliff and above even the trees. All of Aurora hunkered beneath them. Miss Cornelia's house sat on the hill. The town lay below. The barrens spread out like white fields, giving way to woods and mountains. On the beach by the river's mouth, Gran Pie knocked pieces of wood together. Annie waved.

Going down.

Annie shut her eyes as they spiraled back down toward the sea. She clutched the dragon's spine with both hands and clenched her thighs around his back.

Open your eyes.

"Annie, it's so fun," Bloom said, and then he yodeled and yelled. "Yeee-haww!"

Annie didn't know elves yodeled, but she opened her eyes. It *was* like an amusement ride, like a roller coaster, only smoother, and if she forgot about her headache and the cold beating of the wind against her, it was sort of fun.

"Yell, Annie!" Bloom said, punching her in the arm.

"Yell?"

"It's so fun. Just yell." He did again. "Yee-haw. Do it. DO it. Yee-haw!"

Annie cleared her throat. "Erm—Yeee?"

"Yee-haw!" Bloom bellowed again, lifting both his hands above his head.

Annie tried again. "Yee-haw."

Louder, the voice in her head and Bloom said at the same time.

She looked around and felt silly. "Yee-haw!"

"Again!" Bloom laughed as the dragon soared in a whirlpool pattern lower and lower and then zipped back up.

"Yee-haw!" Annie yelled. "Yeee—haaaww!"

It felt glorious. It felt like ice cream at the beach. It felt like a straight-A report card when the know-it-all boy in the seat next to you got a B in Health.

"Yeeee-hawwwwww!" Annie shouted again.

Good, good. Now let's go in so someone can take this arrow out of my tail.

It was only when the dragon said that sentence that Annie realized the mellow male voice in her head was not her own, but it was, actually, the dragon's. She gulped. She lifted up her hand off his back, but she missed the feel of his shiny skin against her fingers so she put it back down again.

"Okay," she said. "I'll do that for you."

In her head, she could feel the dragon smile, and they turned and headed for the middle of the cliff, straight for the black hole of the dragon's cave. As they flew, Annie patted the dragon's back. His scales shimmered like fairy dust, like a thousand tiny diamonds or stars reflecting all the colors of the sun.

The dragon's lair did not resemble the dangerous place Annie had always heard about in Grimms' Fairy Tales. No heaping mound of treasure mixed with human bones and skeletons. Swords and daggers taken from humans in bloody battles didn't cover the floor.

Instead, there were some nice mounds of sea glass sorted into colors. The pile of royal blue was the biggest. Annie slid off the dragon's back taking care not to hit his right wing, which he had folded neatly into his side. She reached into her pocket and brought out the blue and purple glass. She reached them toward the dragon's front legs.

"These are for you."

Thank you. The dragon bowed his head like a gallant knight.

Annie smiled up at him with a feeling in her heart that could only be described as love. "Thank you for saving my life."

Anytime.

Bloom slid off and landed next to her.

The dragon was about eight feet tall and maybe twelve feet long. Even in the cavern he shimmered, but now most of his color was red. His wings were even more beautiful than his scales; they seemed to waver with the wind like ribbons blowing in the breeze.

He is so beautiful, Annie thought. *Why does Gran Pie think dragons are scary?*

It's these, the dragon answered in her head.

He opened his gigantic mouth and showed her seven rows of pointy teeth as long as her forearm. Behind them was a pointy forked tongue like a snake's.

"Oh," Annie said.

"Whew," Bloom said. "Those are huge teeth."

The Big Feet don't like the fire either, the dragon said and blew a tiny flame out toward the ceiling. It turned into the shape of a bird and flew out toward the sea.

"Wow," Annie said and looked up past the dragon's teeth and into his eyes. It was the first time she'd actually looked at them. They were a lovely calm blue. She had never in her life seen anything so beautiful and sad.

Do you like that? the dragon asked. *I can also do a horse.*

With another little puff, he made a winged horse totally composed of red flame. It flapped its wings as it flew away.

Annie clapped her hands, delighted. The dragon smiled.

It's just a little trick, not a big deal. How about another? Maybe an archer such as our elf friend here with a mighty bow and a quiver of arrows.

"Oh, the arrow!" Annie said, hitting herself in her already aching head. "I forgot. Let me get it.

"You hear him, too, Bloom? In your head?" Annie said as she trotted around the dragon to its long forked tail.

"Yes."

That's how we talk, the dragon said.

"Do you hear my thoughts?" Annie asked, looking at where the arrow had stabbed into the tail. It wasn't in very deep.

Yes. And his. And the gull's. And when you are near me, you hear each other's.

Annie tried not to groan. This could all be terribly

embarrassing, like if she had to use the toilet or had grumpy thoughts or something like that. She tried not to think about it and focused instead on the arrow. She wondered how to best pull it out.

If you just pull it up while the elf holds my tail down that should do it. Or I could try to pull it out with my teeth.

"No, it's my fault. I'll fix it," Annie said.

It's my fault, Bloom's voice said in her head.

"I'm the one who fell."

It is no one's fault, and it barely hurts, the dragon said. *No more blaming.*

Bloom straddled the tail and then bent down, pushing all his weight against the appendage. Annie wrapped her hands around the arrow. She didn't want to hurt the dragon more.

You won't hurt me.

Annie shook her head. This mind reading stuff was more than a little annoying.

It can be intrusive, the dragon said.

Annie laughed. Well, she'd have no privacy, that's for sure, but it was worth it if she got to be near a real dragon who might help her rescue Miss Cornelia. "Okay. I'll count to three and pull. No, Bloom, you count."

Bloom wiggled his eyebrows at her. He knew the thought of hurting the dragon that had just saved her life terrified her.

It'll be okay, his voice said in her head. *Breathe deep, Annie.*

Out loud he counted. "One . . . two . . . three . . ."

Annie yanked the arrow up and out and threw it across the cavern floor. A tiny trickle of blue blood spewed out of the wound.

"Oh, no." She clamped her hand over it.

Touch your cheek.

"What?"

Touch your cheek with my blood.

Annie didn't understand why, but she wasn't about to refuse the order of a dragon that had just given her life. She put her other hand on the wound and placed the hand with the dragon's blood up to her cheek. Her face tingled and the world went black. Bloom caught her as her body fell to the floor.

Now we are joined, the dragon said in the darkness. *Annie, Bloom, I am Grady O'Grady.*

It was the last thing Annie heard. Her exhausted body went into a coma-like sleep for almost a half hour.

Bloom used the time that Annie slept to explain to Grady O'Grady what was going on. The dragon, it turned out, knew Miss Cornelia and was a great fan of the old Time Stopper. Just as Bloom was the last elf, Grady O'Grady was the very last dragon, and he and Miss Cornelia (and then Gran Pie, when she discovered him by accident) had agreed that his existence would be kept secret to protect him from humans and to protect Aurora from evildoers who wanted to free the Raiff.

Grady and Bloom talked strategy, and the dragon made Bloom touch the rope burns on his hand with dragon blood so that they, too, were bound. Now there was a circle that linked the three of them.

"Forever?" Bloom asked.

Forever.

Annie's mind woke before her body, and the dragon's voice promising to help echoed through her head.

Traveling through a portal on a dragon's back isn't easy, Grady O'Grady was saying. *It's rougher than regular flying.*

We have no choice, Bloom thought.

No, you don't. Not with the Tree of Many Trunks gone.

Annie opened her eyes. The dragon sat on the floor with his front paws curled gently around Bloom and herself.

You're awake.

"What happened?" Annie asked, staring up into the dragon's mouth. Though she wasn't afraid, his many teeth weighed heavy on her mind. It was like the mouth of a shark. She'd seen one of those in a science book at school. They had rows and rows of teeth, just like a dragon.

The joining was a little too much for you, Grady O'Grady answered. *You were tired. I'm afraid it made you faint. I'm sorry. I didn't quite expect that. Bloom caught you, though.*

Annie tried to imagine Bloom catching her and felt

herself turn a vicious red. *Don't think out loud,* she told herself. *They'll know.*

"Why didn't you come when we called?" Annie asked, sitting up. "And what's this joining thing, and when are we going to go to the Badlands? We need to go now. Miss Cornelia needs us."

In a moment. The answer to your first question is that dragons don't hear with our ears the way humans do.

"But, then, how did you know to save me?"

Dragons hear souls. I could feel your soul and all the despair in it. That's how I knew to rush out. That's how I knew you were good. You let your guard down and I saw right in. I knew that your intentions were noble and that I could trust you.

"So what about me?" Bloom asked.

When Annie fell, your fear flew out with her. You shook with it. You were horrified, overcome with the possibility of her loss. That's how I could tell you were good, too.

Bloom blushed.

I'm sorry I embarrassed you, Bloom, but we dragons are honest. We tell the truth even if it hurts. And we remember things. For instance, I can tell you every time one of the Red Sox struck out, every error in a World Series Game, the name of every elf that the trolls have taken.

Annie could feel the pain shoot through Bloom's heart at Grady O'Grady's words. In her mind flashed two pictures of elves, both with golden hair like Bloom's. Their eyes looked so kind. It broke her heart along with Bloom's and the dragon's. She wasn't so sure how she felt about this dragon code of absolute honesty. She decided to change the subject and itched at her nose.

"You like the Red Sox?" Annie asked.

Of course. I am red. I live in New England.

"I see," Annie said, although she didn't. On each of his feet were three toes that ended in pointed talon-like nails. "You don't wear socks."

The dragon's laughter echoed in her head. His belly shook, but no sound came out into the air with them.

Now, tell me a riddle.

"Tell you a riddle?" Annie panicked. That's what Gran Pie had said. Dragons like riddles. She was awful at riddles. Maybe Gran Pie was right after all. She'd tell it a horrible riddle, and Grady O'Grady would eat them both. Then Miss Cornelia would die and the world would stop.

Stop it with those thoughts. Those thoughts will be your undoing. I will not eat you. We are joined. Plus, I prefer salmon. And those red hot dogs they sell at Red Sox games . . .

Then why a riddle? Bloom asked in his head.

He seemed to be quite comfortable talking without words, but Annie found it hard and kept saying things out loud.

Dragons like riddles.

"What does it mean to be joined?"

The dragon showed her a picture of two souls swirling in

white with ribbons flashing between them. *We are in sync. We vibrate together. We help each other. Your wound is gone and so is my arrow.*

Annie touched her cheek. There wasn't even a cut or a scar.

"Okay," she said. "A riddle."

Think the riddle, but block the answer. It will train your mind.

"For what?"

Not for anything, but against intruders.

That wasn't something she wanted to think about. Mind intruders. She shuddered.

"Okay. A riddle." She searched around the cave frantically for some sort of visual clue to jog her memory. "A riddle . . . a riddle."

The only one she could think of was the one she'd told Gran Pie before. She decided to give it a go, forcing herself not to think of the answer.

What's black and white and red all over?

The dragon's mind was silent for a moment. Then he yelled, *A newspaper.*

"No."

There was no reply.

A skunk in a bucket of red paint?

"No."

A raccoon blushing?

"No."

I give up.

"A zebra with a sunburn."

Grady O'Grady smiled and stood up. *Good one. Good one.*

"Gran Pie didn't like it."

She has no sense of humor. None of her kind do.

"Actually, I don't think she knows what a zebra is," Bloom said.

Well, I do. I've seen them on one of my journeys to Africa, which you should remind me to tell you about sometime. And the riddle is good.

9

The Headless Horror

Jamie couldn't believe what he was seeing when he finally woke up in Aquarius House. Rainbows covered the house, and there were pixies flittering in and out the front door. They twittered when they saw him, circling around his head.

"He's not dead!" one yelled.

"He's not troll!"

"He's rescued Eva and Canin! Look! *Look!*"

Pixies and fairies buzzed around his face, kissing his cheeks, hanging out in his hair, catching a ride on his ear-lobe. It was a huge, noisy commotion, and still Eva and Canin didn't wake up.

"Um . . . are . . . is . . . Annie here?" he asked. A pixie buzzed right in front of his eyes. He resisted the urge to swat her away, reminding himself that they weren't flies or mosquitoes even if right now they were being that annoying.

"Annie is gone!" one shouted in his face. She landed on his nose.

"She saved us!" another said, perching herself next to the other pixie.

In a twittering hubbub of noise, nose sitting, ear tugging, and hair bombing, the pixies told Jamie that Annie and Bloom were off looking for a portal or a dragon or something. They weren't quite sure, but they brought him Annie's note. It took five pixies to fly the piece of paper and hover it in front of Jamie's face.

Two seconds later, Gramma Doris rushed to his side. "James Hephaistion Alexander!" she scolded. "Look at you! If you aren't eaten by trolls, or jailed by our less intelligent townspeople, you're going to starve to death! Pixies, stand back! Let the poor boy through!"

"Are people really looking for me? To put me in jail?"

"Yes. They are blaming you for Miss Cornelia's abduction, for the . . . the trolls," she basically spat out the word, "that have been invading this town, for everything really."

Jamie contemplated this for a moment, his heart sinking. "Because I might be a troll."

"Because people need to blame someone, I think. You'd bet that magical creatures would be above that sort of thing, but no . . . Just as bad as everyone else, I suppose. Just as bad as humans." She paused and hiccupped, straightening her hair and getting gobs of flour in it. "Do you like what I did to the house?"

"The rainbows?" Jamie asked, wondering why they would talk about that when other things were oh so much more important.

"Yes! I thought it would be cheery for when Cornelia comes home, and she is coming home, so help me. I will see to that. And all will be right, and there will be pies for everyone. But for now, we need to keep you fed, safe, and hidden."

"Hidden?" Jamie protested.

"Yes! Hidden!" With a sturdy hand placed on the bottom of his back she pushed Jamie into the hall, down the stairs, and into the room off the front parlor, the one with the Cupid statue, which he and Annie had beheaded accidentally. The cherub's head had been reaffixed with rainbow duct tape, and it now sported a curly blond wig. The statue's plump arm was raised to the mosaic on the ceiling, which had shifted to show a shiny green arrow pointing at what resembled a British pub or hotel.

"Wait!" Jamie protested.

But it was too late. Gramma Doris had slid open the trapdoor by moving the Cupid statue with her foot. She pushed him down the hole with a "sorry" and an added "it's for your own safety" and then "I will bring you some pies."

And that was that.

She slid the trapdoor shut on top of him, and he was stuck there in the darkness.

The door slid open. Hope filled his heart.

"Forgot a flashlight! Here are some books! Have a sandwich." Gramma Doris zinged all the items down on a slide that magically appeared out of thin air. It, too, was made of rainbows.

"Please don't make me stay here," Jamie begged. "I need to help Annie."

"We don't even know where that girl is!" Gramma Doris said, face frowning. "I can't lose anyone else today, Jamie. My old heart can't handle it. I want you safe. No ifs, ands, or bottoms."

The door shut again and he was in the dark. Alone without even a regular-size wolf or chair-size dwarf to keep him company.

The last time Jamie had been trapped in this same hole beneath the floor of Miss Cornelia's, he had company. Sure, they were all terrified of the crow monster who wanted to freeze them for the trolls' later use. Annie, Eva, Bloom, and Tala were all equally petrified—Eva had even passed out—but there had been a certain kind of comfort having his friends with him. Even if he had died then, or been frozen in feathers, he knew that he wasn't going to die alone.

That was kind of a big deal.

Or at least it seemed like kind of a big deal to him especially at this exact moment when he felt very much alone.

"It's all going to be okay," he whispered, turning the flashlight on. "It will totally be okay."

And he spent a good amount of time eating his sandwich and reading *The Magical Burrens of Ancient Ireland and How They Inspired Guinness and Pubs and All Sorts of Wonderful Things*, which was much more informative (although much more boring) than the Irish graphic novel that Gramma Doris tossed down, *Captain Awesomepants of Aurora Defeats the Devil Dog*.

After rereading that for what seemed like the thousandth time, Jamie stood up. "This is ridiculous."

He tapped on the ceiling with the end of his flashlight. He yelled the word "help!" over and over. He tried to create a psychic link between himself and the pixies, which is what Captain Awesomepants of Aurora did to enlist their help to defeat the dastardly Devil Dog. That didn't work either, not that Jamie thought it would. It was pretty obvious by now that he wasn't magic, no matter how much he wished he was.

He began pressing on the walls in a systematic manner, moving from high to low, from one end of the room to another, tapping here, following it by a good press, over and over again until he thought he must have touched every square inch of those walls three times.

Frustrated, he flopped to the floor, and momentarily gave up.

"There has to be something that I'm not thinking of,"

he muttered, but the truth was that when all four of them had been trapped here last time (five counting Tala), they'd done this same exact thing, examining all of the stone walls for secret places and hidden levers that would reveal an escape route.

The ceiling! Maybe it was in the ceiling! They hadn't checked there. Standing on tiptoe, Jamie reached up and began to prod the ceiling with his flashlight. Once again, he worked methodically. He didn't want to take a chance on missing any potential spaces that could lead to an exit. Sighing, he felt as if he was never going to be able to get out of there. Pointless . . . it was all so pointless . . . Here he was stuck, and Annie . . . Who knew what was happening to Annie? His heart beat faster as he pushed his anger back down into his gut. He had to find a way out. He had to. It didn't matter if it was dangerous out there. What mattered was . . .

The flashlight pushed in a stone.

The stone's movement made a scraping noise.

A huge piece of the ceiling retracted.

Jamie jumped back as dust fell. He coughed once, twice, in the swirling cloud of particles. When it cleared, there was a ladder, gleaming and brand-new looking, resting in front of him. He didn't even hesitate, just barreled up, two rungs at a time. It led to a corridor with gleaming white walls and violets sprouting out of them. Some of them seemed to be wilting a bit, probably because Miss Cornelia was missing, but the effect was still dazzling. Gently he touched one of the violets with the tip of his finger.

"Jamie . . . ," it whispered.

"That's my name."

"We've been waiting for you . . ."

"For me?" He pointed at his chest and then felt sort of ridiculous and quickly put his hand back down. "Why? Are you sure?"

Talking flowers were so odd, but everything about Aurora was odd, wasn't it? Standing a bit straighter, Jamie waited for an answer.

"Because you will save us."

Jamie lifted an eyebrow.

"We are dying without them."

"Without who?"

"The elves."

And then he heard it—something thumping down the corridor, which seemed to come to an end and then turn right or left. It was a noise quite different from the lilting, broken sounds of the violets.

There in front of him were hundreds, literally hundreds of rabbits with horns . . . jackalopes, actually. They were on the cover of the *Magical Burrens of Ancient Ireland* book Gramma Doris had thrown down. The jackalopes all rushed forward in a mad cluster. Jamie pressed himself to the side of the wall to resist being trampled. He hoped he wasn't hurting the flowers.

"Whoa . . . whoa . . . slow down," he said as they thumped past him, a thundering wall of fur and noise. "What are you even running from?"

And then at the end of the corridor, he spotted something . . . A small horse. It saw him, met his eyes, and then reared up on its hind legs as if looking about. It screamed out a piercing cry and then followed the jackalopes down the hole, scampering past Jamie as if he wasn't even there. A Grant. That's what that was. That was in another book from Gramma Doris, and there was also one about a bow and arrow made of gold.

Then Jamie heard another noise—altogether different.

"Do you have gold?" the violets whispered.

"Gold?" Jamie asked. Fear and confusion mixed and made his whisper as ethereal as the flowers'.

"It will keep you safe. Hurry."

Gold. Gold. Gold! Jamie's mind raced. He was too young for gold teeth and too poor for gold jewelry, not that he was flashy like that anyway. And then he remembered.

Jamie whisked out the timepiece that the scorpion man had given him in the forgotten room. It shone like gold, but he didn't know . . . It could be fake.

"Is this . . . ?" Jamie didn't get to finish asking his question because a headless man shot out from behind the corner. No, that wasn't right. He had a head; he palmed it in his own hand like a basketball. He thundered toward Jamie, astride a black horse. In his right hand, the man held a whip made of spinal bones. With that same hand, he threw buckets of blood upon the flowers, which shrieked but did not die.

"Jump on!" said the flowers closest to Jamie. "Jump on and tell him where you want to go . . ."

"But you . . ."

The man and his horse filled the corridor. This was not the same black horse that he had seen with the evil crow monster. Jamie sensed that immediately. But what it was, he did not know. There was no time to think at all.

"Just go. We will return in the spring. Go! Tell him who you want," the flowers insisted just as the headless man reached them.

He did not pause; just threw more blood. Jamie ducked beneath the bucket's contents as they spewed across the flowers, and in a flash the man was past him, heading toward the dead end of the corridor. Jamie scrambled after him. The horse pulled a wagon made of skeleton bones.

Three strides. Four. And Jamie was close enough to leap. He threw his body forward and grabbed the end of the wagon, hands wrapped around what appeared to be human legs. He tried not to worry about this, or even think about it, but hauled himself on board, the timepiece chain wrapped around his wrist, secure.

The skeleton head turned to face him.

"Who dares ride with me? I am the dullahan." The creature rasped through the hole where its mouth once was.

Jamie stuck out his watch. "I do. Take me to Annie."

"Gold!" The creature recoiled and its head faced front once more. "So be it."

It picked up another bucket of blood, ready to throw it.

"And no more blood!" Jamie demanded.

The surviving violets made a little cheer, but he couldn't focus on that . . . Instead . . . instead . . . They were heading straight toward the wall, the very solid-seeming wall. They'd smash into it and wreck.

"Hey!" Jamie yelled. "There's a wall! You might want to slow down!"

But instead the dullahan sped up, smashing forward, the bones of the wagon chattering and clanking. There was no way they were going to stop in time even if they wanted to. Jamie screamed and held on tightly to the wagon's side. The dullahan urged the dark horse forward, lashing it with the whip of bones. The horse screeched and kept going—and kept going—and smashed right through the wall without even stopping. The wall stayed there, but the horse and then Jamie's wagon flew right through it without even a hitch or a stop or an anything . . .

"We're like ghosts," Jamie whispered and then realized that they were in the kitchen of Aquarius House and then—smash—they went through the wall into the dining room where a bewildered-looking Ned the Doctor sat with a cup of hot chocolate and the full-size forms of Eva and Canin in front of him. Ned raised his hand in greeting and then—whoosh—they were through the exterior wall and out into the cold Maine air, racing across the barrens and toward the ocean, faster and faster. The speed whipped the air against Jamie's face. He tucked into a ball, trying furiously to stay on the wagon and stay warm. He pulled his hat out of his parka pocket and tucked it over his head, thankful that he had fallen asleep in his coat and hadn't taken it off. He couldn't imagine how cold he'd be without it.

"Excuse me . . . um . . . dullahan . . . um . . . sir . . . ," Jamie began.

The skull in the man's hand didn't turn.

"You are taking me to Annie, right? You aren't just . . . um . . . taking me?"

The skull began to laugh.

10

The Maker of the Town

Jamie was already terrified of the dullahan's headless body, his whip made of vertebrae, and wagon made of bones, but the speed that they were traveling toward the cliffs above the ocean brought that terror to a whole new level. He couldn't jump because they were going faster than a car. He couldn't talk to the dullahan and ask him to slow down. He had tried. The dullahan just laughed. No, that wasn't quite right. The dullahan just cackled. Jamie couldn't make sure that he was even truly taking him to Annie on this hell ride.

And the cliffs were coming closer.

They slammed through trees and past low-hanging branches. They powered across the snowy terrain and through any obstacle as if they were not trees or stones or walls, but just made of thin air.

A tree—right through it.

A rock wall—right through it.

A random troll—right through her. Even as the troll roared and shook her fist, the dullahan tossed a bucket of blood upon her and she screamed, hissing and melting into the ground, leaving a puddle of green and red.

Where were the buckets even coming from?

It made no sense.

And Jamie's poor nerves shattered. Watching the troll die from the sizzling blood, even if it was an evil, hideous, murderous troll, made his stomach churn.

"Hey! That's mean!" Jamie yelled.

The dullahan didn't respond.

Jamie scurried forward in the cart, crawling over the long bones that were fused together to make up the carriage floor. "I'm serious. That's evil right there."

The skull turned to stare at him. Jamie didn't back down. "I mean it. I know it was a troll and everything, but still . . ."

A bucket materialized in the dullahan's hands. The creature's body turned around to face Jamie. His heart stopped. Was the headless man going to throw the bucket on Jamie?

"I have gold!" Jamie thrust the timepiece in front of him.

The dullahan shrugged.

"Well, go ahead then, but I . . . I . . ." Jamie thought about what it must be like to be headless and riding around forever, throwing blood on people, afraid of gold. "I'm sorry. I'm sorry you have to live . . ." Was it even alive? "Or, un-live this way. I'm sorry that you have no head and your horse seems to have an attitude problem and . . . Yeah, yeah . . . I'm just sorry."

The dullahan's attention jerked to the left. A gray-and-white cat slinked across the snow. It was the same cat who had led the rescue at Jamie's grandmother's house, who had shown him where the Gnome of Protection was, who had attacked his grandmother to keep him safe.

"Do not hurt that cat!" Jamie implored him, grabbing for the bucket.

The dullahan easily yanked it out of Jamie's reach.

"I mean it!"

The dullahan's skull turned to face the cat.

"Look!" Jamie's voice rose frantically even as the cat slinked closer, seemingly unconcerned by the headless horseman, the stomping, snorting horse, or the wagon made of bones. "Look! I have gold!"

The dullahan shrugged again.

Jamie thought quickly. He had a gut feeling. He had to take his chance. Sometimes you have to give up your power to get control. Leaning forward and climbing up the horse behind the dullahan's body, he sat behind the skeleton.

The head jerked back in his direction, eyelessly staring at him.

"I'm giving you the gold," he said and dropped the watch into the bucket.

The blood sizzled and turned . . . and turned . . . to something white.

"Milk?" Jamie whispered even as the skeleton in front of him jerked and spasmed, falling to the ground and shattering.

The horse reared, obscuring Jamie's view of the dullahan. Jamie clutched the horse's back, struggling to stay on. Two seconds later, the cat was sitting in front of him and the horse's four hooves all fell to the ground.

Where was the dullahan, though? Jamie scanned the place where the skeleton had fallen. There was no skeleton. In its place stood a man dressed in the kind of clothes that Jamie imagined pilgrims would wear: beige pants held up with tan suspenders.

The man stared at the timepiece as it dangled from his hand. "How clever of him to make me fear the one thing that should save me. Mayhap that's why they call it fool's gold? Although, this is true gold, but yet . . ." His attention riveted to Jamie. "I have the young master to thank, do I not?"

He bowed with a flourish, twirling his arm in the air as he took off his cloth hat. His head stayed attached to his neck, luckily. "I thank thee, young master."

“Y-y-you’re welcome,” Jamie stuttered. “Are you . . . ?”

“I was once the monster of whom you were afeared. Even the best of us can be twisted, young master. Even the best-souled men can be accursed; do not thee forget it.” The man sighed. He was somewhat transparent. He noticed this himself. “I was once a living man, the originator of this magical town, and then the demon spawn himself took vengeance on my soul.”

“The Raiff?” Jamie was piecing it together even as the cat made itself comfortable on his lap, purring. The horse had calmed down as well.

The man grimaced and returned his hat to his head, which Jamie realized was firmly attached to his body. He let out a breath of relief. He didn’t want the man’s head to fall off anytime soon.

“Are you . . .” Jamie racked his brain for the name Sal-Goud had mentioned in his impromptu history lesson so long ago.

“Thomas Fylbrigg. Yes.” The man took off his hat again and bent over with a flourish before righting himself and extending his hand. “Founder of Aurora and Time Stopper. Now dead, it seems, though I can’t recall the moment of my death. I am sure it was at the hands of my former friend and current demon, the Raiff. I was left to wander the secret halls of Aquarius House until I met a young man with a noble heart.”

“Me?” Jamie pointed at his chest.

“Very much so,” Thomas said kindly as Jamie’s shyness

and doubt became obvious in the sad lines of his face. "Not many would mourn the loss of a troll."

"I wouldn't say I mourned it," Jamie admitted. "It just didn't seem like a fair fight."

The ghostly man took a step forward, placed a hand on the horse, and studied Jamie's face. "Young master, you do realize that this world is full of death and there is nary a fight that is truly fair."

"I do."

"And how do you propose to keep your heart noble in a world so full of evil?"

"I . . . I don't know." Jamie's hand stroked the cat's head. She purred.

"Very well, then. An honest answer." The man jumped back up on the horse. The wagon, it seemed, had disappeared for good. "I feel compelled to finish my ride. Do you still wish to seek . . ." He paused. "I have lost my destination."

"Annie." Jamie perked up. "Annie Nobody."

"Annie Nobody," he repeated. "Ah . . . I have located her . . . She is with . . . Oh, well, isn't this interesting? Oh, to be alive again and able to help . . . At least I have my head now, thanks to thee. I shan't complain." He pressed the horse's sides with his feet. "Ho! Let us journey, young master, who has not given me his name. My last journey on this earth, it shall be, so let us make it a good one."

"I'm Jamie! James Hephaistion Alexander!" Jamie shouted as the cat jumped gracefully to the ground.

"I am pleased to make your acquaintance, James Hephaistion Alexander, great rescuer, boy of noble heart, keeper of justice, and ender of curses. Let us ride!"

Jamie swallowed hard, as they moved forward toward the ocean. "Wait . . . Where?"

Jamie's voice returned to a high place that he now called the Panic Place. It was a good octave above his normal voice, like he'd suddenly become a soprano in show choir instead of a reluctant baritone.

"Sir?"

The horseman rode faster.

Jamie tapped Thomas's back, but his finger went straight through his ghostly body. In fact, Jamie was pretty confused how he was even staying up on the horse, since that was ghostly, too. If he survived all of this, didn't turn troll, and didn't get kicked out of Aurora, then he was going to definitely have to look up the physical properties of ghosts, because it just didn't make sense to him that he could be riding a ghost horse and have it feel solid beneath him while at the same time be able to put his whole entire arm through Sir Thomas DeFylbrigg or Thomas Fylbrigg or whatever his official name was.

Jamie tried again.

Yep, his entire arm went through the man.

"Would you be so kind as to refrain from that, young James? It tickles mightily." The rider smiled at him.

Jamie yanked his arm back out. "Sorry! Sorry!"

"No harm done." Thomas turned his head back forward again, rushing toward the edge of the cliffs.

"Sir! I think that we might go over the cliffs . . ." Jamie's breath gushed out in a terrified rush. They were so close now. It seemed impossible for them to be able to stop in time.

"Not at all." Fylbrigg was quite calm. That was probably because he was a ghost and already dead.

Another twenty feet and they'd be over the edge. The waves pounded against the shore. Hard and unforgiving.

"Sir! I think—"

"Hang on, young master," Fylbrigg ordered.

"Sir!"

Ten feet.

Jamie began to scream.

Five feet.

But instead of leaping off the cliff and falling to the rocky shore below, the horse turned downward, heading straight into the snow. Its hooves went through first, then its chest and head. Jamie's scream stopped abruptly as they tilted and were suddenly through the snow and into the rock. They traveled through the rock as easily as they'd traveled through the walls of Aquarius House. Layers of dirt and sediment whizzed past Jamie before he could really understand what was going on. And then—poof—they were through and into a cave, and there in front of him waited a massive red dragon, a yellow-haired boy, and an undersize girl with too-big eyes and limp hair, standing right by the dragon's fearsome mouth with its countless teeth.

"Annie!" Jamie yelled, vaulting off the horse and rushing forward, weaponless. "Don't hurt her! Annie! Step away!"

And then—wonder of wonders—she smiled at him.

"Jamie! It's okay! Everything is okay. Let me introduce you to Grady O'Grady, the dragon, and my new friend."

He stopped dead still. "Friend?"

She smiled gently at Jamie and pulled him into a hug. "Definitely a friend. Now who is that with you? And can you help us with a riddle?"

"A riddle?" Jamie asked, completely confused by the cave and the dragon and how Annie and Bloom seemed so calm about the fact that they were standing next to something that resembled a winged brontosaurus. "You need a riddle?"

Quickly, Annie explained about dragons and riddles and how they needed to really stump him. Plus, it was a nice thing to do since dragons loved riddles. Plus, not to worry, because dragons spoke in thoughts and not aloud.

"Okay . . ." Jamie's face turned thoughtful. "How about this? A wealthy man is murdered on a Sunday afternoon. The police arrive, of course, and they ask—"

"This isn't the story about me, is it?" Thomas Fylbrigg interrupted.

"Of course not!" Jamie exclaimed. "Oh, sorry. This is Sir Thomas Fylbrigg, one of the founders of Aurora. He was just headless, but he's a regular ghost now, and so is his horse,

I think. He was cursed by the Raiff, but I managed to undo that by putting a piece of gold that Plutarch gave me in the bucket, which was cool, although, I mean, I only met him—Sir Thomas—because Gramma Doris locked me away in a secret room so nobody would kill me, which is sort of nice of her, I guess. I mean, she had my best interests in heart, is what she would say, but—"

Is he always like this? Grady O'Grady interrupted.

Annie put her hand on Jamie's shoulder and sat him down by a pile of sea glass. "No."

Bloom came and crouched in front of him, taking Jamie's wrist in his hand and monitoring his pulse. "Are you feeling all right, Jamie?"

"Yes . . . It's . . ." He pulled his hand free of Bloom's and swiped it over his own face. "I think it's just . . . things have been pretty crazy."

"That's an understatement, you poor guy." Annie placed her hand back on Jamie's bony shoulder. "You'll tell us all about it later, if that's okay? We really have to get going on saving Miss Cornelia, and in order to do that, we have to stump Grady O'Grady with a riddle. Or at least amuse him."

Dragon rules, Grady O'Grady said apologetically. *It is good to see you once again, Thomas.*

Fylbrigg moseyed up to the dragon's large red nose and affectionately placed a hand upon its tip. "You as well, my friend."

If it was possible, the ghost seemed to be fading even more.

"I think that now our ride has finished, I may not be much longer for this world."

Jamie stood back up, alarmed. "But—"

The man put his hand awkwardly on Jamie's hair. "You will be brave and save this town without my assistance, young James. Did you say your middle name was Hephaistion? How curious. Nonetheless, I have great faith in your abilities." He moved his hand to tap Jamie's parka in the chest region. "And in your heart."

Something warm seemed to fill Jamie's heart as Thomas Fylbrigg stared at him. Fylbrigg suddenly groaned and shrank back against the dragon. Keeping his voice low, he said, "I feel it is now my time to depart to whatever the next destination has in store for me."

"Maybe you'll come back?" Annie offered. "Are you okay? Does it hurt?"

"Yes . . . perhaps I shall. Stopper strength to all of you. Keep our town a haven, children." Thomas spoke quietly as his horse whinnied and pawed at the floor. Then his body twisted and turned, faster and faster, before becoming a white spinning cloud. The horse's body did the same, and then both launched through the ceiling, a backward tornado, and were gone.

The cave was horribly silent.

"I miss him and I didn't even know him," Jamie said softly.

Annie stood behind him. Bloom muttered strange, quiet words beneath his breath and moved his hands through the air as if searching for something, but whatever it was he was looking for, he didn't seem to find it.

Nothing happened. Thomas Fylbrigg and his horse did not return.

"It's pretty sad," Annie said finally. "He seemed nice."

"I know he was just a headless man pouring buckets of deadly blood on things, but I liked him," Jamie admitted. "It makes no sense."

You saw through to the soul of him, Jamie, Grady O'Grady said. *Thomas Fylbrigg was one of the greatest, kindest Stoppers to have graced this world. Even when cursed, you could probably sense that.*

Annie froze.

Bloom grabbed her hand.

"He was a Stopper?" she whispered. "Like me? And Miss Cornelia? And then he became—a ghost—a headless, evil ghost?"

Nobody said anything. There was nothing to say. Annie already knew the answer.

"We need a good riddle, right?" Jamie asked, awkwardly breaking the solemn moment.

We do! Grady O'Grady announced. *A riddle to take our minds off our troubles, and our recent reloss of Thomas.*

"Okay . . . So . . . Yeah . . . ," Jamie began again, sniffing.

He rubbed at his nose and continued bravely with his riddle. "So, let's say a very wealthy man was murdered on Sunday afternoon and the police officers went to his home to get the body and investigate the murder."

Annie gave him a thumbs-up, but she was obviously nervous. Circles had made homes beneath her eyes. He hated to see her that way—so stressed. He cleared his throat again.

"The investigating police officer questioned the brounie chef, the dwarf butler, and the mermaid in the fountain who was in charge of . . . um . . ."

Swim lessons? Grady O'Grady suggested.

"Right. Swim lessons. So the detective asked the brounie, the dwarf, and the mermaid what they had been doing when the man died. The brounie said she was getting the mail because she'd been expecting a package of special paprika. The dwarf said he was cleaning the front drapes because some vampires had been a bit rowdy the night before. The mermaid said she was setting up cones for a swim race. So who was it that murdered the man?"

They all stared at him. Annie's eyes grew big, and it was obvious that she got it. Bloom stared at him blankly. The dragon was the one who mattered, though. A tiny bit of steam left his nostrils.

Oh, I like that . . . I like that . . . The brounie did it because she lied. Mail doesn't come on Sundays . . . It's good . . ., the dragon said slowly. He lifted a large front arm to give Jamie a thumbs-up.

Annie perked right up. She grabbed Bloom's upper arm, leaning forward. "So . . . So . . . you'll take us to the Badlands?"

"What?" Jamie shouted. "What are you talking about, Annie? You can't go to the Badlands! The Raiff will kill you!"

"We have to go rescue Miss Cornelia," she quickly reminded him. "The portal has been destroyed. What's important is that dragons can bring people over and back. Stoppers can make portals, but I can't. I don't know how. And I'm probably not strong enough, so it has to be a dragon."

I can only bring one at a time on the way back. The dragon sighed.

"I can't just let the Raiff have Miss Cornelia. Not without a fight!" Annie was every bit as passionate as Eva, but instead of yelling, she was whispering. Her intensity almost frightened Jamie. "Can you imagine what he's doing to her? I can't let him hurt her, Jamie. I just can't."

"But . . . but how are you going to stop him?" Jamie asked, looking from one to the other. He couldn't believe Bloom was going along with this. "You need a plan. And weapons or something. You need . . . I just don't think . . . He will hurt you, Annie . . ."

His words trailed off beneath the intensity of Annie's stare.

"You don't have to come, Jamie," she said softly. "It's okay. Nobody will be mad."

"Of course I'm going to come!" Jamie said, but the horror

of what might await them rushed to him—monsters everywhere, the stench of the evil. Trolls, just as bad or even worse than the Alexanders.

I shall take you all. Grady O'Grady heaved out a heavy sigh. *But first you must help me. I just brought someone back from the Badlands, actually. It's a boy and he's sick. My goal was to get him back to Cornelia, but then—Cornelia was gone,* Grady explained. *And I must admit I became flustered. It was—It's all—It's a lot of responsibility, and I am afraid I am not one who can handle a lot of responsibility, not anymore.*

"Why didn't you keep him with you?" Jamie asked, eyes narrowing.

Annie could tell that he wasn't quite sure what to think about the dragon. She had to admit she wasn't 100 percent sure either. She just knew that she wanted to go and hurry up about it.

I am a loner, Grady O'Grady said.

"So you just sent him back to Aurora unescorted? When there are trolls around? How could you just leave him alone?" Jamie burst out.

Annie had never seen him so upset.

I didn't know about the dangers. I had assumed Aurora was still protected, the dragon answered. He coughed. *It was a no-win situation for me. Whenever I go to Aurora, the Big Feet scream. People can't know that dragons still exist. They will torture me and kill me because they are afraid I will breathe fire and burn down their buildings. Or they will use me to fly them places. Fire lighting and portal crossing are rare skills.*

The dragon seems to feel guilty about it, Jamie thought. He knew how it felt to have people just want you to serve them, to make their food and clean their toilets with toothbrushes, to just use you over and over until you forget how not to be used. It was no good.

"I get it. It's okay," Jamie said, placing his hand on the dragon's neck. "We'll help you."

That was that, Annie thought. There was no way they weren't going to go help a boy who had survived in the Badlands, somehow. Plus, he might know something about the Badlands, some way to defeat the Raiff, some way to find Miss Cornelia. Plus, it was just the right thing to do.

"Yes, we will help you, dragon," Annie said. "And then you'll take us to help Miss Cornelia. Deal."

The dragon sent them to the woods where he'd last left the boy, just into the edge of the tree line near the carnival site. And so they left, making a plan to rendezvous on the beach after they found the boy.

"Are you sure this isn't a trap?" Jamie asked as they finally made it across the barrens and into the woods. "Are you sure you trust this dragon?"

"We have no other choice," Bloom answered.

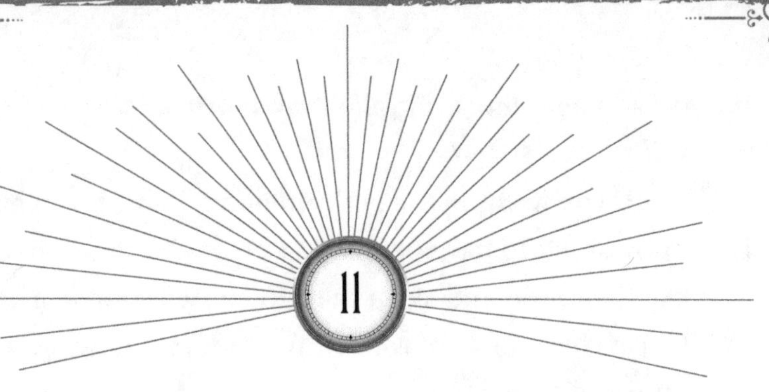

The Boy in the Woods

They searched through the woods. Bloom would touch the ground, hunting for faint imprints in the snow. He would sniff the air. He would get frustrated. And then he stopped, tilting his head; Annie did the same thing beside him. Bloom's magical balls of light illuminated the way as they scurried about.

"He has to be somewhere," Jamie whispered.

They both shushed him, obviously intent on something his human ears couldn't hear.

"I heard a boy's voice come from over here," Annie said, pointing at a copse of trees. "Bloom?"

"Hello?" she called out.

There was no answer.

Bloom pointed. There was a hole in the ground, just

beyond another spruce tree. Annie steeled herself and crawled toward the hole. Once there, she peered into the cave. Reaching inside, she pulled out the things her hands came in contact with: some rubies missing from the Ferris wheel, a sword, a diamond, a dwarf's dagger, and a golden shield, and then she finally found something soft and mushy. It was the hand of the boy himself.

Annie, Bloom, and Jamie heaved the boy out, huffing and puffing before they could get a good look at him. She laid him across the mossy ground and let his head rest on her calves. She was too tired to do much more.

Bloom fell to his knees.

"Bloom?"

Her friend said nothing. Bloom just kept staring at the boy who, like Jamie, had the look of someone who had never had a good meal. He was a skinny, blond-haired, dirty boy who really was much smaller and thinner than even Jamie. His dyed green tunic was torn and dirty and seemed to be sewn together from potato bags. A tremendous amount of blood crusted in some places around his arm. Annie wiped at it carefully, wetting it down with a water bottle. She found a bite mark festering beneath the blood.

Annie studied the boy's eyes but saw nothing there. "I'd like to help you, but you aren't making it easy. We called out to you. Why didn't you let us know where you were?"

"I don't know that I can trust you." His voice was like a sad bird song.

It broke her heart.

"Bloom, a little help over here." She motioned the still-stunned elf forward.

It took a moment for Bloom to realize Annie was talking to him. "Yeah . . . Sorry . . . Okay . . ."

She sighed and took off her jacket. Then she removed her sweater and carefully ripped two pieces of cloth off the sleeve of her shirt. The first piece of fabric she wrapped around the boy's wound. Annie surveyed her work on the boy. On the whole, she thought she'd done quite a good job.

Bloom didn't speak.

The boy's face, in its stillness, looked terribly sweet and not like the face of someone who had been in the Badlands, or at least not how she imagined it.

The boy tried to scuttle back into his hidey-hole. Annie grabbed him by the shoulders, and he turned and bit her hand, drawing blood. She yelped but did not let go.

"I—am—trying—to—help—you," she muttered fiercely. "Will you please stay still?"

He dived to the right, just in front of Bloom, who looked as if he was still in shock.

Annie dived after him since the boys were just standing still. "Look, you're hurt. You have to take it easy. Grady O'Grady sent us here to help you. We just want to know who you are and where you're from. We need to do something about your arm, and you look really tired. Grady O'Grady said you came from the Badlands and that you might know about Miss—"

She caught him by the foot. He twisted around, snarling. In his hand he held a shiny short dagger, and he looked only an instant away from using it. Annie cringed, and without thinking about it she grabbed at the boy's arm with her bleeding hand, using all her strength to keep him from slashing the weapon into her.

The boy's face was devoid of emotion. There seemed to be nothing in his eyes.

Jamie sprang forward and grabbed his other arm. "Bloom?"

There was no answer.

"Please, we want to help you," Annie begged the boy. *This shouldn't be so hard*, she thought.

The boy's expression did not change. He seemed to grow stronger.

"Please," Annie pleaded, her hand beginning to shake.

The boy paid no attention, and Annie lost hope. She could already feel the dagger at her neck. She could imagine the bite of the cold steel.

Bloom's voice suddenly broke out of the darkness. "Let her go or I shall kill you with one shot."

Bloom stood fiercely, finally taking action. The darkness had stolen the color from him, but he glowed silverish in the light of the moon. He seemed taller than normal, more regal.

He never looked much like a normal boy—not if you really looked at him—but he certainly looked nothing like a boy now. He was all elf. Any doubt about his worth, about his heritage, appeared to have vanished from him. He exuded confidence. In his hands, he held his bow. Notched on it was an arrow, and it was aimed right at the other boy's heart. Two extra arrows dangled from his hand.

The younger boy dropped the dagger.

Jamie grabbed the weapon with his hand. He pointed it at the boy and said, "Bloom. Um? Help?"

His name escaped Jamie's lips like a breath, and Bloom was immediately at Annie's side, arrows and bow stashed again, before he took the dagger from Jamie.

"He's wounded you. I'll kill him," Bloom said.

Annie touched his shoulder and leaned on him for a moment. "No, you won't, Bloom. He's just scared. You okay? You were zoning out there for a bit . . ."

Annie pulled herself away from Bloom, feeling instantly colder. She pointed to the young boy, still watching them, as he huddled up next to an oak tree. The boy pushed his blond hair out of his face, tucking the loose strand behind his ears.

They were pointy.

Bloom inhaled and dropped his bow to the ground. He rushed to the boy's side.

"This is no boy," he announced with the weight of a thousand pounds on his voice. "He's an elf."

Bloom moved his hair to reveal his own pointy tips. "I thought there were none of us left. They said all the elves had been killed. I was the last elf."

The boy sighed, and his body seemed so weak and tired that Annie worried for a moment that he might die right there. The boy lifted his hands to her and to Bloom. He closed his eyes and spoke. His voice was low and full of melody, but dry as if he hadn't tasted water for weeks.

"My name is Lichen. And you three, you three will help me?"

They grabbed his hands in their own and kneeled down to his level.

"Help you with what?" Annie whispered.

The boy closed his eyes. "Help me bring the others home."

12

Megan's Room

They huddled around the young elf. Jamie gave him his own parka, but Lichen still shivered.

"Others? Other elves?" Bloom's whisper was intense. He grabbed Lichen by the shoulder. "You mean there are more of us? We're not all dead?"

"We lost some during the battle and others over time, but most of us are very much alive," Lichen explained. "After the Purge, the Raiff took us to the Badlands where he's held us captive ever since."

"My parents . . ." Bloom's voice trailed off, and his hand dropped from Lichen's shoulder.

"Miss Cornelia said something about elves!" Annie remembered aloud. "When she appeared in the fountain . . ."

As Lichen told them what he knew, he sighed a lot and

scratched at his head, his eyes constantly searching the darkness beyond them. The first thing he made them promise was to not tell anyone who was a "mature person."

"You must swear," he said. His voice was adamant. "You must swear on your life."

He stared each of them down, and all three of them promised not to repeat anything he said to "mature people."

"Like grown-ups?" Annie asked, smiling but unsure.

"Yes, no grown-ups," Lichen said, face twitching nervously.

A red squirrel chattered away in a tree, and Jamie jumped. Then he looked embarrassed. He made a mental note to his running list: elves don't jump for squirrels; trolls are a different story.

Annie protested the elf's request a bit because she knew that swearing to keep things away from adults always leads to trouble, and the last thing she wanted was trouble in Aurora.

"Are you okay? Why can't we tell?" Annie had asked Lichen, peering into his face, which was pale and shadowed beneath his eyes.

He looked tired and scared, but serious. To Jamie, he looked so . . . weary . . . That was the word for it: weary.

Lichen nodded he was fine, even though it was obvious to all that he was lying and very not-okay.

"The Raiff can sense adults' thoughts," the elf whispered. "So if you tell them, he will know that I've escaped."

"But, escaped from where exactly?" Annie asked.

The elf groaned, shifted a bit, didn't answer, and listened to the sounds of the woods. He jumped as something boomed in the distance.

"Something comes," Lichen said softly, shuffling backward toward his small cave. "Something large."

"It was just a firecracker . . . ," Jamie began, hoping he was right.

But Bloom held up his hand to hush him as they all listened.

Annie imagined the horrible things that could be lurking out there, waiting. Trolls. Wiegles. Maybe even the Raiff. Maybe he had tortured Miss Cornelia enough to get her to open the portal; maybe he and his goons, his monsters, were marching through the woods to them this very second . . .

No.

She refused to believe they could have lost everything already. Not when . . . Not when there was another elf here, right here. Bloom wasn't the last. They weren't all dead, and that meant that there was hope. And even though she was terrified, Annie was going to hang onto that hope until it disappeared like a ghost.

All three were tense until Bloom whispered, "I hear them. It's just SalGoud and Eva. I can tell from all the thumping and cursing noises."

Lichen scooted back, obviously scared of Eva and SalGoud. Annie tried to ease his fears.

"Oh, no. They are very nice. Well, SalGoud is. Eva's more grumpy, but that's because she's a dwarf and dwarfs are like that. But man, she is someone you want on your side. Really. She's totally a toughie and terribly funny, really. Although, her table manners are super bad . . ."

Annie realized that she had probably said too much, and just as she realized that, Eva and SalGoud emerged into the small circle of trees where they sat in the silvery moonlight. Eva began talking immediately.

"I AM SO MAD AT YOU FOR SHRINKING ME, JAMIE WHATEVER ALEXANDER! SO MAD! AND YOU WILL PAY, but first, good job escaping. Gramma Doris thought you were dead, but SalGoud said they'd be carrying your body around town and celebrating if you had joined the congregation of the dead. But anyway, while she was moaning, we snuck out, which we aren't supposed to do because of trolls and everything, but we had to come looking, you know? And we found blood and followed it. Where did you two go? Canin said you were somewhere sucking face, so that hag Megan ran off crying and I high-fived him, and then Helena gave me a 'talking-to,' which fortunately involved croissants, so it took us a bit to get here."

The dwarf stopped grumbling to inhale deeply as she saw that Jamie and Annie and Bloom were not alone. She pointed her ax at the boy. "Why . . . he's . . . he's an elf. Sal-Goud, that's a freakin' elf!"

Lichen's entire body shook.

Annie blurted, "Okay. It's okay. Eva is a dwarf; she doesn't care for adults and all their rules, their washing tips, their table manners, their firm resolve that chewing with your mouth open is a horrendous sin. She is fierce and always wears pigtails and reminds me of a puppy somehow, but she is totally not going to tell anyone about you if we ask her not to, right?" Annie glared at Eva. "Because it goes against a dwarf's honor, right?"

"Duh," Eva said. She spotted the pile of items Annie had pulled out of the cave and started stowing them in her bag.

"And SalGoud?" Annie asked.

"Stone giants are keepers of oaths." SalGoud adjusted his glasses and slowly moved forward to inspect Lichen. "Annie, he's hurt."

The elf scuttled backward a bit more, but Annie caught the sleeve of his old potato-sack tunic and stopped him from retreating any farther. Bloom was immobile, obviously back in shock. It couldn't be easy for him, Annie realized.

"They are our friends," she whispered to Lichen. "Tell him, Bloom."

"You are safe," Bloom managed to say. "I trust them with my life, even the dwarf."

Eva shook her fist at him.

It took a while to convince Lichen, but he finally calmed down enough to make them swear once more to not tell any adults anything, and then everybody was properly introduced.

As SalGoud tended to the elf's wounds, Lichen finally, finally, began to tell his story again.

"A long time ago a wicked demon named the Raiff took all the elves from the Land of Lights."

Bloom's face hardened, and at the sound of Raiff's name, Annie shivered. No one noticed.

"The Raiff was evil and horrible, a demon-man who lived for centuries, admiring himself, building an army even as he pretended to be good. He had trolls, disgusting things from the night, bind the elves. Some were eaten. Most were tortured. All were taken."

"Except me," Bloom whispered.

Lichen cringed as SalGoud pressed some bark to his wound.

"I'm sorry this hurts, but I have to stop the bleeding. All this moving around has reopened your wound," SalGoud said. "As they say . . ."

"No quotes!" Eva demanded. She explained to Lichen, "SalGoud is always showing off and quoting dead people. Do they have stone giants in the Badlands? Because if not, I may want to move there . . . because there will be no showing off with the quotes all the time."

"It's not showing off," SalGoud protested, still holding the bark to Lichen. "Eva likes to embarrass me, but it's only because she loves me so much. Please, go on with your story."

Eva punched SalGoud in the arm. He didn't even flinch.

Lichen blinked, likely confused, and continued, "The elves were taken to a place beyond this world and held prisoner there, chained and enslaved as the demon harnessed their power. Each month away from Aurora, our people's power lessened. He shackled our feet and hands at night. By day, we were forced to help him build his machine. Those who protested were killed. Once dead, they were hung from the walls of the Tunnel of Despair."

He paused, weak. It seemed as if the entire forest were listening. The night became thicker.

"What machine?" Annie whispered.

"It is in a pit lined with our cages. It is meant to control the power of the strings. To control the strings is to control the universe, for they are the basis of all." Lichen closed his eyes and leaned a bit on Annie, looking terribly young all of a sudden.

"That blasted evil freaky demon!" Eva exploded, slamming her hand into her fist. "I tell you if I get within a mile of him, I'll crush him till his Adam's apple pops out and I'll use it as a puppy chew toy. I'll bash him until . . ."

Jamie tried to not throw up.

"Enough, Eva," Bloom said, raising his hand.

Lichen continued, "We haven't seen the Raiff for over a month, but then we heard he had the Stopper, so I decided to escape. I had never seen Aurora. I was born there, in the cage. I had heard enough stories to know how to get here. And

I knew what I had to do. Once I escaped the pit, I had to find a dragon."

His voice faltered a bit and he closed his eyes again.

"So, you escaped . . . And found Grady O'Grady . . . Did you see Miss Cornelia?" Annie asked, trying to get him to continue.

"Yes," he said. "And no . . . I heard the trolls talking about it. The trolls . . . they talk so much because they think we are powerless . . . It is from them I learned the secret to our escape. It is our only hope for a rescue. His power grows and he is draining the Stopper . . . The old one. So, I escaped one night by pretending to be dead. It wasn't hard. I was just still. The trolls and vamps took me to the Tunnel of Despair, which is where they place all the dead, and . . . I can't explain that place . . . It is too horrible. They strap us to the rock and then . . . They were distracted by the others . . . I untied myself while they raced off to hear what was going on back at the machine . . . We all planned this . . . I was the strongest with the most life force left . . . And when the other elves created a commotion, I fled. My family, though, is still there, and so are the rest of the elves . . . those who still live."

Bloom swallowed. "So there are many elves, still alive?"

Annie glanced at him. His eyes were full of hope.

"Yes," Lichen said, "some are left, but we are weak. The Raiff takes our power. Our energy is sucked into the making of the machine. Our only hope is to pierce the machine with the Arrow of Gold after placing dwarf objects in points around the perimeter, and then it will break and the elves will be freed. That is what I came here to do, and now I've failed."

SalGoud looked puzzled. "Where is the Arrow of Gold? And how have you failed?"

"I don't know where it is, and I'm too weak to return. Just being in the pit brings the machine power. It taints you. The machine takes a part of you inside of it, the best part of you, and the longer I am away, the weaker I am. Soon, I will die."

"No, you won't," Jamie insisted, looking to the others for confirmation. "We won't let you die."

Lichen shook his head. "The machine holds my core; it will not release it voluntarily, just as the Raiff won't release the Stopper. The only way they will release us is if they are destroyed. And it isn't just me. All the elves are dying. As he sucks away our magic, he sucks away our life force. We have not much time left. That's why I had to risk it, had to chance an escape."

SalGoud threw up his hands and accidentally hit a tree branch, sending acorns falling down on them. "But, you have to go back. You have to stop the machine."

Lichen looked defeated, hopeless, and ashamed, but he shook his head. No words came out of his mouth. In the distance, an owl called out that it had finished a successful hunt.

Bloom reacted quickly. "No, he does not have to go back there. I will. I'll go back for him."

Annie's shoulders tightened and her head lifted up to meet Bloom's gaze. "What?"

"We will bring Lichen to Megan. She's a hag. They're great healers. We can bribe her silence," he explained.

"Megan!" Annie rolled her eyes. She did not like Megan. Megan did not like her. The only people Megan liked were boys, more specifically, blond elf boys named Bloom.

"She is annoying, but in this, I think, she can be trusted," Bloom said. "And she is not a grown-up, so nobody will be able to sense that Lichen escaped. And then I will go save the elves and Cornelia. My people are heroes, and I shall not let them down. I shall follow in their footsteps, Annie. That's what it means to be an elf." Bloom stood up and started pacing as he talked. "Lichen will tell me how to get to this place. I will find the Arrow of Gold, break the machine, and save everyone."

"All by yourself?" Jamie asked. He lit a match to see by.

Bloom whirled on him, so quickly that it extinguished the match. "Yes. These are my people. Don't you see? I am not the last elf now, but if I don't do anything I could be again."

"We will go together," Eva said, handing SalGoud her flashlight. "It is only right."

Jamie cleared his throat and turned to Lichen. "Do you actually know where the bow is? It's a special bow and arrow, right?"

"Not exactly, but I can tell you how to get to the pit where the machine and elves are," Lichen said. Using the flashlight and Bloom's orbs to help him see, he drew a map on a piece of paper SalGoud had in his pocket. He explained it all to SalGoud and Bloom and Eva.

Annie said nothing the whole time until SalGoud picked up the little elf and prepared to carry him to Megan's. She put her hand on Bloom's shirtsleeve. Bloom had taught her to shoot a bow, and how to be a friend.

"Bloom," she said, "we are *not* letting you do this alone. You know I've already decided to go to the Badlands to save Miss Cornelia. The elves don't change that."

He looked into her eyes. Behind him another owl called across the darkness, happy to have caught a mouse in the barrens. It, too, would eat tonight.

"It'll be hard, Annie. I don't know if we'll make it back." He swallowed. "The Raiff has been taking the elves' magic. That makes him more powerful than we thought."

"We go together or we don't go at all," she said. "We're friends, Bloom. I won't let you go alone. Not without me."

"Nor without me," said Eva, who had been eavesdropping.

SalGoud paused and looked at the three of them. "I'm coming, too. You might need someone to heal people. Stone giants are good at that. Plus, someone has to handle Eva."

Eva glared at him. "What is that supposed to mean?"

"And me," added Jamie. "Nobody even wants me here right now. Plus, we kind of have to find that arrow first. I think we should be a little more concerned about that.

I mean, there's no point in going to the Badlands and trying to save Miss Cornelia if we can't also save the elves. And to do that, we have to be organized and get the Golden Arrow. Or at least figure out where it is."

There was something familiar about the sound of the arrow that was nagging at Jamie, but he couldn't quite put his finger on it.

"This is freaking complicated," Eva explained.

Bloom sighed and smiled a bit. "Fine, then. We all go to save the elves and Miss Cornelia."

"To save them all," Annie whispered and let go of his sleeve.

They trudged through the darkness of the woods, to bring Lichen to Megan's, and to begin their journey into horrible danger. Not wanting to be noticed by trolls or townspeople, they tried to stay quiet as they moved through the snow-drifts, shadowing each other between tree trunks.

"If you go to the pit," Lichen whispered, before slipping into unconsciousness, "and you fail, you may never return. Once the machine feels you, it taints you. It pulses into you. Do you know what you risk? I cannot ask it of you."

Eva kissed the top of his head and grumped out, "We will not fail."

"Eva, you just kissed an elf!" SalGoud said, shocked.

She shrugged. "Whatever. You have to kiss something before you trudge off to probable death. An elf's head is as good as anything."

Nobody had an answer for that.

"And nobody go telling nobody I did neither," Eva demanded.

They all remained quiet.

"And we will not fail," she repeated. "There is no failing when Beryl-Axes are involved. Not now. Not ever."

Jamie and Eva volunteered to go back to Grady O'Grady and tell him what had happened while Annie, Bloom, and SalGoud carried Lichen to Megan's house. They planned to meet back at Bloom's house before embarking on the hunt for the Golden Arrow.

The hags' house is kind of adorable, Annie thought when they got to Megan's.

With its thatched roof and white stone walls, it was a bit like some sort of fairy cottage that you might find in the middle of a book or a forest. Flower boxes filled with snow were outside each window. Bloom brought them around to the back wall.

"Megan's bedroom is back here," he whispered and tapped on the window.

SalGoud readjusted his hold on Lichen, who was still unconscious. Annie felt the boy's forehead. It burned.

Bloom tapped on the window again. Three short raps.

"Maybe she's not home," Annie said, worried. She was really afraid that Lichen would die. She already liked his feisty self, and it just seemed so wrong to die so young, after trying ridiculously hard to save other people. Plus, Bloom . . . how would Bloom handle another loss like that? She didn't want him to have to.

Megan's panicked face appeared at her bedroom window. She gasped and then smiled as she saw Bloom, but her expression changed into something much more negative as she spied SalGoud, Annie, and Lichen.

She lifted the window. "What is it?"

"We need help, Megan," Bloom answered. "Please."

His voice was desperate.

"The hags are still awake. Be quiet." She lifted the window higher, and Bloom vaulted up the five feet and was easily inside.

SalGoud passed Lichen through the window, accidentally bumping the injured elf's leg against the wall. He cringed. "Sorry . . . Sorry . . ."

Annie went in next with SalGoud giving her an easy boost up. Then he climbed through himself.

"What is going on?" Megan had pulled a sweater over her white nightgown. Her hair was all knotted and twisted up like the hair of the older hags she lived with. She reached up to her hair nervously and tried to tuck it into shape, and Annie realized she must spend hours every morning with brushes and detangling spray trying to get it to behave, which explained why she was always floofing it.

Poor Megan, Annie thought, and then immediately grew mad at herself. *That girl hates me and I'm "poor Megan-ing" her.*

She almost expected Megan to refuse to see them, especially after Megan's prophecy that "Annie would fall with evil," but the young hag didn't seem to care about that at all, right then. Instead, Megan drew in a sharp breath when she saw Lichen, who looked so much like Bloom, her not-so-secret crush.

"Is he your brother?" she asked Bloom, eyes wide. "He's beautiful."

And so they told her the story and she swore secrecy, making a bed for Lichen in her large closet, surrounding him with stuffed animals and dolls in case he grew delirious and rolled about, thrashing as people sometimes do when they are terribly sick. She didn't want him to cut himself or hit his head on her sharp-heeled dress shoes or anything like that.

He had become conscious long enough to spot a gigantic purple poodle with rainbow ears and a red heart on its chest.

"Am I dead?" he asked, poking the dog's heart.

"I love you," a robotic voice squeaked from inside the dog.

Lichen gave a little shriek and fell back asleep. Megan

took out a chest of strange-looking potions, a small rainbow-glitter cauldron, and a book of healing spells called *Hags' Healing Health Spells*. Then she placed a wet cloth on his head and whispered to the rest of them, "I'll take good care of him."

"And you'll tell no one. Not the hags. Not Odham?" Bloom asked, referencing some boy that Annie vaguely remembered meeting before.

Megan's nervous fingers clenched into fists. "I detest Odham."

Bloom smiled and held out his hand for Megan to shake. She took it.

"Welcome to the club," he said.

But Megan had already turned away, pulling a pink quilt off her bed and tucking it in and around her patient in the closet.

She cocked her head, listening, and then her eyes widened with alarm. She shut the closet door and lurched into her bed, gesturing frantically for them to go underneath it. "Hide!"

The children scurried under the bed, except for SalGoud, who couldn't fit and had to hide behind the long drape by the window. He had only just scooted his shoe back behind the long pink drape before the bedroom door opened and an eyeball floated in. The blue eye zipped around the room, hovering over Megan's bed for a moment before rushing off again, the door shutting behind it as Megan started to make fake snoring noises. It reminded Annie of pig snorts, which reminded her of Walden, her obnoxious ex–foster brother.

"All clear," Megan said, jumping out of bed and opening her closet door. "They always use the third eye to check on me. Every night. They tell me it's because they love me. Personally, I think there's some trust issues going on. Hags have a lot of trust issues."

She sighed and looked at Bloom and SalGoud. Annie, Megan ignored. She scurried back into the closet and put her hand on Lichen's forehead and then arranged some of the fluffy stuffed animals around him.

"He won't die here with me," she told them. "You go do what you must to stop this. He'll be safe here for as long as I am safe here. The Council says they've got all the trolls. It turns out there weren't that many who had made it inside while the gnome was gone, but it was enough . . ."

"Did anyone . . . ?" Annie didn't know how to ask the question she wanted to ask, because she didn't honestly want to know the answer.

"Die?" Megan finally looked her in the eye.

Annie refused to look away, but she couldn't make herself say the word, especially not with Lichen right there and so close to death himself.

"There are a couple of fairies missing even though you all rescued them . . . allegedly." Megan raised an eyebrow as she spoke the last word, illustrating that she still wasn't cool with Annie. "The mayor is missing. Canin and Eva were, but they'd just shrunk. And Jamie is missing, but I suppose you've found him. You were missing, Bloom. Since you are here, you are obviously alive. Some vampires were injured. One shifter is hurt. That's about it. There were pretty minimal casualties."

"Except for Miss Cornelia," Annie murmured.

"Yes, except for her." Megan studied Annie for a moment. "I will keep the little elf safe. Try to not make my prophecy true."

"She won't fall with evil," Bloom interrupted before Annie could answer for herself.

"We'll see, but if she does . . ." Megan pointed a finger at Annie. "She better not take anybody with her."

"What do you mean? Why not?" Annie blurted.

"Because these are my friends, and I protect my friends." Megan's answer was a whisper, but it was still pretty intense.

After that, it was a lot harder for Annie to keep disliking her so much. Still, as they excused themselves from her house, she couldn't help worrying about whether or not Megan would really keep her word, or for how long.

13

Grandparents

After talking to Grady O'Grady, Jamie led his friends back to Miss Cornelia's to find the book he had read about the Golden Arrow in the hidden compartment beneath the Cupid statue. They discovered the town was still in an uproar about losing Miss Cornelia, and about the random assortment of baddies that they had to expel. The fairies didn't feel safe any longer and spoke of going to Charleston, South Carolina, where there was a North American Fairy Family Festival going on. The vampires dreamed of a mass exodus to Seattle and New Orleans, but decided that was a bit too cliché. Jamie kept his head low and tried to avoid everyone's notice. He didn't know when the residents' sentiments might turn against him again.

At Aquarius House, Annie watched as the town's magic

seemed to dwindle with the remnants of the night. When she first arrived in Aurora, the sitting room looked like an enchanted forest. An overhead light source shafted rays of brightness down through branches of trees and ivy that covered the ceiling, which must have been twenty feet high. Along three of the walls, thin tree trunks grew into branches, golden flowers and bright purple blossoms twining around the bark. The fourth wall was a mural. Couches, chairs, and statues were nestled among it all. But now, everything seemed a bit drab, like a yellowing lawn that hasn't been watered in the heat of the summer.

She eavesdropped as Gramma Doris said that even the Gnome of Protection wouldn't last much longer. Canin was busy patrolling the woods at night, searching for monsters. Annie hoped Megan was doing a good job nursing Lichen.

Jamie slid back the secret catch to the Cupid statue and scrambled into the hidden hole, retrieving the book Gramma Doris had flung down at him only hours before. He flipped through the pages, which revealed the country where the Golden Arrow had last been seen: Ireland. Annie, Jamie, Eva, Bloom, and SalGoud knew Ireland was a big country. They were going to need another clue if they had half a chance of finding what they needed to save Miss Cornelia.

Annie's patience could take it no longer. Every minute that passed was another minute the elves and Miss Cornelia came closer to death. Every minute that passed was another minute that the Raiff grew more powerful.

Closing the shades behind her, Annie called for everyone's attention.

"We need to find the bow and arrow, and we need to find it now," she said, pulling the final drape shut over the shades. "Maybe we need to think about this another way. If all our research isn't helping, maybe we can use magic to find the bow and arrow."

"Magic?" Eva scoffed. "The only magic we got left around here is the magic of my ax."

"That's not true," SalGoud interrupted. "The town isn't as fortified, yes, and Miss Cornelia's magic is almost completely gone, but each of us still has our own. Bonding together we are still strong."

Eva raised an eyebrow.

"Strong enough," SalGoud faltered.

"How about if Annie uses her magic?" Jamie suggested.

"But I don't really know how." Annie looked at the floor.

"Maybe you could draw it," Jamie said.

Bloom exploded off the couch. "That's brilliant!" He grabbed Jamie by the shoulders and twirled him around, laughing. "*You* are brilliant."

"I am?" Jamie asked.

Bloom kissed the top of Jamie's head. "Exactly." The elf turned his attention toward Annie, kneeling in front of her and grabbing her hands in his. "You can draw the arrow and the bow, Annie. You draw bunnies and they appear. You draw the word "STOP" and it happens. Why not the bow and arrow?"

"Um . . . because I don't know what they look like," Annie offered.

"It's a bow and arrow! Gold. How hard can that be?" Eva asked, stashing her ax and the sharpening stone in assorted places in her belt.

"It's a good point," Bloom said. "And if they are protected by a magic spell of any sort they won't just appear, but we should give it a try, shouldn't we?" He answered his own question, "Oh, yes, we should."

Annie caught Jamie's eye in an attempt to get him to say something, anything, to help her out here. Responsibility crushed her confidence. What if she couldn't make the magic work?

Eva scoffed and Jamie shushed her even as he showed Annie the picture of the arrow in the book.

Bloom pulled in a breath and began to read. "It's gold . . ."

"Duh . . . ," Eva interrupted.

"Could you please shush her?" Bloom asked SalGoud.

SalGoud made hopeless eyes. "How?"

Bloom continued. "The string is gold and it is thick for a string. The bow itself is shaped as if two golden wings reach a point in the middle. This is where the arrow goes. The arrow is gold."

"Duh," Eva interrupted and yawned even as Annie tried to imagine the Golden Arrow.

"And the shaft is gold. The back is notched with three golden feathers for balance, and the front, right before the tip, is bound by shiny green twine . . . or some material like it."

Annie's fingers moved on top of the desk, outlining the object in her head. Her fingers seemed to vibrate as she drew the lines of the bow and the arrow. The wood underneath her hand glowed, and then the entire room lit up.

"Wow," said Eva, sitting back up. "What's happening?"

"Look!" Jamie pointed to the far wall where there was a mural that seemed to change slightly even as they watched.

A golden bow just like the one that Annie had drawn glowed against a backdrop of four-leaf clovers. A prancing unicorn galloped around a field of clover on green hills. Eva rushed over and tried to pluck the glowing bow out of the painting, but it wasn't three-dimensional at all, just flat, part of the painting.

"What the holy heck," she muttered.

"It must be protected," Bloom said, sighing and flopping down on the couch. He seemed heartbroken.

Annie felt that way, too. Still, she petted him on the arm. "It's okay. We'll find a way . . . It's a clue maybe . . . a sign . . ."

The door flew open. Helena and Gramma Doris hobbled into the room.

"What are you children doing? Having a party? I love a good party!" Helena boomed. She had confectioner's sugar all over her shoulders and streaks of chocolate on her cheeks.

"Oh, look!" said Gramma Doris, rubbing her hands together. "The mural glows. It hasn't glowed like that in—" Doris gasped, hand to her heart. "Her grandparents . . ."

"What?" said Annie. "What does this have to do with Eva's grandparents?"

"Not hers . . . yours . . ." Helena pointed at her. Rainbow sprinkles shot out of her finger and cascaded around the room.

Doris squealed, throwing up her hands in disbelief, trying to get Helena to not say anything more.

"Grandparents . . . I have grandparents?" Annie squeaked.

"Everyone does, silly," Helena said.

"Yes . . . yes . . . that's right," Doris said awkwardly, pulling Helena back out of the room and into the hallway, leaving the children alone and in shock.

There was no stopping Annie. She barged into the kitchen just as Gramma Doris was baking bread. Flour and sugar was spread all over the kitchen counter. A mound of sliced apples seemed ready to topple over. Fairies hovered around it with their arms out, ready to catch the slices if it all went to heck.

Doris smiled as Annie and the other children entered the kitchen.

"Gramma Doris!" Annie said with gentle force.

Her voice sounded quite a bit like Miss Cornelia's, Jamie thought.

"Children! Have you come to help with dinner? How nice!" Gramma Doris snapped her fingers, and aprons whizzed toward each of them, wrapping their cloth around the children's backs and tying themselves in place.

Eva scowled at her bright-pink kitty cat apron. "Dwarfs do not cook."

Gramma Doris ignored her.

"Excuse me, Gramma Doris!" Annie didn't pay attention to her own apron, which was struggling to tie itself around her waist as she strode toward where Gramma Doris stood by the refrigerator.

"What is it, Annie?"

"I have grandparents." Annie yanked her apron off.

"Of course you do, dear." Doris seemed nonplussed.

"Are they alive?"

The room went still.

"Yes." Doris began to twist her hands together. "This . . . this is really . . . this is really not . . ."

"I have grandparents." Annie sat on a stool with a thump, face sad and broken. Her forlorn voice seemed to make the entire kitchen sigh. "I have grandparents who are alive."

"Shouldn't that be a good thing?" Eva said, snagging an apple slice.

Bloom threw his hands up in the air. SalGoud thrust an apple into her mouth, silencing her.

"Who are they? And why didn't they want me, then?"

Annie asked quietly. "Why did they shove me off from foster house to foster house? Why does nobody ever want me?"

Jamie started to try to comfort her, but he didn't know what to say, and shoved his hands into his pockets.

"That's not it! That's not it at all, Annie." Gramma Doris's face broke into an understanding grimace, and she rushed forward to try to take Annie up into a hug, but Annie skittered away, knocking over the stool.

Her shaking hand covered her mouth. "Does everyone know? Does everyone know this but me?"

"Not me," said Bloom and SalGoud.

"Hadn't a clue," Eva said with her mouth full of apple.

"Your grandparents never met you, Annie . . . They didn't . . . They didn't approve of the match between your mother and your father," Gramma Doris began. "They later regretted this choice."

"How do you know this?" Annie asked.

"You were born here, Annie. Cornelia failed to protect you during the Purge. We thought you had died. Your mother was dead. Your father—" Gramma Doris's voice cracked. "It is a difficult story, but Miss Cornelia assumed you were dead as well, and the other grandmother and grandfather that you are asking about . . . Well, they never acknowledged your death."

She looked up at Annie, horrified. Some pixies entered

the kitchen as well, and Gramma Doris shooed them away, claiming they made her cakes drop.

Annie's voice steeled out. "I used to live here? Does everyone know *that*?"

"I had no idea, Annie." SalGoud raised his hands.

"Me, either," Eva said, "and let me add that it is freaking rude of everybody to not tell me."

Bloom elbowed her in the stomach. "Eva, this is not about you."

Eva grumped over to the refrigerator, opened it, and looked in. All of the food was quietly whispering.

"What else aren't you telling me?" Annie demanded. "Did you really think I was dead? Or did you just let me go?"

"Oh!" Gramma Doris rushed forward, and this time she truly did gather Annie up into a great big hug. "Oh, you poor little thing. The world was in chaos. We were confused and overwhelmed and so many were dead and so many were gone, and . . . We would never, ever let you go, Annie. Don't you remember how joyous we were to have you back?"

Annie did remember. She tried to take a calming breath. "Then why didn't you tell me? Why didn't you tell me all of it? That I was from here? That I belonged here . . ." She had never belonged anywhere, and the moment she came to this quirky, magical town she had finally felt like she fit. Well, now it all made sense, didn't it? She fit because she was from here. Not because she was special. In fact, she was so un-special that her own grandparents never met her. "Wait. What about my grandparents? What are their names?"

"Thomas Tullgren and Aislinn O'Grahaghan Tullgren," Gramma Doris announced somberly.

"And are they magic?" Jamie asked for Annie, who was now clutching her hands against her chest.

Tala hobbled in, front leg in a cast, and rubbed against her legs.

Gramma Doris looked at the ceiling before saying, "Yes, they are quite magic."

"But they don't live here . . . ," Jamie continued, prodding for answers that weren't too obvious.

"They live in Ireland," she huffed out dismissively, shutting the door without thinking. The momentum pushed Eva right inside the refrigerator with the eggs and milk and radishes.

She began to let out some screams that were muffled by the door. Jamie made his way over, but he knew the moment he let her out, she'd start huffing and puffing and everyone would be too distracted to answer his questions.

He pressed on, ignoring Eva's fists hammering against the side of the refrigerator. "What do they do in Ireland?"

"They run a bed-and-breakfast by the Cliffs of Moher. Half their clients are human. Half are not. It makes it . . ." Gramma Doris searched for a word. "It makes it . . . interesting. It's a lovely place. The Clover, they call it. It's been called that for centuries. Right next to the Ballinackalacken Castle or some such. Aw, in the good old days before the Bugbears of the Clan McFarland came, the unicorns would frolic in the meadows. Bugbears have a taste for any flesh, best hunters, but they do love a unicorn."

Jamie silently repeated the names. That's what they needed. That had to be where the bow and arrow were. It was as good a place as any to start. He made eye contact with SalGoud, who was awkwardly patting Annie on the shoulder with his giant hand, which was actually larger than Annie's head. Jamie opened the refrigerator door. Eva tumbled out. Shredded pieces of cheddar cheese clung to her pigtails. A portion of a carrot stuck out of her ear.

"DWARFS DO NOT GET STUCK IN REFRIGERATORS!" she roared, shaking herself like a dog.

Bits of shredded cheddar flew everywhere, but Tala didn't lick them off the floor. He just stood there next to Annie. His leg could support his weight, now that he was healing and in a cast.

"I want to go," Annie said.

Gramma Doris stepped backward. A timer went off on the stove. "What?"

"I want to go see them," Annie insisted as the stove door popped open and loaves of bread flew out.

One had flattened from the stress. Gramma Doris threw her hands up in the air but only for a moment, before turning back to Annie and commanding the loaves settle themselves down on the counter.

"No. Absolutely not," Gramma Doris announced. "We need you here."

"Everyone was just trying to send Annie to the Badlands! Which is it? Do you need her or not?" Bloom demanded.

SalGoud roared up to his full height. "I know you're upset, but you may not talk to Gramma Doris like that, boy!"

"I am not a boy," Bloom shot back.

"Then what are you?"

"I am an elf." Bloom stood there, taller than any had ever seen him. Strong and angry. He seemed mature suddenly, somehow. He took Annie's hand and didn't even look back as they left the kitchen. "I am an elf and it's time I start acting like one."

Jamie and Eva had to scurry to catch up to Annie and Bloom, but they managed to reach them in the hallway outside Annie's room, all of them crowding together. Annie's face had become even paler than normal and her hair seemed limp.

"I don't know whether or not to feel angry or betrayed or hopeful," she admitted.

"I'd pick angry," Eva said, plucking a radish out of the pocket of her overalls.

"You are allowed to feel whatever you want to feel, Annie," Jamie began, and then Eva clamped her hand over his mouth.

"Now is not the time for feelings. Now is the time for action," she said and let go of his mouth.

"Let's get to the point," Bloom said. "We are going to Ireland to the area of the Cliffs of Moher. We shall find the castle and the Clover Inn that Annie's grandparents run, and then we shall locate the bow and arrow and return."

"It's a good plan," Jamie said, "but how do we get to Ireland? We can't take Grady O'Grady because dragons can't fly across entire oceans, plus Grady said that he's at the Badlands searching for Cornelia and the elves again, plus he'd be seen, which means we have to go the normal human way. By airplane. And then I think there's a significant hike on foot. I saw a map of Ireland in that book about the Golden Arrow. The castle is all alone, nowhere near civilization. I don't even have a passport. Does anyone have a passport?"

"That," Eva said, wiggling both her eyebrows up and down, "should not be a problem. I'll take care of it."

She started scuttling off.

"Eva!" Jamie called after her. "Can you find us some money, too? Enough to pay all of our ways, plus taxis. Plus spending money."

Jamie, who had never gone anywhere ever, had seen enough videos to understand there were certain essentials that you had to have for traveling across the ocean. And who was even going? Him. Annie, of course. Bloom. He doubted Eva would stay home. SalGoud?

"That will be thousands of dollars," Jamie whispered as he silently calculated the cost of airfare.

"No problem!" Eva yelled over her shoulder. "Meet me by the library when you're ready, but give me an hour or two."

"Dwarfs," Bloom muttered. "So annoying."

"But so necessary," Annie added.

"Exactly." Bloom cleared his throat. "Let's get moving."

As evening closed in, they each already had backpacks stowed away. Annie had left hers beneath her bed and filled it with water and food, clothes, and her sketchpad. Now she added her pastels and the phurba Miss Cornelia had given her when they'd first met. She had found matches, too, just in case they needed to make a fire. She tied a pot to the strap so that they'd have something to cook in on the hike. It clanged against her as she snuck down the stairs and past the mermaid's fountain. A nymph waved to her. She waved back.

"Going on a trip?" it asked with its watery voice. It plucked a piece of algae out of its hair.

"A little exploration," Annie explained, crossing her fingers against the half lie.

"Well, have fun. Don't let the Raiff or any trolls get 'cha.

Good fight. Sleep sight. Don't let the demon bugs bite. May you have visions in the night." The nymph began to laugh at her own feeble joke, then choked on the seaweed.

"Ha. Ha," Annie said, awkwardly scuttling away.

Jamie and Annie rendezvoused in the parlor and quietly shut the door behind them. It was the first room Annie had seen when she arrived at Miss Cornelia's house. The drapes were long and velvety green. The couch and floor seemed to be made of moss with delicate flowers growing in them as well. Long vines and treelike plants covered the walls. It was more like an elegant forest room than a formal parlor.

Annie shook her head at the familiar place.

"I can't believe that I used to live here once," she said.

Jamie shrugged. "It's strange."

"And nobody told me, but everybody knew," she grumbled. "How embarrassing. Why didn't they tell me, Jamie? Why haven't they told me about my parents? About . . . well, about anything?"

"Maybe they really were waiting for the right time?" he offered as she leaned the back of her head against the wall and closed her eyes. "I don't think it's because they didn't trust you, Annie. I think—" He searched for the word. "I think it's because they were ashamed. Magic people are like adults. They think that they have to be perfect all the time because they are adulting or have powers or whatever, but when they screw up, it turns them into liars and hiders. They can't admit what they have done wrong."

"I used to try so hard to be perfect. I thought it would make me loved, make me finally belong," Annie said after a moment.

"And now?"

"And now, I don't think I care anymore about being perfect or belonging. I just care about getting those elves back." She opened her eyes.

"And Miss Cornelia, still?" Jamie's heart gave a little jolt of worry. Annie seemed so pained lately. How much had all this changed her? And so quickly?

Annie gave a little sigh as she adjusted the straps on Jamie's backpack.

"Yes, and Miss Cornelia. I love her even though she's not perfect either." Annie put on her hat and turned Jamie back around so they faced each other.

"You're very smart, Annie Nobody."

She looked at him, really looked at him. "And so are you, James Hephaistion Alexander. And so are you."

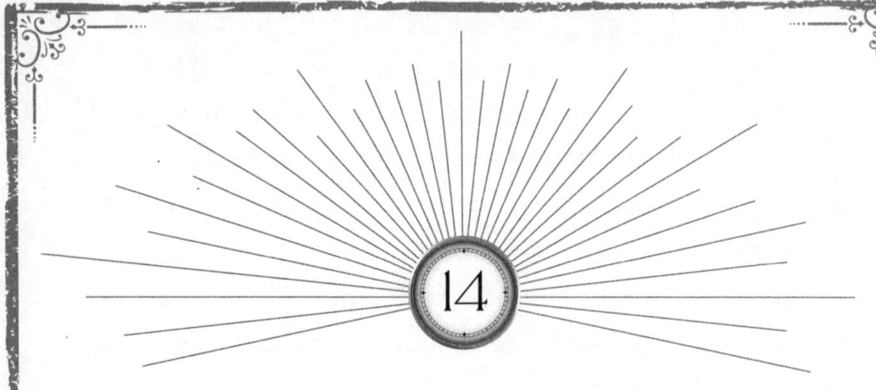

Preflight Jitters

Since Eva's dad's snowmobile was still broken and the skis were completely out of commission, the children used a toboggan to get out of Aurora and into town. Luckily, it was mostly downhill. Even more luckily, Eva was capable of steering the toboggan, and no matter what her faults, didn't crash them into any trees, or even the huge oil truck that steamed up the road just as they crossed it.

They had all their gear stowed on their laps or their backs, and Eva even had pockets and pockets full of cash, which she displayed rather proudly. After he apologized to Bloom for reprimanding him for the way he spoke to Gramma Doris, SalGoud had agreed in secret to come along and pretend to be their "chaperone" since his height and bulk could pass for an adult's, and he and Bloom had done the best they could to disguise themselves as humans. Bloom tugged his winter hat low around his head, hiding his elf ears.

Once they were in the town of Mount Desert, getting a taxi proved easier than they thought it would. They all piled inside the ugly green minivan that read Acadia Taxis on the side. The placard was magnetic or something and Eva wanted to study it for a while, but the others pushed her into the car.

Annie was still angry at, well, at almost everyone who knew that she had grandparents, real living relatives, and had never told her.

"What happened to my father?" she blurted as they drove on the one-lane state highway past an IGA grocery store, the Trenton Bridge Lobster Pound place closed up for winter, and an octagonal building that everyone local called "the cheese house."

"He died in the Purge," Bloom said.

"And my mother?" Annie asked.

"She died a hero," Eva announced. "She lost, though. Sorry. Bad, but still glorious, you know?"

The taxi driver raised an eyebrow and said in a voice that smelled of coffee and sounded like cigarettes, "What are you kids even talking about?"

They sat in awkward silence.

"We are composing a story," SalGoud began slowly, obviously thinking out every word before he spoke it.

"About a video game!" Jamie added, trying to make it

more believable. “And, um . . . one of our characters . . . this Time Stopper girl . . . she needs a back story.”

“You kids are smart. I bet you’ll make a billion dollars on something like that,” the taxi driver gruffed out, finally driving through Ellsworth and making it onto Route One to Bangor. “Is that why you’re heading out to the airport? Meeting some producers? Game execs?”

Nobody answered for another long pause before Jamie got it together enough to say, “Exactly.”

“I don’t even know my mother’s name,” Annie whispered to Bloom. “Someone must know her name.”

“Lilana,” Bloom whispered back as they bounced over a frost heave. SalGoud hit his head on the minivan’s ceiling.

“Do you know how she died?” Annie asked.

Eva unbuckled her seat belt, hauled herself over the seat back, and crawled between Annie and Bloom before buckling in again. The taxi driver didn’t even notice.

Eva didn’t bother to whisper. “She was a hero. She tried to save the elves. Faced the Raiff herself, she did. Stood there and took hit after hit. She’s the one who weakened him enough for Miss Cornelia to be able to send him to the portal at all. That’s what I’ve heard at least. Unfortunately, I wasn’t there or I would have killed him myself with my ax.”

“You kids are weird,” the driver announced, turning up the radio.

Shivering slightly, Annie stared straight ahead and didn’t respond.

"Yes, sir," SalGoud agreed from his spot next to the driver in the front. Being the "adult" seemed to make him the official spokesperson for the group. "Yes, they are."

Jamie leaned forward and tried to touch Annie's shoulder in what he hoped was a comforting way. Annie didn't respond, and after a minute he sat back again, listening to Eva chattering on about the physics of airplanes and how dwarfs were really the ones who invented them and so on. Before long, Eva was peeling off some money from her stash of cash—well, one of her many stashes. Even as she did so, a happy-looking gnome, the size of a pixie, popped his head up out of the center pocket of her overalls. He was carefully peeling off more dollars from midair, plucking them out, and then transferring them to Eva's other hand.

"What is that?" Jamie whispered to SalGoud as they took the suitcase and backpacks out of the back of the taxi.

"Oh, that's a special gnome who has a buy-your-way-forever charm," SalGoud said offhandedly as though it was nothing unexpected at all. "They don't talk, but they are very good at what they do."

"Which is?" Jamie asked.

"Making money out of thin air." SalGoud yawned and checked his watch, then startled back into attention. "We are a mere sixty-one minutes early. We should be checked in at exactly sixty minutes prior to departure."

Eva made a fake moan and put her hand to her forehead. "Heaven forbid."

"Planes run like clockwork, Eva," SalGoud stressed, grabbing pretty much everyone's backpacks and the suitcase and running into the terminal. "Get your picture identifications and follow me!"

"He gets a bit anxious about timetables. He's the same way about getting the bus for school," Bloom explained to Annie and Jamie as they followed SalGoud and Eva into the terminal.

They all had passports ready thanks to Eva, who had vaguely explained that "her people" had handled it. "Her people" had also secured the pixie-size gnome with the buy-your-way-forever charm, and also had *allegedly* found a car to meet them in the Dublin airport since none of them could *actually* drive a car, *legally*. Those same "people" had booked rooms for them at the Clover Inn.

The Bangor International Airport was incredibly small, but somehow managed to have one of the longest runways on the eastern coast of the United States. At the airport, only American Airways and Delta had airplanes with engines instead of propellers, and each of them just had two staff members. The kids tromped through the ground floor of the airport, past the one escalator that led up to the gates and one car rental booth and the two luggage terminals, and to the Delta ticket counter.

"I feel nervous," Bloom said. "I'm not a big fan of planes."

"You'll be fine," Jamie said.

People all seemed to be staring at them as they walked

by. They had to look odd—a motley crew of twelve- and thirteen-year-olds trudging through an airport with one barely passable adult. Plus, SalGoud was so tall and carrying absolutely everything. Add to that, Eva was short and had very stand-out pigtails.

SalGoud dumped all the luggage on the floor as he made it to the ticket counter. There was no line at all. It was nothing like bigger airports that Jamie had seen in television shows and movies.

"We are here!" SalGoud announced. "We are one minute late and I apologize profusely, for as John F. Boyes said, 'Strict punctuality is perhaps the cheapest virtue . . .' and yet we have let you, the customer service ticket agent of Delta Airlines, down."

The ticket agent blew some hair out of his eyes, didn't even glance up from his computer terminal, and said, "Yeah . . . uh . . . whatever. Your final destination today is . . . ?"

"Dublin," SalGoud announced.

"It's in Ireland!" Eva was jumping up trying to see over the counter.

"Any luggage today for any of your party?" the ticket agent asked.

"It will be okay," Annie mumbled as they checked in to the airport. "Everything will be okay."

Jamie grabbed her hand and said, "Of course it will," but he really wasn't sure.

15
Pig Cars

They made it through security fine. The gnome didn't even register on the TSA's whole-body X-ray machine, and the gold in Eva's pockets or any of their weapons in their bags—Eva's ax, Annie's phurba, and Bloom's bow and arrows—somehow didn't either.

Eva winked at Jamie once they were all the way past the listening ears of the security people. "Leprechaun spell. Bought it off Canin last year. Knew I'd need it someday. Hides the property of metal into something more like cotton balls when probed."

"Wow," Jamie managed to say as they strode across the carpeted floor toward Gate 2B.

"Exactly. Wow. I am a wow kind of dwarf, if you haven't noticed," she boasted.

"Oh, I have . . . I . . . um . . . I have noticed."

"Good."

The others joined them, and as they waited to board the plane, Eva began to pull at her pigtails just a little bit. Annie petted her absently on the shoulder. "I know you're nervous but . . ."

"Dwarfs do not get nervous!" Eva yelled, which made everyone in the terminal turn and stare.

"But they do get noticed," Bloom said drolly, putting his legs up on top of the backpacks and stretching out.

"As well they should!" Eva said, and to be fair she said it a bit more quietly.

The older woman who had been gaping at them all open mouthed turned around and muttered to her companion, "No manners at all. Where are their parents? They can't all belong to that strange tall man."

Annie seemed to shrink into her metal and plastic dull-gray seat.

"Annie?" Jamie leaned toward her. "You okay?"

"I just . . . I feel . . . sort of betrayed, you know?"

"And hurt?" he suggested.

"Definitely hurt," she answered, sighing. "I just think they should have told me. Someone should have told me that I had living grandparents, and maybe they should have looked for me."

"I'm pretty sure everyone thought you were dead."

"I might as well have been," Annie admitted. "I know it's

silly, but I just feel like Miss Cornelia or Gramma Doris or someone should have told me the moment I got to Aurora."

"Maybe they wanted to . . . but . . ." Jamie motioned to the air. "Things got pretty wild, pretty quick, with the Raiff and stuff. Maybe they just didn't have time."

"Maybe I just wasn't important enough for them to actually tell me."

"I don't think it's about you being important. You're super important, Annie. You're a Stopper. I think . . ." He searched for words. "I think that maybe it had more to do with the grandparent information not being number one on the list of vital things to deal with."

"Like right now. It's still not." Annie raked her fingers through her hair, combing it. "Like right now, the most necessary thing is saving the elves and Miss Cornelia."

He half shrugged. "Kind of . . . It's not that your feelings don't matter, though."

"My feelings can wait," Annie announced stoically, working out a knot near the ends of her hairs.

He began to say something, but right then the gate agent spoke into her little microphone and said to prepare to board. Poor Bloom's face whitened, and he swayed so much when he stood that SalGoud had to solid him up.

"You're much more likely to die in a car crash than in a plane crash," SalGoud began. "Would you like the statistics?"

"No." Bloom took one baby step toward the boarding door.

"The probabilities involved may comfort you. They comfort me," SalGoud continued.

"Really, I'm okay."

"Stop wussing out!" Eva shoved Bloom forward, smashing her two hands right above his butt and propelling him toward the gate agent. "This is for your people, to save your people. Elf up, man. Elf up."

And with those words, Bloom strode forward, handed the gate agent his ticket, and for the very first time, boarded an airplane.

Bloom inhaled deeply and pulled out the magazine from the seat-back in front of him. "I'm nervous about the flight. Okay? I've never been on a plane before, and it is so detached from all the elements—the natural elements."

"Not wind," Jamie suggested. "We are in the wind. Think of it like riding Grady O'Grady."

Bloom's face lightened. "Good point, brilliant one."

Jamie smiled, and after that Bloom was much happier. Jamie opened the plastic bags that contained tiny navy blue blankets to keep them warm, and the flight attendant passed out pillows. By the time they lifted into the air, Bloom was practically yelling "yee-haw" because he was so excited.

"Look out the windows!" he said, pointing to the side row of seats. "Isn't the sky beautiful? Oh, we're in a cloud. Oh, that cloud looks like a dragon. Oh! We're above it. There is the moon."

Eva began hyperventilating into the airsickness bag

that she'd pulled out of the seat-back compartment in front of her.

SalGoud threw his hands up into the air, hitting his knuckles on the bottom of the overhead luggage compartment. "If it isn't the elf, it's the dwarf. Honestly."

"Eva," Annie whispered, petting the dwarf's arm. "You have this. You are a dwarf. You are strong. You roar and you have an ax."

Eva pulled her nose and mouth out of the bag long enough to sputter, "My ax is in the luggage."

"That wasn't the point. You don't need the ax, Eva. You are strong all by yourself."

"How about we cancel all the New Age, I-eat-organic-foods garbage and just focus on the fact that we are in a steel can thundering through the air without any magic to keep it going and we are all going to die," Eva grumbled.

"You do know they have movies on here," Jamie said from the other side of Eva. "There is one with ancient Greeks and they have axes."

Eva dropped the airsickness bag onto the floor without a second thought. "Where?"

The plane ride lasted hours and hours. The sun set and rose again. Eva spent the entire time eating bags of pretzels and biscotti while watching violent movies during which she would criticize the fighting techniques.

"That's not an effective way to get out of a choke hold," she would mutter, or, "That round kick is so easy to counter. Look, the Spartan monster troll left his entire left side unprotected."

Jamie noticed that Annie had brought a book about demons and was focusing on that. Her hands would clench every once in a while. It took everything he had not to unclench her fingers for her, to just reach over there and try to pry them open. Annie looked a mess and he was worried for her.

SalGoud was watching some sort of history channel, and Bloom seemed just as bored as Jamie for most of the flight, fidgeting occasionally, attempting to take a nap and failing.

"In the world of elves, which ones are the best looking? The epic fantasy movie–kind or you?" Jamie asked Bloom, who just stared at him.

"Don't ask him that," Eva grumped. "He'll start going off about how they make vampires sparkly now in movies."

Mimicking Bloom's voice, Eva and SalGoud said simultaneously, "Vampires are not attractive. Elves are sparkly."

Bloom pulled the little navy blue blanket around his legs again and closed his eyes, ignoring them all. Not long after that the flight attendants collected all the garbage, getting ready for landing.

"I'm sorry . . . Sorry I asked. I didn't realize they'd make fun of you," Jamie said as soon as Bloom sat up straight again.

Bloom looked at him vacantly for a moment and said,

"It's okay. They—tensions are high right now. We are all nervous. I mean, look at Annie."

Annie was twisting her hands again.

"I'm okay," she announced and then lost all her confidence. "Really. I swear."

Eva pointed at her hands. Annie abruptly stopped twisting them and sat on them instead.

"There's just a lot—there's a lot at stake," Annie said finally. "Demons—demons are hard to deal with, to defeat. And . . . my grandparents . . ."

She lost her thought.

"You're afraid they ain't going to like you," Eva said.

"Aren't going to like you," SalGoud corrected as he continued to play solitaire on the same screen that showed movies. It was built into the back of the seat.

"Sort of," Annie admitted.

"People don't like me all the time. Whatever. No big," Eva bragged. "You should take it as a mark of having a larger-than-life personality. A personality that makes people go 'Wow' or 'Uck' is better than one that makes people do nothing at all. Plus, they are trolls if they don't like you. You are very likable. Everybody likes you."

"Not Megan," Annie answered.

"That hag does not count. She's got jealousy issues. Ain't that what you said, SalGoud?" Eva nudged him as he put a queen of spades on top of a king of hearts.

"Isn't. 'Isn't,' Eva. 'Ain't' is not a word." SalGoud kept playing and didn't actually answer Eva's question.

"What. Ever." Eva harrumphed.

The pilot said to prepare for landing, to put their seatbacks in an upright position, and then after hours in a plane they were suddenly there—in Ireland. The plane skidded to a stop on a runway surrounded by other runways in an airport that was much bigger than the one they had used in Maine.

"All that green," Bloom whispered, leaning forward so that he could stare out the window. "All that beautiful green, even in winter."

"And the elf collapses in joy," Eva deadpanned.

Annie petted his arm. "It's lovely."

"It is, isn't it? How does it feel to you, Annie?" Bloom asked. "Does it feel good?"

"It almost feels like home," Annie answered. "Like the whole country is magical, the way Aurora is."

Bloom perked up. "Exactly! That's the way it feels to me, too."

Eva made a fake puking noise and that was it. They were there. In Ireland. Now all they had to do was find a bow and arrow and save the day.

They made it through the customs officials' gate check where their passports were scrutinized and they were asked the reason for their stay (their official answer was "tourism"), gathered up their luggage, and stood in the entryway of the airport right near where the taxis were queued up to collect passengers.

Annie wanted to enjoy all the hustle and bustle of the airport, all the people and excitement of travel, but she was so worried about failing. They all stood there for a moment, clustered together as adults and families bebopped around them, hurrying to cars, buses, and taxis, ready to get on with their day. But Annie's group remained motionless until Jamie stepped one foot off the curb.

A bright pink car screeched to a halt, barely missing him as Jamie leaped out of the way at the very last second. He landed on his feet, but toppled over onto his side. He ached from the impact of landing, but he was perfectly fine.

"Jamie!" Annie was already on the ground, grabbing him and checking for injuries.

"I'm fine, Annie," he tried to say, but a loud, male voice was hollering over his.

"What kind of fool are ya, to jump out in the middle of the road like that? I was like to splatter your guts next way to Sunday," the fellow roared. He was small, very small, and stocky. He had a long red beard and tufts of hair sticking out at odd angles all around his head.

Eva stomped up and yelled right in his face. She was only an inch shorter, which was rather remarkable. "Well, maybe you should watch where you're going, troll breath!"

"Who ye calling troll breath?" he bellowed back.

An Enterprise Rent-a-Car van honked its horn and swerved to avoid smashing into the . . . into the . . . Jamie gasped, finally getting a good look at the car—was it a car?—that almost hit him.

It *was* bright pink and fuzzy—not furry, but fuzzy—and there *was* a pig snout covering the front grill. There *were* eyelashes around the headlights, and two gigantic wing-shaped ears sprouting from the roof.

"Jamie?" Bloom had come to his side.

"Did I hit my head?" Jamie asked.

Annie and Bloom exchanged a glance, and Annie answered for both of them, "Not that we saw."

"So that's . . ." Jamie gestured toward the pink vehicle, "that's really a pig car."

"It appears it is," SalGoud said as Eva head-butted the driver. The driver head-butted her back. Then they fist-bumped.

"I was almost killed by a pig car." Jamie got back to his feet with Annie's arm supporting him around the waist, and he added, "In Ireland. I was almost killed by a pig car in Ireland."

"Because you didn't look both ways before crossing!" SalGoud emphasized as a Hertz Car Rental van honked at them. It was the fourth van to honk.

Annie gestured to where Eva stood with the pig car's driver. "Eva? Are you okay?"

"Why the heck wouldn't I be?" Eva bellowed back, still in the middle of the road. Another Enterprise Rent-a-Car van swerved around her.

"Well, you're head-butting the dwarf who just almost squashed Jamie," Bloom said impatiently.

"That's how dwarfs greet each other," the young driver said, coming toward them, bowing his head toward Annie. Just the look of his massive forehead gave her a headache.

"Oh . . . oh . . . ," she said, backing up into SalGoud who steadied her, "no thank you." She waved her hands in front of her. "Not a dwarf. Sensitive head."

"Humans do have wimpy skeletal systems." He reached out a hand for Annie to shake, then seemed to think better of it and bowed at his ample waist, waving his hand in a flourishing circle as he bent. "Johann Murray-Broadsword of the Doolin Broadswords at your service, young Stopper. It is my honor to be your driver on your first expedition to Ireland and to be a part of your astonishing adventure."

Annie gasped and turned on Eva, but not before Bloom lashed out. "Eva! Did you tell him our mission? You know . . ." His face reddened. "You know that adults can't know . . . If the Raiff senses that—"

Eva threw up her hands. "Take a chill pill, elf."

"Elves are so jumping to conclusions, aren't they?" Johann gave Bloom a derisive glare. "I am only fifteen."

The silence was awkward.

"We age quickly over here. It's the Guinness beer."

Annie's mouth may have dropped open, which sent Johann into fits of laughter. Bloom's anger seemed to only grow, and he pulled Eva aside.

"How do you know he can be trusted, Eva?" he demanded.

Eva bristled and she whispered, "All dwarfs are to be trusted, elf. Don't insult my brethren."

"Eva, no entire species is ever all good or all bad." Bloom threw his hands up in the air, giving in. "It's too late now, anyway. We'll just have to hope he can keep a secret."

"Dwarfs always keep secrets," Eva insisted as Bloom walked back to the group.

"You're doing it again," he tossed back over his shoulder, not even bothering to turn around and make eye contact, which meant he missed Eva sticking her tongue out at him.

Jamie didn't miss it, though. He didn't miss much anymore. The adventure had fine-tuned his senses—that, along with an elevated heart rate and being in constant mortal peril, seemed to heighten his awareness of everyone else's moods and actions. He wasn't actually sure that this was always a good thing.

"Let's get going; that is, unless the black-haired boy wants to keep trying to die via car and the elf wants to glower around and be all moody because his hair isn't perfect or something." Johann laughed at his own joke and Eva punched him in the arm in appreciation and he punched her back.

Jamie decided to make a mental list about dwarfs, and

the first item was: *Dwarfs can be mean sometimes. They can be bullies. And obnoxious.*

Johann opened the back door with a flourish and smiled. "After you, Jamie. I'm sorry that I almost smashed you into the next county."

"Thank you," Jamie said, climbing in and instantly adding to his list: *Sometimes, dwarfs can have manners and be nice.*

Dwarfs, he decided, were just about as confusing as elves, but he settled into the posh seat as the dwarfs threw the luggage in the back of the vehicle. The seats were covered in furry pink upholstery with zigzag stripes on the actual seat cushions and stuffed pig heads for the headrests. Next to the heads were tiny upholstered hooves that rested on SalGoud's shoulders the moment he sat back.

"I feel as if the pig is embracing me," he said awkwardly, grabbing his pink seat belt and strapping in.

"I know! Isn't it the greatest! Dwarf ingenuity at its finest if I do say so myself," said Johann Murray-Broadsword. "Well, come on. Everyone in. We're blocking traffic, and if another rental van carting tourists around honks at us, I may lose my cool and show them the sharp edge of my sword."

Even the steering wheel, which was on the right-hand side instead of the left like in the United States, was covered in pink fuzziness.

"Wow," Annie whispered as she got in the car. "This is . . . This is . . ."

"Pink," Bloom suggested.

"Furry?" said Jamie.

"Piglike?" SalGoud sighed.

"Awesome!" Eva shouted, taking the shotgun seat next to Johann. "Completely and totally awesome."

She held out her hand for a fist bump. Johann bumped it. A car tooted at them to get moving. Johann coughed and turned the engine back on, and the pig made a snorting, roaring noise and they were off, heading through Ireland in search of a magic bow while riding in a car that was outfitted like a pig.

Annie's life was decidedly weird.

"Did you—um—did you 'trick out' this car by yourself?" she asked.

"Why, yes, I did," Johann said proudly, swerving onto a roundabout so erratically that Annie's eyes shut themselves as if they—not she—were too afraid to watch.

They drove straight out of the airport toward Dublin, and immediately it looked so different from Maine. Despite the fact that it was winter, snow didn't heavy down the scarce trees or cover the hills. There were cows pretty much everywhere in fields beside the highway. All the highway signs were blue instead of green and had the words written in Gaelic and English, which SalGoud thought was the best thing ever.

"It's so close to the language of the stone giants," he kept exclaiming.

Johann complained about the cold, saying that it was only forty-five degrees out. That was a full twelve degrees more than it had been in Maine, and to Annie it almost felt balmy.

There was a wee bit of confusion because Johann insisted that they needed to go to Dublin first to pick up a few supplies that were essential to their mission, or as he said, "procure some provisions," which sounded much fancier, especially in his Irish accent.

Dublin wasn't as crazy busy as Annie expected, but she liked all the brick houses with their colorful painted doors, the cobblestones that made so many of the narrow streets, and the pubs and taverns that seemed to be everywhere.

"It's a gray day, it is," Johann apologized as he parked the pig car in a spot near a narrow calm river.

"It's lovely," Annie said and she meant it.

They all scrambled out of the car and stretched their legs. A man pedaling his bike shouted, "Brilliant car."

Johann gave him a happy wave. "We're going to get something that you desperately need. Our first stop is the Ha'Penny Bridge." He pointed at a gently curving pedestrian bridge.

"Is that 'something' food?" Eva asked.

Bloom said that she shouldn't be thinking about food at

a time when rescue was of the upmost importance. Eva countered that being full and strong would ensure a better adventure. Annie stopped listening and instead followed Johann and Jamie onto the bridge.

"I just have to stand in the middle and stomp three times," Johann explained. "Cover for me. Pretend like you're taking my picture or some such . . ."

"What are you getting?" Annie asked.

"I'm summoning a Helper."

"We don't need no Helper person." Eva squinted at him and put her hand on her ax. "What are you getting at, Johann Murray-Broadsword?"

"I'm not getting at anything, okay? And this Helper isn't a who, per se. It's a thing. Something that you will need to help you on your quest. Do you know that the Broadswords have been cursed for many a century, stuck here on the Emerald Island, unable to explore the vast fortunes and riches of the world—" Johann seemed to have found the correct spot on the bridge.

Jamie grabbed Annie's arm.

Bloom cleared his throat. "Eva, I thought you said we could trust him."

"I'm sure we can . . . He's a dwarf. You can always trust a dwarf," Eva stated simply, but her grip on her ax tightened and then Johann stomped three times.

"Aketay usay ownday," he droned in what Annie was 100 percent certain was pig latin.

But before she could translate, the bridge below their feet gave way to a giant slide made of slippery green lichen. Screaming, they fell down and down . . . sliding on their bottoms.

"This. Is. Not. Happening," Eva hollered.

SalGoud was attempting to slow down by grabbing onto pieces of the wet green substance, but it was too slippery and instead he ended up turning topsy-turvy and somersaulting ahead of the rest. He landed with a flop on mossy stones.

He started to stand and thought better of it when he saw what was in front of them. "Guys . . . um . . . be wary . . . there is a beast."

Bloom, Jamie, Eva, Annie, and Johann landed in quick succession around him. The slide disappeared with a screech and came back again.

"A beast? A beast! Let me at him." Eva started to whip out her ax, but then she spotted the creature across the chamber. She stopped midmovement and fainted.

The beast stooped over as it ambled toward them. This smalling down of its true size only made it seem even more frightening. Its huge eyes followed them as the children fell into the torch-lit chamber that glowed with a strange purple hue. Long fangs sprang up into its furry bearlike face.

"That is not a Helper. It's a Bugbear!" Bloom vaulted in front of the others. "Stand back."

SalGoud scurried along the floor, searching for his

glasses, and Eva passed out again, collapsing with a thump on top of SalGoud's shoulders.

They were all too spread apart for Annie to stop time quickly.

"What's a Bugbear?" Jamie blurted.

"It's bad . . . It's really, really bad . . . ," Johann admitted, retreating toward the lichen slide. He tried to scramble up it and failed, just slipping right back down and landing on his rump. "They say the first were born to goblins, meant to help them in the annihilation of the unicorns, and they say this one killed all its siblings so the goblins had to banish it, but I'm not sure if it's true or not because they say a lot of things that aren't true."

"Who are *they*?" Jamie asked.

"Exactly." Johann poked him in the arm. "Ex-act-ly! This Bugbear is not the Helper thing we need to find. And who knows who *they* are who started all these tales."

The Bugbear was definitely toying with them, slowly stalking forward as if positive that they had nowhere to run to. Annie searched the area. They had landed in an enclosed pit far below the bridge and street.

"No offense, but I don't care about its origins right now," Annie said. "We need to find a way out of here."

"I'm afraid there's only one way out," Johann said, pointing toward the tunnel and the beast in front of it. "And the Bugbear is protecting it."

The Bugbear licked its lips.

"Okay," Bloom said urgently. "I need my bow."

Annie gave him his bow and arrows, picking them up off the floor. He shot an arrow directly at the Bugbear. It whizzed through the air perfectly, so fast they almost couldn't follow its flight. But the Bugbear snatched the arrow out of midair, broke it in half, and tossed it down onto the floor. It smiled. There was no doubt in their minds that this monster could easily have killed a bunch of unicorns.

"I think we need a distraction," Annie suggested as the Bugbear took a step—just one step—forward. If it rushed them, they'd be goners. Its paws had claws bigger than her wrists.

"Good idea! Good idea . . . Hmm . . . who can we sacrifice . . . Well, who don't we need?" Johann asked. "I'm guessing him."

He pointed at Jamie.

"We absolutely need Jamie!" Annie hollered. "Why would you even bring us here? Did you know this was going to happen?"

"Maybe *he* should be the distraction," Bloom said, shooting another arrow. Again, the Bugbear snatched it out of midair and broke it.

"Maybe she should stop time. Isn't she a Time Stopper?" Johann asked.

"I'm not very good at it," Annie admitted. Anxiety twisted her stomach into knots.

"Just try, Annie . . . ," Bloom said.

"But you can't help me . . . You're sort of busy . . . ," Annie blurted, frantically writing the word "stop" on the palm of her hand. "It's not working."

The Bugbear stepped closer.

"Someone drag Eva over!" Jamie yelled. "Or we'll be stuck carrying her."

"What are you even talking about?" Johann asked, but he grabbed Eva by the arms and hauled her toward the group.

Annie pressed the top of her forehead between Bloom's shoulder blades. Jamie grabbed her coat and SalGoud's. Johann followed suit.

"Make sure to hold Eva!" Jamie insisted.

Johann touched Eva's pigtail with the tip of his boot, and Jamie gave up worrying and instead tried to use a calm voice. All six were connected with one part of their bodies touching another, even if only barely.

"Just focus, Annie. You can do this. You got this," Jamie gushed out.

"Stop," she said.

Nothing happened.

She hauled in a big breath. She could do this. She had to.

Bloom shot another arrow. His elbow barely missed knocking Jamie in the nose. The Bugbear chuckled. There was no other word for it. It chuckled.

It was all up to Annie.

"Stop!" she commanded, trying to feel the vibrations that

made up every little cell of every single thing. She tried to reach inside of them and make them bend to her will. She wrote the word on Bloom's back, visualizing every single letter. "Stop!"

And the world did. It finally did.

"Can I let go now?" Johann whispered into the stillness.

Jamie thought that maybe they'd all been holding their breaths.

"Yes." SalGoud bent over and started trying to rouse Eva. "We should hurry."

Eva's eyes snapped open. "What did I miss?"

"Everything," Bloom said, stashing his bow and creeping up toward the monster.

It had a sword at its belt, a bow, and several arrows of its own. Bloom stashed the arrows into his quiver and handed the sword to Jamie, who looked at it with disgust.

"Give it to Annie, then. She's not afraid of it."

"I'm not afraid of swords."

Eva harrumphed, yanked herself up to a standing position, and slammed Johann in his chest. "What." One push to the stomach. "Did." Another push. "You bring us here." A mighty push. "For?"

His back was up against the slimy wall. "There's something down here that we need in order to continue our quest . . . A Helper . . . I didn't know . . . about the Bugbear . . . I had heard there was a Helper . . . And you could only get the arrow if you had it."

"That what?" Eva gave him a hairy eyeball worthy of a hag. "That it was a trap?"

"I knew it would be dangerous, but . . . Well, dwarfs laugh at danger." Johann laughed to prove his point, but instead of a hearty chuckle, it sounded more like a fake hollowness.

Jamie reached around the Bugbear to gently pet Annie's shoulder in what he hoped was a reassuring way, but as he did, his arm grazed the Bugbear's own furry arm and something inside of him flipped over. It was as if his stomach rolled in half and then righted itself again. He couldn't tell what that feeling was. He would have expected it to be fear, but instead it felt more like recognition?

Bloom motioned them forward. "Come on. We have to find another way out."

"Wait!" Johann pushed past Eva, moving her ax aside. "We have to find the Helper."

"We don't know that there is a Helper, though." Annie wiped her hair out of her face and said a silent "sorry" to the ghosts who she knew would have headaches again.

Jamie thought she looked tired. Time stopping seemed to drain her.

"And tell us while we walk. I don't know how long the

stop will last, and I want to put distance between us and . . . and . . . what is that again?"

"A Bugbear," Jamie answered before anyone else could.

"Exactly," Johann scoffed. "How can you be magical people if you don't even know what a Bugbear is?"

Eva made a growling noise as they rushed through the lichen-covered passageway. They passed abandoned buildings that had been built over and never removed, doors that led to dark, hollow window spaces that likely hadn't seen daylight for centuries.

"You better not be insulting me or my friends, Shortsword," Eva said.

"Broadsword," Johann corrected, and his eyes glanced over the rest of the children, who were eyeing him rather suspiciously. "I would never insult a fellow dwarf, but to be cavorting with elves and stone giants . . . It seems a bit—"

Eva roared and side-tackled Johann into an ancient inn's outer wall. She tossed her ax to the ground where it squished into the soppy floor that was once a medieval street. Spores rose in great clouds as Johann's head smashed into the moss-covered wall.

"Are you attacking me?" he thundered.

"What do you think?" Eva snarled back as they wrestled around in circles.

Meanwhile Annie was yelling, "Stop fighting! No fighting!"

SalGoud was trying to yank them off each other;

Bloom's face reddened with impatience and then pain as Johann's attempt to kick Eva ended up being a direct smash to Bloom's shin; Jamie stood there, horrified, and then began laughing.

"Why are you laughing?" Annie whispered.

"They look so silly . . . like . . . like puppies wrestling," he explained.

"True." Bloom hopped on one foot. "But they are wasting time, and we don't know how long the stop will last or how to get out of here, and that Bugbear—"

He didn't have to finish his sentence. The Bugbear was not something that they wanted to fight; the Bugbear seemed as if it didn't know how to lose. Plus, it had teeth.

"Dwarfs! STOP FIGHTING!" Bloom yelled.

They ignored him, and kept rolling around on the floor, grunting and insulting each other's weapons of choice and family line. Annie picked up Eva's ax and got it out of the way.

"I wouldn't be surprised if your grandfather was a pixie pacifist," Johann grunted.

"Don't you be insulting my grandfather!" Eva bellowed back.

"Your father couldn't annihilate a peanut butter sandwich."

"Your mother couldn't cut a head of cabbage in half, let alone a freaking zombie."

"Is that an ax you wield or is that a toothpick?"

"Don't you be insulting my ax!" Eva screeched and landed a fist against Johann's cheek.

"Enough!" Bloom yelled, yanking Johann back and away from Eva. "You two are acting like . . . like . . ."

"Trolls?" Annie suggested as she disentangled Johann's suspenders from around Eva's foot.

"Jerks?" offered Jamie.

"Dwarfs." SalGoud sighed. "They are acting like cranky dwarfs."

"We ARE cranky dwarfs," Eva sputtered the words out, sitting on her butt in a pile of dust, broken cobblestones, and what appeared to be chicken bones.

"Well, we don't have time to be cranky," Annie scolded. "I could lose the stop any second and we haven't found a way out of here."

"You keep saying that." Johann straightened out his shirt. "And what kind of Stopper can't make a stop last?"

Annie didn't answer. She just turned away and strode down the corridor again. He was right. She bit her lip to keep from crying and walked a little bit faster down the corridor that was once a street, through the ruins that had once been homes and stores. They were just forgotten, too, weren't they?

"Listen! I, Eva Beryl-Axe, am the only one allowed to insult our Time Stopper, you got it?" Eva bellowed behind Annie. "And I do it out of love. That's why I'm allowed."

"Maybe I do it out of love, too," Johann said sheepishly.

"You don't even know her. Now go and apologize," Eva said and grunted as she pushed Johann forward.

Annie still didn't turn to look. She would much rather be alone at the moment, and she never rathered being alone, ever. She'd been alone far too much to actually think of it as a wanted or preferable state of being.

Three seconds later the dwarf was waddling beside her. He had a cut on his cheek from the fight. She pulled out a tissue and held it there, stopping the blood before he even had a chance to apologize.

"She's ridiculously nice," Eva said as she caught up to them. "Don't look so shocked. She's nice to everybody, even the people who are jerks and insult her. I should know. Now apologize."

Annie checked to see if the bleeding had stopped. It had. She continued walking forward. "Apologies don't really mean anything. It's about actions. A good apology is like a promise not to do something hurtful again."

"That's what I do, then," Johann said, catching up to her once more. "I won't insult your Stopper skills again, Annie."

"Okay. Apology accepted." There was a hitch in her voice as she said it, though, and she turned her head to make sure Jamie was still with them.

He was straggling behind a bit and it worried her.

"Now, where is this Helper thing and why did you make us come here? No lying."

She still didn't trust him. None of them did anymore.

"The Helper is rumored to be down here. Somewhere. There's a society—a sort of secret society." Johann swallowed a gulp of water. Water dribbled into the reddish hairs of his beard. "Well, it's in a book, actually. I wasn't a hundred percent sure it was real. And I thought—Well, once Eva contacted me about the Golden Arrow—I mean, it became obvious it was real . . . And, um . . . And the society is sworn to keep the sacred bow and arrow safe."

"Safe from what?" Annie asked.

"It's 'for what,' isn't it?" Jamie answered before Johann had a chance to reply. Annie was glad he had caught up to them, but a little surprised he answered before Johann did. That was pretty bold for Jamie; he tended to hang back a bit.

"That's right." Johann cleared his throat and suddenly sounded much older and more pompous. "There is a prophecy—"

Eva groaned. "There is always a freaking prophecy."

"Eva!" Bloom scolded. "Let him talk."

"I'm just tired of prophecies," Eva grumped. "Look . . . There is a turn in the street. Maybe we're almost out of here."

And as they turned, they spotted a wall of bones, ascending all the way to the lichen-covered ceiling.

"Those aren't chicken bones . . . ," Annie whispered. "Are they?"

"No." Johann stopped, turned, and continued, spreading his arms wide. "Those belonged to humans."

16

Polka-Dotted Giggles

Somebody better give me back my ax," Eva informed the rest of the shocked, motionless friends. "I don't like to face a wall of bones weaponless. Of course, my hands are deadly weapons, but you all know what I mean."

Annie gladly handed Eva her ax, shaking her head free of the cobwebs that seemed to have gathered there, and she tugged on Bloom's elbow. "Maybe you'd better take your bow out again, too."

"That's a lot of bones," Bloom said in a marveling voice.

"They are the ones who have tried to find the Helper before." Johann reached up into the air and pointed forward, past a hole in the wall of bones toward a chamber where something small glowed red in the corner.

"What is that?" Annie asked, moving so someone else could look through the hole. "Can anyone see?"

Johann peered through. "Well . . . wow . . . it's true . . ."

"What's true?" Annie asked, but Johann jumped backward, startled by movement in the wall.

Hiding in the cobbled-together wall of human femurs and tibias, skulls and rib cages, separated from the rest of the bones by what looked like old, caked mud, was a skull that was bigger than the rest and moving. It wasn't actually coming out of the wall or anything like that. The jawbone was moving up and down, up and down, and then up and down again.

Annie looked expectantly at Johann.

He cleared his throat rather nervously and started to fix his shirt again. Another skull did the same thing—it just began to move all by itself. And then another did, too. In a quick flash, all the skulls started chattering. The ribs, the disconnected arms and toes and legs and hips didn't move. Johann fiddled with his sword and refused to make eye contact with anyone.

"Just tell us . . . ," Eva started. "Just tell us and I will try not to take my ax to your head and—"

"I'm not trying to harm you!" Johann protested. "This is just one of the things that the taker of the bow and arrow must do or . . ."

"Or what?" Annie prompted.

"Or they'll die." He stared at the floor, which was bare here and smooth except for long grooves that resembled ax marks.

"Looks like a lot of people have died here already, so maybe you should just hurry up and get on with it."

"The prophecy is this: *the bow and arrow will bring the world to right, end the darkness screaming, bring the sunlight streaming,*" he began.

"Seriously?" muttered Eva. "It rhymes?"

"A good prophecy always does," SalGoud whispered back.

"Ugh and double ugh," muttered Eva, turning away.

Johann continued, "*In the darkest hour, call upon the Stopper's power, the elf of light, the boy of might, and—*"

"Is there or is there not a dwarf in this prophecy?" Eva stomped her foot on the floor and time rushed back, bringing with it sound and wind.

Before Johann could answer, a roar—loud and fierce—filled the chamber. The Bugbear was moving and obviously upset that his prey wasn't right in front of him, ready to be eaten.

They all just stood next to the wall of bones and clacking skulls and stared at Johann. Every so often one would glance at another as if to say, *Um . . . Do you know what to do? Because I don't, and inside I'm kind of freaking out.*

"Can you stop time again?" Johann blurted.

"I don't think so," Annie admitted.

Eva moved toward the turn in the road. "I will meet him with my ax," Eva said. "And prove myself worthy of a prophecy. Any prophecy."

Bloom grabbed the back of her coat. "No, you won't."

Lifting her beneath his arm, he rushed to the wall of bones and shoved her rather ungraciously through the hole. She landed with a clatter on the other side of the wall and protested with a string of swears that involved troll bottoms and hag eyes.

Jamie ignored her. "What do you see?"

"A feather . . . It's beautiful and obviously magical . . . And stairs . . . ," Eva answered. "Let me get through."

Her head poked out of the hole. Johann pushed it back in. "We're all coming through. Get out of the way. That feather is the Helper thing!"

"We're not fighting?" Eva scuttled backward as Johann hoisted Annie through. She landed on her feet and moved out of the way as Jamie blasted across.

"SalGoud, you next," Bloom ordered.

"No, you." SalGoud shook his head.

"I'll use my arrows to hold the Bugbear off." Bloom nudged the stone giant forward.

"That didn't work the last time, brother." SalGoud pushed his head through the hole and then started to wedge his shoulders through. "I might be too big."

He made a groaning noise. The bones around him didn't budge.

"Grab him and yank, Annie," Jamie suggested, taking one of SalGoud's long slender hands and his wrist.

Annie grabbed the other, and they pulled as hard as they could, bracing their feet against skulls and leg bones.

"Oh for dragon's poop, make room for me!" Stowing her ax, Eva scaled up a stack of vertebrae and slipped her arm around SalGoud's chest. "On my mark . . . heave!"

Annie and Jamie tightened their holds.

"Hurry up!" Johann bellowed. "I hear the Bugbear."

"One . . . ," Eva said.

"It's coming!" Johann added.

"Two . . . ," Eva announced.

Johann pulled Bloom back toward him. Bloom stowed his bow and began pushing at SalGoud's bottom, trying to hoist it up and through the hole in the bone wall.

"Really . . . it's running!" Johann yelled, helping, too, using his back as a bigger pushing surface. Bloom flipped around and did the same.

"Three!" Eva grunted and yanked.

SalGoud exploded through the hole like a cork blasting off the top of a champagne bottle. He popped right through, sending Annie, Jamie, and Eva flopping onto the floor. One moment later Johann scuttled through the hole right after him. His eyes were terrified.

"It's here! The Bugbear is here!"

"Bloom!" Annie yelled, picking herself off the floor. "Bloom! Hurry!"

One second seemed to last a thousand minutes, but Bloom's bright yellow head poked through the hole and his body quickly followed. He dropped smoothly to the floor in front of the opening, whisking out his bow and notching an arrow before anyone could draw in a breath. The arrow whizzed through the hole. Two more followed.

The Bugbear bellowed in pain and rage.

"Finally!" Bloom said, smiling. "Finally, I got him."

Eva yanked him forward and away from the wall, hands shaking a bit. "No time to bask in your glory now, elf. We have stealing to do."

Johann carefully turned toward the glowing feather as the Bugbear raged on the other side of the bone wall.

"Aw, there are booby traps . . ." He rubbed his hands together. "How exciting!"

"I don't understand dwarfs," Annie whispered to Jamie as she eyed the object they had come to retrieve.

It was a feather, a single feather, but it truly did glow red and vibrant and magical.

He lifted his shoulders to indicate he didn't either. "Do you think the wall will hold?"

"It's enchanted. It seems it will." SalGoud studied it.

The Bugbear's arm reached through. SalGoud leaped back gasping, but Eva surged forward.

"Feel the sting of my ax!" She swung down hard, hitting the tops of the Bugbear's claws and neatly clipping all of them.

"You gave it a manicure," Bloom said as the Bugbear's hand retreated back into the hole.

"I gave it a warning!" Eva insisted.

"A manicure."

"A warning."

Jamie cleared his throat.

"We should probably get out of here as quickly as we can," SalGoud suggested.

"How do we get the feather, and what do we do with it when we have it?" Annie cleared her throat awkwardly.

"It is part of the arrow that is part of the bow," Bloom explained. "It must be the Helper like Johann said. It helps the arrow fly true."

"You know this, how?" Eva demanded.

Bloom pressed his hand against his chest. "I feel it in here. In my heart."

Eva harrumphed, but Annie took him at his word and lifted his hand off his chest. Bloom seemed moved, absolutely in awe of the feather.

Annie knew it had to be special. It had to be, didn't it? There was a wall of bones keeping it safe. But there was also a staircase leading up and out of the chamber.

"What is the staircase for?" she mumbled.

And the skull closest to her spoke up. "Last Chance Staircase. Make the decision to live."

They all jumped at the voice, high and tinny.

"Um . . ." Annie exchanged a glance with Jamie.

"If we go up can we come down again?"

"No," the skull answered.

"Can you tell us if the feather is booby-trapped?"

"Of course it is. How do you think I got here?" The skull probably would have rolled its eyes if it had any.

"Shouldn't it be floating?" Annie asked. "In a book it would be flying and we'd have to try to catch it. It's just lying there on the floor."

"I give up talking to you." The skeleton's jaw snapped shut.

"No, really? I meant it . . . Was that a bad question?" Annie looked to the others to help.

Johann and Eva both went to the skull and threatened its kin and ancestors with their sword and blade and blah, blah, blah . . . Jamie tuned it out. He was busy trying to think of what the booby trap might be. The Bugbear kept raging behind the wall, and it was hard to concentrate.

"Maybe we should just go up the staircase and come back for the feather after we find the bow and arrow . . . ," SalGoud suggested because he honestly didn't want to deal with this anymore. He would much rather read a book and sit by a fire somewhere.

"Then we'd have to fight the Bugbear or avoid it again."

Bloom grabbed Johann's sword and ignored Johann's sputtering protests. "Maybe I could jab it out of place."

Annie placed her hand on top of his, even as he bent into a crouching position, stopping him. "We need to think, Bloom. We have to be clever. I'm sure one of those people tried that already." She motioned to the wall behind them. "Maybe if we could figure out what the booby trap is, then we could figure out how to avoid it."

"And how do we do that?" Eva blew hair out of her face and took a swipe at the Bugbear, who was reaching his hairy arm through the hole again despite his neatly shorn claws.

"Well, what happens to the people who fail?" Annie asked.

Jamie motioned toward the wall. "They get stuck here."

"And how does that happen?" Annie peered at the bones as if they had an answer.

"This is so boring!" Johann shouted. "Can we just grab the feather, and can I have my sword back, elf? I feel naked without it. Plus, the longer you hold it, the more elf cooties it gets."

But Bloom wasn't about to give anything back. He was still peering intently at the feather, transfixed.

"I could get it. It's right here . . . ," he murmured, leaning in.

Annie scuttled back to him, grabbing his arm again. "Bloom. Look at me. Do not touch the feather until we figure out what will happen."

"What will happen is we get the feather and we skedaddle

out of here," Eva said, taking aim at the Bugbear's hand, going right for the knuckles. She swung the ax. It whizzed through the air and clattered against the floor under the hole in the wall. "Darn thing moved back." She put her face up to the hole and shouted, "Coward!"

On the other side of the room, over by the stairs, a small table sat covered in dust. There was indeed a pot—more of a cauldron, actually—sitting on top of it. SalGoud gestured toward it.

"Did any of you notice that before?" he asked, approaching it cautiously, but in the next moment he stopped frozen. "That's a pot of acid, isn't it?"

"Acid indeed!" Annie said sharply, sounding remarkably like Miss Cornelia somehow.

Striding toward the table, she seemed to forget about all notions of booby traps and potential entombment in a wall of skeleton bones and occasionally talking skeleton heads. She stopped just short of the table, motioning for someone to join her. Jamie did, rushing along the exact same path she followed. Their footsteps made prints in the thick dust, breaking its thick covering. There were no footsteps around the table, Jamie noticed.

"Magic. It's part of the magic," he said, motioning. "No marks around it. The table . . . It just appeared there."

Annie twirled around, a light sparking in her eyes. "Everyone. Listen. That means you, too, Eva. Stop toying with the Bugbear's arm and listen to me."

Eva harrumphed but notched her ax with her penknife to record the strike against the Bugbear and faced Annie. The Bugbear's hand stretched out in the air, searching for something to grab, but got nothing. Its fingers spread out. Still nothing.

"Look. The skeletons are those who tried before and failed. There are a lot of skeletons in that wall. I mean how thick is it, honestly?" Annie squinted at it.

"Four feet," SalGoud answered, stepping a bit away from the wall. "That's how thick it feels."

"Exactly. That's a lot of bones." Annie pointed at the feather, glowing and resting on the dusty floor but surprisingly not dusty itself. "A feather should not cause you to die and be entombed in a wall, but acid would . . . Well, not the wall part, but—"

"But it would burn the flesh and muscle off your body," Jamie finished for her, and he, too, took a step away from the wall.

"Look at the placement of the acid," Annie continued. "It's right by the staircase, so people must grab the feather and just run up here to escape, but they can't because—"

"Because the acid attacks them or something!" Eva finished. "Holy vampire garlic dogs! That's brilliant."

Annie bit her lip. "But we're going to have to try to bypass this acid part somehow."

Jamie took one more step so that he stood next to her, mere inches away from the table and its acid cauldron. He craned his neck, staring up. "It looks like there is some sort of trapdoor at the top of the stairs."

"What's it made of?" SalGoud asked.

"Wood." Jamie's eyes lit up and he pivoted. "Bloom. Can you attach a rope to an arrow? Then maybe we could climb up it and bypass the first part of the stairs."

"Why would we want to bypass the first part of the stairs?" Eva asked.

Annie knew what Jamie was thinking and watched as Bloom attached a rope, pulled out of Eva's handy knapsack, to an arrow.

"Maybe the acid touches their feet, or the bottoms of their shoes or whatever and then—" Jamie snapped his fingers, making everyone, even the now-quiet Bugbear, jump. Or at least it looked like he jumped because his arm jerked upward. "The acid just eats all of you from there."

"And the bones . . . ? How do the bones get in the wall?" Johann asked.

Annie shrugged. "Magic? Maybe? I'm not sure and I don't want to waste time figuring it out. Just . . . Just . . . Whatever you do . . . Whatever happens . . . Try to avoid the acid."

Jamie swallowed hard as Bloom shot the arrow with the rope attached up to the trapdoor. It struck on the first try. Bloom tugged on the rope to make sure it would hold their weight. While everyone else was watching the rope and judging if it was secure, Jamie eyed the cauldron. The acid inside kept bubbling but didn't leak out or spill over.

"I say we all get near the bottom of the rope . . . ," Jamie suggested. "One of us grabs the feather. And we climb."

"I think you should start climbing before I grab the feather. It seems safer," Bloom suggested.

"I will stay down with Bloom," SalGoud said over the protests. "We are the fastest climbers and the tallest."

Eva and Annie objected, but they were talked down, and within minutes, Johann, Eva, Annie, and Jamie had started climbing the rope. It wasn't easy, actually. The rope's fibers rubbed against their hands. Annie's bled a bit from the chafing, and a drop of blood hit the floor . . . a drop so small that nobody really even noticed it . . . But the moment it touched the ground, the cauldron's bubbling grew more chaotic, more passionate . . . Bubbles . . . bigger and bigger bubbles began to pop inside it.

"It's boiling over!" Jamie announced. He was closest and could look down upon the boiling mess.

And it did. The acid sloshed over the side and began spreading across the ground, edging toward Bloom and SalGoud.

Bloom rushed to the other corner and snatched the red feather. For a moment nothing happened. A giant creaking noise filled the room. It came from the skeleton wall.

"Jump up, man," Bloom urged SalGoud. "Let's go."

SalGoud bypassed the rope completely, leaping over the acid and to the edge of the staircase. His fingers caught the edge of a step, and he clambered up, immediately racing toward the top and grabbing the rope, hauling it up, trying to get the others to safety.

But below them, the bone wall had started to move. The skeletons were leaving it, breaking free of whatever magic bonded them to each other. They creaked out of the wall, one after another, all edging toward Bloom, who stood near the bottom of the rope.

"Bloom!" Annie yelled as Johann jumped from the rope to the stairs with the assistance of SalGoud's long hand.

A skeleton lunged toward Bloom. Its hands gripped his neck, choking him. He tucked the red feather in his cloak pocket and pulled out his dagger, stabbing at the skeleton, but there was nothing to stab into, no flesh, no muscle; it was all just bones.

The skeleton's hands tightened around Bloom's neck, and he gave up on the dagger, instead trying to get out of the skeleton's grip even as others converged on them.

"Bloom!" Eva bellowed and started down the rope, climbing over Jamie and Annie, stepping on them without a thought. "Don't you touch my elf, you nasty bag of bones!"

Annie made it to the top of the stairs. There was no way she could stop time and help all of them . . . They had to be touching and were too far apart . . . "Eva, come back! The acid!" The acid hit the end of the rope and easily climbed up it. The rope sizzled as it dissolved, spreading up and up toward Eva's feet. She stopped, rushing back to the top of the stairs.

And on the other side of the breaking skeleton wall, the Bugbear howled. Skeletons attacked it. More and more skeletons joined in the skirmish . . . And on Bloom's side, too, they left the wall, arms out, ready to kill, surrounding him. He used his forearm, pulling it up and in between the skeleton's own arms and smashed outward, breaking the hold, and as he did, he rolled on the floor, knocking several of the attacking skeletons right over.

"The acid!" Annie yelled.

He switched directions, rolling in the opposite way.

"He's like a bowling ball, and the skeletons are the pins," Eva whooped. "Way to go, elf! Way to go!"

SalGoud yanked Jamie up onto the stairs just as the entire wall tumbled to the ground, revealing a Bugbear smashing one skeleton after another. It set its sights on the elf, now in the farthermost corner of the room. It smiled.

"Get. The. Door. Open. Now!" Annie ordered, and Johann slammed up the remaining steps, smashing at the trapdoor with his shoulder.

"It's not moving," he said with a grunt as SalGoud sprang up there with him.

Bloom stood up effortlessly and pulled out his dagger, but it was not going to be much of a match for the Bugbear, who even now was casting aside the attacking skeletons as if they were nothing—just air.

"Bloom!" Annie yelled. "The rope! You can't use the rope!"

It sizzled, dissolving faster and faster.

The acid had spread across the floor, a giant bubbling puddle of it. The skeletons that Bloom or the Bugbear had smashed over lay in it, twitching and slowly liquefying. Bloom sheathed his dagger even as the Bugbear lunged toward him.

At the last second, Bloom vaulted into the air, one foot landing on the confused Bugbear's shoulder. He powered off it even as the Bugbear made a startled attempt to grab him. Landing on first one skeleton head and then another, he rushed toward the stairs, feet never touching the acid. Finally, running out of heads, he leaped forward and up, bounding toward the stairs. Jamie's hands shot down and caught him. The weight of Bloom almost yanked Jamie off the stairs, but Annie and Eva grabbed him by the waist and staggered backward.

One second later Bloom was smiling. "Let's go!"

He urged them up the stairs.

"The feather?" Annie asked.

"Still got it."

Johann and SalGoud had managed to get the trapdoor open, and the sunlight streamed down into the chamber. They stood on a green lawn surrounded by big white buildings and walkways. Tourists snapped pictures of them as they urged Annie, Jamie, Eva, and Bloom to hurry up and out.

Below them, the Bugbear howled, and it was such a strange and unpleasant sound that the tourists went still.

Then they began to applaud, thinking it was a play or street performance.

Eva bowed as she popped through.

Annie didn't seem to even notice. She yanked Jamie up and out, and then Bloom rushed through onto the street.

"Shut it!" she ordered.

She was almost too afraid to look at what was happening down below, but as the trapdoor closed, she could see the Bugbear still fighting off skeletons, could smell the acid stench of bones and dust evaporating. Then the wooden door shut completely, and she was grateful to not have to hear anything else.

"Well, would you look at that," Eva said, admiringly. She went down on her hands and knees, feeling around the grass for the trapdoor, prodding her thick, strong fingers into the dirt. "You can't find it again. It's just gone—poof!"

"Must be one way," Jamie reasoned as some tourists snapped pictures and yelled for an encore.

Eva stood up. "I'll give you an encore!"

She started to do a happy little dwarf dance right there, all stamping feet and ax throwing.

Bloom sighed, exhausted, and smiled. "She's such a show-off."

While Eva played to the crowd, a sweaty Johann explained that they were on the College Green inside Trinity College, which was established by an English queen centuries ago.

"Where are the secret societies?" Jamie interrupted, studying the fronts of all the large government-looking buildings, all white and seemingly marble, and all facing in toward the square.

"Underground and hidden in plain sight," Johann blurted and then looked a wee bit embarrassed. He started explaining how dwarfs built the subterranean parts of the library that had over five million books, but abruptly stopped his boasting. "I'm sorry about all of that. But I know you've got to get the feather to be successful. I just know it."

"Because of the prophecy?" Annie asked.

"Yes."

They all stared at him. The tourists applauded for Eva and began to drift away.

"I've got more!" she bellowed, wiping the sweat off her brow despite the chilly air. "I could ax dance all day."

"She could," Bloom said, "or at least until she passed out."

Johann led them past the Berkeley Library and Arnaldo Pomodoro's Sphere Within Sphere bronze sculpture, which sat on the stone patio outside the library's walls.

"The artist has made a bunch of these," Johann said, pausing to touch it reverently. "The craftsmanship is almost worthy of a dwarf, I say."

They all paused by the sphere, although Bloom's impatience showed in his foot tapping on the ground. Annie, however, was awestruck by the spinning globe within a globe. It was so beautiful. The bronze shone in the sun, which had just managed to come out from behind a sheath of clouds. Tourists hopped up the steps to the platform that the sphere sat on, ready to take a picture. They were quite cheery and laughing; Annie smiled, happy that some people didn't have to deal with boiling acid and could just be joyful. But her attention quickly turned back to the spheres. They seemed to resonate somehow. They reminded her of time stopping, of the vibrations of the strings . . .

"What do they do? The spheres?" Annie whispered, reaching forward to touch it.

"Nothing—" Johann began.

Pink liquid exploded from outside of the inner sphere. It sprayed the tourists posing nearby and both Annie and Johann, who were closest to it. The tourists screeched. Eva drew her ax as Annie staggered backward, hitting SalGoud but not knocking him over. Johann began to laugh hysterically as did the tourists on the other side of the sphere.

"Oh!" Annie gasped as Bloom started trying to wipe the pink liquid off her face. "Oh!"

"That is not nothing!" Eva bellowed.

In the confusion, the tourists who had been sprayed began laughing uncontrollably as their companion looked on helplessly and then began clicking away, taking photo after photo as if the spraying sphere was the most natural thing in the world.

Annie started giggling, too.

"Annie?" Bloom asked, pausing in his efforts to wipe

the pink liquid off. He studied the corner of his cloak, which he had been using. None of the liquid had come off Annie. In fact, it seemed to be seeping into her skin. Johann's, too. "This . . . this isn't coming off you. Why are you laughing?"

"They're taking pictures . . ." She giggled, pointing at the tourists and then falling on her butt—bam—right on the cold stone surface.

Johann snorted and started giggling, too. He plopped down next to Annie and made his feet wiggle in the air like babies do.

"Hahahaha!" Annie laughed. "Oh—hahahaha! Your feet!"

"It's not actually funny, is it?" Jamie asked SalGoud. "I mean . . ." He motioned at Johann and Annie who were pretty much rolling around on the ground, giggling.

"To be laughing this hard," SalGoud finished for him. "No. It is not. While laughter may be the best medicine, forced giggling while your skin is turning . . . Wait . . . Are those . . . ?"

Everyone huddled around Annie and Johann examining their faces.

Eva threw her hands up in the air, disgusted. "You're both polka-dotted."

"Hee . . . Hee . . . Hee . . ." Annie kept giggling, pointing at Johann's yellow-and-green polka-dotted face, which contrasted nicely with her purple-and-orange polka-dotted skin. "We look like we're in a kids' picture book."

"With heffalumps or something . . . ," Johann added. He

was having a hard time talking while he laughed. "Or helphants or eggplants. What am I even saying? Ack . . . giggle . . . I am so giggly giggling . . ."

"*I* would not be giggling if *I* were covered in polka dots," Eva exclaimed, hustling them forward. "Where is your pride? I expect this from Annie, but you—Johann Murray-Broadsword! You are a dwarf. Dwarfs do not giggle."

"I am not giggling. I am chuckling," Johann retorted as he giggled. "Chuck-chuck-chuckling—upchuck buckling—chucky-chukasauris."

Eva threw up her hands. "Let's just get you back to the car before anyone else notices anything. It will be freaking fine. It's all going to be freaking fine. First we fall into some abandoned underground city, then there's a Bugbear and burning acid and skeletons that attacked my elf, and now this . . . Seriously, you all cannot stay out of trouble for one sec." She paused, thinking, and shrugged. "Actually, that makes me kind of proud of you. Now try to blend in and not giggle so loud or be so spotted."

But as they trotted through the streets of Dublin, past the police officers and tourists, the double-decker buses, the bicycling college students and foreign workers, everyone *did* indeed notice. People cheered and gave thumbs-up signs, applauding Johann and Annie's "excellent use of face paint."

"That must be for the game," some footballers said coming out of a pub whose dark wooden exterior walls were brightened with green shamrocks. "Brilliant."

A weird tickle of doom began stirring in Jamie's chest. It wasn't exactly anxiety. It wasn't exactly panic. It *was* a feeling that something terribly bad was about to happen.

They hurried past the shops and pubs and the tourist knickknack places selling woven Irish sweaters, tweed hats, and stuffed-animal sheep emblazoned with the Irish flag. A stray cat, gray and white, trotted behind them for a while. It reminded Jamie of the one who'd helped him at his grandmother's house, the one with the dullahan, the one who had appeared in Aurora, the one who kept showing up, impossibly often.

He tried not to stress about it and instead pay attention to the street, the tourists, the cold against his face, and Annie and Johann, who seemed to still have an impossible case of the giggles.

"I've touched that sphere a million times before, and that has never happened. I'm telling ya, not ever." Johann giggled even though his words were gruff. "Why now?"

"Maybe it's because Annie touched it," SalGoud answered.

Johann giggled again. He rubbed at his cheeks as if they hurt from laughing so much. "But why would that do anything? Why would it do that just because Annie touched it? It makes no sense—unless . . . What if it's some sort of trap? Like a Stopper detection device or something?"

Just then a group of footballers heading out of another pub pointed at the sky.

"Would you look at that?"

"How do they do that?"

"You're seeing that, right? Because I feel like someone may have put a little extra something in my shepherd's pie!"

Turning his head to see what the football fans were talking about, Jamie gasped. Three winged creatures—each half bird and half woman—were soaring down the street. Their metal wings made clanging noises as they flapped in the air, propelling them.

SalGoud whispered, "Snatchers . . . I don't . . . I thought they weren't real."

"What?" Eva stopped dead still, face suddenly ashen. SalGoud didn't even look again, merely seized her and carried her beneath his arm as they all ducked into the pub that the football jersey–wearing men had just come out of.

"Hurry . . . Hurry . . ." Bloom held open the door and popped inside.

They all scurried to a window booth and stared out onto the street.

"Oh . . ." Annie giggled. "They are so beautiful."

"Ethereal. 'Ethereal' is the word." SalGoud sighed.

"And deadly." Eva moved some malted vinegar and packets of brown sauce out of the way, crawling up onto the table to get a better view. "Look at the sight of them, just soaring away, la-di-da, not even caring if the humans see them. And who are they about to snatch? Huh? You know they don't just randomly appear somewhere. The Snatchers have a mission. They always do . . . My dad says—"

A lilting voice came from behind their table, female and knowing. "Why, I would say that the Snatchers are most likely after you."

17

Hovering Snatchers

Skinny with birdlike collarbones herself, the waitress who had spoken was shaped like a pear. Her shoulders seemed too small to carry the giant tray of steaming dishes in her hands, and her neck seemed too narrow to support her head. And her head seemed too little for all the thick, brown hair that fell around it in waves.

"You . . . What . . . I'm sorry, ma'am, why would you think that?" Annie asked, trying to be polite. She giggled. She groaned. Giggling was not polite. She giggled again.

Eva clamped a hand over Annie's mouth. It smelled of dirt and metal.

"Well . . ." The woman's eyes twinkled and she shifted her weight to her other foot. "The fact that you and the lad over there are polka-dotted and neither of ya can stop giggling is evidence number one to saying that they are looking for you." She nodded sagely as if proud of herself, and then her stance stumbled a little under the weight of the tray of shepherd's pie, colcannon, fish and chips, and some sort of meaty stew. "Why don't you settle in? Hide the polka-dotted giggling ones from the window and check out the menus. I don't think you'll be leaving for a bit with those things out there. I'll be right back to take your order."

"But—" Bloom started to protest, but the waitress had already whirled away, vanishing through a narrow doorway that seemed to lead to another part of the establishment.

The entire pub wasn't what Annie expected. She imagined more of a scary, seedy bar with dark lighting and beer smells, but this place smelled more like ground beef sautéed with onions. There were tons of booths and tables, not just a big bar with stools, although the pub certainly had those, too. Along the walls were crooked black-and-white photographs of mostly men. Jaunty Irish singing lilted through the loudspeakers. It was quite a different atmosphere from what was going on outside as the three Snatchers swooped down the street, talons out and ready to grab anyone in their path.

Annie, still giggling, motioned everyone forward. They all leaned over the wooden table, knocking the silverware about and displacing it. The little moneymaking gnome in Eva's pocket whimpered and popped out, looking slightly smooshed. He scampered onto the table, slid across it, and then dived into Eva's side pocket before anyone really noticed he'd moved.

The children's heads were all close together as Annie asked, "What do you think? Should we stay?"

Johann giggled. "Those . . . things . . . are out . . . so, yes . . . I vote . . . plus, food."

Jamie's stomach growled loudly, agreeing.

Annie's eyes met his and he gave a bit of a nod. She shifted her gaze to Bloom. "It seems like the wisest course of action. Plus, I'm hungry, too."

Eva flopped back onto the upholstered bench. "Good. I'm famished. You still got the feather, Bloom? Good."

She didn't actually wait for Bloom to answer and yanked a menu out of the holder at the end of the table and didn't offer it to anyone else. SalGoud passed the remaining menus out courteously. Just as he gave Annie hers, one of the Snatchers paused outside the pub window.

Eva shoved Annie beneath the table. "Get down. Get down!"

Johann clambered below it himself, meeting Annie among everyone's smelly feet. They both giggled even though they were much too scared to be feeling giggly at all.

"What's happening?" Annie pulled on Bloom's pant leg and giggled.

"The Snatcher is looking inside," Bloom explained. "Her face is pressed against the glass. She's really pretty."

"Totally pretty in a creepy, kill-you-soon-by-ripping-you-apart-with-my-talons kind of way," Eva agreed. "I like it. I mean I would if she wasn't after you guys," she self-corrected. "I mean I would if she was only after Johann or something. Wow. I am totally getting the Irish stew. Did you guys see that plate go by?"

"Eva!" Bloom scolded. "Focus. There is a Snatcher . . . Right. There."

His voice squeaked a little.

Jamie swallowed hard, his appetite suddenly gone. The Snatcher's dark-brown eyes stared into his.

"Not you," she mouthed and moved on, staring at Bloom, and then SalGoud. Each time she said the same two words. *Not you.*

Relief flooded Jamie's heart. Not him. She did not want him. But then he remembered who she really, probably did want . . . He crossed his legs, kicking Johann in the shoulder. There was a big *oomph* noise and then more giggling.

"I'm not a football." Johann laughed.

"Shh . . . Stay hidden. Just . . . just . . . stay hidden." The words sounded panicked, but Jamie didn't care. He *was* panicked.

The Snatcher hit the window with her fist. More people in the pub noticed her.

"Would you look at that?" the bartender said.

"That can't be natural," a granny sort of woman said,

standing up at her table to get a better look. "What do you think she's doing? Some sort of stunt for a TV3 show?"

"I'd be staying back and praying if I were you," said one man, making the sign of the cross across his chest.

"I think she must be a supermodel," the granny said. She fished some glasses out of a large, fabric purse. "Oh . . . she's so pretty . . ."

The Snatcher hit the window a second time. Everyone at Annie's table jumped. Annie was so startled her head hit the bottom of the table, jerking it.

"Stay still. Stay quiet," Bloom hissed.

"Oh . . . ," the bartender said, spotting Annie and Johann. "Are you kids hiding from her? Is that your mum?"

Another man from the bar peered at them. Annie giggled and gave a little wave. "Oh, they're spotted. I bet that's why they're in trouble."

"Should we tell their mum? She might be worried?" the bartender asked jovially.

"Worried?" The granny shook her head, standing up. "She looks like she's ready to kill someone. And look at the wings on her. And the talons. That's not their mum. This is a television show stunt, and these children aren't involved at all. Are you?"

None of them answered for an awkward moment.

Annie giggled.

Johann giggled.

Jamie cleared his throat.

But Bloom was the one who finally answered, "She's not our mom, ma'am, and we don't think she's very nice. And there are two more of them outside. We'd all rather they just go away."

The music stopped.

The bar went silent.

For a moment, Jamie thought that maybe Annie had stopped time, but no—everyone just went quiet by their own choice. Glancing around the room, he tried to locate an escape path. The people of Aurora had taught him to never trust a crowd or a crowd mentality again.

Jamie wondered about the folks in the bar. What could they possibly be thinking as they stared at a Snatcher; two polka-dotted, small-size kids; himself; Eva; a ridiculously tall boy; and a remarkably handsome guy wearing a cloak? They had to seem pretty weird. The police at the airport had certainly thought so. The customers and workers at this pub place didn't even know them. Maybe they would turn on them, grab pitchforks and . . .

Jamie's imagination created a huge, terrifying scenario that involved them all running across burning fields, chased by Snatchers AND bar customers wielding farm tools. He shook his head. Nobody even kept farm tools like hoes and pitchforks and rakes in a bar. Did they?

He cleared his throat again and whispered to SalGoud, "I bet there's another exit in the back in case . . ."

"In case what?" SalGoud whispered back.

"We aren't going to do anything to you kids."

The bartender hopped over the bar and, reaching over the kids' table, pulled down the long thick shade that obviously hadn't been shut in years. Dust flew about the air. A random pixie was dislodged, but she blended in with the dust so much that nobody seemed to notice even as she sneezed out a big blob of glitter.

The bartender just moved to the next table as the Snatcher moved to the next window. He shut the shade there, too. "None of us objects to a little privacy this afternoon, do we?"

"Makes it cozier!" one man at the bar said. "Plus, no garda—that's the police—or weird flying things can peek in."

"Exactly!" the bartender agreed, motioning for another server to help him with a shade that was stuck.

They leaned over the empty table just as the Snatcher got to the window. She knocked.

"Nobody home, love," the bartender called cheerily.

Meanwhile the waitress hustled over to their table and ignored the fact that Annie and Johann were still sitting under it giggling. "You best stay here till they're gone," the woman said. Then she made the sign of the cross over her chest. "Well, if it isn't—I say . . . You poor thing. Which of you is the Stopper?"

Annie twittered. She raised her hand. "Me."

This just made Johann chortle even louder.

The waitress cleared her throat and whispered reverently,

"I am so honored—so very honored—to meet you. Are you the one who was lost at sea?"

Annie pulled on Bloom's pant leg. "Was I?"

"Not that I know of," Bloom answered.

"The one who will fall with evil?" The waitress cocked her head. "I'm Shauna, by the way. Horan is my last name. And I'm pleased to meet you."

The waitress reached out her hand and Annie shook it. The waitress used the opportunity to pull Annie all the way out from under the table. She put her arm around Annie's shoulders and announced in a voice that was worthy of a dwarf because it was so loud, "Ladies and gentlemen and others!" She took a side step away from Annie. "Let me introduce you to my new, lovely friend from America. Miss Annie Nobody."

Annie smiled awkwardly and tried to hold in a giggle.

"You know my name," she said.

"Everyone does, Annie. Tales of your adventures run far and wide."

"But I've only just started having adventures."

"Not here. Not in Ireland. Here you are famous."

The bartender came over with a bunch of graphic novels. There was a girl on the front that vaguely resembled Annie, or what Annie thought might be a better-looking version of herself. Jamie thought otherwise. Either way it was the title that got her: "Time Stopper vs. the Demon, How Annie Nobody Saved the World."

"That is definitely my name," Annie whispered as she began leafing through the booklet. She sat back down at the table and Johann crawled out, too.

"This is weird," she said quietly in between giggles. "Undeniably, unstoppably weird."

"I am going to be so jealous if you have your own fan club," Eva said, snatching the book away and flipping to the last page where there was a link to an Internet site where you could join the Annie the Time Stopper Fan Club. Eva hit the table with her fist so hard the silverware bounced around. "You have your own fan club. That was fast. I want my own fan club."

"Of course she does!" The waitress shook her head at Eva as if she was the silliest goober in the entire universe. "And these books were written years ago. So, I'm not sure what you mean by 'fast.' Now, what will you all be having while you wait out that winged woman at the window?"

They all ordered food even though it was hard for Annie and Johann to eat because of all the giggling. And the worry. Jamie didn't feel safe. He wasn't sure why the Snatchers didn't come into the actual buildings, but they didn't.

"Must be some sort of binding spell like with vampires. Maybe they have to be invited in," Bloom said.

"In your books it says it's the cross and the clover above the doorway," the waitress said as she refilled their water glasses.

Bloom flipped to page 57, and sure enough there was a picture of a cross and a clover above the door. He peered up at Shauna. “Do you know who wrote these books?”

“Sure and enough, I do.” She got one of the novels out of the stack and showed them the front cover, which made them all feel foolish, especially when she pointed at the name. “It’s by someone named Tully. Quite mysterious. I heard he lives out near the cliffs.”

The kids exchanged a glance. It was by the same author who wrote the book Gramma Doris had given Jamie when she’d hid him under the floor.

“In the books, does it mention anything about . . .” Bloom cleared his throat. “Does it mention anything about Snatchers? Or the Secret Society?”

Johann kicked him under the table. Bloom grimaced and flicked a chip at him.

“It does!” Shauna’s face lit up and she sat down next to Annie, perching precariously on the edge of the booth. “It says that the Snatchers are part of the demon’s detection system, set up throughout the world in an attempt to find Annie because she is hidden, you know? Nobody knows who she is. Most people foolishly think the Stopper is the dwarf or the elf companion.”

The waitress paused for a moment.

“What is it?” Annie said, managing to actually suppress a giggle.

"I just—I didn't think it was actually real." The waitress bit her lip.

Annie thought she might actually cry.

"Oh, it's not . . . ," Eva blurted.

"Then what's this?" The waitress waved her hand about. "Don't tell me you're just actors because I won't believe it. There's magic in this world and we all know it, and you lot—you lot and that thing hovering outside are perfect examples of it."

They didn't really know how to respond to that. Shauna went on for a bit about how much she loved the books.

"What about the Secret—" Jamie began, and then Shauna was called away by another customer.

Johann's polka dots turned red.

Eva whirled on him. "What is it?"

He coughed and sputtered. "Nothing."

"Do I need to get out my ax?" she asked. "Or sing show tunes?"

"No jazz hands!" he exclaimed. "Fine. I'll tell you."

And as they ate, Johann hesitantly told them about the Secret Society. "It's in the books," he said. "I wasn't sure if it's real or not. But the Helper—I only knew about it because of the books. I didn't know about the Bugbear. I swear."

"And the books said what exactly? What is this Society?"

Johann didn't have the easiest time of it as he tried to explain that the Secret Society was really just kind of an

Annie the Time Stopper fan club and he wasn't 100 percent sure if it was real or not. He was a dwarf so he knew magic existed, but he didn't know if *Annie* actually existed or was just pretend. Once Eva called and told him she needed his help, he was all for helping. He was MORE THAN all for helping. He was enthusiastic and delighted and psyched. So he reread his graphic novels because he wasn't all that good at remembering details in things he read, joined the fan club on the Web, and when he did, got a notification that he was now a part of the Secret Society.

"Which does what exactly?" Bloom asked.

Johann shrugged, giggled, and pounded the wall. "Don't know. That's the secret."

Eva threw her hands up in the air and began muttering. Bloom excused himself to use the bathroom.

"Plus, my computer began to smoke after I accepted the membership." Johann coughed. "It turns out this is normal. I was just lucky the keyboard didn't start flaming. That's happened, too. Or at least I've heard so. That's a powerful magic to do, that it is."

They all stared at him, but his entire attention was on the plate in front of him and his polka dots were reddening again.

"So, you brought us to retrieve a Helper, not really knowing if the Helper, which turned out to be a feather, was real, or if the Secret Society is good, or even what the aim of the

Society is. Then you brought us to the sphere . . . Was that in the books?" Jamie prodded.

"No!" Johann blustered. "Maybe . . . I'm not sure . . . There's a sphere for certain. Oh, maybe . . ."

He started to slink under the table, but Eva grabbed him by the collar and hauled him back up as Bloom came back from the bathroom. They all sat there, finishing their food, which was still difficult for both Annie and Johann thanks to the giggles, and they occasionally peeked out the window to see if the Snatcher was gone. She wasn't.

"We're going to have to sneak out somehow," Annie said, frustrated. "We can't just stay here forever. It's wasting time while Miss Cornelia and the—"

"Don't say it out loud." Bloom clamped a hand over her mouth. "You don't know who is listening."

So, Annie didn't finish her sentence, but her point was still obvious. They needed to hurry. They needed to save the elves who were suffering for so long and losing their power, and Miss Cornelia, who was probably being tortured or hurt or something equally horrible.

They motioned for Shauna to come to their table, and thanks to Eva's moneymaking gnome, they easily paid for all their meals and had money to give a tip.

Bloom leaned over the table conspiratorially and whispered, "Look. We need your help as part of the Secret Society of . . ." He paused. He didn't know the proper name.

"The Stoppers of Evil," Shauna filled him in, even as Eva rolled her eyes and murmured something about that being a completely dorky name.

"The Stoppers of Evil. I need your help," Bloom said, being as charming as elves can be, which is honestly, ridiculously charming. He then explained their need for an alternative exit so that they could sneak out of the pub without the Snatcher seeing them leave.

"We don't want to be snatched," Annie added and giggled. And clamped her hand over her mouth until the giggling stopped. "It would be so kind of you to help. I mean, I can't thank you enough. I mean, I am so sorry I am giggling."

"Anything for you, Stopper." Shauna made a thumping motion with one hand against the other.

"It's the secret symbol of solidarity," Johann explained. He giggled as he did it, too. "I hope this giggling wears off soon. It's likely to make me go mad."

"Well, you sound pathetic," Eva said as they got up to leave. "Now, everyone try to not be noticeable."

"Oh, that's easy," said the polka-dotted Annie.

Jamie looped his arm in hers as they skirted around the bar, past the restrooms, and then into the kitchen, which was bright, loud and shiny, full of grease smell and cooked-meat scents. "It'll be okay, Annie."

She managed to whisper back, in between giggles, "The Stoppers of Evil. Have you thought about that name? It could mean Stoppers who stop evil or Stoppers who are evil."

He paused. A chef pointed at Johann. "Look at the wee man. All polka-dotted he is. Ah, isn't that a sight?"

Johann tried to glower, but he just giggled instead. The rest of the cooks stopped stirring gravy and frying beef. They turned and stared, openmouthed. Some grease lit up on the griddle. Someone stomped a pan on top of it. The flames flickered out of the sides.

Jamie tapped Annie, obviously slightly distracted by the chef and the fire but more concerned about the Secret Society. "That's not cool," he said.

"No," she agreed as Eva charged out the back door into the street. "No, it isn't cool at all."

"But . . . how do we know about the name? How do we know which one it is?" he asked.

Annie bit her tongue to keep from giggling. Blood popped into her mouth. She let go and blurted before she could giggle again. "We won't know until it's obvious. I think." She paused, biting her tongue again. The pain kept the giggling back. "And when it's obvious . . ."

She let her words trail off, but Jamie finished for her.

"Then it might be too late."

"Exactly."

Piggy GPS

Eva declared that the little back alley behind the pub was clear of Snatchers, and the others followed her out onto the brick street, with SalGoud gently shutting the kitchen door behind him.

The sun had gone down quite a bit and the air had gotten colder. They hurried down the road, watching the darkening sky for signs of the Snatchers.

"The car is just a bit this way." Johann giggled as they ran.

Jamie pulled a hood up and around Annie's face, an awkward maneuver as they were moving. "That should help disguise you."

Bloom tried to do the same with Johann, who fended off his kindness with a stiff forearm. "No dwarf hides his face."

"They should," Bloom muttered back angrily. Bloom was in such a foul mood lately. It was obvious that the stress of trying to save Miss Cornelia and the elves was getting to his good nature.

Fortunately, neither dwarf heard him. Bloom spread out his arms, blocking the others from following him into the street.

"Do you see any Snatchers?" SalGoud asked.

"No . . . Yes . . . To the right. She's facing the other way."

"And the car?"

"To the left," Bloom said. "Johann, unlock it with the key fob. Let's see what happens."

Johann hit the fob. The pig car beeped as its doors unlocked. The Snatcher whisked around at the noise and whizzed past them, heading directly for the car. It was not the same Snatcher who had been waiting outside the pub. This one had blond hair.

"What's she doing?" Annie whispered.

"Hovering above the car," Bloom answered.

"We can't wait all day," Eva groaned. "We need to get going."

"We can't risk her snatching Annie," Bloom protested.

Jamie cleared his throat. "Okay," he said. "This is what we do."

And he detailed how he, the un-magical one who really didn't know how to drive, should just go and get the car. He wasn't giggling. He wasn't polka-dotted. They wouldn't try to snatch him.

Annie shook her head. “But what if they do?”

“Then we’ll freaking save him.” Eva grunted. She pushed Jamie out into the street before Annie could protest anymore. “Go. Do it. Drive the car here and stop.”

Jamie was casually walking down the road before Annie could protest again. It was too late. He was already in danger. Her heart sank and she crossed her fingers and murmured, “Please be okay . . . please be okay . . . please be okay.”

“Freaking toad breath, Annie. Chillax.” Eva shook her head. “You sound ridiculous murmuring and giggling. He’ll be fine.”

Jamie tried to act like walking toward a pig car was the most natural thing in the world. He was halfway there before he remembered he didn’t have the car keys. Smacking his forehead with his hand, he pivoted, heading back to the alley.

“What are you doing?” Eva asked, agitated.

“The keys,” he mouthed back.

Bloom took them from Johann and tossed them to Jamie, who caught them with one hand. He turned back around again. The Snatcher was sitting on the car now, just hanging out on top of it with her legs crossed in front of her as if it was the most natural thing in the world. Tourists stopped and whisked out their iPhones, taking pictures. One of them posed in front of the pig car. The Snatcher smelled the happy tourist’s hair, but didn’t grab her up in her long talons.

"Thank you!" the tourist called as she walked away. "You look lovely. Best costume ever."

Jamie held his breath as he approached the Snatcher and the pig car. Every single nerve in his body shook. The Snatchers were beautiful—yes, beyond beautiful—but that beauty hid a big heartless evil. He could feel it . . . And those talons! They could pierce right through his skin like ten thick, horrible daggers. He let out a breath. Why would someone make such a horrible creature? Why would anyone want to kill or capture Annie? Or another Stopper? It was all about the Raiff. It had to be him.

Jamie held his breath again, trying to look like walking to a pig car was an absolutely natural thing to do. Closer and closer he came until it was all he could do to look normal. He tried to hum a jaunty tune, which is what he imagined any normal person would hum when they walked toward his pig car that was guarded by an evil Snatcher.

"Totally normal . . . just a normal day . . . just a normal guy walking to his car." Jamie smashed his lips together, realizing he was singing . . . actually singing. Normal people didn't sing under these circumstances. He stopped dead still and hit himself in the head with his hand hard enough to make himself sputter out an "ouch." It was enough to make him move forward past a parking meter and an abandoned bicycle, closer to the car and those terrible talons.

He was almost there . . . Almost . . . He readied the keys in his hand. He'd yank open the pink car door, dive in, and slam the door shut behind him. Yes, he could do that, he thought. He'd be fast and do it all in one smooth, fluid motion. He'd duck right under the Snatcher's foot and be inside before she blinked. He'd be fast and swift and—

He made it to just about five feet away from the car before the Snatcher leaped off the roof. She stood in front of him, magnificent, massive, at least a foot taller than him and spread out her wings, effectively blocking his entire view of the car. Slowly, she leaned forward and sniffed.

"What are you smelling me for?" he gasped out.

"Magic."

Jamie waited. Her breath moved his hair as it left her nose and mouth. She reeked of horse poop.

He held his breath again.

And tried not to gag.

"You have been near much magic." She still hovered over him. "But you are no Stopper."

Leaning back, she eyed him. "What are you? I have never smelled anything like you."

"A boy," he managed to say. "I am just a boy."

She scowled at him. "You are not just a boy."

And with that she lifted into the sky and flew up and up, above the two- and three-story buildings, until Jamie couldn't see her anymore. But he could still feel her rancid breath in his hair.

The others rushed out from the alleyway. Annie's hood fell as she ran to the car. Jamie flung open the doors and tossed Johann the keys.

"Brilliantly done." Bloom slapped Jamie on the back.

"Fearless. Never would have thought it of you," Eva agreed, smashing herself into the backseat after clapping Jamie's back in a show of dwarfy commendation. Annie squeezed his hand and gave him a small peck on the cheek. Jamie's hand went right to his face, stunned. No girl had ever kissed his cheek before. SalGoud's eyebrows raised up so high that they almost hid in his hair. Jamie quickly removed his hand from his face and got in the car. Johann had settled himself back into the driver's seat, but every time he tried to put the key in the ignition, he collapsed with giggles.

"Johann. Stop it," Eva sputtered from the backseat, leaning forward and smacking the other dwarf in the back of the head. "We need to go. We are off to the Cliffs of Moher and the Ballinackalacken Castle! To Annie's grandparents! Do you still have the feather, Bloom?"

"You keep asking, Eva. Of course," Bloom answered.

Johann just kept laughing.

"It looks like I am going to have to drive," SalGoud stated.

"It's okay," Bloom assured everyone as SalGoud and Johann switched seats. "SalGoud has been driving tractors and all sorts of things since he was a baby. Stone giants are very good drivers."

"I think it's illegal." Annie snickered. She clamped her hand over her own mouth, obviously frustrated by the continuous laughter.

"Illegal-smeagal." Eva snorted. "We stole a police car before."

"I try to forget that," Annie said. She giggled inappropriately. "And we *borrowed* it."

"I'm not sure we officially ever gave it back," Jamie added. "I'm sure they found it, though."

"It doesn't matter!" Eva stormed. She punched the back of the pink upholstered headrest of the driver's seat.

SalGoud turned on the pig car. It oinked happily. "Okay, everyone buckle up. We are off!"

SalGoud turned out to be an incredibly good driver who stayed in the lane, never honked the horn, and didn't seem to have issues with being on the opposite side of the road.

"In Maine, we tend to drive in the center of the road anyway," he said. "So this isn't much of a stretch."

Annie and Johann's giggle fits and polka-dotted skin gradually faded. So they would only burst into laughter once every fifteen minutes or so, and then not at all. The biggest problem they had was figuring out exactly where they were going. Luckily the car had its very own GPS system, composed of tiny flying pigs who kept pace with the vehicle and sent out scouts. They'd oink directions into the car's antennae and the directions would translate onto a screen that showed the pig car looking like a regular pig running down roads, heading toward a giant feed bucket, which when you zoomed into the screen said, YOUR DESTINATION IS HERE; GET THERE, YOU HUNGRY PIG!

"I would like this car better if it didn't remind me of Walden," Annie murmured without one single giggle.

"You still like it because it's cute," Bloom disagreed, and he was right. But Annie was having a hard time. They'd already dealt with so much. Trolls. Miss Cornelia's abduction. Walden. Bugbears. How could they deal with more? As if he read her thoughts, Bloom whispered, "It will be okay, Annie. We'll rescue them all."

"And we'll survive?" she whispered.

"Of course we are going to freaking survive!" Eva yelled, waking up Jamie who had fallen asleep. "For brounie's sake, Annie. Don't be such a doubting dork."

But Annie didn't know how *not* to be a doubting dork.

"I'm just being realistic," she said, flushing.

"Realism gets you nowhere," SalGoud said. "You've just got to believe."

They drove through the countryside on narrow highways as late day became early night and then middle night. The little pig GPS flyers oinked out directions. Eva fell asleep, snoring heavily, and Johann joined her. Annie nestled herself in between Bloom and Jamie and strangely, felt safe.

Jamie, however, was silently freaking out. He didn't trust a magical GPS system and was totally terrified that the Snatchers would find them even though both Annies and Johann's giggles had stopped and their polka dots were 100 percent gone. And who was this Secret Society, actually? And those books? How did someone know enough about Annie that they could write books about her?

Annie stirred in her sleep and then jolted awake.

"What is it?" Jamie whispered.

"I had—I dreamed I was falling." Annie stretched her arms over her head. "It's . . . it's not a big deal."

They both kind of felt that it was, indeed, a big deal, but neither of them said so. They were both far too polite.

"Are you stressed about meeting your grandparents?" Jamie asked.

Annie realized she was sort of wringing her hands together. She tucked them into her pockets instead and said, "That and everything. I worry we won't be able to . . ."

She didn't want to say that she was terrified that they wouldn't be able to save the elves, because she didn't want Bloom to doubt her. Plus, when you say your fears, that somehow makes them more true.

"I keep wondering which one of us will go missing next," she said, fidgeting with her thumbnail. "Or get spots."

There was an awkward silence. Annie imagined that both Bloom and Jamie were frantically hoping, *Not me. Not me.*

"Do you ever think," Annie asked, "what the point of it all is? If we fight the Raiff and manage to save Miss Cornelia and the elves, do you think that will be the end of it all? Will we be safe? Will Aurora?"

"Even if we aren't . . . even if Aurora isn't . . . It's still worth it, you know, because to not fight . . . to not try . . ." Jamie's words trailed out.

"Would make us as bad as him?" Annie suggested.

Jamie exhaled. "Exactly."

Just a little bit later three tiny, winged pigs flew out of the heating vents and into the car announcing, "Oinky Oink Oinkki Oink. Snort."

"Huh?" said Eva, waking up and rubbing her eyes.

"We are here!" the pigs announced in heavily accented English.

They then disappeared back into the heating vents, and who knows where else, as SalGoud steered the car up a tiny drive that ascended a hill. A large Georgian house with two small strips for parking was all lit up and glowing—welcoming.

"Is this it?" Annie whispered, unbuckling so that she could lean forward and stare out the window.

"The pigs say so and they've never gotten me lost before,"

Johann said, stretching and yawning. "Ah, and it's nice to not be giggling anymore."

Jamie expected Annie to agree, but she wasn't really saying anything. She seemed paler than normal and a little shaky around the edges.

"According to MagicVacationAdviser, it is the number one hotel or bed-and-breakfast in the Doolin area, known for being a "model B and B experience, full of charm and character, surrounded by grassy hills and views of the sea . . . One can spy the distant Cliffs of Moher from the dining room where the wine selection is exquisite. The appetizer selection—"

"Enough, SalGoud. Please . . . ," Annie said quietly. "Thank you, but I'm just . . . I'm not . . . Sorry. I don't mean to be rude."

Jamie opened his mouth, ready to see if she needed anything, but she bolted out of the car, leaping over Bloom's legs rather gracefully.

Bloom's surprised face turned to Jamie. "Well, I guess she's ready, then."

Annie strode up the grassy bump that separated the two parking areas. Modest spotlights lit up the smooth, yellow front of the manor house, which was one story but sprawling, with large windows and a curved portion that seemed to house a restaurant. People were dining inside, seated at nice tables with white linen tablecloths spread over them. The seven short yellow chimneys that she counted quickly felt sort of impressive, she reasoned. She didn't stop to savor the moment, though, because inside her chest was the thought beating away at her, *My grandparents live here.*

They were the first relatives she would ever meet. At least that she remembered. She must have met her mother and father, but she couldn't remember them at all.

"It will be fine," she said to herself. "And if it isn't fine . . . Well, I've dealt with un-fine before."

And she had. In so many foster homes. So many times.

Three long stone steps led up to the front door. To the left, on another rolling hill was a bench, also lit up with a spotlight, and beyond that the ruins of a square tower castle claimed the area. She'd always imagined castles to be bigger, but it was still impressive and foreboding, perched at the highest point. She could almost imagine well enough that she thought she spotted archers at the windows, arrows pointed, ready to thwart invaders.

She shook the image away as the others tromped up the hill behind her.

"Wait up, Annie." Eva snorted, huffing. "My legs haven't woken up yet."

But Annie didn't want to wait. She didn't even want her friends to be with her. She wanted to do this alone.

"Stay here," she said, turning around, spreading out her hands to make them stop.

"What?" Jamie asked, coming to a halt.

"Just stay here, please. I need to do this myself." Her heart raced.

"I don't think that's a good idea, Annie," Bloom began, but Annie turned back around, ignoring him even as she felt bad about it, and pushed open the manor house's front door.

The reception room had two doors leading out. One, immediately to her right, led to the restaurant where the happy chinking sounds of glasses settling onto tables and silverware meeting plates filled the air. The other door seemed to lead to the bedrooms and was situated right next to a broad, heavy wooden reception desk. Upholstered chairs, stuffed grandly, were scattered about, and a large table full of flyers advertising things to do in the area dominated the room. Across a wall hung a large ancient-looking mirror. A huge fireplace, framed in granite, sat below a thick mantel that held two huge stuffed buzzards and an assortment of books, including the Time Stopper graphic novels.

Annie resisted the urge to touch the books and flip through the pages. They were all about her. Or a version of her. So strange . . . She checked her reflection in the mirror. She hadn't even combed her hair. She was hardly presentable enough to meet her grandparents for the first time. She nervously pulled her fingers through the limp strands of hair, trying to straighten it out.

"Ah . . . You've seen the mirror, then, have you? As old as

the castle, it is. There's tales that the mirror is one of the first ever created, but you know how tales are . . ." The voice ended in a hearty, knowing chuckle.

Annie turned quickly, knocking her hip into the table, which was so solid it didn't even move. The voice belonged to a woman, a tall woman with thick silver hair braided and then balanced on the top of her head. The braid defied gravity and stood straight up toward the ceiling. Annie's mouth dropped open.

"It takes a lot of hair spray to get it just so," the woman said, smiling. She zipped up her green fleece vest and eyed Annie. "So, will you be needing a room for the night? Are your parents staying here?"

Annie remembered her manners. She reached out her right hand. "I'm Annie."

The woman took her hand and shook it. "And I am Aislinn Tullgren. It's a pleasure to be meeting you."

"The pleasure is mine." Annie remembered to say the right things, the polite things, but her hand trembled and the woman seemed to notice.

She cocked her head and didn't release Annie's hand. "You've much magic running through you, don't you, lass?" She turned Annie's hand over and examined the palm. "So much magic and so unused . . . It's ready to overflow at any second. Do you have a hard time taming it?"

Annie was so taken aback that she didn't know how to respond. "Yes . . . no . . . I . . . ," she sputtered and resisted the urge to take her hand away from her grandmother. “I only . . . just . . . I just . . . I didn’t realize that I was magic until recently . . .”

The woman’s eyes drooped at the corners the tiniest bit, in the same exact way Annie’s did.

“I . . . um . . . I draw things and then . . .”

“Do they come out of the paper? Alive?” The woman’s voice lowered to a whisper. “Sorry. We have some regular people in there—non-magical.” She motioned toward the restaurant. “Will you be needing a room, lass?”

“Yes . . . I think so.” Annie pondered the woman who had suddenly tensed up.

She released Annie’s hand and turned her back to her. “Are you from America?”

“Yes.”

“Whereabouts in the States?”

Annie didn’t want to lie. But she didn’t want to say. “New England.”

“Anyplace in particular in New England?”

“Maine.”

The woman’s shoulders began to twitch. “What did you say your last name was?”

“I don’t think I did.” Annie watched the woman grab a room key. But the woman didn’t turn around again. Did she know? Did she figure out who Annie was?

“Ah, well, I need it for the records, dear.” The woman’s

voice had gotten high, raised a whole octave. She was nervous. She knew. She had to know.

"Nobody," Annie said. "I am Annie Nobody."

The woman's right hand pressed a yellow button. The restaurant door and the door to the rooms slammed shut, locking without anyone touching them.

"Wait . . . What?" Annie sputtered out as the two giant buzzards leaped from the mantel above the fireplace and snatched her arms in their talons. They flapped their wings, going airborne toward the ceiling, which had opened, giving way to the star-filled night sky. "Wait?! What?"

"No vacancy!" her grandmother yelled below her, waving, still holding the room key. "Please go away now and don't come back!"

The cold air whooshed against her face as the buzzards whisked her up and away from the manor house and closer to the old, deserted castle. They flew over Eva, Bloom, Jamie, Johann, and SalGoud, who began shouting and running after Annie and the birds. Annie struggled at first, but then realized she was much too high to be able to drop down safely.

Bloom notched an arrow on his bow.

"No! Don't!" Jamie yelled. "She's too far up. They can't drop her."

And the birds just kept flying; it was not graceful, nothing like soaring eagles, but more of a lumbering sort of flight. Annie didn't know if she should close her eyes or open them as they soared past the ruined castle and toward a herd of cows, all staring up at her with big moony eyes.

The buzzards started to descend, gradually getting lower. And then just as they were ten feet or so above the cows, they let her go. Annie tumbled to the ground, not making a sound until she landed—oomph—in a cow patty. Well, only her left foot, but it was enough.

"Uck!" she yelled, trying to scrape the cow dung off her shoe and onto a rock as the cows watched and the buzzards flew off. "Uck. Uck . . . Uck . . ."

The closest cow turned her head toward Annie and mooed.

"I'm not mad at you," Annie said, satisfied that most of the bad-smelling substance was gone from her shoe. "It's just smelly. I know it's a natural part of the digestive cycle and everything. It's—yeah . . . Wow." What just happened hit her, the realization grasping her heart with a horrible sadness. "My grandmother just threw me out of the house. She didn't even say hi. Not that I was expecting a hug or anything. Only Miss Cornelia hugged me. Ever. It's just—I was . . . Wow."

Eva bellowed her name from beyond the fence.

"Wow," Annie repeated. "I'm talking to a cow." She nuzzled the heifer on her nose. "No offense. You're a very good listener."

Eva yelled her name again and added, "YOU BETTER NOT BE DEAD OR I WILL KILL YOU!"

"I'm not dead!" Annie yelled back, but Eva didn't answer. She might not have heard Annie, whose voice, even when she was yelling, was never as loud as Eva's.

Annie gave the cow one more fond pet. It followed her as she weaved her way around the cow patties and back toward the manor house. The other cows trailed behind them, and they skirted the outside of the castle. Annie kept glancing up at the dark rock walls, partially covered with ivy, and the gaping holes where the windows once were. She swore she could almost smell meat cooking and hear laughter, but they were just memories of the past, she assured herself. Weren't they?

Finally, she got to the fence and gate. Bloom had climbed the fence and hopped over, while Eva was trying to pick the lock. He rushed to Annie, scooping her up in his arms and inspecting her. There . . . there was a hug . . . a real hug . . . She may not have family, but she had friends. Friends could be even better than family, couldn't they?

"What happened? Are you okay?" Bloom's ears twitched as his questions rushed out.

Annie did her best to answer them as the others listened through the gate. Finally, Eva managed to pick the lock and they all slipped through, the cows trying to follow behind.

"Um . . . Guys . . . What about the cows?" Jamie asked as the cows barreled through the hole, one after another after another, all suddenly silent as if they were afraid that mooing would hinder their escape.

"We should free the cows!" Eva bellowed. "They are prisoners here."

"They are cows," Johann said dismissively.

"PRISONERS!" Eva insisted. She left the gate open and dared them all to shut it.

The cows meandered through, following them back to the manor house. One of them expelled some gas.

"My kind of cow," Eva said, slapping its rump. "I name you Eva the Cow of Glorious Glory."

The cow expelled some more gas, which inspired Eva to dance around singing a Magical Toot song that she explained was known to all dwarfs since they were born, taught at the cradle and so on. But none of the others were listening (except Johann, who recited the Irish dwarf version, which was much naughtier) because Annie had just been evicted by buzzards via her grandmother and that was kind of a big deal.

"Not kind of," Bloom corrected Annie. "It's a really big deal."

"We should probably have a plan before we go back in there," Jamie said as they stared at the front door. All the shades in the restaurant had been pulled down.

"They had my books," Annie said, thumping to the ground next to a cow. "They had them all lined up on the mantel in between the buzzards. They were like prized possessions or something."

Jamie hopped forward. "SalGoud, can you check on the

MagicalVacationAdviser website and see if it says anything about the bed-and-breakfast owners being writers?"

SalGoud whisked out his phone.

Annie wandered over to the manor house and began peering into the windows, trying not to stomp on any bushes or plants.

"What are you doing, Annie?" Jamie asked.

"Trying to see in. Can someone give me a boost? This window over here is . . . Annie grabbed the edge of the window and was sucked right inside.

"What the heck!" Eva bellowed.

Bloom was the first one over, and the moment he grabbed the windowsill he, too, was sucked inside with a great squelching noise.

Eva rushed right after him even as Jamie hollered for her not to get too close, that it wasn't safe. SQUELCHING SQUASH. Eva's feet flapped for a moment as if she were struggling. The wall seemed to open up somehow and suck them right through, headfirst. No, Jamie realized that wasn't how it seemed at all. It was more like the wall of the manor house stayed solid, but all the molecules moved and blurred somehow just as they were sucked through—like they were being zoomed up by a giant invisible vacuum nozzle.

SalGoud stepped softly toward the area, investigating even as Johann charged ahead, sword in front of him. The dwarf took a wild whack at the side of the building, and his sword flew out of his hand and vanished—*floop*—right into the wall.

"Hey! My sword! Nobody takes a Broadsword's sword, you trolls!" And he hit the wall with his fist.

A moment later he was gone. SalGoud turned to say something to Jamie, and then it was as if his left foot was getting sucked up behind him. He staggered, left leg now straight and backward. Jamie lurched forward and grabbed SalGoud's hand. "Hold on!" he commanded.

SalGoud's face twisted with concentration. "I'm trying. As Yoda says in the original Star Wars trilogy, 'Do. Or do not. There is no try.' Or something? Right?"

In the next instant, SalGoud was gone. His hand ripped out of Jamie's clutches. Jamie staggered backward, giving himself some distance between the house and his own body, which he definitely did not want to get sucked up and transported somewhere.

Because that was what had happened, wasn't it? One after another, the children had been sucked away. Jamie ran back down to the car and opened the trunk. He had to be prepared. He had to save them from—from whatever or whomever—Annie's grandparents? He had to hurry, but he had to be ready.

But for exactly what? A giant invisible vacuum?

No, he decided. He wouldn't even go that way. He'd try a direct approach to the front door. He wasn't magic. They wouldn't smell it on him or whatever. The Snatchers hadn't even thought he was a threat or worth snatching. So . . . he would use that lack of magicalness and take them by surprise.

He scooped up some loose money that had fallen out of Eva's pockets. He patted his hair into shape as best as he could, and tried to straighten his shirt and jacket and get dust off them.

"There," he said, trying to give himself a pep talk, "so human. I am so completely human. No troll blood. No magic. Just human."

He headed off toward the house, carrying Eva's suitcase with him and his own knapsack. He had decided that a suitcase seemed the most normal, plus Eva had packed a lot of weapons. He was hoping he wouldn't need them, but you never know.

The front door was still shut and a sign had been flipped around to read CLOSED. He rang the bell anyway. It buzzed like a swarm of angry bees. He was sure it wasn't an actual swarm of angry bees . . . was it? No . . . no . . . of course not, he told himself.

A moment later, a man's lilting voice sang through a speaker. "Why, hello and welcome to Ballinalacken Castle Hotel and the Clover Inn. How may I help you?"

"I'm—I am looking for a room." Jamie cleared his throat, deciding to keep it simple.

"You are, are you?" the man's voice said slowly. "May I ask you a series of questions?"

"Of course." Jamie shifted Eva's suitcase to his right hand.

"Are you fond of pigs?"

"I—I'm fond of all animals really."

"Where did you hear of our fine establishment?"

"The Internet," Jamie lied.

"What's your reason for visiting Ireland?"

"I'm—ah—" Jamie stumbled for a bit. "I am hoping to do some sightseeing. I've always heard how beautiful it is. I thought I might hike to the cliffs . . ." He couldn't remember the cliffs' name, and faltered for a moment, but it didn't matter. The door swung open and a smallish-size man met him. The man's face was finely chiseled with thick brows low over piercing, dark-brown eyes that somehow managed to be both intimidating and kind all at once. He had a widow's peak in the middle of his forehead, just as Annie did, and the uniformity of his features reminded Jamie so much of Annie that he must have gasped.

The man lunged forward, grabbing Jamie by the shirt, whisking him inside and slamming the door behind him. "What is it?"

Jamie couldn't exactly say, *You look just like Annie*, but he didn't want to lie. He decided on, and said, "I thought I heard something."

The man launched himself back on the front steps, looking to the left and right while taking the suitcase that Jamie had dropped. He hurried inside again, and stood a mere inch or two away from Jamie. "What sort of something?"

"A vacuum sort of sound." Jamie decided to be as close to the truth as possible. "Like a swooshing, squelching kind of noise. Sorry. I am sure it was nothing."

The man petted Jamie's back and said, "Of course it is. Of course, probably just a housekeeper vacuuming up the rubbish from unwanted guests. I mean unruly guests. I mean messy guests. You know what I mean . . ."

He led Jamie over to the big front desk. Jamie eyed the buzzards on the mantel. You couldn't tell they had whisked Annie off less than an hour ago. They were motionless, still, and very stuffed looking.

"Ah! You're admiring Odin and Thor, are you?" The man smiled at Jamie and his smile was dazzling—full of charm, lightening his face the same way Annie's always did. "They're my wife's favorites. Beautiful boys, they are."

Jamie agreed, frantic inside about where the others might be, but he managed to remain composed as he paid for his room and asked about the cliffs and other things he thought real American tourists would ask about. To his relief, the innkeeper didn't say one thing about Jamie traveling alone. Just as he was being handed the key, an older woman with an upright braid began escorting some diners out of the restaurant.

"I'll just be taking you to your car," she said, shooting the innkeeper a knowing look, "while my husband helps the young lad here. It gets dark out there, and I wouldn't want you to twist an ankle or stumble about." She held the door open. The innkeeper mouthed the words "be careful" as she went out the door, and she gave him an "okay" sign.

The innkeeper man coughed awkwardly. "Did you see that, did you?"

"Is that your wife?" Jamie asked.

"It is! It is! A lovely woman. Lovely." He stepped out from behind the desk. "Very cautious, she is. Very considerate of her guests."

Unless she's having them escorted away by buzzards, Jamie thought.

"What was that?" The innkeeper turned around. "Did you say something?"

"No!" Jamie's heart froze. Could Annie's grandfather read minds? He pointed at the books on the mantel between the buzzards. "That's a lot of books!"

The man's smile came right back and Jamie's heart beat again. He resembled Annie so much when he smiled. Only Annie didn't have wrinkles or gray hair or such thick eyebrows . . . But still . . . Annie's grandfather skipped over to the books. Actually, it was more of a hopping step.

He pulled out the first one. "I wrote these books."

Jamie's mouth dropped open.

Mr. Tullgren laughed. "I see you're surprised, aren't you, that an innkeeper such as myself could also be a graphic novelist? But it's true. I love to draw, I do. And stories? Well, every Irishman loves stories," he teased, winking at Jamie. He handed him a book. "Would you like to be borrowing it?"

"I'd love it," Jamie said, clutching the book in his hands even as Mr. Tullgren hauled Eva's suitcase up the three red-carpeted steps to the hallway behind the entry room. The hallway didn't lead straight back, but went to the right and the left. The left way, Mr. Tullgren explained, was to the bar and a back way to the restaurant. The right turned a corner and led to the guests' rooms. Jamie searched for signs of Annie or the others as they walked, even hoping for a glance of the Golden Arrow, but all he saw were carpets and big, white-painted wooden doors with ancient locks, gilded mirrors, antique settees and desks in alcoves, and overstuffed chairs. He didn't know how he would ever find anything here.

Behind one door, it sounded like a group of dwarfs was playing ring-around-the-rosy.

"That lot had a bit too much at the bar," Mr. Tullgren said knowingly as they passed, giving Jamie another happy wink.

A few doors away came the sound of a woman crying. "Our resident ghost, Colina Farrela O'Brien, a woman in white. She was married here, but her groom ran away. Killed herself on the spot. She's up at the castle sometimes, but at night she tends to go back to what would have been the honeymoon suite, crying away and waiting for him. Poor thing. We'd exorcise her and send her off to another realm, but she refuses. Plus, she likes to do the dishes."

Jamie's cheeks sort of sucked in, and Mr. Tullgren laughed.

"Just kidding. Just kidding."

They turned a corner and passed a couple of doors before he announced, "Well, then, here's your room, young James. I hope you'll find it to your liking."

The door opened to a poshly carpeted room with two giant beds. Huge drapes covered a window. Striped wallpaper in varying hues of yellow covered the walls.

"There you go, then!" Mr. Tullgren said, turning to leave.

Jamie's hand shot out before he could stop it. "Sir . . ."

Mr. Tullgren's face retained its pleasant aspect. "Yes?"

"I've—I've always wondered where authors get their ideas for their stories," Jamie sputtered out.

"Oh!" Mr. Tullgren said brightly. "People do! People do. That's quite normal. Nothing to feel odd asking about."

"Thank you for lending the book to me. It looks amazing." Jamie pretended to study the cover, but felt totally fake doing it. He asked again, "Where did you get the idea for it? I mean, it seems so incredibly imaginative."

"There are all sorts of things in this world that spark the imagination." Mr. Tullgren sat on the edge of the bed, crossing his legs politely at the knee. "But this book was inspired by my own granddaughter."

"Really?" Jamie perked up. "Is she here? Can I meet her?"

"Oh . . . no . . . She is long lost." Mr. Tullgren sighed, staring straight at Jamie.

"I'm sorry."

"As am I . . . These books . . . They are . . ." His hand fluttered about as if the words he was looking for were floating in the air somewhere. "They are my imaginings of her life, if her life could have continued. With magic thrown in, of course. Not that magic exists . . . Obviously."

"Obviously," Jamie repeated.

The man stared at him, long and intense, as if he were indeed trying to see inside Jamie's brain. Jamie thought about ice cream. Mint chocolate chip ice cream.

Mr. Tullgren sighed, smiling, and stood back up. "You seem like a good lad, Jamie. I hope you'll enjoy the first book and your stay here. You have big plans for tomorrow?"

"I was—um—thinking of doing some exploring . . . Maybe seeing the cliffs." Jamie flustered about, moving Eva's suitcase a bit closer to the wall so it wouldn't block Mr. Tullgren's path to the door. There had to be a way to get some more information out of him. Somehow . . . He just had to think of it. "This is an amazing place. And that castle. Wow!" He cringed inside. He sounded so fake. "It's so cool. Do you own that, too?"

"It's been in the family for centuries. As has the house. The castle is in disrepair, you know. We're trying to raise some funds to renovate it, put the floors back in at least, and a roof." Mr. Tullgren helped Jamie remove his backpack. "It's locked, but I bring tours up every afternoon around five if you'll be liking to join us tomorrow after your adventuring."

"I'd love to." Jamie walked behind Mr. Tullgren, setting his pack on the bed. "Does it have a dungeon or anything?"

Mr. Tullgren laughed. "Not like you'd be imagining, I'd say. The house has some secret rooms, though, corridors that lead to nowhere. It's a bit like life, this house."

"How so?"

"You never know where it will take you. What you'll find. That's why books are better. You've got your heroes and your villains. Your story moves forever forward, never stalls out, and when you get to the end . . ." He let his sentence dangle and his face looked horribly sad, like he almost might cry.

"And when you get to the end?" Jamie prodded.

"That's when you write the sequel!" Mr. Tullgren gave a Santa Claus–style laugh and shut the door behind him, calling out to Jamie that he wished him a good night, and he was gone.

Jamie decided to wait a few minutes to make sure that Mr. Tullgren wasn't lurking about outside. He didn't seem like the kind of man who would lurk, but he also didn't seem like the type of man who would be okay with his wife snatching away his own long-lost granddaughter and dumping her in a field full of cow poop.

He pulled out an extra ax from Eva's backpack and placed it on the bed and then hopped up there with the book that Mr. Tullgren had given him. The entire room smelled clean, like cinnamon and Christmas trees. The bed was soft enough that he half longed to plop down on it and go to sleep. Maybe it could all be a big dream. But it wasn't. He knew that. So, instead, he opened the book and checked his watch. He would read for ten minutes. That was all.

The book began with character images and little bios beneath them. Jamie sucked in his breath. The likenesses weren't perfect, but they were close enough.

AVA: The dwarf girl who passes out whenever there is danger.

TREE: The last elf who doesn't know how to be an elf, constantly doubting his abilities.

SGGATSLEAHCIM: The stone giant with the heart of gold, love of quotes, and hatred of violence.

MISS AMELIA: The Time Stopper whose fading powers and guilt make her as much a liability as a help.

Jamie paused at that. He would never imagine Miss Cornelia a liability. Mr. Tullgren obviously didn't like her much. He wondered why. Maybe he blamed her for the Purge and the battle with the Raiff, maybe for his son's death. There was no Jamie in the list of characters, no boy with dark skin, nobody raised by trolls. But everyone else? They were all there, just with different names.

He wasn't sure what to think about it. He flipped into the book and saw a section where Annie nails the Corvus Morrigan to the earth. In real life, Jamie had been there. In the book, he wasn't. But how did Mr. Tullgren even think to write this? It was so close to being real. He flipped to see when it was printed. Three years ago.

"Wow," Jamie murmured, flipping through the pages again. "Just, wow."

He came across an image of a woman standing inside the walls of a castle. Her hair billowed out behind her and she was sobbing. A golden arrow with a red feather notched at its end was on the wall above her, and archers stood at all the windows. A beheaded man lay at her feet.

An arrow.

It had to be the one they were looking for. It made sense that it would be in the castle, all locked up and protected. Wait. But then why would Mrs. Tullgren have the buzzards deposit Annie so close to it? Maybe she didn't realize that was why Annie was here? But why wouldn't they want Annie to be here in the first place? He stood up. He couldn't figure it out. And he couldn't just stay on the bed forever, looking for clues in a book that didn't have the whole story right, could he?

"I am going to look for them," he announced to the room. "And if I can't find them, I'm going up to that castle and get the Golden Arrow and the bow and I'll go save the elves and Miss Cornelia myself. You can be human or troll or whatever and still do good. I know it. Right?"

The room did not answer.

"There are no snakes in Ireland," Johann kept repeating. He paced around in a small circle, rubbing his head with his hand.

"So then, these are not snakes." Bloom swept his flashlight around the small dark room into which they had all been deposited.

As he did, the slithery creatures jumped back and away from the light, retreating into the shadows in the corners of the room that seemed to be made of mirrored glass.

"I think they have wings," Annie whispered, rubbing at her head, which she'd fallen on.

"Wings on snakes! That is offensive. That's like—that's like—I don't even know . . ." Eva snorted. "It's just wrong!"

She smashed her ax into the floor and started to do a cranky dance, swearing the whole time and sort of, basically, stomping around in a circle. Johann joined her.

"Ancient dwarf ritual," he said.

Annie worried about the snakes themselves and gestured toward the floor, past the dancing dwarfs. "Do you think they'll attack us?"

SalGoud took Bloom's flashlight and moved it quickly, back and forth across the closest winged snakes. They were hissing and baring their fangs. It looked like the remains of a ripped-apart shirt was scattered among them. "Yes."

"And they haven't because?" Annie asked.

"Too many? The flashlight? They like to scare their prey first? There's a lot of reasons," Bloom said.

"And none of them good." Johann stopped dancing. "What say you? We just start killing them?"

"They haven't actually hurt us yet. 'Blessed are the peacemakers,'" SalGoud misquoted nervously, "'for they shall inherit the earth.'"

"Unless they die first," Eva grumbled.

"Yes, there's that," SalGoud agreed and kept moving the flashlight back and forth even as one of the winged snakes slithered behind them, unnoticed.

"And what about Jamie? Do you think he'll come through the wall, too?" Annie asked, turning around to look. The mirrors stayed solid. "How did that even happen? A giant vacuum?"

"Magic," Eva said. "Duh."

Sometimes Annie really wished Eva wouldn't answer questions. She pressed her hands against the mirror, searching for a trapdoor or something, but the surface was so smooth and the room was so dark except for where SalGoud shone his light. "SalGoud, could you swing the light over here? Maybe there's some sort of way out."

"It's a prison room. There ain't going to be a way out." Eva hauled her ax up out of the floor.

"Maybe you could hack a hole through the floor," Annie suggested, trying not to be annoyed.

"Maybe I could hack one through your head," Eva countered, which was mean even for Eva.

"Is anyone else feeling—irritable?" Bloom asked. "I mean, Eva's always cranky, but are you feeling crankier than normal, Eva?"

"Of course, I'm feeling crankier. We're trapped in a freaking mirror room. You probably love it, Mr. Pretty Pants Elf, but the rest of us don't need to be seeing our own faces all the time. Plus, these winged snakes."

"They are not snakes!" Johann insisted, trembling. "There are no snakes in Ireland."

"Just because you are *from* Ireland doesn't mean you know everything *about* Ireland," Eva countered as Bloom turned his attention to SalGoud.

SalGoud shone the flashlight toward the snakes again. "I must admit that I, too, am cranky."

This stopped Eva. "He never *is* anything. He's stony and quotey. SalGoud, you do not get cranky."

"Don't tell me what I get, Eva," SalGoud countered, shining the flashlight directly in Eva's face.

She blinked wildly and hard. "You are blinding me, you giant stone poop."

"I am not a piece of poop! Also, you said 'ain't' before. You know that's not proper." SalGoud frowned. He never frowned. He pointed the flashlight right at Eva's face. "Not. Proper. At. All!"

Eva stepped forward, swinging her ax. "I will show you what's proper."

"According to Frederick Douglass, 'Man's greatness consists in his ability to do and the proper application of his powers to things needed to be done.' "

"What are you freaking quoting about? You make no sense! You never make sense!" Eva blasted back.

Annie's scream broke the standoff.

"What is it? What is it?" Bloom rushed toward her, bumping into her, and she fell on the floor.

"The snakes!" Annie yelled, batting them off her hair. "Everywhere. They're everywhere."

"SalGoud! Light!" Bloom yelled, but at that same moment he seemed to remember that he could make light himself. A glowing ball shot out of the palm of his hand followed by another and another, each hovering over one of the children's heads, encasing them in a dome of illumination.

Eva bellowed, her ax slicing through the air and cleaving a winged snake in half even as the other snakes retreated out of Annie's hair and into the corners of the room. The room erupted into confusion as Annie kept stomping her foot up and down. Half an attached snake flailed in the air as she moved. The fangs were still sunk into her jeans and the skin beneath.

Eva slapped Bloom on the head. "You just remembered? JUST remembered? What kind of elf are you?"

"A bad elf." Bloom's face showed he was almost crying. "I'm a bad elf, all right?"

Annie staggered toward him. "You are not bad. You're

just learning. That doesn't make you bad." Her own voice sounded like crying. "You are good. You are. I promise you are."

Eva scowled and turned to SalGoud and Johann. "What the heck is wrong with them? They are all wah-wah. Bloom should be hitting me back." She kicked Bloom's shin. "Why aren't you hitting me back?"

"What good would it do?" Bloom asked as Annie hugged him. They both started sobbing.

"Okay . . ." Eva backed away. "This is just weird. Like, even for an elf, it's weird."

"People are allowed to have feelings, Eva," SalGoud said.

"No. I'm with her. It's weird." Johann poked at Annie and Bloom, who were clutching each other, crying. A flying snake fell out of Bloom's cloak. Johann stabbed it with his sword and lifted it up to examine. "I think it bit the elf."

"And now they are both crying . . . ," Eva said. "Great."

"What does that mean?" Annie sobbed.

"It means that in one day you've gone from a giggling mess to a sobbing mess. It means these stinking snakes—"

"THEY ARE NOT SNAKES. THERE ARE NO SNAKES IN IRELAND!" Johann screamed.

"Get out of my face, Johann." Eva pushed him back. Snakes slithered out of the way. "And let me freaking finish before I make mincemeat pie out of your face. Now I was saying that these stinking snakes must have some sort of depressing venom that makes a normally okay, tough elf—well, tough for elves—into a whimpering emo mess. And Annie? Well, she's human and wimpy but not usually this bad."

"Annie's not wimpy," SalGoud said, smashing his hand into the mirrored wall. It cracked. "Hey!"

"Do that again, SalGoud," Eva ordered.

"Don't order me around, Eva." SalGoud did it again, smashing his fist against the mirror. "I think this room is affecting all of our moods. I'm so angry. I am never angry." He punched the wall over and over, and the mirror's crack grew larger and larger until it broke completely, jagged pieces of it falling to the floor.

"You did it," Eva said.

"But it's—it's just concrete behind it. Concrete!" Johann growled and lifted his fists to the air. "I HATE BEING TRAPPED!"

"'Hate' is a very strong word," SalGoud said, rubbing at his knuckles. "But I completely agree."

19

The Boy Who Goes Unnoticed

Jamie ended up tucking the book into his backpack, putting the room key in his jeans pocket, and then hiding the ax inside his sweater. It looked peculiar, but he didn't want to have to try to get it out of the pack if he needed it in an emergency, and the way Ireland was going, it felt pretty likely that there was going to be another emergency.

He slowly shut the door behind him and crept down the hall, not exactly sure what he was looking for. Where would you go if you were sucked inside a manor estate? How did the rules of such magic work? Would you stay close by or end up halfway around the world? His gut told him that his friends were probably close by. Weren't they? Maybe it wasn't his gut telling him that. Maybe it was his hope.

If he was magic, he could probably do some sort of locator spell. Instead, he just went around, slowly rapping on walls, checking for secret rooms, anything. He found a corridor that led to a spa. He found stairs that stopped right at the ceiling. He found a room that was full of swirling disco balls. But he couldn't find his friends. Frustration tightened his stomach.

He bumped into Mr. Tullgren just as he was knocking on a section of wall beneath a picture of leprechauns.

A tiny rainbow hovered over Mr. Tullgren's head. He blinked hard at Jamie. Jamie stepped back. Mr. Tullgren smiled.

"Oh . . . this . . . yes . . . um . . ."

Jamie made a pretend surprise face and stuttered out, "You . . . you're magic?" Trying to make it sound convincing, like he'd never realized magic could exist before. He added for good measure, pointing at the painting, "Are you a leprechaun?"

Mr. Tullgren's eyes grew wide and the rainbow above his head sputtered out. "Oh, no! Of course not. Ha! I'm not anywhere near short enough or fixated on gold."

"But, you're magic?" Jamie stepped back, still trying to act surprised when he was anything but surprised. If Mr. Tullgren thought Jamie was okay with magic, that he knew it really existed, he might figure out that Jamie had arrived with Annie and kick him out via buzzard or something. Jamie couldn't risk that.

"I am. But just a magical human. Sometimes wish I was the kind of magic that could made people pick their wedgies in public over and over again, but I'm not that kind of magic either. "

"That's not very practical."

"Practical. No. Fun? Yes." Mr. Tullgren sighed. "But instead I am the kind of magic that draws the future."

"Always the future? The real future?" Jamie asked.

"It is a possibility. The future is truly a bit of a pain in the neck. It likes to flounce around. You think you catch it, but no . . . off it goes in an entirely different direction because some random person or animal enters the picture. You think you have a good handle on everything that's going to happen and then—boom—here comes a talking hippopotamus messing up the order of things. Oh! The stories I could tell you, young James, about the random things that have ruined the future. Such sad things. But sad things are not so good for a boy who has just learned about magic while on his vacation to Ireland. Ha. No. No. No. I won't be doing that to you."

"And what happens in your books' future? What happens to your granddaughter? Does she save the world from the evil demon?" Jamie reached for a book, the last book in the row on the mantel. It had to have some sort of clue, even if Mr. Tullgren's vision of the future wasn't perfectly accurate. He bet the book could at least tell him if his belief that the Golden Bow and Arrow were in the castle was correct.

Mr. Tullgren snatched the book away. "I can't let you see it."

"Because . . . ?" Jamie prompted, but he saw the title, *She Falls with Evil*. It was the same thing that Megan's prophecy had said.

"Because Annie dies. She dies. For real." Mr. Tullgren's lip shook, and he pulled out a huge bottle of Irish whiskey from the inside of a large metal helmet that looked as if it had once encased a knight's head.

Jamie's heart broke in half. "That can't be true," he said vehemently. "I won't let that be true."

"I'm sorry, lad. Most of my readers don't like it either." Mr. Tullgren tipped his head back and took a huge swig, wiping his mouth off with the back of his sleeve as Jamie vaguely paid attention. His heart was racing. There was no way Annie could die. No way. Mr. Tullgren took another swallow of booze. "Don't tell the missus, my boy."

"Don't tell the missus what?" Mrs. Tullgren stood at the door, hands on her hips.

Mr. Tullgren passed Jamie the bottle, which Jamie stashed behind a buzzard. "Nothing, love. Nothing but how much I love you."

She harrumphed and turned, retreating back into the restaurant.

"You can't tell her I've told you, okay? You can't let on that I said the story is true. She's . . . she is terribly upset. Just before you arrived, a girl who said she was Annie Nobody showed up right at my very door! Here. In this very inn! If she was telling the truth, that means . . . That means Annie has been well and truly alive all this time. The missus is in a bit of a shock despite the message we received about a week ago from the Americas saying much the same thing. The Missus . . . ? She's spent the last years since the Purge trying to ensure that Stoppers were kept safe, that Miss Cornelia and the others who are still left on this earth don't fall into the Raiff's evil clutches. She uses my books as a way to reach other Stoppers across cultures to keep everyone on their toes and now—"

"Now this Miss Cornelia is kidnapped?"

"Exactly!" Mr. Tullgren whispered. "And the sphere in Dublin went off, meaning a Stopper was about. The missus had them all accounted for, too. She's got a computer program that keeps track. And then! Poof! Annie shows up here. And if she's alive that means my books aren't just dreams of her, but that she will die again, a horrible, miserable—"

"So where is Annie now? Did Mrs. Tullgren just get rid of her? Her own granddaughter?" Jamie squinted at Mr. Tullgren, unable to contain his anger. "And you let her?!"

One of the buzzards blinked.

"My wife thinks if Annie is here, the Raiff will be close by. She's worried she can't protect her."

Mr. Tullgren dropped the last book back on the mantel. Jamie edged his fingers toward it, but the buzzard clomped its foot right on top of it, wrapping its talons around the cover.

"But the Raiff is in the Badlands," Jamie said. "He can't get here without a Stopper."

"Which he has."

"Miss Cornelia would never let him across," Jamie blurted, realizing too late that he wasn't supposed to know about Miss Cornelia, wasn't supposed to know about the Badlands, or about any of that at all.

Mr. Tullgren eyed him, crossing his arms over his chest. "Who are you exactly, young man? And how would you know what Miss Cornelia would or wouldn't do?"

"I'm the character you didn't see," Jamie said. "The boy who goes unnoticed."

At last, Annie's and Bloom's sobbing ended and a quiet that was just as ominous filled the room of broken mirrors and winged snakes. The concrete walls that SalGoud's fists exposed showed no ways to get in or out, leading them all to believe that the entire room was part of some magical protection spell—a strong one.

Annie and Bloom both felt dizzy, but Annie felt it much more than the elf, which Eva and Johann both blamed on her human blood. Unfortunately, the others were still just as cranky as they had been when they were sucked into the room. It seemed like a fight could break out at any minute. Bloom's light balls seemed to last, even as he bemoaned the fact that it took so long for him to remember how to do it. It didn't matter, though. The light kept them safe from the winged snakes' fangs, but it didn't get them out of there. And they all really wanted out.

"My ax should be strong enough to break these walls," Eva complained. "Maybe you should try your fists again, SalGoud."

The stone giant lifted up his hands, which were still bleeding at the knuckles. In fact, they had bled all the way through the socks Annie had wrapped around them. Using her socks on a wound reminded her of when she first met Tala and had tended to him after a dogfight. She missed Tala so much she felt like she might begin to sob again. Instead, she bit her lip. The dizziness increased.

"Annie, are you okay?" Bloom asked.

"Maybe . . . Does anyone have anything I could draw with?"

"Oh, she's lost it . . . ," Johann said.

"Shut up!" SalGoud said, uncharacteristically, taking a pen from his pocket.

"SalGoud said 'shut up,' " Eva sing-songed. "SalGoud said 'shut up'! And he wasn't quoting it."

"I could have been quoting it," SalGoud said, flustered. "A lot of people say 'shut up.' "

Bloom and Annie, who were no longer cursed with crankiness, gave each other a look of sympathetic understanding.

"That isn't important, no offense. It's totally okay that SalGoud said 'shut up' whether he was quoting it or not. I mean, it's a cruel thing to say, but we are all obviously under some magical influence—a magical influence that is linked to moods . . . Which makes me think . . . ," Annie said as she reached for a pen that SalGoud had taken from his pocket. There was blood on it.

It was a black Sharpie.

"Perfect."

"What are you thinking, Annie?" Bloom prompted.

"That—well, that . . . both this place . . . this trap place . . . and that sphere . . . it involves our moods. Being in here made us cranky and is still making SalGoud, Eva, and Johann cranky. When we were bitten by the snake—just one bite—Bloom, you and I got so sad. Imagine what would have happened if we were bitten more than once?" Annie said as she uncapped the Sharpie and sat on the floor, legs wide apart in front of her. In between her legs she drew a circle.

"We would have died of broken hearts," Bloom said solemnly, guarding her with his light, stalking around her in a circle.

Eva muttered, "Oh, brother . . ."

"Schmaltzy," Johann agreed.

"You are both so ignorant." SalGoud coughed. "Sorry! I just—agh . . . I hate being cranky."

"I think you're past cranky and well into mad," Eva said, tossing her ax between her hands.

"Could you please stop with that? It's making me nervous." SalGoud glared at her.

Johann laughed. "Oh, poor liddle stone giant is nervy wervy."

SalGoud lunged for him, knocking him into the concrete wall with an oomph. They wrestled in the darkness, their light balls halfway across the room. Rushing over, Eva and Bloom broke them up, but not before snakes bit both fighters. Eva hacked the creatures with her ax. They detached and stilled. Immediately, SalGoud and Johann clutched each other, sobbing into their coats.

"Oh this is just—ew—so much baby crying." Eva hit her head against the wall.

Bloom ignored her, making sure that SalGoud and Johann were once again protected by a ball of light. He handed them both a tissue and asked, "What were you trying to say, Annie? Before all this, you were saying something."

She had filled in almost half the circle and opened her mouth to speak but didn't get a chance to actually say anything.

"And what the heck are you doing?" Eva demanded, stomping back over even with the blood running from her forehead.

"I'm trying to make a way to escape," Annie said. "If this place is magic, the only way out is probably magic. Only Bloom and I are that sort of magic, so . . ."

"You can't time stop your way out." Eva shook her head, disgusted. Blood dripped everywhere. Bloom handed her a tissue. Annie would have asked if she was okay but she worried it would make Eva even crankier and scream about how dwarfs are always okay.

"I'm not doing that, Eva." Annie tried to be patient as she filled in the circle. She was about seven eighths of the way through, but the marker was drying out. "My magic has to do with drawing, right? I mean even when I stop time I have to visualize the words in my head. Every time I draw a bunny, a bunny appears."

"So you are drawing a hole . . . ," Eva said.

Johann started wailing.

Eva kicked his shin. "You sound like a banshee. We're trying to have a conversation here."

He began to hiccup sob instead. "You're so mean."

"She's terribly mean," SalGoud agreed in a big sob that was barely understandable.

"I am not mean!" Eva shouted. "I am just cranky!"

"Anyway, what I was saying before," Annie said, pressing down hard with the marker, concentrating, "is that the globe thing that sprayed Johann and me was a mood thing, too. We giggled. Remember? I think it's all connected."

Annie stared at the hole she had drawn. It was just wide enough for SalGoud's shoulders. She stuck her hand through it.

"Whoa . . ." Eva swore under her breath. "That totally worked. Would you look at that."

"Where do you think it leads?" Bloom asked.

"Our doom?" SalGoud sobbed. "A worse place?"

"Everything leads to our doom!" Johann fell down crying and rolled right into the hole.

Annie made big eyes at Bloom.

"I'll go first," he said. "I'll tug once if I need to get pulled back up and twice if all is safe."

He tied a rope to his waist and gave Eva the end to hang onto, just in case. Annie was not fond of "just in cases," but she said nothing as she watched Bloom jump into the hole.

"Two tugs!" Eva announced.

"Are you sure?" SalGoud asked.

"Of course I'm freaking sure." She kicked him toward the hole. "Go down there. You, too, Annie. Hurry. Bloom's light balls are fading."

Indeed they were. Annie followed the scurrying, sobbing SalGoud and lost hold of the rope, landing with a thud in the middle of the hotel's reception area. Eva plummeted down next to her, landing squarely on Annie's lap. They sat in the middle of the room on top of the massive table that was full of pamphlets and papers about tourist destinations.

Jamie stood there at the end of the room, his arm around the sobbing SalGoud. Annie's grandparents stood next to him. Well, she assumed they were both her grandparents. The little man looked so much like her, he had to be.

"Where were the children?" Mr. Tullgren demanded in a whisper that was much scarier than a full-blown yell. He wiped a tear from his cheek.

"I didn't know . . ." Mrs. Tullgren's lips trembled, and she gave up being tough and mean and instead rushed to Annie, engulfing her in her arms. "I'm so sorry, sweet girl, so terribly sorry."

Annie seemed to not know how to respond. For a moment, her arms stayed down at her sides, but then . . . they lifted. She circled them around her grandmother and murmured, "It's okay."

Her grandmother felt soft and smelled of the woods and cooked potatoes. For a second, Annie let herself relax into the hug—a real hug—and tried to forget about the buzzards and the snakes and the cow poop. She sighed. Her grandmother was hugging her . . . Annie!

"She can never stay mad. It's ridiculous," Eva huffed, but even she smiled the tiniest of bits.

"I'm sure you have a good reason for treating your own relative so badly . . . Don't you?" SalGoud asked, sobbing still.

Mr. Tullgren snapped his head up. "You boys need to be doctored. Was anyone else bitten?"

One by one, Eva, Johann, Bloom, and SalGoud confessed they had indeed been bitten, and the Tullgrens snapped into action, sending the buzzards into the night to pick up supplies. Eva, they said, was an easy fix with the magical first aid supplies on hand in the hotel. Mrs. Tullgren created a potion and poured in hot chocolate, which ended up smelling like white sugar cookies. Eva gulped it down, and Jamie wished he'd been cranky if that was the treatment.

Mrs. Tullgren made a lot of excuses about how she hadn't realized the children had been trapped in the room, that she'd been too busy trying to determine if the Raiff was still in the Badlands and so on. At first, Mr. Tullgren wasn't hearing any of it, actively blocking his ears and singing "la-di-da-la," but eventually he gave up, putting his arm around Mrs. Tullgren's slumping shoulders and kissing the top of her head.

"I love her too much to stay mad," he said.

"Not me," said Eva.

"Me, neither." Johann shuddered. "It's not right for there to be snakes in Ireland. I can't believe you put snakes in there."

Bloom studied him. "I thought you said they weren't snakes."

Johann began sobbing again, which made Eva curse and everyone wish the buzzards would hurry back. While they waited, Mrs. Tullgren explained that the Raiff was known to be terrified of snakes, which is why they were set up in the trap room.

"And the emotions?"

"Oh, that's just my added touch." She flushed.

"She's a genius with emotional warfare." Mr. Tullgren beamed proudly, coming back into the room, even though nobody had noticed him leave. He carried a plate of cookies.

"Could you make the dwarfs less grumpy?" Bloom asked.

"Oh, sweet elf, why would I? They are adorable just the way they are." Mrs. Tullgren tweaked Eva under the chin.

"I am not adorable," Eva said, but it was obvious that Mrs. Tullgren's charm was working because Eva smiled with half of her mouth.

Jamie wished that they could just tell them what they were here for, but Lichen had demanded that no adults know about the arrow and bow and rescue mission. He had insisted that the Raiff would know if an adult knew.

The buzzards landed, carrying a massive purple flower in their talons. Mrs. Tullgren thanked them and tossed them dead fish as treats while Mr. Tullgren sprinkled what looked like rainbow pixie dust onto the flower, which suddenly grew to ten feet tall, its tips touching the ceiling.

"Wow . . ." Annie's eyes shone.

"Here, help me," her grandfather offered. He held a yellow crayon in his hand. "Take this and touch the stem. Think of something happy."

Eva started to say something, but Bloom clamped his hand over her mouth and whispered, "Be still, Eva. No snarky comments."

SalGoud slumped into the farthest chair, still sobbing. "Taraji Henson said, 'Every human walks around with a certain kind of sadness. They may not wear it on their sleeves, but it's there if you look deep.' " He coughed. "How could you not know that Annie was alive? That's so mean. She was stuck going from foster home to foster home and not one of them was nice. NOT ONE! She was never loved. Never. Agh . . . It's so sad. So sad."

"Maybe you should have covered SalGoud's mouth," Eva suggested as Bloom's hand dropped.

Both the Tullgrens had horrified expressions, and Annie's lip trembled. She refused to make eye contact with anyone, and the fingers in which she held the yellow crayon seemed to twitch. Her grandfather pulled some more crayons out of his pocket and offered them to her.

"I might not be able to think of anything happy right now," she said slowly.

Mr. Tullgren sighed. "Me, either."

But Mrs. Tullgren's eyes watered and she fluttered up in the air to the top of the center table, scattering pamphlets about the Doolin Cave. "It has nothing to do with *not* loving Annie. It has everything to do *with* loving Annie." She snapped her fingers and Annie began to float, too, drifting toward her grandmother. "We didn't know you were alive until just a few days ago, and even then we couldn't believe it—not really. All that time in the past, we truly thought you were dead. And when the globe alerted us that a Stopper was here and actually in Ireland, well, we didn't think it could possibly be you . . . And even if it were, we couldn't bring you here with us because if you were with us, you'd be in danger."

Mr. Tullgren sighed and added, "It was easier that way."

"Easier that way?" Annie raised an eyebrow. "To just let me flounder out there, to leave me unprotected?"

"Annie, I couldn't—I couldn't feel you," Mrs. Tullgren said.

"Feel me?"

"I usually can feel those I love. Feel their emotions, their hearts beating, their distress."

"Even if you aren't with them?" Jamie asked, excited. It sounded a bit like what happened with him. Sometimes it felt as if others' emotions were his own. Like when his grandmother was angry, even if it wasn't at him, he felt it battering away at his insides. Or when Annie was really scared, Jamie felt that way, too . . . Only different. Lighter and frantic.

"Even if I'm not with them," Mrs. Tullgren said. "And then suddenly I felt Annie. Felt all of her emotions and her fear and her grasping at happiness . . . And my heart . . . my heart . . . it broke . . . When Miss Cornelia sent the arkan sonney to tell us what had happened, about Annie's miraculous return . . . Well, I . . . I was overwhelmed. What had happened to you for so long . . . Those people you lived with . . ." She turned white. "It's hard for a grandmother to deal with."

Annie hovered above the table again.

"Please put me down," she whispered sadly.

"I'm not doing that." Mrs. Tullgren's hand went to her mouth. "You poor thing, you know nothing of your powers, do you? You are so vulnerable to him." Mrs. Tullgren turned to Mr. Tullgren. “See? *See!* I was right! She is totally unprotected!”

Eva bristled. “I will protect her!”

“As will I,” sobbed Johann.

“And me.” Bloom grabbed Annie’s hand and pulled her back down to the ground.

Jamie swallowed hard. He would protect Annie, too. He would. He would protect all of them. He just didn’t know how.

Annie tried to calm her nerves and think happy thoughts as she and her grandfather—her grandfather! Who could believe it!—clutched the yellow crayon, but she had so many questions about everything. About them and their magic, about her dad, their son. Annie knew nothing about him. Nothing about anything.

“Just take the crayon and think of something happy. Then draw that happiness on the stem of the flower,” her grandfather coached as he did that exact thing.

Annie peeked over at his drawing. He had drawn her scrawny arms and too-big eyes and limp hair. She was hugging a man, her grandfather. She was what he thought of when he thought of happiness. Her heart hiccupped a bit and she focused on her own crayon, drawing yellow lines across the green stem. First came the legs, then the body and shaggy waggy tail, and then the face: Tala. Tala made her happy. He always did.

The flowers burst into rainbow-colored raindrops, and Mrs. Tullgren hurried to catch the drops in two goblets. She brought one over to SalGoud, who was still flopped in the big chair by the door, quietly crying, and she took the other goblet to Johann, who was full-on sobbing while curled up under the table.

"Drink," she said calmly. "Drink in the happiness."

Once SalGoud, Johann, and Bloom were cured, Mrs. Tullgren proceeded to worry intensely that the Raiff or his minions would find Annie. Her grandparents' home was the first place he'll look, she had insisted. But she couldn't bear to kick Annie out again, certainly not in the middle of the night. Mrs. Tullgren stalked and paced, fretting while the rest of them watched. Eva had taken residence in the big chair that SalGoud had been in previously, and she started to fall asleep, but her own snoring kept jolting her back awake.

"We should just send you off right now. That would be safest," Annie's grandmother said.

Annie gave everyone a panicked look. If they left now, they wouldn't be able to find the Golden Bow and Arrow. Plus, she'd finally met some relatives—real relatives, her dad's parents. And they were a bit quirky—okay, a lot quirky—but cool. She sniffed.

Mr. Tullgren stood up straight and wrapped his arm around Annie's shoulders. "We will not be sending our granddaughter off into the night. We will soldier up, increase the house's defenses and alarm systems, and she will have a good night's sleep at least. We will decide what to do in the morning." He clapped his hands authoritatively and then rethought it. "Unless, we have a party?"

Mrs. Tullgren's eyes lit up. "A party?"

"Wake up our guests! I think it's time for a celebration!" Mr. Tullgren roared.

A party seemed the exact opposite of what people hiding from the Raiff should do, but Mr. Tullgren explained that it was not what a demon would expect. A demon would expect them to hunker down, to boost up their defenses and security (which is what Mrs. Tullgren was doing), and try to hide. A party, he explained, would throw the Raiff or his minions off, confuse them.

"We would never draw attention to ourselves if the Stopper was here," he explained as he drew a picture of how he wanted the restaurant to look for the festivities. There were trees and lights filling the entire room and tables full of happy faces.

And so it was determined that they would have a party, but Annie still had a big question, which was why the Raiff would even want her now that he had Miss Cornelia.

"She doesn't know." Mr. Tullgren's hand went to his mouth.

"Know what?" Annie asked, but Mr. Tullgren frantically paced away and called for his wife.

"What is it?" she yelled down to him. She was hovering up by the ceiling, installing spikes of garlic to keep any bad vampires away. Sadly, there were no good vampires in Ireland.

"SHE DOESN'T KNOW! CORNY DIDN'T TELL HER!" he shouted.

Annie bristled. Miss Cornelia, it seemed, hadn't told her a lot.

"Oh, dear . . ." Mrs. Tullgren fluttered down. "Let me hold your hand. I need to make sure you don't— Well, people have been known to spontaneously combust when they hear news like this."

Bloom raced to Annie's side. "News like what?"

Mrs. Tullgren took a deep breath and stroked Annie's hand like a frightened puppy. "Annie, my dear. Annie, you are no ordinary child. And I don't mean because you are a Stopper. Your power is strong because you come from many lines of magic. You're the strongest Stopper there could ever be. In your blood, there's my magic and Mr. Tullgren's, plus your father's. Plus . . . well, Annie, the other side of your family is magic, too. Your mother was . . . Well, she was the daughter of a very magical woman. And her grandfather, your other great-grandfather . . . He's . . . There's no easy way to say this, dear. Your great-grandfather is the Raiff." Mrs. Tull-gren petted Annie's hand absently, and stared into her eyes. "He wants you because you are his blood. And if you turned evil, the way the Raiff wants you to, you would be the strongest demon alive. Together you two would be . . ."

"Unstoppable," Annie whispered, stomach clenching. "We would be unstoppable."

The Arrow

All this time, I thought I was supposed to be saving everyone," Annie said bitterly, as the buzzards hung streamers for the Party of Midnight, which is what Mrs. Tullgren decided to call it, "but it turns out that I might be the biggest evil of all . . ."

It hadn't been exactly easy going from the kid nobody wanted to the girl who was supposed to save the world to the girl who may ruin everything by turning evil, but Annie was struggling to maintain her calm. Nothing had been easy about her life; she didn't know why she expected it to suddenly change.

"No wonder everyone wanted to believe I was dead. It would have been easier," she muttered to Jamie.

Blue, green, and yellow paper vines made of cut-leaf shapes and twirls dangled from tree branches that sprang up out of the tables and from the ceiling. Mr. Tullgren clapped his hands, delighted. "Just as I drew it! Do you like it, Annie?"

"Of course," she said, smiling because it was beautiful but also because she wanted her grandfather to be happy.

"You aren't going to be evil at all," Jamie said. "Do you remember the Raiff? Do you remember his eyes, Annie? You are nothing like him."

She wanted Jamie to be right, but she just . . . She was *so* worried. All these emotions twisted up in her head and confused her. Happiness at finding her grandparents (well, the good ones at least) and the feather, worry about failing to find the arrow and bow and not being able to tell them about it, fear of the Raiff and horror over the news that they are related, stress at trying to save Miss Cornelia and the elves. Annie's heart fluttered anxiously. So much stuff was just pounding around in her head that it hurt. She decided that she was just going to have to ignore all of the emotions and instead focus on what they had to do.

"After the party," she whispered to Jamie, "we will all pretend to go to bed, meet up in your room, and go looking for *it*."

She didn't want to say what "it" was out loud. It seemed too risky to say "bow and arrow." Jamie had already told them his idea that it was in the castle, and it made perfect sense to her. Jamie always seemed to make a lot of sense. She smiled fondly at him as he admired the paper trees, vast and brilliant. He was a good friend, the best kind of friend, and she felt so lucky to have him.

Mr. Tullgren blew on a tin whistle and all sorts of creatures and people streamed through the front door, not just hotel guests, but magics who lived in the surrounding town and hills. There were cliff dwellers with rocky hands and algae hair, leprechauns who already seemed tipsy and cantankerous, dwarfs who began arm wrestling upon arrival, several ghosts of kings and queens, a banshee who had tape over her mouth to keep from howling, brounies, shifters, a unicorn, and a few ponies and cats who could talk.

The buzzards began dancing on the table a mere fifteen minutes into the festivities, and Mrs. Tullgren flew mugs of Party Pizzazz Potion and Joyful-to-Jolly Juice around to the guests. Pixies and fairies cavorted in between the paper leaves, and for a moment Annie felt almost content. It was beautiful and good and magical and special.

"Pretend your name is Emily from Canada and you are a nice low-level witch," her grandmother said. "If you don't mind. That should be a good cover."

And so that's what Annie did, introducing herself as Emily from Canada over and over again, even as Eva and Johann began dancing some strange, magical line dance that involved a lot of stomping and hovering. She hunkered in a corner with Jamie and Mr. Tullgren as the fairies began preening Bloom's hair and SalGoud discussed philosophy with a cliff dweller.

"It's lovely." Annie sighed, admiring the party decor and the happiness, then asked her grandfather if their magical community was set up like Aurora's.

"No, we've got no Stopper here, nothing to protect us other than your grandmother's little traps. Most of us who can pass interact with non-magical humans daily. Others hide. There's an acceptance of magic here in Ireland; they call it myth or fairy tale, but it isn't as huge a deal as it is in the States. Magic gets found out and someone will blink hard and wonder, but that's about it," he explained, and when Annie asked why they didn't need a Stopper he added, "We'd love one, but there aren't that many of you, you know. Hardly enough to go around. You are all precious, but few and far between, if you know what I'm saying."

She did. They stood together watching the fiddling and the dancing, the arm-wrestling and then floor-wrestling dwarfs, the banshee and ghosts twirling through the tables in impossible fox-trots and tangos, and the pixies getting tipsy and passing out into the drinks and the stew. Mrs. Tullgren survived it all, too, with a smile plastered to her face but worry in her eyes.

"Annie, you may be thinking of doing dangerous things," her grandfather said after a long pause. "Please don't."

"What do you mean?" Annie asked, untangling a pixie who

had passed out in her hair and gently placing her on a table. She put a napkin over her like a blanket, tucking it in, and wadded up another one beneath the pixie's head for a pillow.

When Annie looked up again, her grandfather had tears in his eyes. "This . . . this is what I mean . . . This kindness . . . I don't want you to lose that."

Bloom sidled over, obviously eavesdropping. "There is no way Annie will ever lose that. It's part of who she is. But what she may lose is her rest. Do you think that we could all head off to bed now?"

"Of course . . . of course!" Mr. Tullgren flushed and called over his wife. Mrs. Tullgren gathered Annie up in her arms, apologizing again for what had happened earlier in the evening. She was unprepared, she said. She was terrified, she added. She had not handled it well.

She walked them all to their rooms and took Annie aside for a moment, fondly touching her cheek. "I will understand if you never forgive me, but I—I am so scared for you. To suddenly have you alive, but then . . . you know that your grandfather writes these books."

"About me."

"About who he thought you might become. But we never thought they could be part of his visionary powers because we thought for so long that you were dead—just dead and gone like your poor mother and so many others." She sighed. "And now that you are alive—the first thing I thought is that maybe those books are prophetic, too, and maybe some terrible things might happen to you. I do not want terrible things to happen to you."

"They already have," Annie said, patting her grandmother's arm. "I'm sure it will be okay."

Her grandmother shook her head. "That is not the sort of thing that a grandmother wants to hear."

Annie bit her lip, feeling a bit sorry, but she had work to do. "Why is the castle locked up?"

"To keep it safe," her grandmother said, eyeing her oddly. "And to keep visitors safe. It needs to be renovated."

And that was the end of the conversation. Her grandmother abruptly whirled around and unlocked the room that Eva and Annie would share. Once they were inside, Annie checked the doorknob.

"She's locked the door," Annie said, disappointed.

"Of course she did," the dwarf said, whisking out her lock-picking tools with a mischievous glint in her eye. "It's a good thing I've got these."

Jamie ended up sharing his room with Johann, which he was not particularly happy about. He didn't trust the dwarf much, plus Johann made a huge mess the moment he got in the bedroom, pulling up the covers on the bed so that it looked more like a nest than a bed, throwing pillows around, and putting the lamp shade on his head for a hat before abruptly falling into a snoring slumber.

"We're supposed to all be meeting up," Jamie told him, shaking his leg.

"Just tell me when the others get here," Johann murmured before he started snoring again.

Jamie glared at him. Then he went in the bathroom and ran the shower so that he wouldn't have to hear the snores. He actually jumped in the shower because he suddenly felt dirty and icky. He wasn't sure if that was from Johann or the long flight and hectic day. He felt much better when he got out, dried himself with a super puffy white towel, and dressed in some clean clothes he had packed. By the time he was done, everyone else was waiting for him in the bedroom.

Annie was sitting on the bed next to Johann's nest of covers. Eva bragged a bit about her door-unlocking skills and then nestled right in there near Annie, pulling a comforter around her.

SalGoud stood by the door, listening for footsteps, just in case the Tullgrens decided to check up on them. Bloom paced back and forth. Jamie stashed his dirty clothes in his backpack and sat in a chair.

Bloom began. "So, where do you think the arrow is?"

"The castle. It has to be," Jamie said. "Did you see how frantic they were when the gate was left open? That wasn't about the cows."

"That's what I think, too. My grandmother acted kind of

sketchy about the castle. I mean—I think we should go now," Annie said nervously. "If we wait, they might hide the arrow or . . . I don't know . . . We should just go now."

Eva flailed about on the pillows. "But the bed is *so* comfortable."

"Dwarf? Are you choosing a bed over a mission?" Bloom demanded.

Her snore seemed to be her answer.

"It's okay." Annie swallowed hard. "We don't need her. Let her rest."

"She'll pummel us if we don't bring her," SalGoud said, but they decided to let Eva rest there anyway. Johann was snoring away next to her. So they were out two dwarfs.

Annie, Jamie, Bloom, and SalGoud gathered up their supplies and snuck out the window, not daring to risk going down the hall and alerting the Tullgrens. The party was still going full tilt in the restaurant. The sound of fiddles and whistles and dancing happiness spilling into the outside air. Annie paused for a moment.

"What is it?" Jamie asked, stopping next to her.

"I just want them to always be happy. I don't want the Raiff to ruin it."

"He won't, Annie," Jamie said as they continued walking toward the castle.

But she wasn't so sure. The Raiff had taken all the elves, had kidnapped Miss Cornelia out of her own home in a town that should have been safe. Whatever his plans were, the

Raiff obviously didn't care how many people or creatures died. She had to stop him no matter how worried her grandparents were about it. She wasn't going to let some demon ancestor of hers ruin the whole magical world.

Magical was the perfect description of the ruined castle on the limestone outcropping above her. It was at least a two-story house that resembled a tower. Holes gaped in the rock walls. They'd once been windows.

"It looks more like a fortress than a castle," Jamie whispered.

She agreed and stormed up the hill to the castle, the cold night wind whisking her hair up off her shoulders and behind her. She imagined she looked like a witch. Bloom and SalGoud caught up with her.

"They relocked the gate," she said, pulling on it.

"No problem." Bloom scaled up with a rope. He tossed it down and pulled each of the others up and over. They landed in the soft grass. There weren't any cows around, but a couple of sheep milled nearby. Something moved in one of the castle's upper windows.

"Did you see that?" Annie's breath came out in a tiny whisper, but the others heard it, stopping still and staring up at where she pointed.

None of them saw anything, but she insisted it had looked like an archer.

"I'm not going crazy from the stress," she said. One of her foster moms used to think that about her when she saw things.

"Of course not." Jamie looped his arm through hers and Bloom got out the flashlights, giving one to each of them. They seemed terribly modern for magical people, but they were all glad to have them, even if just to help avoid stepping in cow patties of unnaturally good-looking cows.

"Why do they call them patties?" Jamie asked. "And not just poop?"

Nobody had time to answer because a great rattling came from their left. Bloom whisked out his dagger and Annie did, too. Jamie didn't even realize she had it. He was surprised by how easily she grabbed a weapon.

"It's just the dwarfs," Bloom said, sighing and heading back to the gate. "Hold on, sleepyheads. I'll haul you over."

"Can't believe you left without me," Eva said, once she and Johann had joined the others. "I should kick you in the neck for that."

"It's not our fault you dwarfs are all about the sleep." Bloom strode off toward the castle, not waiting for anyone.

"I don't think anyone is thinking about Bloom's feelings enough . . . ," Annie said but was cut off by Eva cursing about feelings being ridiculous. She began again. "I mean, we have to save all his people. That's a really huge responsibility, and he already has feelings of doubts and worry about his own abilities as an elf."

Jamie was going to agree with Annie, but Eva slapped her leg and started laughing. "You sound like a guidance counselor. Oh my freaking banshee brains. Feelings."

With that she strode off after Bloom, still laughing. The others followed in an awkward sort of silence. Now that they stood right in front of it, it was obvious that the castle was much taller than they had thought. The castle rose at least four stories high. Vines covered the bottom stones that were gray from age. A huge wooden door, heavy and thick and ancient looking, blocked the entrance, which was on the opposite side of the manor house and the hill. Bloom stood there, staring at it.

"It wouldn't budge," he said. "I tried. I think maybe I should scale the sides and go up a window, then throw down the rope."

"I can't climb no more ropes," Eva grumbled. "Rather just haul myself up."

"Any more," SalGoud corrected.

"Whatever." She harrumphed and kicked the door. The door didn't move. "I think this is a stone giant's job, hate to admit it. Unless I use my ax. Maybe I should use my ax . . ."

"SalGoud?" Jamie asked.

Bloom looked to his stone giant friend. "Have you ever noticed how big SalGoud's bones actually are?"

"Big," Jamie admitted.

"Big? They are like, if you took an elephant's bones and then multiplied their thickness by two. It makes him very strong."

"How strong?" Annie asked.

SalGoud used his right hand to chop the door. It cracked in half.

"That strong," Eva said as they followed him into the castle.

Towering pillars supported thick walls. A chamber overgrown with moss and littered with pieces of crumbled ceilings lay in front of them, and to the right was a staircase, narrow and steep. Their flashlights didn't seem to emit nearly enough light, so Bloom made balls, one after another, illuminating the first floor and the staircase. They searched the chamber of the main floor, doom and dread filling their bones.

"It's a two-stage manor house," SalGoud whispered, "built on a limestone outcropping. That's what the pamphlet said."

"When did you have time to read a pamphlet?" Annie asked.

"When I was sitting in the chair, sobbing, it made me sob more," he admitted. "It belonged to the O'Brien family. They are gone now, all their power just gone. Poor family."

Annie petted SalGoud absently on the shoulder, glad he wasn't crying any longer. That feeling of dread seemed bigger, thicker. She mentioned it, and since they all felt it, Jamie guessed it might be part of the security system her grandmother had set up. Maybe she was manipulating all of their emotions so that the dread feeling would make intruders want to get out of the castle right away and hide. He had to admit that he wanted to do so and was resisting the urge.

"Maybe we should look upstairs," Bloom suggested.

Jamie pointed at the collapsed ceiling. "Is there even an upstairs?"

"There's a stairway," Bloom said.

Bloom led the way up steps so narrow that the children had to climb them sideways, except for Annie who had strangely small feet. They all hunkered at the second-floor landing, balancing precariously on a small piece of remaining stone slab. The rest of the floor was gone.

"This is a bit of a dead end," Annie said. "Should we go straight up to the top of the castle?"

Pointing, she showed them. The other floors above them were completely gone, too, which meant that the shadows or archers she thought she saw at the windows those times weren't real. She had imagined them, she guessed.

Bloom looked utterly defeated.

Eva started back down the stairs. Johann followed her.

"We'll pound some stuff and see if it shows up," he announced.

"Don't pound too hard!" Annie called after them. She had a feeling they could make the whole castle topple if they really got going.

"Maybe I'll go babysit them," SalGoud suggested. "As Chuck Yeager said, 'You don't concentrate on risks. You concentrate on results. No risk is too great to prevent the necessary job from getting done.' "

That left Annie, Bloom, and Jamie balanced on the outcropping of floor at the second-story landing. Annie peered down across the floorless room and then up, before asking, "What do you think, Bloom?"

"I . . ." He cringed, seeming to doubt himself. "I think I can feel it. I mean . . . It feels like there is something powerful and elfin here. But . . . I should see it, shouldn't I?"

"When you say you can 'feel' it," Jamie asked, "do you mean like, feel it in a way that you can find it? Like follow-the-feeling-to-it kind of thing? Don't you think you should use that feather?"

"Of course!" Bloom stashed his dagger in its hilt and took the red feather out of his pocket and let it go. It moved straight through the air, unaffected by wind or gravity. Following it, Bloom took a step forward right into the open air and Annie shrieked.

He was standing in midair.

"Bloom?" Annie's voice squeaked out.

"What the heck is he doing? You ain't supposed to walk on thin air!" Eva hollered from below, rushing so that she was directly underneath Bloom, her arms out to catch him, but he didn't fall.

"It feels solid," he said. "I mean, it *is* solid."

Eva kept her arms outstretched. "I'm not taking any chances."

Jamie stepped forward, testing the floor with his foot. "It's not solid for me."

"It must be enchanted because of the feather," Annie said nervously. "Hurry, Bloom."

"I'll be okay, Annie." Bloom gave her an encouraging thumbs-up, and stepped forward again, one foot after the other, following the red feather. Annie held her breath until he reached the far wall. He touched it with his hands, feeling the stones. The feather scurried into his hair. He didn't seem to notice, his attention totally focused on the wall in front of him.

"What is it? Do you see it?" Johann yelled.

"We really should stop yelling. Someone is going to hear us," SalGoud scolded.

Johann growled at him, but stayed quiet.

"I feel something," Bloom said, groping the stones on the wall. The castle seemed to shake, and suddenly there were archers, real-looking archers at every window. Like the elf, they seemed to levitate in midair.

"Bloom . . . ," Annie whispered.

"See them," Bloom answered.

The archers didn't seem to notice him, but they did notice the others. Two archers turned and pointed their bows at Eva, Johann, and SalGoud.

"Run!" Jamie yelled, "Get outside!"

Jamie rushed down the stairs, meeting up with Eva,

Johann, and SalGoud. They barreled through the castle doors and out into the fields, where the cows surrounded them, mooing protectively.

Bloom reached his hand into what looked like a solid wall and pulled.

"Got it!" he yelled, rushing across the floor, the Golden Bow and Arrow in his hand and the red feather still stuck in his hair.

The archers bowed at him as he passed. "Good tidings, elf. Take what is likely yours. We will deal with the others."

"They are my friends," he ordered. "Do not shoot!"

The elves merely repeated their message. "Good tidings, elf. Take what is likely yours. We will deal with the others."

Bloom stood in front of Annie, stopping, protecting her with his own body and said again, "Do NOT shoot. They are no danger. They are my friends."

"They are not elves and have not the red feather of finding," the archers said and repeated once more, "Good tidings, elf. Take what is likely yours. We will deal with the others."

"They are entranced," Bloom said over his shoulder. He stashed the bow and arrow into his cloak, hiding them.

Annie swallowed cautiously. Something strange was happening inside of her. She could feel a calling, a pull. The feeling of dread expanded and seemed to squeeze at her heart. She crumpled at the waist, reaching out to Bloom.

"Annie?" He whirled around, trying to hold on to her, but she was being yanked up toward the next flight of stairs. Her legs leading the way, straight up and out. "ANNIE!"

"I can't . . . Something is pulling me, Bloom." She cringed. It was like invisible hands were on her ankles. One second later, she was ripped out of Bloom's grasp and zooming through the air, up the staircase.

Bloom came thundering after her, hollering her name as she flew through the darkness, through a door and to the rooftop. But there was no roof, just a ledge. And the door she flew through slammed shut behind her. A moment later, Bloom threw himself against it, trying to rend it open. Annie landed on a six-inch-wide ledge, illuminated by the moonlight and stars. All around her were the rolling hills of Ireland, the Burren, and then the sea. A car zipped down a winding road. She could see Jamie, Eva, and Johann down on the grass. It looked like some sort of force field surrounded the castle, greenish and spherical. They were pounding against it the same way Bloom was battling the door, trying to get back in despite the archers' arrows.

"Annie!" Bloom pounded on the door. "Are you okay?"

She was not okay. She was not. But she couldn't tell him why, not yet.

"Yep. I'll be down in a second. Go wait with the others," she called out.

"What?" Bloom stopped pounding, his voice incredulous.

"Totally fine. Just have to pee, do girl things, I'll be right out."

"Um . . . okay . . . yeah . . ."

Annie finally looked at who was waiting for her up there, looked at him straight on as if she wasn't terrified, as if she didn't want to beg for Bloom to come save her, but she couldn't do that, couldn't put her friend in as much danger as she was in. No way. She refused to be that kind of girl.

Unleashing the Power

The Raiff demon stood at the top of the parapet, waiting. Annie knew it wasn't him, but she also knew that it *was* him—just not his real body. He had somehow materialized there, like a ghost—real but not real. And even in this form he was strong enough to drag her up here against her will. She hated to think how powerful he was in person.

"You aren't here," she said bravely.

"I am and I'm not. My body is still trapped in the Badlands, obviously." He sighed softly. "Miss Cornelia is proving to be a tough nut to crack. Sorry for the cliché. They are tiresome, I know. But my mind and my spirit are indeed here, talking to you, my great-granddaughter." He eyed her. "I see you are not shocked, so they've told you that you are my descendant."

"They have."

"And still you tremble. Do you think I would harm my own blood?"

"Yes. You already have. I know you killed my mother." Unclenching her fists, Annie grabbed the side of the castle's roof wall. It was rough against her fingers. "I don't think you care who you harm."

"Or what." He laughed slightly. "Don't forget the 'whats.'"

"Did you make that force field down there?" Annie asked. "Are you the doom sensation I've been feeling?"

"Of course. Silly questions." He waved them away. "Don't you want to know why I'm here? How I found you? Why I've sought you out?"

"Not really," Annie said, and she wasn't sure if she was lying or not. She knew it couldn't be good, though. Nothing was good right now. Miss Cornelia and the elves were still trapped in the Badlands, her friends were cut off from her, and she was alone with the demon who had stolen all the goodness out of her life. He'd killed her own mother. He'd probably killed her father, too, and now . . . now here she was powerless, stuck on the top of a half-ruined tower castle, shivering in the night sky while he toyed with her. There was no way she'd get out of this. No way at all. This was a demon who didn't care about killing or pain or anything. Just his own wants.

"The hag's prophecy says that you will fall with evil." He looked down to the dark ground below them. Annie peeked over, too. Her friends were banging on the force field. The bow and arrow were still safely hidden. That's what was important. She hoped that the Raiff didn't realize that this was why they were here. He'd said nothing of it. Instead, he seemed focused on creeping her out.

He continued, "I don't think this is what the hag meant. You will not tumble off the top of this ruined castle and die with me on the rocks below. Not that I would die, since I'm not really here . . . yet."

Annie unpressed her lips, which she had pushed together so firmly that it seemed they had stuck together. "I am not going to be like you. I am not going to become a demon."

"Of course not. Too much tainted blood, too much Tullgren in you." He arched an eyebrow. "Isn't that right? You think that goodness will protect you, will stay inside of you? You do know that I was once good, too, and it was so terribly, terribly dull."

Annie had nothing to say to this. She found it hard to believe. She crossed her fingers behind her back, letting go of the wall first. She was so scared.

"You need to let Miss Cornelia go," Annie said.

"Are you ordering me?"

"Yes." Annie's knees shook.

The Raiff just laughed. "Well, then I guess we are related." He paused for a moment. "You do know that the old woman didn't tell you things. Who you were. Who she was to you. That you had grandparents here."

Her mouth went dry. "I know."

"And yet you say she is the one who is good?"

"Goodness is complicated. Adults are, too," Annie said. She turned back toward the stairs, pulling at the wooden door. It wouldn't budge.

"I didn't say you could leave."

"I don't care what you say. You aren't even here." Annie turned back, glaring at him. Anger soaring inside of her.

"You won't have a choice, Annie. You will join me or you will die. And your precious Miss Cornelia will die and your pathetic little elf. Neither of you know your power. Neither of you have any idea of your potential."

"I don't want power." Annie turned to look at him, to really look at him, and what she saw made her stomach turn. Because what she saw was pure evil.

"You will." He shook his head as if he cared enough to be disappointed in her. "Everyone does. Fear will make you care only for your own survival, and you will twist into something I can use. Or you'll die. You don't want to die, do you, Annie?"

"If you aren't there, death doesn't seem so bad," she said bravely.

He scowled at her, and then out of the air, Miss Cornelia materialized, broken and pained looking. Blood ran from her forehead. Her rainbow skirts were torn and her eyes hollow.

"This is what goodness gets you, Annie Nobody who will always be a nobody, a nothing, just like her beloved, weak

Miss Cornelia." His scowl deepened. "Perhaps, I should just kill her now as you watch. That would be fun, but naughty. All naughty things are so fun . . . Such a shame for do-gooders, always stuck in the land of boring."

"No!" Annie yelled.

"Annie?" Bloom's voice called through the door.

"He's going to kill her!" Annie hollered back, surging forward even though the Raiff and Miss Cornelia weren't really there.

The Raiff pulled out a dagger, pressing the blade against Miss Cornelia's throat.

"He can't kill her, Annie. She is his bargaining chip," Bloom yelled from behind the door. "He's tricking you."

But Annie was past reason. Emotion roared through her and love—pure, true love for Miss Cornelia—and that love shot out of her body like a giant white light, rippling across the castle's top parapets and down into the Raiff's force field and straight through it, waving over Eva, Johann, Jamie, SalGoud, and all the cows, filling every living thing with light, illuminating them with a brightness and then passing through. The cows shivered in a burst of rainbows and became unicorns. Eva hugged the boys standing with her and proclaimed they were the best boys in the universe. Jamie's heart almost exploded with love and happiness.

And that light spread all the way around the world, and for one moment—one beautiful moment—the world was full of the magic of love, pure love, and for that one moment not a single person hurt another person, magical or non-magical.

And then it was gone.

The Raiff arched an eyebrow. "You, my dear, are far more powerful than I thought."

Annie turned, openmouthed, exhausted, to face him again.

He was gone. Disappeared. And the image of Miss Cornelia was gone with him. The door behind her unlocked, and Bloom flung himself through it, catching her as she started to crumple.

"What did you do?" he whispered, wrapping his arms around her waist as he kept her from tumbling off the castle.

"I don't know," she told him honestly. "I think—magic? Some sort of magic? Do you have the bow and arrow?"

"I do." He smiled, but his eyes were concerned. "We've got them, Annie. We can do it now. We can rescue them now."

She tapped his side with her fingers, trying to solid herself up, allow herself to be more happy and relieved than scared about what the future might bring. "Bloom . . . When I did that . . . that thing I just did . . . What did it feel like?"

"It felt like love," he said as he helped her down the stairs.

She took a step forward and down, elf by her side, and said, "I think maybe it was."

And So It Continues

The castle stairs were dark and unlit; Bloom's elf light had died a long time ago. Annie had to feel her way down, moving her hand along the wall, sensing for each stair with her toes. It took a while, but when they got to the bottom, their friends were waiting for them. Eva thundered toward Annie, snatched her around the waist, and hauled her up into the air in a dwarf hug.

"Don't know what happened in there but don't you go away like that again, Stopper," Eva demanded.

"Did you get it?" Jamie asked.

"We did," Bloom answered as the unicorns came forward, one by one, bowing to him and to Annie.

"Oh, no! Get up! Get up!" Annie urged them. "Oh, please, don't bow to us."

But they did anyway, and after a second, Johann, Eva, and SalGoud did, too. Despite her exhaustion, Annie yanked them all back up.

"We are equals," she insisted. "You should never ever bow to me. Or to anyone else. Not ever."

Eva shrugged. "Okay."

It wasn't until they got back to Jamie's room that Bloom felt safe enough to pull out the Golden Bow and Arrow. Eva *ohh*ed and *ahh*ed and touched it reverently. Annie told them what had happened with the Raiff at the top of the castle, and they allowed themselves to celebrate just the smallest of bits.

The sun rose in the sky before they finally went to sleep. Annie slept fitfully, fretting that the Raiff was right and that all good could corrupt to evil, that she didn't stand a chance of rescuing poor Miss Cornelia. They had come a long way already, but their quest was far from over. They still had to go back to Aurora for Grady O'Grady and then make their way to the Badlands.

As he slept, Bloom hugged his bow and arrow to his chest. Johann embraced his sword. Eva snored out earsplitting burp-songs in her sleep, but Annie was so exhausted she never woke up despite her anxiety and Eva's loudness. Being a stone giant, SalGoud needed little sleep and spent the time arranging a car to the airport and flights home.

And Jamie? Jamie worried. They had the bow. They

had the arrow complete with red Helper feather. But how would they survive? How would they get to the Badlands and rescue Miss Cornelia? Would the dragon be able to carry all of them? The problems seemed so big to him, so utterly impossible.

He wandered out to the restaurant and met up with Mrs. Tullgren, who served him black pudding and scones, eggs, and baked tomatoes. His days of only eating canned goods seemed so long ago and far away.

"How come I've never seen Mr. Tullgren's books about Annie at home?" he asked as she poured him some orange juice. "I think I saw another one, about a devil dog."

"They are bestsellers here, but they haven't been released overseas yet, not like his other series." Her nose twitched. "Something seems a bit off. You smell a wee bit magic, James. Has something happened? Do you feel different?" She sniffed at his hair, lifted up his hand. "Have you been up to the castle?"

She let go of his hand after she sniffed it, and stared at him.

"Your scones are really good," hc said awkwardly.

She gave him another long, hard look. "You won't be telling me, will you? I am going to hope you have good reasons for that, but you've given me no reason not to trust you, so trust you I will."

He cleared his throat. "Thank you."

"Just don't be mentioning it to the mister." With her elbow, she indicated Mr. Tullgren, who was busy telling stories to a table of golfers who were laughing uproariously. "He tends to imagine the worst-case scenario all the time, which is not a helpful thing when your imaginings become real."

Just as Jamie was going to promise not to tell anything to Mr. Tullgren, Annie entered the room and he was completely forgotten. Both Mr. and Mrs. Tullgren rushed toward Annie and flung themselves at their granddaughter, gathering her up in their arms before setting her down next to Jamie, and asking after her sleep and what she'd like for breakfast. She stared after them longingly as they scurried off to make the food.

"Part of you wishes you could stay here, doesn't it?" Jamie asked.

"I do," Annie said quietly. "But we have to try to save Aurora. I just—I worry that I'll never get to come back . . . that this will be the last time I see them, you know?"

He thought he did know, but he couldn't find the words to comfort her so instead he petted her on the hand and poured her some tea. A passed-out pixie had flopped in the sugar cubes. Annie gently moved her out of the way.

When the Tullgrens returned, she told them everything that had happened in Aurora, about how she was rescued by Eva, how they had saved the town from the trolls—but some had obviously snuck in and hid, striking when the time was right—how Miss Cornelia was taken from her own home, how the Raiff had threatened them, and how the town had turned on Jamie as if he was the one who had done all the horrible things.

They listened raptly, sitting at the table with them, as she told them about Grady O'Grady. Mr. Tullgren sighed happily; he'd thought all the dragons were gone, dead, or in the Badlands, turned into evil tarasques by the Raiff. Annie had a hard time talking so much, and her voice grew thin and weak, especially when she said how mean some of the townspeople had been to Jamie and how responsible she felt for failing to get across to the Badlands to get Miss Cornelia.

"But why are you here?" Mr. Tullgren asked. "How did you end up here?"

Annie looked to Jamie for help. His mouth opened, but no words came out. More than anything, both Jamie and Annie longed to tell them about the elves and what had happened in the wee hours of the night, but they couldn't. Lichen had been so insistent that no adults know. They couldn't risk ruining their attempt at rescue by telling the Tullgrens—no matter how badly they wanted to do so.

"I—I'm not a hundred percent sure," Annie admitted, which was sort of true.

The Tullgrens let this pass.

"And you're going back home already?" Mr. Tullgren said slowly.

Annie's head jerked up. "How did you know?"

"I could feel it." Mr. and Mrs. Tullgren exchanged a look

before he said, "We are terribly sorry about how we treated you when you first got here, lass, but we want you to know that you are welcome to stay as long as you like. Your friends, too." He gestured toward Jamie. "It doesn't seem as if Aurora is treating the young man well at all, and we here . . . Well, you'd be welcome here, Jamie, even if you did become a troll. I'm guessing you'd be the nicest troll that ever was."

Jamie allowed himself to smile, and Annie grabbed his hand in hers, squeezing it and saying softly, "Jamie, I would understand if you didn't want to come back with me. I wouldn't be mad at you or anything."

He shook his head. Part of him longed to stay with the Tullgrens and their quirky bed-and-breakfast and their magical happiness and love. In just a couple of hours they had made him feel something he had never felt before: completely accepted. But his loyalty was with Annie.

"We made a promise a long time ago, remember?" he asked. "That we would always look out for each other, always be friends?"

"It wasn't actually that long ago." Annie laughed. "But I remember."

She squeezed his hand again and let go. He wished she didn't always let go.

The Tullgrens had remained silent throughout the whole exchange, but now Mrs. Tullgren smiled, leaned over, and wrapped Jamie up in a big bear hug, smelling of flour and sausage. "I am so glad that our Annie has a friend like yourself, James Hephaistion Alexander."

"So am I," Annie said. "So am I."

The rest of the morning was a bit of a sad blur for Annie. Her grandparents explained that the Snatcher was not part of Mrs. Tullgren's warning system, which made them terribly worried about the extent of the Raiff's powers and influence.

"It may be worse than any of us supposed," Mrs. Tullgren fretted.

The others woke up, and Eva and Johann both spent far too long stretching, complaining, eating, and then eating some more. SalGoud walked the grounds with Jamie because they both ached for some sunshine. Bloom seemed happy, happier than normal, and when Annie got him alone for a bit, he explained that he was the only one who was able to retrieve Lichen's core from the machine because he was the only elf still free. Plus, he was very proud of having recovered both the feather and the Golden Arrow.

"You've always known you were an elf," Annie said. "Nothing has changed."

"How I feel inside has changed." He leaned against the car SalGoud had ordered. "I feel like I know who I am now, like I have a point, a destiny."

They had packed up the car and were just waiting for Eva

and Johann to finish up their third breakfast. A unicorn ambled over to them, and Annie petted her muzzle. Bloom's hand went to the unicorn's mane. The creature nuzzled him, getting drool mixed with grass all over his cheek. He laughed as Annie wiped it off with a napkin she'd stashed in her pocket in case her nose got runny again on the airplane.

"I've always known I am an elf," he said, "but I guess I still felt like an imposter somehow. Like I was untested or maybe unworthy."

"Why?"

"Because I survived when all the others were"—he broke off, dodging another unicorn kiss—"when I thought they were dead. I thought maybe I was such a bad elf that the Raiff didn't want me, didn't think of me as a threat, or . . . I told you it was silly."

"It is silly," Annie agreed. "But not because you felt it. Just because it's so wrong. What happened last night proves it. You were so brave. The ghost elves guarding the Golden Arrow recognized you as one of their own. Your people would be proud of you. I know I am. You're a great elf, Bloom."

He blushed and couldn't meet her eyes, focusing instead on the unicorn. "I hope to be."

The rest of the day passed too quickly for Annie. She hugged her grandparents good-bye, and Johann drove them in the pig car all the way to the Dublin airport, through fields of grazing cows and sheep and horses that lifted their heads as the pig car passed.

"They are saluting us," Eva claimed. "They know in their hearts that greatness is before them and that we go on a quest to save the elves."

Annie wasn't so sure this was true, but she was fine with the dwarf thinking it. Her own heart was so full of mixed emotions. She wanted to get on with it, to get to the Badlands, to try to save Miss Cornelia and the elves. But she also just wanted to hunker down and hide, to stay here with her grandparents, to be hugged every day, to not have to save anyone at all, to not be taunted by the Raiff and all his evil.

So quickly, they were saying good-bye to Johann and on the plane again, customs forms filled out, passports checked, seat belts buckled. And then hours later they were home in Maine, and ready to begin.

The taxi dropped them off outside the town line, the same place where they'd struck down the crow monster. Annie paused, inhaling deeply. Aurora lay just ahead, around the bend of a snow-covered road.

"We can do this, Annie. We will do it together." Jamie gestured toward Bloom, who pulled out the Golden Bow and Arrow from his luggage.

"It's still there." He stashed it away again. "We're good."

They started walking down the road, and Annie said,

"Once we get to the Badlands and the elves and Miss Cornelia, and if we actually can rescue them—"

"No freaking 'actuallys' about it. We will rescue them. Dwarfs do not fail," Eva interrupted.

"Okay," Annie began again, stepping on the snow, watching it engulf her boot, "when we rescue them and I make the portal to get back here, how do we close it up again?"

There was an awkward silence, which SalGoud broke. "You won't be able to. The Raiff will come through. He will bring his army."

"But she has to make a portal to bring us back," Jamie said.

"And the elves," Bloom added.

Annie swallowed hard and they got their first glance at Aurora, nestled between the ocean cliffs and the blueberry barrens, the mountains of Acadia, and the sea. "So our town . . ."

Jamie took her hand, dread filling his heart, and finished her sentence for her, "Will have to prepare for war."

They didn't talk about Jamie's declaration of war as they hiked into town, but the possibility resonated in their heads, dampening their spirits. As they entered town proper, Eva paused.

"We're going to Megan's. We're going to talk to Lichen and then we're going to get moving. Action!" Eva held her arm up like she was holding a sword in the air while sitting astride a horse in front of millions of heavily armored troops.

SalGoud startled and dropped his suitcases and Jamie checked behind him to make sure there were no actual troops there. There weren't.

"Um . . . have you talked to Annie or Bloom about this?" Jamie asked. The others were all trying to help SalGoud load the suitcases he had dropped back into his arms.

"Why would I talk to them?" Eva roared.

Some mice that had been listening nearby skittered into a mouse hole in the trunk of an old oak tree. Jamie could see why. Eva could be—well, she could be loud.

And grumpy.

And loud.

And bossy.

But she was good inside.

"It's just that . . . Well, Annie and Bloom seem to be . . ." He didn't want to finish his sentence. Eva was pretty competitive with Bloom.

She stomped up to him. "Seem to be what?"

Jamie shrugged and wouldn't meet her gaze.

"Leaders? Are you trying to say they seem to be leaders?" Eva demanded. "I'll have you know that no dwarf has ever been led by an elf. Not in the history of ever. A Time Stopper—well, maybe. But an elf? Never! You take that back."

She lifted her nose to Jamie's chest. Her breath smelled of the cheese they'd had in the airplane.

"I didn't say it, Eva. You did." Jamie stepped backward.

Eva crossed her arms over her chest and harrumphed. "Where's the arrow?"

"Bloom has it."

"Bloom has it? All by himself? Like one puny elf can protect the important tool that we need to save an entire species! What is wrong with us? We shouldn't even be walking except in a protective diamond formation. We have important assets to protect!" She rolled her eyes. "We went all the way to Ireland to get that thing! We fought creatures. Someday the magical beings of this world will sing our glory because of our exploits, and the only one protecting the arrow is Bloom?" She flopped on the ground, obviously too distraught to stand.

"You trust Annie more than Bloom?"

"It's not about trust! It's about protection! Annie is wimpy and weak, but she's getting tougher and she is an actual Time Stopper. Protection is in their bones, in their DNA, or whatever that science word is. It's what they do. Now the elves . . . They are hardly better than fairies."

"Eva. You are far too mean to the fairies." Bloom stood there with a backpack slugged over his shoulders and his hands on his hips.

Eva hopped back into standing position, landing solidly on her two feet. "Oh, please . . . Fairies aren't good for anything except flitting around and taking care of flowers."

"Flowers are important," Bloom said, almost smiling.

Jamie couldn't tell if he was kidding or not.

"Harrumph." Eva stomped over to Bloom and poked him in the stomach with her finger. "Where's the arrow?"

"In my quiver. Stop asking!" Bloom tapped the portable container that held all his arrows. Cylindrical, it was suspended from his back with straps. The nocked ends peeked out above his left shoulder. He then tapped a cloth bag attached to his belt. "I have others in my arrow bag."

Something hard and solid seemed to form in Jamie's throat as he stared at Bloom nonchalantly showing off his weapons. Violence. Fighting. Death. There was no getting around it. It was inevitable. It just mattered who was going to die. The good guys or the bad guys. But he didn't want anyone to die. Death dominated everything, even the world of magic. Violence cultivated it. It reminded him of the Alexanders.

He stared out at the dark sky. Why did it have to be like this? When he lived with the Alexanders, he thought he'd never feel calm and peaceful. When he saw his grandmother turn into a troll, he had lost all hope of a good life, a calm life, a life where he didn't have to be afraid all the time. And then Eva and Annie came on a hovering snowmobile and brought him here to this magical town and for a moment he felt—well, he felt like he belonged. Sort of. Sure, everyone was a little afraid that he'd turn troll, too, but Annie and Miss Cornelia and Helena—who had the most amazing bakery—and Mr. Nate and everyone . . . They'd . . . they'd accepted him. They didn't think he'd turn troll, and Annie said she didn't even care if he did. He'd always be Jamie and they'd always be friends.

That's what mattered.

That's always what mattered.

But he didn't want to have any of them hurt, and he didn't want to have to hurt anyone, not even the Raiff.

But people were already getting hurt, weren't they? The demon had Miss Cornelia now. Who knew what he was doing to her.

A hand touched his shoulder and he jerked back. Annie.

"Are you ready, Jamie?" she asked. "I think it's time. We have to go to Megan's."

He swallowed hard. "Now?"

Annie frowned next to Jamie. She was not a big fan of the hag who didn't think she was good enough, who prophesied that Annie would "fall with evil."

"Hags are fine," Bloom said, ushering them forward, obviously responding to Annie's frown and knowing it was about Megan. "You just have to remember they always expect the worst. Once Megan envisioned that all the vampires and werewolves fought over this boring human girl—no offense to the girl—and it turned out that she was just watching a movie. Same thing with her apocalypse dream. The one where all the humans killed each other in some weird game. You will be fine."

"You're braver about dealing with the Raiff than with a hag." Eva shook her head. "Sometimes you make zero sense."

"Sometimes," Annie said, echoing some of Eva's words as they walked into town, "it's easier to deal with true evil than the kind of evil that pretends to be your friend."

"Only way to deal with either is a swift kick to the neck," Eva enthused.

They crept through the dark night on guard. Finally, they came to Megan's strange little house with its ramshackle roof that slanted in too many directions and the walls of white stone. It smelled like lasagna. Eva sniffed at it. Her stomach growled.

They climbed through Megan's window into her bright pink room.

The young hag glared at Annie and smiled beautifully at Bloom, who didn't seem to notice. "You're back! Finally! Did you get it?"

Bloom nodded. "Lichen?"

"In the closet, hidden. I've kept good care of him. He still—he is still sick. His life energy is low, but his wounds are healing."

Bloom swallowed hard. The words seemed to stick in his mouth. "So he is . . . still alive?"

Bloom's eyes filled with hope as Megan opened the closet door and whispered for them to keep their voices low even though the hags were watching their favorite show, *The Real Hags of Hapsburg*. Lichen lay at the edge of the closet, covered with a puffy pink quilt and several stuffed unicorns. His color was still not right—sort of dusky rather than bright—and his eyes were dull, lacking Bloom's spark, or any spark really.

Annie knelt in front of the boy.

Megan snatched a baby Big Foot stuffed animal that Annie's knee almost landed on and blurted in a whisper, "Yes. He is alive. I wouldn't be much of a hag if he died."

Bloom's breath exhaled. He moved into the closet next to Annie and squished a stuffed turtle beneath his shin. Megan didn't seem to care about that.

"Lichen?" Annie whispered. "Bloom has something to show you."

The others gathered just outside the closet door, staring at the three of them as Bloom quietly pulled the Golden Arrow from his back quiver. Lichen's eyes slowly followed Bloom's movement and then widened in surprise. The edge of his mouth tilted up in a feeble smile as the entirety of the Golden Arrow was revealed.

"You got it," Lichen whispered.

"Annie did," Bloom replied.

"We all did," Annie corrected him as he laid the arrow across Lichen's lap. Behind them Megan made a scoffing noise.

Lichen's hand came out from beneath the quilt, and he touched the arrow with reverence, carefully tracing the shaft of it with his index finger. "It's so beautiful."

Bloom agreed. "It is."

"So there is hope?" Lichen met Bloom's eyes and finally—finally there was a spark. "There is hope you will save them."

Eva roared, "OF COURSE WE WILL SAVE THEM!"

Megan squeaked. "Eva! Shh! The hags!"

The television in the other room suddenly went silent. Megan's eyes grew round and huge with fear.

"Hide . . . hide . . . ," she urged them, shoving them all inside the closet and closing the door behind them. Eva fell onto Annie's back, flattening her. Jamie tried not to, but he was pretty sure he stepped on Bloom's leg. "Get under the stuffies!"

There was a frenzy of activity as they frantically worked to bury themselves under Megan's pink, glittery clothes and stuffed animals. What if the hags found them? How would they explain Lichen? The moment an adult knew about him, then the Raiff would know he had escaped. That couldn't happen. Someone stepped on Annie's hair and she yanked some clothes down, hoping that the extras would cover them enough to hide them if the hags checked in the closet. They wouldn't, would they?

"What was that?" came a crooked, broken voice from beyond the closet door. It was one of Megan's hag relatives. Annie wasn't exactly sure how they were related or even if they were. She'd have to ask someday.

"What?" Megan asked. Her voice sounded . . . nervous.

"Sounded like a dwarf yelling," the hag said. "Are you hiding a dwarf in here?"

"Ha! Like I would hide a dwarf." Megan fake-laughed. It wasn't very convincing.

The hags obviously didn't think it was convincing either, and one of them threw open the closet door. Light poured in. Annie crossed her fingers and stared at the pink gauze of the tutu that covered her face. Beside her, Lichen seemed so still that she worried he was dead. She could feel Bloom on the other side, holding his breath. She wasn't sure about Jamie's location, but Eva definitely seemed like she was still sprawled across Annie's lower legs at the end of the closet closest to the door.

"What's this?" a hag shrieked.

Annie's breath hitched. Someone grabbed her hand and squeezed. There was no hope. They were caught.

Helping Hags

The hag peered into the closet.

"Someone's in this room with you!" she accused as Megan gasped, her fingers with perfectly manicured nails curled into fists.

The other hag had flattened herself on the floor, lifted up the bed ruffle, eyes peering beneath it, and announced, "Under the bed is clear."

"All right . . . all right . . . ," Megan announced. "I'm hiding a dwarf."

The hags gasped.

"She needed help with her homework and I—well, I know the rules about no late-night visitors and—" Megan's lie was losing steam.

Everyone in the closet collectively held their breaths for one second, two, three.

There was a great flurry of commotion and a scattering of stuffed animals and Eva bounded out of the closet, standing in front of the hags and Megan, yanking a loose unicorn saddle out of her right pigtail.

"It's true," she said, dejected. "I came for help. NOT THAT DWARFS NEED HELP!"

Inside the closet, Jamie tucked Annie's foot back under a purple sweater and then hid his hand back under a stuffed bunny. One of the hags pulled out her eye. It hovered in the air and then zigzagged around the room as if hunting for other intruders.

Eva back-kicked the closet closed just as the eye approached. It ricocheted off the closed door and launched toward the ceiling fan, barely missing it, and causing much commotion in the panicking hag who did not want to permanently lose an eye to the swirling fan blades.

Eva took advantage of the confusion and added to it, yelling, "CAN WE NOT TELL ANYONE ABOUT THIS! Dwarfs, as you know, do not ask for help. It could be the end of my reputation. My dad will never let me hear the end of it. Please . . . You cannot say anything! Promise! If you don't, I swear you'll see the end of my ax!"

A hag hissed. "Don't be threatening me, dwarf."

In the next instant, Eva was wrapped up in bedsheets,

arms fastened to her side. The hag popped her eye back in her head, while the other made a series of intricate hand movements that seemed to cause the bedsheets to tighten around Eva. Eva lifted off the ground, levitating through the door and down the hall. The front door opened and Eva was forcibly floated right out of it, before she landed with a thud on the front lawn. The bedsheets unwound and slithered back inside the house. The hags had followed her to the door and now stood triumphantly, smiling. A lot of teeth were missing, which may have been a good thing, since the remaining teeth were black with rot.

"Never threaten a hag," they said simultaneously. The door banged closed, and Eva was left in the middle of the lawn, unceremoniously dumped.

Inside her bedroom, Megan reopened the closet door and whisked the clothes, stuffed animals, and jewelry off the others.

"Really," she said. "Dwarfs. So much drama."

In the next moment, her voice softened and she turned all her attention to Lichen, who was still clutching the Golden Arrow, protecting it in all the ruckus. "Are you all right?"

His words came out slowly. "Yes. Thank you."

They all stood up, except for Lichen who was too weak

and Annie who was too hopelessly entangled in multiple pastel feather boas that she assumed were for dress up. But knowing Megan, maybe they were just regular clothes.

Annie put her hand on Bloom's shirtsleeve, stopping him as he made his sad good-byes to Lichen.

"Bloom," she said, finally disentangled from all the boas, "you don't have to go."

Bloom touched her hand on his sleeve. "It'll be hard, Annie. I don't know if we'll make it back, but I'm the last elf here. I have to go."

Megan gesticulated wildly. "That means you shouldn't go! We can't lose the last elf . . . other than Lichen, obviously."

Her tone made it obvious that she didn't think Lichen was much longer for this world.

"We go together or we don't go at all," Bloom announced. "We're friends, Annie. I won't let you go alone. Not without me."

"Nor without me," said Eva, who had been eavesdropping through the window.

They all shushed her. Megan rolled her eyes and said something again about all the dwarf drama.

SalGoud paused. "I'm coming, too. You might need someone to heal people. Stone giants are good at that, right? Plus, someone has to handle Eva."

Eva glared at him. "What is that supposed to mean?"

Bloom sighed. This conversation was so familiar. They

said good-bye to Megan and trudged through the darkness of the woods to begin their journey into horrible danger.

When they got to the beach, Annie focused her thoughts.

Grady O'Grady. We are here. There are . . . There are a lot of us . . . She hoped her voice sounded apologetic. The dragon's back was big, but she couldn't imagine he would want to carry a stone giant, two humans, a dwarf, and an elf.

Coming . . .

Bloom touched her shoulder. *It will be okay.*

Not if we start hearing Eva's thoughts.

He gasped, obviously stricken by the possibility, but before he could respond, the air above them whooshed with a violent force and in the next moment, the dragon had landed on the rocky shore right next to them.

Hello! he said, smiling and showing all his teeth.

Eva fainted dead away.

SalGoud opened his arms. "I somehow failed to anticipate the fainting."

"She'd been doing so well." Jamie made the excuse for both of them. "Sir, can we please have a ride to the Badlands?"

Absolutely. The dragon bent a bit at his knee, and SalGoud and Bloom hoisted Eva up. Annie and Jamie climbed up themselves, and soon they were all on the dragon's back.

Grab a scale, he recommended. *The crossing can be rough.*

Annie shuddered as she thought of the Badlands, of

facing the Raiff in the flesh. *He was bad enough when he was just projecting himself.*

Yes, little Annie, shiver. It is an evil place we go to. But hold on to my back, and we will do what we can to save your Miss Cornelia and end the devastation of the Raiff.

Bloom sat behind her and restrung his bow.

"Just in case," he said. "Do you still have your phurba, Annie?"

She checked. It was still tucked to her belt beneath her coat. "Yes. And the bell the ghosts gave me."

Good, the dragon said. *I think you will have to use both of them.*

He faced the clouds and storm, and without even a second glance or a second thought, he pushed off his massive hind legs and leaped out into the open space of the sky with the children clinging to his back. The mighty wings unfolded and stroked the air, slicing through it and moving it to fit their needs. The sun was beginning to rise behind them.

As the wings flapped, the air made a faint humming noise. Warmth filled Annie. Every part of her seemed to be full of blood and strings, resonating.

We are joined, Grady O'Grady said. *Your power is greater with me.*

Will you come with us to the Raiff? Annie asked in her head, desperately hoping he would.

I may not be able to. We shall see. I have enemies there just as you do. It may be more dangerous for you to be with me.

That is not encouraging, Jamie thought.

They headed out to sea directly toward the storm. The lightning broke the sky in vibrant yellow vertical streaks. They were on their way.

"Here we come, Miss Cornelia. Here we come," she whispered.

"Don't look down, Annie," Bloom said, grabbing her by the shoulder. His voice was husky with concern, but she didn't need it.

She did look down. She could. Her heart leaped. She wasn't afraid of heights anymore.

Fly with me, Annie, Grady O'Grady said. *Feel the wind. Call it to you. Make it your friend.*

She opened her arms and lifted them up to the clouds. Behind her, Bloom did the same thing. Jamie held on tight, and SalGoud clung to the still-unconscious Eva, but Annie and Bloom with arms wide open flew toward the storm, flew away from the only world they knew and headed into the arms of danger without ever once looking back.

24

The Badlands

A great swirl of clouds greeted them as they flew straight into the storm. The lightning screamed against their ears, and the rain beat at them with slashing pellets. Annie hunkered down low, pushing her chest to her knees, and Bloom leaned his body over hers, protecting her back from the worst of the pellets. She clutched Grady O'Grady's scale right below his neck, but her hands were rapidly turning red from the cold and the lashing water.

"This is not the best," Jamie mumbled.

She tried to keep her eyes open, but it was almost impossible to do anything more than squint.

Hold on, children. Crossing into the Badlands is never easy, and of course, the Raiff has given us a storm.

Up! They climbed higher into the sky. Lightning struck

past the group, missing them by merely a foot, and thunder came with it like a monster's smack across the face. Bloom's body tensed, as did Annie's. She wished Tala were here. She would bury her face in his fur.

"Please," she said between clenched lips, "let Tala stay safe."

She thought of Miss Cornelia.

"Please, let Miss Cornelia be okay, and let the elves be okay. And my friends, please don't let him hurt my friends."

Despite her fear, not one of her worries was for herself.

Bloom was chanting *Hold on, Annie. Hold on, SalGoud. Hold on, Jamie.*

"We'll be fine," she yelled toward Bloom. But he didn't hear her words, only the reassuring thoughts that went with them. The rain was too heavy, the wind too loud as the thunder became a cacophonous noise that pressed against their heads and made them feel small.

The dragon smashed against the winds that swept the air in opposition to their flight. He roared and beat his wings with groaning moans.

Bloom gritted his teeth and his mind reached out to his friends. His hands clenched Annie's jacket. There was something about this storm that wasn't right, and he was determined to fight against it. He remembered a storm similar to this one when he'd lost his parents to the trolls. His mother had kissed his forehead and smoothed it with her hand. Her lip trembled although he could tell that she was trying hard to be brave.

They won't smell you here, she had said. *Remember your words.*

He'd grabbed her hand. She pulled it away and kissed his knuckles one by one.

We'll be right back, she said, and then turned and ran, her long white dress flowing behind her. The rain took her. Her wet blond hair clung to her green cape, a cape like he wore now, tucked beneath his jacket.

His breath came too fast.

Annie stilled her mind. There, in the back corners a terrible solid lump, stuck in her brain like a piece of not-very-well-chewed-chicken in the back of your throat. The lump felt dark and cold and watchful. She tried to push at it, to move it out. It wouldn't budge.

I feel him, she thought and shuddered, half from the cold and half from the horrible darkness that was somehow inside her, waiting. Bloom's fingers tightened around her arms.

Jamie's thoughts came tumbling into her head. *Annie . . . are you okay? What's that darkness? Are you . . . ?*

A moment later, a nasty blast of wind smashed against Grady O'Grady's left side, pushing him off course and into a spiraling descent. Annie lost hold of the scale with her weakening fingers. Her legs kept their tight grasp around the dragon's lower neck. Bloom rocked backward and lost his grip. Twisting, she lunged for him, and her hand caught his by the wrist. His fingers wrapped around hers and he dangled there, wind lashing into his face and legs kicking at air.

Hold on! she screamed. *JAMIE! SALGOUD!*

SalGoud couldn't help because he was holding Eva. Jamie scurried forward, one arm hanging onto a scale. The dragon flipped upside down, and Annie's arm twisted as did Bloom's. His eyes opened wide and his mouth set in a line of determination. Annie grabbed the dragon's scale with her free hand, and Bloom managed to fight the wind to get his other hand up high enough to grab Annie's lower arm. Her shoulder burned from his weight, and the socket considered whether to pop out or not. Jamie got close enough to grab onto Bloom's arm, too, and they pulled. Bloom did not get up.

Dragon!

The dragon didn't answer. He was doing all he could to straighten out his wings and to stop their downward spiral. They fell, wing over tail, overhead, upside down, and then right side up, until Bloom's feet touched the top of a green wall of ocean water and the biggest wave Annie had ever seen. It was the kind of wave mariners dreaded, the kind that toppled barges, tore apart lobster boats, the kind that made widows. Her eyes widened with fear.

The boy gritted his teeth and closed his eyes, murmuring elfish words that Annie and Jamie couldn't quite hear. Her heart lurched at the sight of him and caught in her throat, somewhere behind her tonsils, making a gigantic lump there that threatened to explode out. He seemed so strong and calm despite the obvious fear that pumped throughout his body.

"You will not die!" she yelled. She pleaded, "Please, Bloom, I need you."

There was a silence then, as if the storm paused for a moment to see what stuff the three of them were made of, to see if it had to do anything else to destroy them, or if they'd destroy themselves just fine.

Anything frantic in Annie fell with the raindrops and was lost in the massive sea. She focused all her energy on her thoughts, all her strength in her arm.

Flip your legs up, she yelled to Bloom in her head. *Pull up to me. Come on.*

You're not strong enough to hold me.

Yes, I am. I am with Jamie.

Annie . . .

Do it, Bloom. I won't let you go.

The elf closed his eyes. He was afraid the momentum of his pulling and tossing himself up onto the dragon's back would be too much for Annie and Jamie, that they would drop him and he would end up in the sea. Lost.

There's no time. Do it now. Now, Bloom. Now!

He bit his lip, drawing blood. He swallowed. Then in a movement full of grace and elfin power, he swung his legs back and forward, vaulting up toward the dragon's back and tossing himself over. At the height of his momentum, he let go of Annie's arm and lunged. Grabbing the scale in front of her, he twisted his body around and seized the dragon's neck between his legs. Relieved, Annie wrapped her arms around his waist, ignoring the ache in her shoulder. They clutched each other, sobbing and laughing. Jamie hung onto the both of them.

You're safe. You're safe, she thought.

Because of you.

The dragon righted himself finally and they skimmed over the tops of the waves. *You were all brave.*

His voice sounded infinitely weary.

And you? Bloom asked Grady.

She strained to hear his thoughts, they were so shaky, so unlike the brave Bloom she was used to, that she already depended on. Well, she'd shown him he could depend on her, too.

He was so scared, she realized. *He thought he was going to die.*

He did almost die, Jamie thought.

Would you all like a quote? SalGoud asked. *I have several motivational ones that might bolster our spirits.*

I am fine, Grady O'Grady answered. *My wing is a bit roughed up. Nothing a good Scotch and a pennant win over the Yankees wouldn't cure.*

They all thought brave things and quotes to one another, but they knew they had to go back up and face the storm. There was no use talking about it. With a sigh, the dragon turned again toward the sky. Below them, a dolphin crested the waves, wishing them luck, trying to give them hope.

It's so beautiful, Annie said as Bloom righted himself, facing forward.

Life is beautiful, he said.

Yet they flew from it.

Directly above them, the clouds turned black and the only light came from far behind them, back in Aurora, and it had to fight its way through the clouds just as they did. It faintly touched them and barely gave any warmth at all to dispel the bitter cold that the dark storm brought with it. Annie thought it was like flying through squid ink that pressed against them, growing thicker and colder with every inch they managed to surge forward. In a shocked silence, the four flew through it. Eva didn't wake.

Fight with me, Grady O'Grady commanded them, his wings struggling to flap up and down.

They focused their minds on the dragon, focused their minds on the flight. Their brains were half in a trance and half-awake. Their eyelids heavied, but they focused everything in their beings on one word.

Up!

And so they did. With a mighty heave, they went up and up. The storm battered them, tried to knock them off, but with each blast, Grady O'Grady was ready. The children's bodies tensed and trembled.

The storm was a formidable enemy, swift and untouchable, cold and dense, but they held their course and suddenly the sky shivered before them like a miracle. Thousands of threads of every color radiated and vibrated in front of them like a gigantic ribbon that stretched across the sky. The whole of it shone like it was made of infinite particles capturing all the shimmers of light in the world, like tiny diamonds of all colors.

Annie gasped. The brilliance of it forced her to blink. It reminded her in all its shimmery highlights of Grady O'Grady's wings. It streaked down the entire skyscape in front of them like the aurora borealis, the northern lights, she sometimes saw in the winter sky, only much more vibrant, much more real. She could almost pick out the individual filaments of color, stretching and moving.

"The strings," Jamie whispered, sounding as awed as she was.

The storm wailed in anger with a rough and horrid noise, but they paid no attention. They headed straight for the strings, and toward the Badlands.

As they entered the strings, Annie's heart thumped hard with joy. From the moment the dragon's first front foot passed into the gleaming lights, her body shook with absolute happiness. It was glorious, like suddenly coming home, like suddenly being able to do a back layout and back tuck in gymnastics.

She knew the danger of the Badlands lay ahead of her; the

knowledge caught in her throat and threatened to rip her to pieces, but she couldn't help but smile and pat the dragon's back.

"I could stay here forever," she said. Her voice sounded like a melody of flowers.

Bloom turned his head and smiled. "It's glorious."

Annie laughed. It was exactly the right word. Glorious. The syllables of it reverberated in the strings.

Bloom turned back around. His body and the dragon's seemed to pixelate a bit, like a computer picture when you magnify it a lot and can see all the little dots of color. Only the colors weren't dots but tiny, tiny moving strings within the dots. Her body pixelated, too. In her head, the music of a million stars resonated with her.

Glorious.

SalGoud started quoting things, and Jamie breathed in, happy, finally happy. And then the strings shifted . . . Something was . . . Something was off . . .

We cross, Grady O'Grady said. *Ready yourself for the Badlands.*

Annie grabbed onto Bloom's back. Behind her, SalGoud clung to Eva and a scale, and Jamie clung to Annie.

But Grady O'Grady's words didn't prepare any of them for the searing jolt of pain that racked their bodies as they left the strings and entered the wretched land of the Raiff.

The Awful Place

The dragon landed immediately after crossing, thudding down onto the hard, deep-red land, which reminded Jamie of the pictures he'd once seen of Mars. Above them, the sky was the deep brown of chestnuts and UPS trucks.

The ghastly landscape created a despair in the children so profound that they gasped from the weight of it. Jamie's heart became a leaden mass behind his ribs.

Annie's hope sank to the bottom of her feet, and she slid off the back of Grady O'Grady. Bloom and Jamie jumped down with her. It was as if an important part of them had gone missing. It was that part that finds joy in a flower, that knows an *F* on a geography test can be fixed by extra credit, that knows no matter what, a mother will hug you at the end of the day, kissing your forehead as she tucks you into bed at night with your favorite stuffed animals and a pillow.

A sob racked SalGoud, shaking him all the way down to his feet.

"This is an awful place," Annie tried to say out loud, but her words came out like gasps and gulps and turned into something akin to a wail that echoed across the fetid land. Grady O'Grady moved to her and wrapped his long neck around her. She clung to it, finding comfort in the brilliant scales, in its long strength.

Brave, Annie, he said, his own voice quivering. *We all must be strong.*

"What the heck? Did I miss the crossing!? Oh bat boogers!" Eva's voice bellowed out.

"Eva's awake," SalGoud said, rather unnecessarily, wiping at his eyes before Eva spotted his tears.

Bloom stood alone, scanning the landscape, searching for the horrible things that he knew must be lurking in the distance. A great fierce focus turned the boy into more of a warrior than the goofy elf that Jamie thought of as a friend. He had almost died when he fell off Grady O'Grady. He wanted to protect his world and his friends. He wanted to protect Annie and save the elves and Miss Cornelia.

Something on Grady O'Grady caught Bloom's sharp eyes. He began inspecting the dragon's wing, touching it lightly with his fingers. He gently took the edge and unfurled it. A horrible five-inch-long gash marred its shimmering beauty.

It will be fine, Grady O'Grady said, grumping and shuffling away sideways. *My arteries are like a horse's, you know. Corny told me that once.*

"Corny?" Annie asked.

Miss Cornelia. I call her Corny. Did you know that her mother was an ambassador to England? Oh, I could tell you stories.

He was trying to distract them.

Bloom rolled his eyes. *Let me help.*

Fine, Grady O'Grady said. *But it's not a problem at all. My bronchitis, however, you could fix. I've been up a few nights with that. Two in the morning it wakes me. Coughing and wheezing. Have you ever heard a dragon cough? It's like an elephant expelling gas out the rectum. You do not want to be around.*

Jamie laughed.

Bloom simply smiled and placed his hand against the dragon's wing and began whispering in that soft, deep tone Annie had become used to already, "*Arli pullnor. Arli pullnor yearnho. Arli pullnor.*"

The words resonated in the air and in Jamie's mind. Bloom traced the wound on Grady O'Grady's wing with his palm. It shimmered as his hand slowly went over the wound mark. Once his hand moved on, the gash became a scar, puffed up a bit from the thin filament of the wings.

Thank you, Grady O'Grady said.

"If we were back home it would be perfect," Bloom told Annie. "It is harder to do here. Everything is harder to do here. The magic is off."

Bloom's eyes narrowed in anger at the ugliness of the world. Jagged mountains stretched out halfway toward the horizon. Bare trunks of trees ripped in half marked the dirty landscape. Thornbushes and pricker bushes rolled along in the fetid wind. Sharp ridges of stone jumbled up through the earth. The smell was intense. The air blew in fear like it would waft in the salt smell of brackish water.

Right near where they stood waited fifty large wooden boats, crudely made and hollow inside, but full of oars.

Jamie swallowed hard before he spoke. "This is how they will cross, now. Trolls are afraid of water, but the Raiff must have convinced them to cross here."

But that means . . . Bloom let his thought dangle. He did not wish to pursue it. Annie had no such qualms.

It means that they can all come at once. It means that he will have one of us stop time soon and make the portal.

She imagined the trolls storming the Aurora beach, pulling in their nasty boats and pillaging Aurora, searching for feather boas and high-heeled shoes and pixies to eat. They would tie up the pixies and fairies. They would kill the stone giants. Annie moved closer to the dragon's side. She had never seen anything so ugly or thought anything so ugly in her young life.

"Is it day or night here?" she asked.

Day, the dragon answered. *Night is the blackest of black. Even one of your most powerful flashlights would only break the darkness a foot at the most. The light is so weak here that trolls and vampires, all the things of the dark, can travel in the day if forced to.*

The children pulled off their winter coats. It was far too warm here to wear them. They stripped off their sweaters, too. The rank air clung to them, curled Annie's hair damp against her scalp.

Eva wiped the sweat beads from her forehead, and Bloom rolled up his sleeves. SalGoud didn't seem to notice the heat.

From the distance came a rhythmic pounding, a loud bass beat. *Thump. Thump. Thump. Thump.*

Squatting down, Bloom placed his hand against the red dirt that comprised the ground in the Badlands.

"What is it?" Annie asked. "That pounding?"

Trolls, Grady O'Grady answered, spitting out the word.

Bloom snapped his head up to meet Annie's eyes with his own. "They are marching. There must be five hundred, at least five hundred."

Annie gulped. The air vibrated with fear. The strings were still there, behind her, beckoning and swaying, a gateway back to her world. It would be so easy to just go back, to just go back and get away from this place. All she had to do was stop time, bring her friends in a boat with her, and go. But what would she be going back to and who? Everything that mattered was here. And if she opened the portal, the Raiff, those trolls, they could cross, too. There was no shutting it once it was opened.

They climbed back onto Grady O'Grady's back, even Eva, who managed not to pass out again.

"How do we go?" Eva asked. "Where?"

In the belly of the mountains is Raiff's fortress. We'll fly low to avoid the orcs spotting us in flight.

As they flew, they tried to devise a way to rescue Miss Cornelia and the elves, and get rid of the Raiff and round up all the trolls and get them out of Aurora once and for all. They exchanged ideas and thoughts, and slowly an idea started to form in their heads. They jumbled over one another's thoughts, stepping on them as a plan developed.

"We will have to stop time to get her," Bloom said. "Then take her with us to rescue the elves."

"But the ghosts . . ." Annie let her sentence hang there. She remembered her promise to the ghosts. She thought of the Woman in White holding her head. She thought about the sweet little girl ghost with her teddy. "We can't. The ghosts can't stand it. I promised not to do it unless I really, really had to. Maybe I won't have to."

Grady O'Grady skimmed over some broken treetops, jagged needles jabbing the sky.

They know it's necessary, Eva argued.

"But I promised," Annie muttered. "It doesn't seem right to expect that I'll have to. Maybe there will be another way."

"We get to the fort and then we link up, and stop time.

Then we go in, Annie, and we grab Miss Cornelia and bring her back to the dragon. Grady flies her through and we go rescue the elves," SalGoud announced.

It sounds good to me, said Grady O'Grady.

It sounds too easy, Annie thought. *I don't have a good feeling.*

Nobody seemed to hear her. Grady was too busy explaining what he knew of the inside of Raiff's fortress, how he thought Miss Cornelia would be in a room in the bottom of the fort, beneath the ground. He had never been in there, of course, why would he want to go to such a place, plus he was far too big, but he'd heard some things. Dragons are good gossip gatherers.

Grady O'Grady flew tirelessly, zigzagging here and there to avoid the legions of trolls marching toward the sea and the strings.

He could not avoid the watching eyes of the crows, though. The birds' black pupils stayed on them as they soared through the sharp trunks of trees.

They decided that the dragon would drop them off just outside the fortress. Then, they would all sneak in, find Miss Cornelia, and only stop time if absolutely necessary. Annie insisted.

A half hour later, their skin had scorched from the heat. Their faces sweltered as they flew over once-gigantic lakes that were now pools of molten sulfur. The odorous liquid belched up toward the sky whenever they passed, as if the land was trying to attack them. Fortunately, Grady O'Grady was much too fast for the liquid to ever come close.

Annie gulped after another near miss and asked, *How old are you, if you don't mind me asking?*

Older than old, Grady O'Grady answered. *Centuries.*

Do you remember being young?

It wasn't that long ago.

How long ago was it?

It was before baseball.

Bloom started laughing. *Everything is about baseball.*

Yes, it is.

Well, Annie asked, *were you ever scared?*

Constantly.

Really?

The thought of a dragon being frightened made her feel much better, somehow.

What were you scared of? Bloom asked.

The Red Sox losing.

No, seriously, Annie begged.

Failing.

Did you ever?

Ever what?

Fail?

Grady O'Grady's answer never came. A gigantic weight crashed down on him, and on Annie and the others. Vampires. They were caught.

26

The Meeting

The vampires lashed them into a special fireproof net, hoisted it into the air, and took wing toward the fortress.

I am sorry, children, Grady apologized.

It's where we were headed anyway, Jamie offered.

"Not like this we weren't," Eva grumbled. "Nobody puts a dwarf in a net."

For the most part, the vampires ignored them and spoke only to one another in hissing voices that reminded Jamie of snakes. The undead flyers didn't seem to care that everyone overheard their conversation. They all listened while trying to find a somewhat comfortable position, which was basically impossible because they were all heaped together. Dragon and elf and dwarf and giant limbs entwined with humans. Annie managed to wrap her arm around Eva's trunk, and she pressed her head against the dragon's rib cage, listening to the comforting beats of his heart. Eva was not so lucky. She had the dragon's rear end smooshed right up against her face. She turned her head, but it wasn't much help.

"Why does this happen to me?" she asked Annie, glowering.

"Can you squirm up?" she suggested.

"I can't get anywhere." Eva's voice was cold. "I was supposed to be rescuing Miss Cornelia, and now I'm in a net. Dwarfs do not get in nets."

Annie reached out her hand to try to comfort her, maybe pat her on the shoulder. She got her knee instead. "It's okay."

Eva kept glowering instead of answering, which was fine because a vampire yelled at them, "No talking."

Grady O'Grady growled.

"No growling either."

They flew in silence. Jamie strained to see the landscape, but SalGoud and Bloom were in the way. He hoped the net would hold their weight. He wasn't sure they'd survive the fall. His hope sank. *But we're all together. We're all together. That's good.*

Jumbled up together in an undignified assortment of limbs and cloaks, Annie struggled to get a good look at the structure carved out of deep-orange rock, complete with turrets like a castle and barbed wire like a jail, but she saw it well enough to know that only something hideous would call it “Home Sweet Home,” which is exactly what was written on a gigantic latch-hook banner over the drawbridge doors.

“Weird,” she said.

SalGoud was fretting. “We’ll have to be careful, Annie. We can’t split up. Maybe as soon as we get to the ground you can stop time. Make sure you’re touching us, though . . .”

But there wasn’t a chance for that. Just as they hit the ground, a massive vampire wearing a fluorescent-yellow muscle T-shirt beneath his cape yanked Annie out of the net and pulled her arms behind her back. He must have been the cowboy vampire. The rest did similar things to the others. They muzzled Grady O’Grady and tethered him to a giant post and lashed the children to a long pole. Two trolls held the ends of the pole from which everyone hung upside down.

It made Annie’s heart ache. She tried desperately to make a plan as they were marched through a mostly deserted common area and taken through a huge door into the inner sanctum of the Raiff. She could stop time, but the cowboy vampire never let go of her. She knew she couldn’t outfight a vampire.

He used his free hand to knock on the door. “Well, here we are, then. Home sweet home.”

Light from hundreds of cream-colored candles filled the room. Along the walls hung portraits of a man in all sorts of different costumes. The man had blond hair and brilliant blue eyes and the strong, square sort of chin that cartoonists always give to superheroes. In one picture he was dressed as a priest, in another as a pirate. He had on a white powdered wig in one. The paintings seemed to come from several different centuries. In one he wore a toga.

Annie couldn't help but stare at them as they passed, heading toward a high table and the fireplace.

The man seated at the table spoke indulgently, "Admiring my portraits, Annie? I do say I'm a comely devil. Don't you agree?"

A shudder rumbled up from inside her soul, all the way from her core.

The Raiff stood up and smiled. She balled her hands into fists.

"A little angry, Annie?" he asked, waving his finger at her. "Not a good idea. Anger is bad for the complexion. Ask the trolls."

Annie bit her lip. She willed herself to be calm as the vampires released her from the pole. She was the only one they had freed so far. She imagined the Raiff as a pirate, doing this to innocent seafarers.

"Yes, I used to have a black beard," the Raiff said. Then he ran his perfectly manicured nails down his lapels. "They even used to call me that."

Annie shivered but wouldn't move a muscle on her face. Had he read her thoughts?

He moved his hand up to smooth his cheeks. "Hated the name. As if that defined me? I shaved it off. Didn't match the hair."

Annie refused to turn away. The vampire holding her arms kept sniffing at her neck, which made her queasy. They released Bloom from the pole and allowed him to stand. Bloom tensed and raged. A night stalker held his arms twisted behind his back. They'd taken his bow just as they'd taken her sword and Eva's ax, leaving them all at the Raiff's feet like offerings.

She knew the others were behind her and wanted to look, but couldn't. She wasn't going to let the demon out of her sight. He left his position standing in front of his chair and strode down the marble stairs toward them. He kicked Eva's ax a bit out of the way, nonchalantly.

"My ax!" Eva bellowed.

"Muffle the dwarf." He snapped his fingers. "Dwarfs get on my nerves."

The fireplace flames snapped and blazed higher with each step he took toward them. He stopped maybe five feet away from them. Annie steeled herself.

The Raiff paced in front of them, stopping to stare at Bloom's face.

"Release the girl," he said. "But keep a finger on her at all times. We don't want her getting any ideas, do we?"

Her arms suddenly free, Annie brushed the hair out of her eyes and reached out to touch Bloom's arm.

"No, no, no. We don't want you touching anyone, Little Annie Time Stopper, except maybe me." He plucked Annie's hand off Bloom's shirtsleeve and forcibly pressed it against his own face. "We could stop time right now. Just the two of us, in control of the world."

Annie struggled against him, but he was too strong. He pried her fingers out of the fist she'd made and placed her hand against his cheek. It was ice cold, so cold that it sent prickly stings into Annie's own skin.

"Leave her alone," Jamie growled the sentence out.

"Muffle him, too." The Raiff stared into her eyes, and the pain spread past her hand and up her arm, and with it came an absolute immobilization. She gasped when she realized what was happening. She couldn't move her fingers. Soon, she wouldn't be able to move her arms. He was showing her his power, she knew. He didn't need to. She could sense the evil of him just by the way the air vibrated around him. He seemed to fill things with shadows. She would block her thoughts, the way Grady O'Grady taught her.

"Leave her alone," Bloom said. The same as Jamie. The words did not help.

The Raiff dropped Annie's hand. She immediately began rubbing it back to life. She hoped she was good enough. The Raiff meanwhile focused his attention on the boy.

"Do I sense a hint of jealousy from the last elf?" Raiff smiled. "How fun!"

Bloom didn't flinch. Raiff preened in front of him, taking

a piece of invisible lint off his shirt cuff. “Would you like to hear how your parents died? It wasn’t the trolls who got them, you know. Would you like to hear how they begged, how they pleaded, how your father lost all control, sobbing for his life?”

Annie could take it no more. “You horrible, awful monster!”

Without thinking about it, she pulled back her good right arm and made a fist. It connected—*smack!*—into the side of the Raiff’s face before she even thought about it. His head jerked back and to the side. The vampires gasped. Bloom’s eyes widened with shock.

The Raiff turned back to her.

“Horrible, awful monster?” he asked in a mocking voice. “My feelings are hurt, Annie. And to think I thought we could be friends.”

He pivoted on his loafers and slowly stepped up the stairs. He pointed a long, crooked finger at a troll. “Bring in the old one.”

Bloom leaned toward her.

“You shouldn’t have hit him, Annie,” he whispered.

“Ah, like you didn’t want to.”

The vampire grabbed her by the neck. “No talking.”

The vampire needn’t have bothered. Truth was, the moment a side door by a bookshelf opened and a woman entered, neither Annie nor Bloom had any desire for words. Annie took a deep breath and let her gaze rest on the figure.

The woman's body bent and her head struggled to stay straight up on her shoulders. Her gait was like one who had been kept awake for days, and indeed she had. The torturers refused to let her sleep. Her rainbow-clad socks were brown and dingy and full of holes, as was her dress. Her hair fled her bun and knotted and frayed, spilling out this way and that, as if trying to escape her head. A vampire and a satyr held on to each of her elbows. So little and fragile and spent, she seemed nothing like the strong proud woman who led Annie up the hill to her house that first day in Aurora. Annie had felt so safe then, safe for the first time in her life.

Miss Cornelia lifted her head and faced Annie. Her lips moved but no sound came out. It didn't need to. Annie knew what she said.

She said, "I'm sorry."

Annie gulped, confused, and the Raiff heard her.

"She hasn't really been keeping herself up, has she?" he said. The difference in his tidy elegant appearance and Miss Cornelia's was striking. "Now tell me, who do you really think is the bad guy here?"

He held his nose. "Even when I was a pirate I dressed better than that. Did you remember I was a pirate, Annie? Oh yes, a long time ago, I sailed up and down the Atlantic stealing from the rich and giving to the poor."

"Pillaging and looting is more like it," Bloom said. His words were responded to with a sucker punch to his stomach administered by the vampire, Brian, holding him.

"No interrupting," the vampire hissed.

"Yes, it's very rude. You've been consorting with incredibly rude people, Annie. Did you happen to notice their lack of manners? Have you been to that wretched tavern? Fights all over the place. Yet, Aurora is supposed to be a haven for the misfits, isn't it? A place for the fae and the other kin, the Stoppers, to be safe? Is that what she told you?" He pointed at Miss Cornelia. "Well, she lied. It is just a zoo of her own amusement, a land of her own making. What I want to do is free everyone, make the entire world safe for us others."

Annie's mind whirled. It hadn't been Miss Cornelia who said that Aurora was a safe haven. It had been Bloom or the mayor. Her heart stiffened when she thought of the mayor and his pride in Aurora. It would kill him if the Raiff's plan succeeded.

"I can't imagine that stopping them in time will make them any happier," Annie said. "They'll be stuck, helpless while your nasty trolls eat them. And those . . . those . . . vampire thingies suck their blood. Instead of a zoo it'll be a horror movie."

The Raiff's face contorted into an expression of concern. "Is that what they told you? That we'd go around eating and pillaging? No. No. No. Well, it's no wonder you hit me. That's not the plan at all. Why even the mayor is in favor of my plan."

"Which is what? Kidnap Miss Cornelia when you should have just kidnapped me?" Annie asked. "Why didn't you just kidnap me?"

"Oh . . . So many reasons. You are untrained. Miss Cornelia is trained. Who knew if you were powerful enough to even make a portal. Obviously, now we know you are. Cornelia was a sure thing. Except for . . . Well, she doesn't cooperate. But you . . . If we tortured you? I think she'd cooperate then. One of you will do my bidding. Either way it's a win-win for us. Isn't it, Mayor?" The Raiff clapped his hands together. "Mayor? Mayor?"

Nothing happened. He rolled his eyes. Annie moved a centimeter closer to Bloom and then another one. No one seemed to notice. The vampire still had a finger on her, though.

The Raiff turned to the trolls. "Will someone get me the mayor?"

The troll pounded out and returned in a moment with the mayor. Annie's whole body relaxed when she saw the familiar man with his ruddy face and huge hands. He'd taken off his parka, of course, and wore just a simple blue T-shirt with suspenders holding up his large pants.

"Mayor!" Annie moved a step closer and the vampire pulled her back, but as he did she leaned another inch closer to Bloom. Soon she'd be able to touch him. Unfortunately, a vampire was touching him as well, so if she stopped time they'd have two vampires to contend with. Then she had another idea.

She forced herself to have a mind as innocent as a two-year-old's. She made herself feel like the mayor was her daddy coming home after a long day of work. Shrugging off the vampire's hand, she bounded toward the mayor and jumped up into his arms while the Raiff smiled indulgently.

"So sweet," he murmured, licking his lips.

But Annie wasn't being sweet at all. She was being sneaky. She clutched the mayor's large chest, and squeezing with every ounce of her body, she forced herself to the right resonation. She could feel the power surging and yelled, "Stop!"

And, of course, time did stop.

And, of course, it was very much the wrong thing to do.

A Traitor Revealed

Mayor, oh thank goodness." Annie broke away from the stone giant and started searching the room for ropes and chains. "Now we have to hurry and tie them all up. Are there more in the fort? We should tie them up, too, I suppose. Hopefully, it won't take long. Stopping gives the ghosts an awful headache, you know."

The mayor grabbed her arm but said nothing. His face was cold, terribly cold.

"Mayor?" Her voice came out like a squeak. He smelled . . . spicy.

"You've misjudged, Annie," he said, his hand squeezing tighter. "You've misjudged badly."

She tried to back away toward Miss Cornelia but couldn't move an inch. He held her fast.

"You're filthy," he spat out. "No better than a troll. Now start time again."

She closed her eyes, had to think of something to do. Nothing came. She was desperate. Maybe she could stall.

"Was it you? Were you the one who betrayed Miss Cornelia?" Annie asked.

He shrugged and didn't loosen his hold.

"But why? She loved you. The town loves you. The fairies and pixies . . . all your speeches."

"The fairies are a nuisance, always hanging on me. Plus, they were all too content; they never wanted anything more. Why stay in Aurora? I asked them. Why not expand?" His voice grew big like it did when he gave speeches. "It was like we were trapped there."

"But you could leave." Annie scanned the room. Everything was frozen. Bloom's face trapped in a fierce expression. Eva, SalGoud, and Jamie all stuck in various stages of entrapment. The vampires resembled wax figures. The Raiff had a horrible TV-actor-style grin plastered on his face. It was much too wide.

"What good would leaving be?" the mayor asked. "We have to hide who we are in the human world. You were there. You know."

Annie thought back to her life before Aurora, how she never really fit in. But there were plenty of good humans, too. Not all of them were like Walden. There was that nice foster father she'd had who made her peanut butter and fluff sandwiches before he had to go to the hospital. There was Mrs. Ballard, her second-grade teacher, who brought in cupcakes on students' birthdays and said that everything always came in threes. When she was in second grade, she was sure that teacher was magic.

"Are you worrying about the humans?"

He then went back to the high table and grabbed some newspapers with his free hand, heaving Annie the entire way as if she weighed no more than a pillow. Her feet dragged on the floor as he strode. Plopping the papers down in front of her, he gave her his familiar mayor smile—kind and knowing. He fanned the papers out in front of her.

"See these headlines," he said. "Read them. See what humans have done to the world. 'Soldiers Torture Prisoners.' 'Air Quality at Its Worst Ever.' 'Forest Fire Caused by Arsonist, Kills 200.' 'Bombing Stuns City.' "

He gloated toward her again, put his finger beneath his chin. "That's what humans are doing to the world, Annie. They have already destroyed it. Don't tell me you don't know that, Annie. You lived there. You've seen the worst of them."

She closed her eyes. She thought of Mrs. Betsey telling her she was worthless. She thought of her foster father who used to chase after all the kids living in his apartment every time he drank too much. She would hide on the roof until he fell asleep, bringing one of the smaller foster sisters with her, holding her so that she wouldn't slide down the steep pitch onto the busy street below.

"How did you get here? The portal is gone. How did you?" Annie shook her head.

"I came before the trolls destroyed it—as they destroyed it, but there are ways that you don't know," the mayor said. "Magic that even Cornelia is not privy to. A Stopper is not a god. You are just magical humans, not all-knowing beings, no matter how often you think you are."

In the distance, a ghost wailed. The bell. If only she could get a hand free, she could fish it out of her pocket. She could get help. She squirmed but the mayor simply wrapped his arm around her trunk, smashing her arms useless against her sides.

"Start time again, Annie."

"No." She swallowed hard. "I don't know how."

She didn't want to think of how angry the Raiff would be when time started again. The cold of him was unlike anything she'd experienced before. She had no desire to relive his freezing touch or withstand his wrath.

"Do it."

"No." She shook her head. How had she liked him? She'd been so stupid. Hadn't her motto always been: *We must. We must. We must never ever trust.* "No, I can't."

With his free hand, the mayor pulled out a knife and held it to her throat. "I'll kill you, Annie, so help me."

His eyes were glassy, nothing eyes, like someone who'd done too many drugs, seen too many things about themselves. They were eyes that couldn't stare back. She didn't doubt him for a minute. The blade of the knife was cold against her skin, cold like the Raiff's eyes and touch. She thought quickly.

"Then time will be stopped forever. You'll be all that's left." She talked slowly, hoping he didn't know better. "You can't kill me because then you'll be alone and you can't abide that. The whole world will be silent except for the beating of your heart. Thump. Thump. Thump-thump."

She stopped herself because she thought she might be pushing it a bit, maybe a little too dramatic even for the mayor.

The mayor shuddered. She grinned to herself. It was working.

"There'll be no one to applaud you, Mayor. No one to listen to your stories." She squirmed her hand up a bit; she could almost reach the bell.

Before she could grab it, the mayor had an epiphany. She could almost hear him say "Ah-ha!" but he didn't. Instead, he squeezed her more tightly, lifting her up in the air with her feet dangling, and took a step toward Miss Cornelia. He shoved the knife beneath the woman's bent chin. He pricked her skin, just a little bit, but the blood didn't come out that should have, which must have been because when time stops so does the blood.

"Start time or I'll kill her," he growled. A big bead of sweat barreled down his forehead and fell off the tip of his nose onto his arm, which made him move it a bit, slightly loosening his hold on Annie.

Annie took the opportunity to grab the ghost bell. Her hand wrapped around it, and she began clanging it desperately. It made no sound.

Oh, they lied, she thought, *the ghosts lied.*

She gulped, staring at Miss Cornelia's sweet face.

"I'll kill her, Annie. She's just a stupid old witch." He glowered and repositioned his knife. "We don't need her anymore. She's useless now that we have you. Too stubborn by half, anyway."

Desperation took its hold on Annie. The ghost bell didn't seem to work. The man she'd trusted had betrayed absolutely everyone. She was in a bad-smelling fortress in a godforsaken place where all her friends were frozen in time because of her, and her best foster mother, the best foster mother ever, was about to have her neck sliced by a power-hungry giant. So, using all of her newfound wisdom and strength and Time Stopper knowledge she did what any young girl with her hands pinned to her sides would do. She kicked her leg back and managed to strike a direct hit on the mayor's left knee.

"Ha!" she yelled as he dropped her.

She fell to the marble floor and scurried a foot away while the mayor grabbed his now-throbbing knee.

"Start! Stop!" she murmured as fast as she could, wishing that maybe, just maybe, she did have the power to start time after all.

The effect was exactly what she wanted. The mayor was

frozen hopping on one leg. Annie took a deep breath, felt the cool marble beneath her hands for just one second, and then pushed herself up off the floor. *The world is extremely peaceful this way. Everything is so calm*, she thought.

Except her heart.

She walked to Miss Cornelia and put her hand along the side of the woman's wrinkled face. In the moment between starting time and stopping it again one single drop of blood had left the lovely old lady's neck.

"I am sorry, too," she whispered.

Then she set about moving her toward the center of the room. It was much harder than she imagined. Miss Cornelia seemed so frail but she was rather heavy, at least for Annie. She heaved and pulled, but the sight of Miss Cornelia being pushed across the floor like a dead mannequin mixed with a sack of oatmeal was just too much for her morale. She gave one more push and managed to get Miss Cornelia a step or two past a goblin who had been caught in the time stop midscurry, his skinny gray-green legs in midstep making him an inch or two above a beetle on the marble floor. When he would step down he'd squash the bug. Poor little beetle. Annie moved it out of the way. Then, thinking better of it, she picked it up and held it in the palm of her hand, staring at the iridescent shell, the little legs.

Sighing, she slumped down to sit on the floor for a moment. She had to catch her breath. She had to think. But all she did really was stare at the beetle, wondering if it had to spend all its time wondering over life or if it simply scurried from place to place, searching for food.

It would be so much easier to be a bug, she thought. *No responsibilities.*

"What are you doing?" a loud male voice demanded.

Annie's hand tightened on the beetle, and giving a little embarrassing shriek she whirled around, startled beyond belief. Who could possibly be talking to her? She didn't see anything. Then all of a sudden the body that went with the voice began to materialize in front of her. First, two fat legs in long socks and old-fashioned shoes appeared. Following them, a rotund belly materialized, and finally the white-wigged head of the grumpy ghost from Miss Cornelia's house arrived. He glared at her with beady eyes.

"You forgot your arms," she told him. And indeed he had. The rest of his body had materialized perfectly, but he'd foolishly forgotten his arms. His sleeves hung there, empty.

"Dragon's teeth," he muttered, and a second later his arms appeared.

Annie stifled a giggle.

The ghost raised his eyebrows and pointed a finger at her. "You've stopped time."

Annie couldn't believe it. He was lecturing her, like a teacher at school. "There wasn't much of a choice, was there?"

Her arm swept the room. The ghost turned his bulbous head around and took in a toppled Miss Cornelia, the demon Raiff still grinning maddeningly, her friends hanging upside down, the mayor in midleap, the countless vampires and trolls and goblins all frozen in their evil tasks. He said nothing.

Annie put her hands on her hips, then started tugging at Miss Cornelia again. "And you guys certainly took a while."

"Sorry." He hung his head sheepishly. "We were playing charades."

The Woman in White appeared next to him.

"I won!" she said in her frothy voice. She flitted over to Annie and glanced sadly at Miss Cornelia. "Oh, my dear friend."

"You cheated," the grumpy ghost snapped back. He implored Annie, "She took her body apart to show the word 'dismember.' That's hardly fair."

A ghostly book materialized in midair. The Woman in White snatched at it and began flipping through it.

"Find that in the rule book. There are no stipulations against taking apart a body. Now, turning solid and moving things—that is clearly against the rules. Yes, right here on page 39."

Annie had her hands beneath Miss Cornelia's armpits and heaved her over toward Bloom. She had hardly been paying attention to the spirits' quarrel, but she paused and said, "You can move things?"

The Woman in White smiled, dropping the book. "Oh, of course we can, dear. Haven't you ever heard of poltergeists, always shutting doors, and rearranging drawers and things?"

Annie smiled a true smile. She hadn't felt so good in ages. "Are the rest of you here?"

In answer, dozens of ghosts suddenly appeared, filling the chamber. They overlapped one another and circled around Annie. The little girl ghost, Chloe, wrapped her arms around Annie's leg. Annie laid Miss Cornelia back down on the floor so that she could give Chloe and her teddy a proper hug. The other ghosts waited impatiently.

"Our heads . . . ," they said.

"The ache . . ."

"Oy, could I use some aspirin. With a head like this, I feel like death warmed over."

"You *are* death warmed over."

"Of course I am, you idiot, but do I want to feel this way? No, no, I do not want to feel this way, I can tell you that."

They talked over one another, voices growling more cacophonous as they talked, turning into quite a din, echoing off the marble walls. Chloe clung to Annie and covered her ears.

"Make them stop," she whispered, turning solid. Annie pulled her into her arms. She'd had enough of the complaining, too.

The Woman in White saw the Raiff, frozen, and shrieked. "Oh! Oh! It's him . . . It's my—"

The stern ghost wrapped his arm around her, and she

tucked her head into his chest before disappearing. Her sobs echoed off the walls.

"They have some history," the ghost apologized for her. "They were married once. He was . . . She . . . Ahem . . . Well, this is awkward."

Annie cleared her throat as the Woman in White's sobs seemed to float out the door. *Wait. Did that mean? Was she her great-grandmother? Or something?* She couldn't worry about it right that second. "Okay . . . Um . . . Well, that's . . . That's not cool. Anyway, I have an idea. You help me with this and I'll start time again. Now, here's the plan . . ."

Basking in the Glory of Ickiness

Annie didn't have much time to bask in the glory of her own genius. The ghosts turned solid. Then they hauled the Raiff, the mayor, and all the trolls, vampires, and goblins, along with any other unsavory ghouls such as kelpies and satyrs, into the dungeons that filled two levels of the fort. All of the dungeon rooms were empty, but they'd been well used. Blood covered some of the floors. Writing on one wall resembled old Celtic runes Annie had seen once in a book on Ireland. A lonely sock was bunched into the corner of a cell. In another, a long green cloak like Bloom wore was draped across the barred window, blocking out the view.

As they worked, Annie and the spirits really didn't come across many of the Raiff's cohorts. There weren't really that many around anymore. Annie figured that most had already started across the sea toward Aurora. Some were probably already there.

"A dungeon won't hold them long," the grumpy ghost said, straightening his wig after the strain of turning solid and helping to heave a bulky troll had caused it to fall over his forehead and all the way down onto his nose. "The Raiff can't be held by such things."

"I just want to buy a little time," Annie explained. She adjusted Chloe, who had spent the whole time sitting on Annie's shoulders in a marathon piggyback ride. "Any seconds we can get and use to stall the Raiff are important."

The ghosts also gathered together Bloom, Miss Cornelia, SalGoud, Jamie, and Eva, moving them close to one another so that they were all in a group huddle like football players. Standing in the middle of the room, Annie rubbed her hands together and surveyed their work.

"Good job," she told the ghosts, meaning it. "Thank you. Really. I couldn't have done it all without you."

Chloe curtsied. "Nothing to it."

The grumpy ghost rolled his eyes. "Right. Now, about our heads . . ."

Oh, Annie hadn't forgotten; she'd just wanted to properly thank them and return the ghost bell before she started time back up again. If the ghosts hadn't helped it would have taken her forever to get everything done. Truth was, she was also a little nervous about starting time up. She had done it once. But that didn't mean she could do it again. She wanted to see and talk to Miss Cornelia and Bloom, true, but she was so nervous about the Raiff. So nervous about everything—all those wretched vampires sniffing at her neck, the loathsome trolls.

Stalling another moment as the ghosts gathered round, Annie fetched the ghost bell from her pocket.

"Here," she said, handing it toward the grumpy ghost. "Thank you for the use of it."

He shook his head and made his hand turn solid. He grabbed the bell and Annie's hand and brought it back toward her heart. "You keep it. You might need it again someday."

"But—"

His eyes softened but his lips frowned, and his hand dematerialized and vanished. "Just start time, Annie."

"But—" She swallowed hard. "I'm not sure I can."

"Just start it, Annie," the Woman in White moaned, suddenly materializing again now that the Raiff was no longer in the room. "Please."

Annie pocketed the bell. She reached out to touch Jamie and Cornelia, who were closest to her. They touched Bloom and SalGoud and Eva. She would start time and then stop it really quickly, as the ghosts knew. That way she could update the others about what had happened and they could make a plan.

She closed her eyes and took a deep breath. She tried to calm down, to feel the resonation of the strings that controlled time.

"Annie," Chloe's little voice implored.

Annie took another breath and whispered, "Start."

Nothing happened.

"Draw!" Chloe said. "Use your foot and make the word."

Twisting so she could write in the dusty floor, Annie began the letters. S-T-A—the A didn't really show up—R-T.

"Start," she whispered.

Life came back into Miss Cornelia's hands. Eva took a ragged breath. SalGoud's muscular back heaved, and Jamie's shoulder moved beneath her hand. She'd done it. She allowed herself to smile. The ghosts cheered. Chloe threw her teddy up into the air and caught it. Bloom's astonished eyes caught her own as she clutched Miss Cornelia's sturdy hand. The old woman instantly stood up straight, losing her crumpled and defeated posture.

"I was faking it," she said to Annie, who was staring at her with her mouth wide open. "Oh, I'm hurt, but not all that bad."

Miss Cornelia grinned. "It's best to let your enemies assume you are worse off than you really are. They underestimate you then."

Her hands went up to fix her hair back into a proper bun. Annie wanted to bask in it all, but knew that there wasn't any time to lose, so to speak. She grabbed Miss Cornelia's elbow and Jamie's shoulder and shouted, "Stop."

Sounds rumbled up from the dungeons.

Oh no, it hadn't worked.

She tried again. “Stop.”

Chloe shook her head. No aches.

Terrified, Annie looked up at Miss Cornelia. It wasn’t working. She tried again. “Stop.”

Nothing.

“Stop.”

Jamie had sympathetic eyes.

“Stop.”

It was no good. She couldn’t stop time at all anymore. She’d lost it. The noise of the monsters, the demon, and the vampires rumbled up from the dungeon, coming closer.

Powers May Fade

Miss Cornelia's gentle hand cupped the back of Annie's head, and the girl opened her panicked eyes.

Miss Cornelia's voice rang out strong and echoed in the chamber. "Stop."

All the ghosts immediately grabbed their heads and started moaning and rolling their eyes.

"They are so dramatic," Eva shouted as one spirit dressed as a nun started rolling her eyes and ripping at the top part of her habit.

"Try not to take too long," the spirit who resembled a Civil War doctor said.

Miss Cornelia turned her attention to Annie as all the spirits simultaneously disappeared. It was a little eerie to have them suddenly disappear at once, to have a room that was completely filled suddenly go empty. Annie didn't notice. She was shattered. She'd failed. She hadn't been able to stop time. If Miss Cornelia hadn't been there . . . She dropped her hands and grabbed her stomach. The thought made her sick.

Miss Cornelia bent a bit to peer into Annie's eyes and spoke quickly, "You don't have unlimited resources, Annie. The body gets tired. Stopping is a great responsibility."

"But it didn't work," Annie murmured. She was trembling all over.

"I gather you've done it a lot. Has she, Bloom?"

Even as he searched the room for the vampires and trolls, Bloom said, "Too many times to count."

"ENOUGH!" Eva bellowed. "Where'd the vampires go? Nobody hangs a dwarf upside down! Where's the Raiff? He kicked my ax! Nobody kicks a dwarf's ax."

No one answered her questions.

"It's like running or drawing, Annie. You get tired after a bit. You need to refuel," Miss Cornelia said, walking quickly toward the door and beckoning them to follow. "It's a skill that has to be refined, and unfortunately, it is also a skill that begins to fade with age."

She sighed and Annie thought she suddenly seemed frail again. They all followed, except for Bloom who was busy peering into hallways and through doorways. He'd even checked beneath the high table. Miss Cornelia would have none of it.

"Come, Bloom. How do you all feel?" she asked. "Well enough to run, I hope. Because we have to run for the border, for the sea. I can't hold the stopping as long as I used to, and goodness knows that the ghosts would prefer that we do not hold it long at all, but we must speed toward Aurora as fast as we can."

"You mean time might start without you?" Annie asked. "Like it does for me?"

Miss Cornelia stepped over a goblin. "I am very old, Annie. My power fades. In a place like this, it's hard to use at all. That's why we were all so grateful to find you. The Raiff does not know this. We won't tell him, will we?"

Annie tried to process all this new information as they strode quickly through the halls of the fortress, passing the Raiff portraits. The one where he was garbed in pirate clothes and had a rascally grin seemed to wink, but Annie knew that was impossible.

At the entrance to the room, Annie found more of the weapons that the vampires had stripped off them. Bloom seemed especially happy to have his bow and quiver back. He kissed each arrow, counting them as they walked. The Golden Arrow was still there, mixed in with the others. They passed door after door, so many that Annie lost count.

"The mayor—" SalGoud began.

"Yes?" asked Miss Cornelia, her eyebrows arching up with her question.

SalGoud didn't seem to know how to continue, and Annie struggled for the words to help him. "You trusted him."

"Yes. Yes, I did."

"And you trust us?" Annie asked.

Miss Cornelia touched her hair. "Yes. Yes, I do."

"Well, how can you trust anyone again?" Annie asked. "After that? He gave you to the Raiff. He was ready to forfeit the whole town. He was—he was—"

He was horrible. He had held Annie on his shoulders. She'd felt safe up there, safe walking with him through the night. He had danced with the fairies, sung for the town, given speeches and praise and told them that he loved them, and all the time he was ready to let them all fall.

"Trust is not generally something you choose. It is like love and friendship. Most of the time it is just there whether you want it or not. You grab it between your hands, Annie, and you hold on to it like you were holding on to the back of a dragon. Not for anything do you let go. Not until it is ripped out of your grasp. It is that precious."

"But—" Jamie muttered.

"Remember, he will not want us to stop time while his trolls and vampires are all still here," Miss Cornelia told them, lifting up her skirt so it wouldn't snag on a troll that she leaped over. A tiny drop of blood from the mayor's knife trickled down her neck and caught in the collar of her dress. She wiped at it. "Don't doubt that he will find the ways. But, it won't come to that. No matter what, Annie and I will not stop time for him. Aurora has a chance in a battle if it must be, but we will have no chance if we are frozen, no chance if it's a surprise. We must warn everyone."

But the elves . . .

They couldn't go back yet, not without the elves. And Miss Cornelia didn't know and they couldn't tell her.

At the threshold, they found Grady O'Grady, frozen. Working quickly, they un-netted him and Miss Cornelia laid her hand across his face. "My old, sweet friend."

Annie touched SalGoud's arm, searching for help in telling Miss Cornelia what Annie didn't have the heart to tell her.

"Miss Cornelia. We have determined that we cannot all go back." The stone giant's voice came out calmly.

She lifted her head, peering at him. "What do you mean?"

"If you open the portal now . . . If Annie does . . . They will all cross. Only Grady O'Grady can go back and only with one. That one is you. We are here to rescue you," Jamie explained.

She stood up straighter. "No. One of you children will go back."

"Aurora is dying without you," Annie insisted. "And you have already been through so much. You need to be there and prepare for war, for when we do cross over."

"And what . . . what will you do?"

This time it was Bloom who spoke. "We are here to rescue others. We can't tell you who because if you know, the Raiff will know."

She seemed to take this in. "He will hunt you down."

"We know," Jamie said.

"He will try to take Annie," she said.

"We will keep her safe," Eva said. "With my ax."

"He will try to kill you all."

"He won't," Annie said, pulling Miss Cornelia into a massive hug. "We have to do this, and we will have to open the portal when we're done. But for now, you need to go . . . prepare Aurora. Call in all the magics that you can. Hurry. Make it strong so that we have something good to come home to, something good to protect when we return, something to fight for."

The old woman kept shaking her head. "No . . . You're just children . . . You're just . . . I can't possibly let you."

"It isn't about letting us. We have to, Miss Cornelia. There is no other way. Not when you love someone." Annie let her go, but Miss Cornelia grabbed her back into another hug.

"Remember, bravery does not trump mercy, and glory doesn't mean anything without kindness," Cornelia said as they finished their good-byes. "It is love and kindness that matter more than anything."

"More than life?" Annie asked.

"Always," the woman said, turning so the tears in her eyes would stay hidden.

They'd run for an hour without her, careening past frozen trolls, stuck satyrs, still monsters of so many kinds, when

Miss Cornelia lost the stop and the world came rushing back again. It came with a foul smell and a howl of the Raiff that echoed across all of the Badlands. The terrible undead shriek of pure evil forced Annie to stumble in her run and clamp her hands over her ears.

Bloom's arm wrapped around her waist and he pulled her along. "Come, Annie."

They sped up their pace, but they knew that it might not be good enough, might not be fast enough.

"We did it, didn't we?" Annie asked Jamie in a quiet whisper. "We saved her."

"Yes." He stared into the distance. "And now we have to save some more."

He paused for breath and his fingers tightened around Annie's hand. "No matter what, you must not stop time. No matter what he does. No matter whom he threatens, Annie. We must not stop time."

Annie said nothing. In the distance, a red dragon and a beautiful white-haired woman soared for the strings.

"We'll do this," she whispered. "We'll get them for you."

They had to.

"No time to celebrate, wimplings!" Eva hollered, ax held triumphantly in the air. "To the elves!"

"To the elves!" the rest of them echoed, and they ran forward, hopeful and terrified, triumphant and vaguely lost, all at once.

30

Evil Keeps on Eviling

The demon waited in his lair, anger coursing through his skin, impatience filling his cold bones and blood. Darkness pervaded everything.

Around the demon, trolls and ogres, evil vampires and satyrs bustled and stomped, getting ready for their escape from the Badlands back to the world of humans, a world where their wickedness could run wild. The demon couldn't wait. He missed that world, missed the beauty of it. He wanted it for his own.

It was all going exactly as he'd planned.

He moved quickly toward the window. Trolls shuffled out of his way, bowing their heads. He ignored them and instead went to the window, reaching his hand out of it, into the hot, humid air. It smelled of rotten eggs and cooked broccoli. He missed the smells of Aurora, the pine trees, the clean mix of snowy air and ocean. There were tiny parts of the Badlands like that, but not enough.

"Soon," he whispered.

He whirled around, still smiling. His pale blond hair was nearly white, matching his teeth. "The elves have outlived their usefulness. Do with them what you will."

He thought of Annie Nobody, the girl who was at the castle, the Stopper girl who came from his own blood, and he smiled. He had made her, his magic had touched her, and she had rebuked him; but in doing so, he had felt her power and now knew how great it was. She was the power he needed to drain. If he hooked her into the machine, his own power would be almost endless. He would be able to change the essential nature of the strings fully, open portals again, go back to Aurora.

He smiled.

Life was good.

But evil was even better.

Acknowledgments

Thank you to Emily Ciciotte of the Glory-Filled Land of Wisdom and Super Stardom, who—like most brilliant and amazing people—wanted a certain kind of story. I am so lucky to be able to give it to her. Her heart and gumption and mind inspired so many of the characters in these stories. You can see pieces of her everywhere.

Thank you to my agent, Ammi-Joan Paquette of the Agent City of Goodness, for taking me and all my neuroses on and doing it with such magical grace.

There is no greater editor than Cindy Loh of the Editor School of Amazingness. Just like Emily, this book wouldn't exist without her magic. Thank you, Cindy, for believing in quirkiness and for putting up with so much goofiness. You are brilliant and so good.

Like Cindy, the amazing, passionate Bloomsbury team does this book-making thing for a living, but they fill the process with so much love, hope, and intelligence. Thank you to Donna Mark, John Candell, and Owen Richardson, who made this into such a beautiful book. Thank you to Hali Baumstein of the Land of Awesome Patience, and to Brett Wright, Linda Minton, Sally Morgridge, Pat McHugh, and Melissa Kavonic, the managing editor. They are all unsung heroes. As are Cristina Gilbert, Lizzy Mason, Courtney Griffin in publicity, as well as Erica Barmash, Emily Ritter, Eshani Agrawal, Shae McDaniel, Beth Eller, Linette Kim, and Brittany Mitchell in marketing.

Many thanks to the People of Mike and Lynne and Grayson Staggs' House of Wednesday Fun, who inspired joy and story in me almost every Wednesday night, with special thanks to Samantha Spellacy and Nate Light, John Bench, Davis and Alisa, Jon and Sarah Day Levesque, Joe Pagan, Thom Willey, Kaitlin Matthews, Michelle Bromley Bailey, Mike Brzezowski, and Nicole Ouellette. They see the worst of me and still talk to me, which is saying a lot.

It is always good to have friends who adventure with you, and therefore many thanks to my own troop of wandering funsters—Steve and Jenna Boucher, and Lori Bartlett and Maryanne Mattson. Thank you to Marie Overlock, who always has my back even when I don't see her, which is very Eva of her.

Many thanks to my brother, Bruce Barnard of Handsome Land, for putting up with my dwarf ways.

Thank you to the readers, librarians, teachers, writers, kids, and other humans. I still can't quite believe how awesome you are and that you read my books and support them. It means everything to me.

And finally, many thanks to Shaun Farrar of the Awesomest Man Ever, who somehow always manages to love me and save me, over and over again. There is no better man for me than you. There is no better love.